The Club at Eddy's Bar

'*Kávéházban*' by Ferenc MARTYN

The Club
at
Eddy's Bar

by

Zoltán Böszörményi

PHÆTON
PUBLISHING LTD.
—— Dublin ——

The Club at Eddy's Bar

FIRST PUBLISHED IN IRELAND & U.K. 2014
by Phaeton Publishing Limited, Dublin

Zoltán Böszörményi has asserted his right
to be identified as the author of this work

Cover illustrations from drawings by
Ferenc Martyn; book design copyright ©
O'Dwyer & Jones Design Partnership, 2014

The author gratefully acknowledges Paul
Sohar's assistance in the preparation
of the final manuscript of this book

Printed and bound in the United Kingdom
by T. J. International Limited, Padstow

*British Library Cataloguing In Publication
Data: a catalogue record for this book
is available from the British Library*

ISBN: 978-1-908420-07-7 HARDBACK

[ALSO IN EBOOK: ISBN 9781908420084 EPUB]

The body should not give in to its appetites at the expense of the soul; but isn't it also true that the soul should not make demands at the expense of the body?

—Montaigne (1553–1592)

—Chapter 1—

TAMAS SCRAMBLED ONTO the airport bus, carried along by the rush of his fellow travellers. He had the papers of a stateless person in his pocket, the fear of death in his soul, and was on his way to a country unknown to him. Like the other passengers, he was glad to leave behind the dangers and the foetid dormitories of Traiskirchen Refugee Camp, but he did not share in the exuberant mood of the bus. His thoughts were with his wife, Iren, and their two children, still trapped in Eastern Europe. He had to leave them behind when he fled across two borders, and now he could not stop worrying about them, and wondering when and if he would ever see Iren again.

His wife did not know the reason he had to run. No one did. He clutched tightly in his hand the thick school notebook in which he had set down the awful story.

The big airport bus was the first step on his journey to a new homeland – Canada. As it pulled away, camp residents left behind gave a salutatory wave to the lucky group on board, now promoted to the status of emigrants. Tamas was touched by this demonstration of fellow feeling.

Leaving the bus at Vienna airport, they followed one another in single file, mostly young women and men; the few straggling children among them were constantly reminded to behave themselves and told how important it was to keep together. If they get lost, none of us can set out on this long journey, Tamas was thinking to himself. Without them the plane will not take off. His worries were echoed loudly by a short-haired young woman in a denim skirt speaking to her brood.

The motley group was being led by a fortyish man,

wearing a white shirt with a red tie and holding an overstuffed briefcase. Halfway between the bus and an office building he stopped and called for attention, loudly addressing this small island of humanity gathered around him. Even before he had opened his mouth his appearance spoke of a bureaucrat who was not going to tolerate dissent. His gestures were measured, almost theatrical. He scanned the faces in front of him with a piercing stare, taking his time as if he had nothing else on his schedule that day. He was silently taking a headcount while he waited for all talk to die down, until even the children were turning their startled faces toward him.

Only then did he beckon to all to follow him.

He led the group into the building and then to a conference room inside. Accompanied by the subdued conversation that had sprung up again in the meantime, they took their seats in the rows of chairs. Then suddenly silence returned. The man greeted all present in a ritualistic monotone. Gradually he slipped into a cadence of emphasizing every word and raising his voice at the end of each sentence as if wanting to put more weight into his instructions.

He explained the process that lay ahead, step by step.

Releasing the catch of his briefcase, he produced a large stack of manila envelopes. He opened the one on top and, tilting it upside down, spilled out a pile of documents. He picked out a brownish booklet that looked like a passport. He checked inside and read out a name. One of those present got up to receive his package. He was followed by the others, one by one.

When Tamas heard his name called, he rose from his seat and quickly made his way to the table to receive his bona fides. He wanted to say thanks, but the official's eyes were already on the next envelope on top of the stack. Tamas carried his documents like a cat its prey back to his seat and checked them: the passport, the immigration permit, the entry visa, the airline ticket, the names of immigration officials, and the addresses of their offices at his destination — they were all there. Only then did he start examining the data entered into them, beginning with the brownish passport.

His name had been typed without the accents.

Looking at his photo he felt a sour smile pucker his lips. It had been taken at the beginning of his stint in the foreign refugee camp. All the agitation was still vivid in his memory, the time when he was filling out emigration applications, always in a hurry — he had to run to the corner photography shop to get there before it closed. From the photo the sad eyes of a thin face looked back at him. And he could not help noticing the date of expiration on the passport: EXPIRY JULY 15, 1983. Void in thirty days, he observed bitterly. Just in case I am tempted to return.

Next his eyes latched onto the line concerning citizenship: STATELESS. In block letters. Unmistakable. Reading it again, he felt he had been jabbed in the guts. To be fair though, what other word would you use to describe someone without a country? He swallowed the lump in his throat and repeated to himself: STATELESS.

He carefully scanned all the other documents, one at a time. All seemed in order. He separated the passport and the airline ticket from the rest and slipped them into an inside jacket pocket.

One by one, the envelopes slowly got picked up from the table.

'Attention please.' The official's voice was firm and hard, 'I want everyone to make note of the gate number on their boarding pass and to be there at least forty minutes before boarding time. Don't get lost gaping at the duty-free shops; you might miss your flight.'

As if he had suddenly run out of words, he paused, took a deep breath, then clicked the briefcase shut before he started speaking again. His voice went back to its initial ceremonial tone.

'I wish you *bon voyage* and much luck and happiness in your new homeland!' He marched out of the room with his eyes focused on the floor.

The table, only minutes ago occupied by a mound of vital documents, was now empty except for a small pool of reflected light.

Here and there voices started mumbling, and soon the small conference room was echoing the repeated phrase: 'Thank you, thank you, thank...'

There was already a long line at the security gate when Tamas ambled over there. His imitation-leather bag contained little in the way of personal possessions – a very few items of clothing and toiletries, a copy of Goethe's *Faust* given to him as a birthday present in the camp, and, most important of all, the thick notebook he had decided to put inside the bag before going through security. If questioned about it, he would say it contained a novel he was writing, which was true in a way, as he had changed the names of everyone in it, and it read like fiction.

At security, however, the notebook attracted no interest. The quick-eyed woman checking his papers raised an eyebrow as if to say: so you're homeless, you good-for-nothing! At least that was the message Tamas read on her face.

Then at passport control, the uniformed border guard remarked loudly enough for others behind Tamas to hear: 'Sir, I assume you know this passport only entitles you to enter the country of your destination. It is not valid for re-entry into this country!'

Tamas knew that to be untrue. There had been cases of would-be emigrants returning after a few weeks with expired passports. He had witnessed just such an incident the previous autumn.

It was about noon on a Saturday when the police shoved a young man with short blond hair into the mess hall. He was wearing a leather jacket and was in handcuffs. He had big, gold-rimmed sunglasses that he placed on the table in front of him. According to the police escorting him, he had arrived from overseas.

At first the boy looked scared and couldn't say a word. He just sat there with his head bowed. By the evening though, he slowly perked up, asked for bread, ordered beer, and began to tell his story. The words came pouring out of him about his experiences overseas. On one occasion in America he had to work twenty-four hours without sleep. None of the workers had the courage to push the on/off button of the coffee-packing machine, even though they started having visions by the twentieth hour of non-stop work. They were laughing at one another at first, pretending to collapse. At the end they stopped paying attention to the machine; instead, they were helping one another stay upright. The coffee packages were falling on the floor, making a sizable mound by the time the owner walked in.

It turned out that the boy was returned to the camp in handcuffs because he had re-entered the country with an expired passport.

As this episode flashed across Tamas's mind, he stared bashfully at the floor. He did not respond to the official's admonition. He did not want to cause trouble. He merely nodded in acknowledgement.

The next step was easier – walking down a long, wide corridor, lined by brightly-lit, inviting shops, the ones he had been warned to avoid. However, it was early yet, and he felt free to make-believe he was a regular there, a transit passenger at leisure between flights, and if he should find some knick-knack that caught his eye, he had the money to buy it and he had someone at his destination to buy it for. He stopped in front of the window display of a stationery shop. He looked wistfully over the fountain pens of various shapes and colours, the marking pens, the retractable pencils. After a while the young saleswoman came out of the shop with an eager smile. 'Can I help you at all?' she asked. 'Are you looking for anything special?'

The young man replied in German he was just looking, but following her with his eyes as she walked back into the shop, Tamas noticed a board in a corner with inexpensive ballpoint pens hanging from it. He bought one of those, with red ink. He did not expect the purchase would impress the young woman. It was the cheapest pen in the shop, although it still cost twice as much as it would have in town.

He headed toward Gate 10, which now had a red sign over it: ALIA FLIGHT 414 TO TORONTO, DEPARTURE TIME: 11:30 A.M.

*　　　*　　　*

Before settling himself in his allocated window seat in row 24, Tamas took his notebook out of the bag that he was stowing in the overhead compartment.

In the detention camp, Tamas had almost filled that notebook with his small script, but his writing had been hurried, even unthinking. He had re-read nothing. Now, armed with that expensive new red biro and on his way to Canada, he felt able at last to look at the whole story from the beginning.

He had fictionalized every name in the notebook, and he had been careful never to describe his own family, so that if the notebook should be lost or seized, no one reading it could know that the story of Vilmos was his own story, his account of the grotesque events that had turned him into a fugitive – a refugee. Of course it was also true that he did not have enough information to write about the events as non-fiction. As an innocent bystander, he was not privy to all the facts of the case; although as a novice newspaperman, he had heard more about it on the grapevine than most. But he did – unfortunately – have almost exclusive knowledge of the true and unhappy ending; he too had been unwittingly drawn into the vortex that shattered the lives of the main players.

He liked to think that the book would be published sometime, but only when Iren and the children were safely out of the country too. For now, he just wanted to set down a record of those sordid events, and then clear them out of his head. When he had reached his destination, he planned to put the notebook safely away. Once there, he needed to immerse himself in the English language and forget about the past until he got himself established and reunited with his family. He wished he had learned English. He was fluent in Romanian and Hungarian, somewhat conversant with Slavic languages, and, of course, German. But neither Hungary nor Germany was far enough for a safe haven. To feel safe, he needed to be in another continent, either North America or Australia, and that meant learning its language.

The tentative title of the story he had put in his notebook came from a newspaper headline of several months ago about the events that had led to his fleeing the country: *MURDER IN HOTEL ODÉON*.

He opened to the first page.

—*Chapter 2*—

Murder in Hotel Odéon
—I—

A FOUR-STOREY APARTMENT HOUSE near the city
lake had collapsed during the night. Vilmos was
awakened by his next-door neighbour with the news. The
old man was yelling through the half-open window, his
voice hoarse from excitement. In the produce market he
had heard about a catastrophe. That was all Vilmos was
able to get out of him – only that one of the buildings
in the housing development constructed about a decade
earlier suddenly fell into total ruin for no obvious reason.

When he had dressed and stepped out of the
building the old man was still hanging about; apparently
the sensational news had got the better of him, and he
didn't know what to do with himself.

'Go find out all about it, and hurry back to give us a
detailed report!' he yelled after Vilmos.

It was a twenty-minute walk to the scene. The
picture waiting for him was shocking, the kind of thing
he would see only on TV News about an earthquake in
a far corner of the world.

The apartment house was nothing but a pile of
rubble, as if smashed by a giant hand. The scene was
closed off by the police and firefighters. There was a
lot of confusion, emergency crews were coming and
going. As he burrowed his way through the crowd he
recognized, in a small group beyond the yellow police
tape, the designer of the complex, who it seemed was
being questioned by the police. He had worked with
that engineer and now started out toward him, but the
security guards would not let him into the cordoned-off

area. He had to stay among the horrified but gawking bystanders. He started questioning some of them, but he got contradictory answers. Among the popular theories was that the building had been built on the site of an old garbage dump, and the recent heavy rain had softened the soil. Then he discovered a familiar face in the crowd, Markus Frankel, a senior editor of the local paper; but as arts section editor, Markus's responsibility was for cultural topics, so he was probably at the scene by chance or for personal reasons. He was not representing the paper any more than Vilmos, who was only an occasional contributor. Vilmos was anxious to hear what Markus had to say about the collapse. He pushed his way through the mob, ignoring the elbows that jabbed him in the stomach and the feet that stepped on his.

He had known Markus for some time and often sought his advice in literary matters when he had a finished essay or a short story. They usually met in the café of the editorial offices on the second floor. The senior editor was known as the stern guardian of the language against the onslaughts of barbarians in the popular media, and the ultimate arbiter in matters of grammar.

Beyond his role at the paper – or because of it – Markus belonged to an élite group of intellectuals in the city. There were four or five of them who regularly got together, visited each other's homes, played bridge with bloodthirsty zest, discussed the local civic leaders and political developments in no uncertain terms, and even hinted at criticism of the bigwigs in the national government.

Whenever he found himself among this so-called 'élite', Vilmos got the feeling he was sitting in a theatre with the actors of an unfamiliar drama coming to life. He felt their performance was artificial and a bit strange; it had nothing to do with reality. He tried to interpret what was taking place before his eyes, but he saw mostly mouths opening and closing, accompanied by flashing eyes.

That clique included an attorney, Dr Artur Liptak, the life and soul of the party. A shortish man with a difficult gait, he had a bright face, and was always ready for a duel of wits. He was not one to mince his words. He had never married and had no children, even from his earlier long-term relationships. He claimed marriage was a prison with no possibility of escape. He was happiest voicing these views in female company, as if he enjoyed the enmity of women.

*   *   *

Having slowly fought his way through to the yellow police tape around the ruins, Vilmos jumped up and down with outstretched arms to catch Markus Frankel's attention. He was eager to know what had brought the arts section editor to the scene of the disaster.

'It's a real tragedy, my boy,' Markus said, finally walking over. His voice was a mixture of sorrow and awe. 'I heard the news first thing this morning, and it frightened me. I came out at once because I have an aunt living here, but she was lucky. It seems she was away visiting relatives in the country. All her possessions are gone, of course, but…she was lucky.'

Vilmos asked him about the cause of the collapse. Markus mumbled something about structural problems with the building. The occupants had been complaining about cracks in the walls and how rapidly they had widened in the past few weeks, the cracks growing into gaps with daylight showing though them. Inspectors from the City Buildings Department came out twice, examined the condition of the structure, prepared reports, and then departed arguing among themselves.

As Vilmos was taking his leave of Markus, the eminences of the city administration came on the scene, the collars of their trench coats fluttering in the occasional gusts of wind. They marched from one point of interest to another. Two officials from the Buildings Department reported and explained. The fire chief summarized the rescue efforts in progress, while the representatives of the local and national news media besieged them with questions. Hugo Wagner, the Mayor, whose tall, gaunt figure dominated the small group of officials, had to raise an arm to fend off the attacks of the microphones repeatedly shoved into his face.

'While the investigation is in progress, I'm not free to answer any questions,' he maintained, almost shouting as he pushed the journalists out of his way.

One of the reporters, however, stubbornly held his place with his camera set for a direct broadcast.

'Is it true that the occupants had been pestering the Mayor's office for months, begging the Buildings Department to do something before the walls completely came apart? If you had intervened in time, could the tragedy have been averted?' The reporter rattled off the questions, all in one breath.

The Mayor gave the journalist an icy look but no answer. The aides straggling behind him, galvanized into action, quickly formed a protective ring around him. The reporter was pushed back into the crowd of spectators.

Vilmos was already far from the scene but still under its spell. He could not stop seeing the crushed, lifeless bodies. On his way home, his surroundings made no impression on him, and he only became conscious of them again when he found his elderly neighbour waiting for him at the door of his apartment. He told the old man as much as he knew, and said he hoped he would find out more when he went in to work at noon.

—*Chapter 3*—

FLYING DID NOT COME NATURALLY to Tamas – if sitting tied into a cramped space like a hostage had anything to do with flying. The plane was in the air only a short time when he had to ask a passing stewardess for headache pills and a glass of water. The captain's voice came on and explained they had another nine hours before landing, and... But Tamas paid no attention to the rest. He closed his eyes and let his thoughts wander back home to the Carpathian mountains, to the streets of Varad, to the courtyard of a small apartment house, still his family's residence.

The hodge-podge of buildings where they had lived for ten years had been built by two butcher brothers for their large families at the turn of the twentieth century. The original long, L-shaped, one-storey structure enclosed a spacious courtyard. Over the years, however, its function underwent several changes, especially when the brothers began to disagree about exactly who owned which portion and called in a real-estate agent. The most recent owner had the building enlarged with an extra floor and chopped it up into apartments. He even built a single-family home in the back of the courtyard with its own small garden in front. The centrepiece of the courtyard was a linden tree. This tree with its straight trunk, symmetrical branches, and perfect cone of foliage was the pride and joy of all the tenants, its fragrance the stuff of legend. While linden trees are all alike, and even their flowers resemble one another like twins, each one has a unique fragrance. In early summer the whole neighbourhood was blanketed by its intoxicating scent.

There were three families living in the original main building: Tamas and his family in the first apartment, two retired brothers in the second, and an engineer couple, Tibor and Marta Nadas, lived in the third with their fifteen-year-old daughter. There were no small children other than Tamas's two little boys. The tenants all got along well. No one made excessive noise, no one harassed anyone else. Loud words hardly ever disrupted the usual slumber of the courtyard.

All that was to change however, when one day State Security agents appeared unexpectedly – knocking on doors, going from one apartment to the next, questioning the residents. Their inquiries concerned Tamas. They wanted to know all about him:

What time did he usually leave the house and where did he go?

What time did he usually get home?

Did his parents ever come to visit him?

Who were his visitors?

Did they know any of them?

Did they ever overhear their conversation?

If so, what was discussed?

What kind of a person did they think he was?

How did he behave at home with his family?

Did he have any female visitors?

Did they notice anything unusual in his behaviour?

Was he a heavy drinker? A carouser?

What kind of a husband, father?

Any domestic fights?

How did he relate to the other tenants?

Did he talk about politics?

Was he a churchgoer?

Was he a complainer?

A troublemaker?

Did he ever speak ill of the authorities?

The neighbours answered the agents' questions – they had no choice.

That evening, when Tamas appeared at the gate of

the building, the two elderly brothers retreated to their apartment, making a show of avoiding him.

But not so Tibor and Marta Nadas, the engineer couple. As soon as they caught sight of him, they raised their hands high, indicating they had something important to tell him. Urgently. They beckoned him toward the bottom of the garden.

Down there, well out of sight, in breathless whispers they told him all about the investigation. Tamas was in real trouble. He was suspected of some terrible crime. They didn't know of what kind, they had not been informed. Not even a hint. For that very reason they had concluded that something of great importance was happening, something vital to the authorities, otherwise they would not have sent two plainclothesmen. 'And not just once,' they whispered to Tamas.

Tamas knew exactly what they were talking about. While the two men from State Security were dealing with the tenants, he too was interrogated for 26 hours in a basement room at police headquarters. He had just been released that afternoon. The engineer couple looked horrified, yet he pretended not to be too concerned. Summoning all his powers of persuasion, he tried to put them at ease. 'Well, now, it's only a routine investigation concerning someone else. This can happen to anyone, anywhere in the world. This is a cancer in every society; the powers-that-be are always curious, searching, distrustful of their subjects,' he said quietly, almost inaudibly, as if talking to himself.

Nevertheless, Marta's hands had a tremor when she left the garden. Tibor followed in his wife's tracks with a nervous shrug of the shoulders.

Tamas was bothered that he was unable to make himself sound more credible and convince them they had nothing to worry about, that the whole thing was just a mix-up, a glitch in the system, as temporary as a power failure: the lights always come back, and life resumes its normal course as if nothing had happened.

The news of his skipping the country spread like wildfire, and when it reached Tibor and Marta Nadas, the man and his wife outdid each other in pointing out their prescience. No question about it, they saw the danger looming ahead. Their suspicions were not unfounded. And neither was their fear for themselves and for Tamas. They confided their worries to Iren.

She reported these developments to Tamas in letters that had to be smuggled from Varad into Yugoslavia for posting to the detainee camp at Traiskirchen in Austria. These letters, although delivered with considerable delay and fairly crumpled, were endless. They were full of longing, hopelessness, and despair. Iren described the boys' activities in vivid details, what happened to them every day, how they behaved in the day-care centre, and how much they missed their father. After reading them, Tamas felt painful thoughts churning inside him, as if he had drunk milk gone sour.

Yet he kept re-reading these letters in the long months spent in camp, drifting from one wave of despondency to the next, because these letters were the only nourishment for the hope that one day they would be together again. He felt guilty whenever he thought of Iren struggling alone back home, but he couldn't change the past; he could blame himself for one moment of impetuosity, but as events developed, he knew he had chosen the lesser of two evils. If he had stayed, he would have found himself in a prison camp in the marshlands of the Danube Delta on the Black Sea, with little chance of survival or of ever seeing his family again.

On learning about Tamas's impending departure from the camp and emigration to Canada, Iren enclosed a four-leaf clover between the sheets of her letter: '...may it bring you luck. The wheel of fortune is bound to keep turning and, who knows, some day you may have this clover to thank for your success.'

*   *   *

His wife kept haunting Tamas's thoughts.

When he had started going out with Iren, he had no immediate thoughts of marriage. At that time, he was going out with a lot of girls. Not that he was out to rack up conquests – he was looking for a steadfast companion, that was all.

He had read somewhere that early mariners were careful in their choice of shipmates, meticulously avoiding worthless, immoral, and godless characters. Such a trait meant a bad omen, bad blood in the future. If anyone on board turned out to be such a person, he was put ashore at the first chance. Or tossed overboard if the ship was too far from land.

Marriage to him was like a long voyage by sea: unique, filled with dangers, and impossible to redo.

This caution had kept his courtships sedate.

Before meeting Iren, he was going out with Iris. She was a Jewish girl, very attractive, a little chubby. Her sophisticated, seductive personality, her sky-blue eyes, her freckled face, attracted hordes of men. Tamas often dropped in on Iris, who inherited and shared a five-bedroom apartment with her brother, Abel, in Oradea. Abel was a compulsive gambler who tried to live by his wits. He had a daily fight with their uncle, a lawyer, whom their late father had appointed as their guardian. Their uncle had control over Abel's weekly allowance, and Abel always wanted more. When he was not in the 'casino' – the illegal gambling den behind The Corner Bar – he was torturing his violin, but with such artistry and success that he was often able to cover his gambling debts from the tips he demanded and got for his performances. He never spent any time at home; he was either in a stuffy gambling casino or a cheap restaurant, making the stagnant air even more stagnant in the opinion of Tamas, who did not much like Abel.

With Iris, on the other hand, he spent many happy hours, and he was convinced for a time that she was deeply in love with him. One of their favourite pastimes was to hike through the labyrinthine, huge old apartment, lingering in various large rooms stuffed with heavy Biedermeier furniture. Tamas had the feeling he was touring a museum. 'My Dad used to practice medicine here until the day he died,' the girl explained in front of the wide window of one of the rooms. The place looked not just extra-large, but full of unanswered questions and unsolvable mysteries. The walls were covered with medical diplomas, certificates of recognition, honorary memberships in various scientific and benevolent societies, all printed in exotic Gothic lettering. Between the two windows an enormous mahogany desk gave the impression of a sarcophagus. On either side were two heavy leather armchairs whose well-worn, faded, brownish colour dominated the room. The opposite wall was lined with shelves, full of dusty old books that seemed to Tamas to be begging for human hands to caress them.

And then came a terrible day when he hurried up to Iris's sanctuary only to find her weeping.

'I don't really know why I've been crying,' she sobbed. 'I've always wanted to get out of this country, but now that it's possible, I can't make a move.'

'I don't understand what you're talking about.' Tamas stepped closer to the girl and pulled her down on a sofa beside him.

'Abel has decided to emigrate. He just told me. He had another great row with that wretched uncle of ours. He barged in today holding some papers like a flag of victory – a permission for both of us to emigrate, made out in our names. But we must leave the country within a month.'

From his relationship with Iris, Tamas took the memory of a few kisses and very warm handshakes.

His courtship of Iren was even quieter, but it seemed to suit her as well as it suited him.

She was a kindergarten teacher, and when she was not at work, she stayed home. She did knitting and crocheting and saw to the household chores. Her mother had left her father a decade earlier, so Iren did the cooking and washing for him.

Tamas took Iren to the theatre about once a week, but other than that, they went out very little. Sometimes they spent rainy afternoons sitting in the opposite corners of the sofa, each of them reading a novel. It was these uneventful, contented afternoons that made Tamas think how nice it would be to be married to Iren. But for a long time nothing happened.

*   *   *

Tamas came from a broken family. He had first-hand experience of the hell that can be created by two people not getting along.

It happened every Sunday. It started with his mother and father raising their voices. They screamed accusations and counter-accusations at one another, their bodies shaking, and then there was no turning back. The screams grew into howls and then finally into sobs. Their hands, raised high in the air, were shaking. 'It's the money, the money, and the money that will be your ruin!' his father was shouting. 'Nothing is ever enough for you, no matter how much I bring home, you always want more. But where do you want me to get it? You want me to steal, or go become a mugger?'

Tamas became nervous. And fearful too when he heard his father yell: 'I'll smash you, cut you up into pieces, I'll kill you...you've ruined my life!' Tamas wanted to run away. Any place where things like that didn't happen. Where people lived in peace...

At that time he had no idea how one would go about running away from home. He surmised it might be like when neighbour Betty's brother went off to Palestine not that long ago. That was the first time he had heard of that country. He even doubted its existence. But if someone actually went there, he reasoned, it must be real, even if it sounded like a seven-headed dragon in a tale.

Clearly, to move to Palestine is to run away into the unknown world, he concluded.

Every time there was a fight, Grandma wept until her eyes turned red. She held Tamas in her arms, as if never to let go. Sometimes she pressed him so tight he could hardly breathe. He was eager to wriggle out of her embrace and holding her hand he would urge her: 'Let's run away! Granny, let's go out into the big world, do you hear? Let's run away from home!'

But the way things turned out they never went anywhere.

—*Chapter 4*—

Murder in Hotel Odéon
—II—

As soon as he got back to his office, the Mayor, Hugo Wagner, was given the fire chief's report on the rescue operations. Of the 67 residents known to have been in the building at the time of the collapse, 42 had been found in the rubble, so far all of them dead. Since the first floor had sunk into the ground almost intact, there was a good chance that many of the still-missing 25 could be found alive.

Shortly afterwards, he received a phone call from Bucharest. The Minister of Internal Affairs was on the line. His tone was loud, his language vulgar: '…I order you at once…a list of those responsible…irresponsible murderers…fire the lot…arrest them all immediately…' Only fragments of phrases managed to penetrate his consciousness. This could not be happening to him, Hugo kept thinking.

Then the telephone rang again. Hugo reached for the receiver with a trembling hand, letting out a sigh of relief when he heard his wife on the line. Nina had called only to say something nice, something to put his mind at ease. But feeling that her encouragement was falling on deaf ears, she cut her call short. Hugo promised to keep her updated on the latest developments.

A week after the tragedy Hugo was summoned to Bucharest. He came home devastated. Out of the 67 residents at home they found 66 bodies in the ruins that they could identify. One person remained missing.

Nina did all she could. 'They have no business accusing you of anything,' she said. 'If there were warnings about

20

the building, it was the professionals who should have paid attention.'

'Was the building constructed during your administration?' she asked Hugo one morning as he was stepping out of the bathroom. 'It wasn't, was it?'

'No,' he answered dully, 'it was built eleven years ago, as you've probably heard.'

'Right, so then why blame yourself? Did it collapse in the middle of the night on your orders? No, it didn't! Did you do everything to ensure immediate rescue operations? Of course you did! Didn't you spend three nights at the scene hoping to find survivors? Didn't you do everything to help those who found themselves without shelter or the support of their families? Then what's bothering you? What more could you have done? Answer me, I beg of you!'

Hugo remained silent. He could have told her about the accusations made against his office, how the many complaints about the building made by the residents had been ignored, but he saw no point in burdening her.

Her husband's behaviour was so extreme that Nina began to wonder if there was something else behind it, something more than the building collapse. She began to change the focus of her search.

Nina was forty-one years old, curvaceous, and wore her hair short since she had let the hairdresser in the beauty parlour talk her into it: this kind of style was supposed to suit her elongated face. 'This cut will bring new life to your features,' the hairdresser explained, 'and we need that to hold on to our husbands, because nowadays men are bored with marriage. They want adventure. And there are plenty of younger girls with attractive figures. At least, with this "new look" we can try to hold our own.'

Nina did not set much store by this kind of chatter; instead, she was examining her green eyes, arched eyebrows, and the crows' feet developing around her eyes,

as if taking inventory of her face to convince herself not to worry: with proper makeup and expensive creams she could keep herself attractive. She was never a showy dresser; she usually covered her full hips with dark skirts or dresses. Hugo often commented on her good taste; everything she wore looked good on her. She didn't really welcome these compliments; she found them meaningless and routine. She wanted to hear something more specific, something deeper, more personal.

She was not indifferent to Hugo's good points. He had more empathy than most men, and told the truth more than most of them – she thought. There was no doubt however that he was lacking in originality, didn't enjoy banter, and usually fluffed the punch line when trying to tell a joke. And recently, after being elected Mayor, he began to drift into a melancholy state, and they hardly ever saw each other except at weekends. They had no children, and their social life was restricted to official dinners and other political events. This was a strain on Nina, because a Mayor was expected to be always attentive, to listen to interminable stories and patiently suffer endless complaints. She too had to be careful to avoid seeming superior or antagonistic, even to arrogant people she despised. Nina wanted something else. She dreamed about long trips abroad; she dreamed of the fabulous views she saw on travel posters – seashores, white sands, mountains bathed in sunlight.

As time went by, it became more and more obvious that she had to say goodbye to her dreams forever; she would never see them come true by Hugo's side.

—*Chapter 5*—

ZENO LANGDON was in his Calgary office by nine o'clock, earlier than usual for the owner and CEO of the Farm-Fresh Poultry Processing Company. Dora, his personal assistant, handed him five telephone messages, already arranged in order of urgency, and started dialling the callers one by one as soon as Zeno shut his office door. None of the calls seemed to go his way. As he finished each of them, his body slumped more deeply in his swivel chair and his face sagged – a temporary state of collapse only Dora was ever allowed to see. He felt middle-aged.

He ordered a big mug of weak coffee with lots of milk. He liked to sip this during the day – his concoction, as Dora called it.

The morning wore on like this for a while before Wanda came on the line. The call surprised Zeno; immersed as he was in the day's problems, he had forgotten all about the girl. He raised the telephone receiver automatically to his ear and only recognised the caller when she introduced herself in a distinctive, singing tone.

'Yes, now, of course, I remember, we met yesterday.' Zeno's mood immediately lifted. He made an appointment for Wanda in his office for that afternoon to discuss a possible summer job for her. She had one more year to go in business school, and the job would be in the sales department.

Zeno had met Wanda's father, Henrik Karady, only weeks earlier in the THLM bank, in the office of the mortgage manager. Henrik, the head of the computer support section, was demonstrating a newly developed program. Zeno paid little attention to him at that time, but a few days later, he ran into Henrik again at the opening session of the Conservative Party's new campaign season. Henrik had sought him out. He walked up to Zeno with two glasses of mineral water in his hands, offering him one. Zeno could not place him at first but accepted the drink while searching his mind for a clue. Henrik spoke with a guttural accent, which Zeno found strangely in contrast to his meek demeanour.

'I've got it!' Zeno blurted out cheerfully. 'Mr Karady. I know you from the bank.'

Henrik nodded, and then, as if observing a fact of little importance, he added: 'So you too favour the political right.' It would not have occurred to him to think anything else; a manufacturer, a solid businessman, can only belong to the right of the political spectrum.

'I put it a bit differently,' Zeno said. 'I call myself a liberal conservative.'

'I don't mean to pry,' Henrik said, embarrassed. 'It's just that I think a lot about politics. You know how it is in the old country. My father was a revolutionary there. He wanted to overthrow the ruling party. I think he had fantasies of a Platonic republic. I shared his dreams for a time. Then, shortly after the triumph of the revolution, my father was taken away by the soldiers of the new order. He never came back. My mother and I looked for him for a long time, but without success.' He slowly turned the glass back and forth in his hand. 'I can never get that scene out of my mind, the soldiers breaking into our kitchen and dragging my father away. It's like a bad dream that keeps haunting me.'

'Did you ever find out what happened to your father?'

'Yes. We were given precious little information immediately after his arrest, but years later, under the new regime, an official statement arrived saying his body was in an unmarked mass grave.'

Seeing Henrik so disturbed by his memories, Zeno did not want to pursue this conversation.

'So, what's your opinion of politicians now?' Zeno asked.

'I'm not sure,' Henrik answered. 'Some politician always comes up with a new way to sound convincing when he promises something, and before I know it, and in a weak moment, I cast my vote for him.' Henrik shrugged bashfully, like a child caught at some prank. 'And how about you? What brings you here?'

'Walter Wallmeyer mainly – the man on the podium. He's a good friend of mine.' Zeno pointed to the speaker at the other end of the hall. 'Do you recognize him? He's one of the best-known journalists in the country. He's been with the *Monitor* for the past ten years. When he decided to run for the National Assembly he asked me to support his nomination. I agreed, of course. He's not like other politicians. If he promises something he'll go through hell and high water to get it, he'll fight for it with his bare knuckles if he has to. But look, here he is.' Zeno turned to the tall, bespectacled, bearded man approaching them. 'Walter, let me introduce you. This is Henrik Karady from the THLM Bank; my friend, Walter Wallmeyer, your next representative.'

Their conversation was interrupted by a petite blonde, still of college age.

'I'm Wanda,' she said, making an almost theatrical bow. 'Sorry to barge in like this, but I'd like to speak to my father.'

Her turquoise eyes and slender figure caught Zeno's eye. He was also taken by her directness.

'My daughter.' Henrik pointed toward her as if to avoid any misunderstandings. Then he asked to be excused as he walked away with Wanda.

'I was only looking for you because I want to go home. This political rally bores the hell out of me. Is Mom home yet?'

'It wouldn't hurt you to stay till the end. There are a lot of people to meet. You might make some useful contacts,' Henrik pleaded.

'The only contact I'm interested in at the moment is

someone who'll give me a summer job. I'm not going to babysit a snotty eight-year-old again this summer. You and Mom have to accept that. You'll have to make some other arrangements for Patrick,' she said, glancing back in some annoyance at the group they had just left.

Then she hesitated, her eyes having landed on Zeno. 'Wait a minute. Isn't that the owner of the Farm-Fresh factory?' she asked her father.

'Yes it is,' he confirmed.

After a moment, she started to pull her father towards them. 'Come on, I'll take you back to your friends.'

Wanda let go of her father's hand only when they got back to the small group, which had grown by two newcomers. She stood silently by his side, letting him speak for both of them. Henrik did so with some reluctance.

'Wanda, my daughter, is looking for a summer job,' he said hesitantly. 'She was wondering…'

Without hesitating, Zeno reached into his pocket, took out a card from his wallet, and handed it to Wanda.

'Take this and call me tomorrow in my office. In our marketing department we can usually use extra help during the summer months. If you're interested…'

'You see,' she turned to her father, 'you only have to speak up and someone is always willing to help. Thank you Mr Langdon.'

The others standing around them smiled triumphantly, as if each of them had contributed to the happy ending of this little drama. It took a few minutes for the conversation to return to politics – how the upcoming election was to be a turning point in the economic life of the country, and so on.

It was hardly noticed when Wanda quietly slipped out without saying goodbye. Only Zeno followed her with his eyes.

—*Chapter 6*—

WHEN IN THE AFTERNOON LULL Dora announced on the intercom that a Miss Wanda Karady wanted to see him, Zeno had the blueprints of the new installation to the poultry processing plant spread out on his desk, and was examining the sketches of the scalding and feather-plucking units. Taking his time, Zeno rolled down his shirt cuffs from his elbow and put on his coat.

As soon as the girl stepped into the office, it seemed to Zeno that the room brightened.

She was wearing a brown skirt and green silk blouse with matching green earrings. When she crossed her legs, her red Italian high-heel sandals matched her lipstick and called attention to it. She wore little make-up – just a touch of colour on her cheeks and eyebrows.

The flimsiness of her blouse distracted Zeno. He was trying to visualize the girl's breasts under it. On the right there was a small bump indicating the absence of a bra. Having made this discovery, he continued to undress her with his eyes. Wanda sensed what was on the man's mind, and with a slow, hardly perceptible move she pulled herself up on the chair, putting her swelling nipples on unequivocal display, letting them almost poke holes in the silk.

It seemed to Zeno the girl was posing for him. She's offering her body, he thought to himself contentedly.

He's swallowed the hook, the thought flashed through Wanda with a pleasant tingle. He's mine to reel in. I wonder if his body's still all right; she ratcheted higher her imagination.

There was a knock on the door. Dora came in but after one whiff of the heady air in the room she felt superfluous.

With a hand still on the doorknob she asked if she could bring anything for the guest.

'Coffee, tea, or mineral water?' she asked Wanda.

'Mineral water, please,' Wanda said, as she reached for the manila envelope she had brought. She pulled out her CV and handed it to Zeno.

Dora slipped out and was back in a moment with a glass of water. She placed it in front of Wanda. She too noticed the girl's nipples stretching the surface of the blouse. She left the room with a discreet smile.

Zeno took a cursory look at the CV without paying much attention to the words. The sheet of paper in his hand somehow turned into green silk.

'Why don't we meet for dinner tonight and go over the whole thing at our leisure?' He looked her in the eye, waiting for an answer with uncomfortable impatience.

'I have no objection…I mean, gladly,' she said, carefully hiding a surge of joy.

Yes, yes. He's caught! He'll be mine tonight, she felt like shouting, but she let nothing show on her face.

Zeno saw her off to her car.

'Well then, I'll see you at eight at the Hot Island restaurant,' he said as he closed her car door.

'I'll be on time.'

The afternoon saw a procession of visitors marching through the office.

'It's a madhouse today,' Zeno sighed to Dora who was running in and out with glasses and cups.

Dora did not say goodnight until after seven o'clock.

'Behave yourself tonight,' she smiled, knowing perfectly well what her boss's plans were.

Zeno was delayed leaving. When he was halfway out the door of his office the phone rang again. The chief engineer of the firm that was supplying the equipment for the expansion of the poultry processing plant was asking for additional information about the conveyor belts in the scalding unit. The set-up consisted of a series of machines where the already-stunned birds were killed with an electric charge. The birds hung head down from hooks on the belt, their beaks touching a trough of water below with current going through it. The method allowed them to enter into the hereafter without any pain. The live chickens always suffered some stress during transport, and also while being placed on the hooks; that was when harmful hormones could accumulate in the animals about to be sacrificed, and any further stress should be avoided according to the technical literature.

The chief engineer wanted to know whether the stainless steel trough should stay within specifications or be enlarged to match the size of the hall where it was to be installed. Zeno was peeved by the question; to him it seemed obvious that the size of the trough should follow equipment design regardless of available space. They had an exchange about it; what seemed logical to Zeno did not seem as unambiguous to the chief engineer. Finally they agreed that the installation should follow the original plans.

The Hot Island restaurant was in an outlying area, and one look at his watch told Zeno he would not make it on time for the date. He pulled out of the parking lot with a feeling of annoyance at himself, even forgetting to say goodnight to the gate guard.

Wanda was sheltering in her car from the drizzle in the restaurant parking lot. Zeno apologized profusely when he ran to take her hand as she stepped out.

Inside, the restaurant was pleasantly warm. The South-Sea-Island theme was meant to transport the guests to another world, far away from the cares outside.

Zeno had reserved a corner table, where they would have the most privacy. They had a champagne toast. Zeno was aware of the girl's scrutiny. But what can she see in a man of fifty, he asked himself, while enjoying Wanda's curious glances that sent tingles through his body.

The appetizers were served. Mixed salad for Zeno, and cold lobster for Wanda.

Zeno was looking at the wine bottle. From the bottom of his consciousness some lines of a German poem started to surface:

> *'Warum gibst Du mir die Hand*
> *Scheu und wie geheim ?*
> *Kommst Du aus so fernem Land*
> *Kennst nicht unseren Wein ?...'*

She listened with an expression of surprise written on her face.

'Heidegger, the German philosopher, fell in love with a student at the university,' he explained. 'Her name was Hannah Arendt, and she wrote these lines to her professor:

> Why do you give to me your hand
> So secretly and shy ?
> Are you coming from so far a land
> That you do not know our wine ?...'

'It's a sad poem,' Wanda remarked with her expression turning more serious. 'I know very little about literature. Especially poetry. I've been avoiding those courses in college that involve poetry interpretation. But there's no missing the longing in the words. What brought them to your mind just now?'

'The wine!' Zeno burst out laughing. 'Wine can not only lift your spirit, but can flood you with certain moods and memories, too. In my younger years I used to read a lot – with no discrimination – anything that fell into my hands. I was a great fan of poetry and philosophy. I couldn't tell you precisely where I read those lines. But they stayed in my memory. Probably I was subconsciously thinking about the age difference between us, how young you are compared to me.'

'But that's ridiculous. Nowadays that doesn't matter. Actually, it didn't in the old days either. My grandmother was eighteen when she married a man of forty-five. They got along just great.'

'Maybe you're right. But how can one tell in advance?' While talking, Zeno reached out to squeeze Wanda's hand. Immediately she reciprocated.

The waiter gave good service. He spent just enough time by the table to serve the dishes, and he only refilled the glasses when they were empty.

Zeno had not laughed so much for a long time as that evening. Wanda was good company, telling one funny story after another. And they were not exactly counting the glasses either. Zeno was beginning to worry about how they would get home. It wasn't his safety he was worried about, but the girl's.

It was past midnight when he backed into his own garage; after dinner Wanda had invited him to her apartment for a nightcap. He astonished himself when he, a man who was always cautious and never impulsive, didn't even think about saying no. He liked the young girl and was enjoying the adventure.

The evening redefined the concept of sex for him: pure pleasure, free of all the obligations and commitments that tied him down. It had been magnificent, the girl, the night, the whole experience. Its afterglow stayed with him all the way home, dispelling feelings of guilt and pangs of conscience.

The night's sexual excursion seemed so natural, so inevitable. There was no doubt about it – he had wanted the girl at first sight and knew he was going to get her. He was not some lovelorn swain longing for an inaccessible object of desire but consciously driven by all the power of passion. He wanted to conquer Wanda, to take her away from the world. Nothing could stand in his way – he made his own way.

*   *   *

Sylvia, his wife, had to wake him in the morning. Where had he been? Why did he come home so late? She was already in street clothes with her luxuriant honey-coloured hair done up, ready to go out. Zeno was slow with answers; his head was still buzzing with the wine of the night before and he had trouble producing a passable alibi. 'I was in the Club,' he said finally.

The Club on 13th Avenue was always a handy excuse, somewhere he dropped in almost every day. Who would recall exactly what night he was there, especially how late he stayed, Zeno was trying to convince himself.

'Walter had called a meeting of the members of the election campaign committee, and we stayed on talking. You know how politicians are, they never know when to quit.'

Sylvia was saying something about his stumbling into bed some time after two in the morning, but seeing the clock on the wall, Zeno did not stay around to listen. 'I'm late,' he said, jumping out of bed.

He peeled off his pyjamas on the way to the bathroom.

'I have a heavy schedule today,' Sylvia declared, stepping into the bathroom. 'Do you think you could have my light-blue outfit picked up from the cleaners by any chance? The ticket is on the kitchen table. Try not to forget, will you?' Blowing a goodbye kiss, she glided off.

Zeno relaxed in the hot tub. Shutting his eyes, he could see Wanda's body and feel the imprint of her hot lips on his own. He gave himself up to the memory.

*　　　*　　　*

Later, at his desk, he had just finished signing a stack of requisitions when Wanda stepped into his office. She ran over and kissed him. Zeno let it happen. A little later he reminded her they were in the office, but then he immediately regretted saying it.

'If meetings are awkward, you could send me letters,' Wanda suggested.

'Letters?' He was surprised.

'We could use the in-house mail. Your mail is never opened by anyone else, and no one would dare open any mail coming from you to me. What do you say? It would be exciting.' Her eyes gleamed. 'I'm afraid to call you, anyone can eavesdrop on phone calls. There are four of us in the office, I'm hardly ever alone, and when I am, you might not be free. Say something, isn't this a good idea?'

Zeno looked at her astonished. He said nothing at first, and then he nodded. 'All right. We'll try it. But send only office documents at first, and we'll see how it works out.'

Wanda gave him another hug, but not the way a mature woman hugs a man; there was something clumsily hurried about it, something that reminded the man of a gawky teenager.

Left alone, Zeno absentmindedly shuffled some papers on his desk. What's the idea of writing letters, he mumbled to himself. The tattered images of last night emerged in his mind. Wanda's bare body. Her embraces. Hot kisses. The shadows dancing on the grey walls. The heavenly post-coital calm.

He wondered what the girl thought of him. One dinner, and she was ready for bed. Who conquered whom, Zeno asked himself with an anaemic smile on his lips. Dangerous game, he thought. Never in my life have I had to keep secrets. Now I'll have to hide, lie, and pretend. No, this cannot go on. And Wanda is so heartbreakingly young.

But why not go on? Another voice spoke up inside him. You do need a little playtime, relaxation. Take advantage of the opportunity. Why be so worried? You're not hurting anyone. Enjoy yourself. And was it you who initiated the whole thing, were you the seducer? Maybe the girl too needs someone, maybe someone she can look up to.

She needs me, of all men? Me, the knight on a white stallion riding to the rescue? Me the idol of every teenage girl?

Look, you're not all that old. What is fifty? You're in good shape. You work out three times a week. You have money, social position, friends in high places. Don't you think all of these things are attractive to young girls? The other voice went on insistently.

Yes, but Wanda is not just any girl!

Oh yeah? Then what kind of a girl is she?

She's different. There's some kind of inexplicable sadness about her, even when she seems to be happy.

Isn't she playing with you?

I don't think so. She acts so natural. I feel she tells me just what's on her mind.

And what is that?

I haven't figured that out yet. I'll have to try harder. But enough of this for today, I've already wasted too much time on her. Let's see what's next on the agenda?

Escaping? Your conscience is bothering you?

Maybe. It seems I can't resist her.

—*Chapter 7*—

THE EVENTS surrounding his parents' divorce had faded from Tamas's memory. The passage of time jumbled them all together into indistinct impressions. The past appeared to him in flashes – like shadows on a filmstrip held up to a flickering light. The small village with its streets of whitewashed cottages was a sea of dust in summer and a sea of mud in autumn and spring. Only the highway bisecting the small settlement was paved. That was where all the long-distance traffic rumbled through, mostly trucks and buses.

They would go by bus to a nearby town. A twenty-kilometre trip would take an hour and a half. Tamas usually travelled with his grandparents or his father among smelly sacks, luggage of various shapes and colours, and live animals too: chickens, lambs, pigs, all packed into the vehicle until it almost sank to the ground. The rattle and clamour filling the airless inside of the bus made conversation impossible. Passengers perched uncomfortably on top of their luggage like chickens roosting on the rods of the coop, the bus and the passengers jolted by potholes.

Then another memory. His grandfather's face with the inevitable fire-flower – the hand-rolled cigarette – aglow in the corner of his mouth. Dad stands next to him. He's questioning Tamas.

'Your mother is a sinking ship. I can provide safety and a warm home for you. Which one of us do you want to stay with, Son?' he asks. 'Do you want to go aboard a sinking ship?'

'Yes!'

'And why? Why do you want to go there?'

'I like it there! I want to stay with Mom!'

'You want to live in an unstable household?' yells the man.

'Mom is not unstable. Why do you say that?'

'Your mother cannot support you, cannot send you to school.' The man raises his voice again.

Tears are trickling from the boy's eyes, their sparkles obscure his vision.

'Why can't she? I can walk to school by myself,' he stammers.

The well of memory is filled with stones.

*   *   *

After he left school, Tamas's life underwent a crisis. He was not only trying to find himself and his place in the world, but also the road to success. He had no resources beyond his honesty, diligence, and willpower – all of which were old-fashioned virtues, inadequate in a world that demanded obsequiousness, two-faced playacting, and unlimited compromises for the sake of a personal agenda that had to be disguised. He did not feel qualified to play that game.

He earned his living, from necessity, as a bricklayer with the city's largest construction company. After graduating from school, his way to higher education was blocked (for unexplained reasons – this happened to many) and he could not find any better way of making a living. In the employment office he was offered a choice of several openings. The one on top of the list was for bricklaying. He had some experience, so he accepted the job without hesitation; it was spring, a time when there was plenty of work in construction, and it was nice to work outdoors. In time, he hoped to work towards a college degree at night school.

He had spent his last few summer vacations working with a bricklayer. It was from him that Tamas had learned all the tricks of the trade, everything the old master was willing to share, which was a lot, because, for some reason, he had taken a shine to Tamas. He found the boy was skilful with his hands, eager to work, and generally a good sort. During lunch breaks, but sometimes even on the job, the old man liked to talk about his adventures in his younger days. He called his memories his most precious possessions, the things that made life worthwhile. He especially liked to talk about the times he had spent working in Budapest, the capital of neighbouring Hungary. Between the two world wars, there was a great deal of construction, the restoration of lost structures and the building of new ones – only for everything to be destroyed at the next turn of history. The old man kept retelling the same stories with minor variations, adding a little extra colour, playing with the scenes, rearranging them, describing places he had set foot in only in his dreams. But he was a compelling storyteller. In Tamas's imagination the whole cast of characters appeared in costume. Hats towered on heads, frills rustled in the breeze, walking sticks went tap-tap on the sidewalks. Horse-drawn cabs rolled by on cobblestones in discreetly lit streets. Here and there, one could come upon noisy, lively bars. Such was the story-telling gift of the old man that Tamas felt that he would only have to stretch his arm out to touch the objects in these scenes, and he too could walk alongside these gentlemen wearing top hats in the fashionable streets of the city, passing shop windows crammed full of merchandise. It was like sitting in a movie theatre, watching an old silent film.

Whenever the old man fell into an uncommunicative, gloomy mood, Tamas was always able to get him out of it by asking him to talk about his experiences when he was young. The old master-mason usually had to ask where he had left off the last time, where to continue so as 'not to repeat what cannot possibly be repeated.' The never-to-be-repeated story always started with his arrival in Budapest. That seemed to be the main railroad junction of all his memories; every train from and into the past had to pass through there on a worldwide web of tracks. Tamas got the impression that stories distracted the old man from the miseries of the present. Hands and thoughts nimbly followed their course while the bricks quickly and obediently lay down on top of each other in a perfectly straight line.

There came mornings, however, when Tamas did not feel like getting out of bed. With difficulty, he convinced himself to go back to work with the old man. But he had to find a reason other than his paltry wages. He thought about quitting, telling the old man he'd had enough of building walls, hauling bricks and mixing mortar, constructing arches over hallways. He wanted something else.

He said nothing, however. Days passed, buildings continued to rise, and in time, he became reconciled to his own restlessness, thinking perhaps it wasn't such a bad thing. Without it, what would happen? Without restlessness and high expectations, was anything likely to happen?

Chapter 8

Murder in Hotel Odéon
—III—

T HE MAYOR was having nightmares about the collapse of the building on Balzac Street; he could see the structure start to give way. He would run and try to hold the walls up with his bare hands, but in the end he was buried under the rubble. He usually woke up with his back drenched in perspiration and his heart pounding.

Nina showed him understanding, patience, and even kindness in the weeks following the disaster; but she became more and more convinced that something other than the building disaster was troubling her husband.

In the past Hugo had never seemed withdrawn and taciturn to the degree he had become of late, never as restless and impatient.

One Friday late afternoon they were packing up for a trip to the summer house when the phone rang. Nina picked it up.

'It's for you,' she said as soon as the receiver touched her ear.

Hugo quickly took hold of the receiver. He recognized immediately the velvety feminine voice. It was Lidia.

'No, this is not a good time, I'm on my way out. How about Monday? What time? I'll be free only in the afternoon. Very good, then let it be Monday afternoon. Have a nice...'

'Who was that?' Nina asked with more sharpness than curiosity.

'Miss Novak. I usually meet her for coffee at the City Hall coffee shop; she works for the city publicity department.'

'And why did she call you today?'

'She thought I was in the office today. But when there was no sign of me she decided to call my home number. Monday morning she's supposed to turn in the plans for an advertising campaign to the media group, but first she wanted to have it vetted by me. So that's the story, that's why she called.' He was being very careful with his explanation.

'Isn't it strange she could not deal with this during working hours?'

'As I said, she had hoped I'd come in Saturday morning like I often do.'

Nina went on with the chore of packing, but her eyes kept returning to her husband who claimed to be similarly occupied.

His mind, however, was somewhere else. No matter how he tried to calm himself, he could not concentrate on packing. Lidia's husky and mysterious voice kept echoing the same words in his ear over and over again: 'I want to see you. As soon as possible.'

Artur Liptak had introduced him to Lidia at a friendly get-together in Eddy's Bar. It was a strictly private party, by invitation only, reserved for the select few. At first Hugo was surprised to see someone there who was not only a stranger, but a woman, too. He had not been told about this. Finally Artur revealed that she was the surprise of the evening, and that there was nothing to worry about; the girl was utterly reliable, and he, the attorney Artur, as the unofficial 'security officer' of their group, would accept all responsibility for her.

The bar was located in a spacious cellar with a high vaulted ceiling and a look of quiet luxury. It had curtained booths on one side, a scattering of comfortable armchairs in the middle, and on the other side an inviting bar with stools. Everyone had a partner, except Hugo. He had been drinking for a while when Lidia sat down with him, gently took him by the hand, and led him into one of the booths. It was only then and there, behind the drawn curtain, that he understood why the girl had been invited without prior consultation with the members.

Later, much later, Hugo was sitting by himself at the bar, glancing constantly at his watch like someone anxious to leave. Artur stopped by. He looked at Hugo with a question written on his brows.

'Well, were you disappointed?'

'No.' Hugo looked at his friend with sadness, like someone who has a lot more to say but is reluctant to go into details. At last he added, 'There was nothing said about her being a hermaphrodite.'

'I told you to expect a surprise.'

'Why didn't Viktor show up?'

'I asked him to find something else to do tonight, because I wanted to introduce you to Lidia.'

'But you know I am fond of Viktor.'

'Yes, I know, but I thought you'd appreciate a little variety. What's the problem? You're not mad at me, are you?' Artur patted his friend's shoulder. 'Are you telling me you got nothing out of it? You got no pleasure from Lidia?'

'Let's just drop the subject. I want to go home now.' Hugo got up from the stool and extended a hand to say goodbye.

'Then we'll say goodnight. But tomorrow, if you can spare a minute I'd like to look you up,' Artur said.

'Call my secretary before you come. And tell Viktor never to stay away again.'

—*Chapter 9*—

I N HIS IDLE MINUTES Walter Wallmeyer often caught himself trying on the habits, behaviour, and speech pattern of people he knew. It was a compulsion he couldn't understand. He wondered if it came from his chronic feeling of discontent, from a feeling that something was missing from his life, even though he had enjoyed considerable success in his career as a journalist and had always achieved whatever he set his mind to.

Once he had made the decision to leave behind the daily greyness of a journalist's life and to set his sights on a political career, he was systematic. As a first step, he had to beg his way back to Melanie, the wife he had abandoned two years earlier.

Melanie had grown up in a strict, religious family. She lived an unusually pious life – so much so that Walter occasionally wondered if she were atoning for some supposed sin. She even had the look of a saint; with her immaculate, oval face and dark, shoulder-length hair, he sometimes imagined she could have modelled for the Madonna. In time, his wife's insistence on doing the right thing became too much for Walter. He felt he was living in a cloister where he had to account to his fellow monks, and to his Maker, for every moment and every thought. He needed freedom.

Even then Melanie did not blame him when he announced his intention to leave her, but let him go on his way with a look of merciful forgiveness.

They remained good friends after they separated, calling each other almost daily. Melanie even took in Caroline, Walter's teenage daughter from a previous marriage, and arranged for her education as if nothing had happened.

At a meeting of the Conservative Party, Walter was

nominated as the most promising candidate in an election district that was more or less owned by the opposing party. The committee, however, made it clear that Walter would have to put his family life in order, one way or the other, to qualify for the nomination.

After a few sleepless nights, Walter called Melanie and arranged to meet her. He said he had something important to say to her, that couldn't be dealt with over the phone. They met at five P.M. in Bistro Alberti, a fashionable restaurant in the downtown area.

The flush on Melanie's face betrayed her curiosity.

'I'll tell you what this is all about,' he said immediately, as soon as they sat down. 'Yesterday I was nominated to stand as candidate for the National Assembly from the tenth district. But I've been advised to settle my marital problems before my nomination is submitted to the national committee. I was asked either to make a clean break and get a divorce, or else to get back together with you.'

Melanie listened with her eyes wide open, and then rearranged the napkin slightly under her glass.

'Which solution would you prefer?'

'Truthfully?'

'Yes.'

'I'd prefer reconciliation. You know how grateful I am to you for taking in Caroline and looking after her like your own flesh-and-blood daughter. I feel that's a good enough reason for all of us to live together again as a family.'

Before this conference Walter had mulled over the alternatives, thinking which would benefit him most. Melanie was of secondary consideration in his mind, only a bit-player in this drama.

It's not Melanie who will have to face the other candidates, he reasoned. She doesn't have to shoulder any of the burdens, dangers, and sacrifices connected with the nomination. The election campaign would demand his blood nearly, but only his. Melanie would be just a bystander, necessary so he could present himself to the electorate as a married man, a family man – even if that marriage was known to have had its ups and downs.

Still Melanie would get something out of it too: his party would be appreciative, and he himself would feel honour-bound to pay her back.

Walter did not have a clear idea of how he was going to adjust, but he thought he would work it out when the time came. He made a bargain with himself not to hurt her any more. He would simply ignore everything about her that used to irritate him in the past.

Melanie reached out for his hand. Her expression was loving but contrite. 'The problem is that I can't change, Walter. Not even for your sake. I am what the Lord made me. I can't think and behave the way you do or have the opinions you approve of, no matter how hard I try. We got along much better when we lived separately than under the same roof. No matter how much I love you I can't change.'

'Then think of it as an experiment,' he pleaded. 'Let's try it, even if just for appearance's sake, for the time of the election campaign. When the elections are over we can think again. Please do that for me, for our future, for Caroline.'

Walter felt drained, and was already beginning to regret what he had undertaken, although he felt close to achieving his objective. He decided to mention the material benefits.

'You'll be treated differently at work,' he pointed out. 'In the school you'll get the best classes, the most sought-after hours. And I won't be home very much, I'll manage to stay in Ottawa even for the weekends, if that's what you want.' Walter was ready to negotiate.

Then Melanie spoke. 'I'm not sure that moving back together is the ideal solution for either of us,' she said softly. 'Maybe we should get a divorce, if that's what the party wants.' Her voice was silky, but to Walter every word felt like a stone she was throwing at him.

'No, please, don't choose this road. Today we go home from here...the two of us and...we make peace. Now, what do you say? I'm certain that's the best solution for both of us...'

At that moment, as he was looking hopefully at Melanie, Walter froze, and almost bit the sentence in half. He had just remembered that he had promised to spend the evening and night with Barbara.

He studied Melanie anxiously, but relaxed when he saw she was hesitating, still unable to decide; so there was no danger of the two of them being back together that night.

'Fine, let it be tomorrow. Tomorrow I'll move my things back to the house. At least I'll have some time to pack.' He clung to the words as to a life jacket; he did not want to give up the night he had planned.

Melanie cast a tender glance at her husband, saying softly, 'Fine, I'll do that one more favour for you, my dear.'

*   *   *

That evening was a perfect one for Walter.

He had got back with his wife, and that, combined with the prospect of spending a night with his lover – and not just any night, but the last one for some time – intoxicated him.

If there was a negative, it was they were both married, and worse – not without some degree of recognizable public image. They usually picked a quiet, romantic suburban restaurant for a dinner, and from there they adjourned to Barbara's place. They followed the same programme that night.

It had been a long time since Walter had felt as liberated and as full of energy. Barbara too, it seemed, wanted to savour this last night.

The next day, however, brought Walter back to reality. He spent all morning loading his belongings into his large sedan, dismayed at the number of possessions he had accumulated in the past two years – things he would probably never have any use for. He drove out of the parking lot of his apartment house with a heart that was heavy and a back seat that was full of bulging suitcases.

Before he knew it, as if guided by the invisible hand of reawakened habits, he arrived back at the home he had abandoned and now wanted to reclaim. After the huge sedan came to a reluctant halt by the curb, Walter took his time getting out of the car. In the meantime his wife appeared at the front door.

'Wait,' she said, 'let me open the garage door. It'll be easier that way, and the neighbours won't have to watch. Caroline will help you.'

As soon as he and his daughter had unloaded the car, Walter collapsed into one of the big armchairs in the living room like an ordinary husband; his wife brought in a tray with two wine glasses and an open bottle on it.

'I thought we'd celebrate your homecoming,' she said as she placed the tray on the coffee table. She emphasized the word homecoming as if she had been Penelope welcoming home Odysseus.

Walter forced a smile, but a faraway look remained; in his thoughts he was still with Barbara. He was only jolted back to the present by Caroline's appearance. She sat down on his knees and put her arms around his neck. Watching the two of them together, Melanie was moved and even had to wipe tears from the corners of her eyes. She went out to the kitchen for a glass of water.

Later, Walter was putting away his books on shelves in the family room in the basement when Melanie called down to him that he was to be featured on the evening news.

The discussion was about the upcoming national elections. Among the candidates of the Conservative

Party, his name was mentioned with the comment that, even though his chances of winning were good, he still had big problems ahead of him; he still had to prove that the rumours surrounding his family life were unfounded.

'I expect this is only the beginning,' said Melanie, who had joined him in watching the broadcast. 'The liberals will do everything in their power to drag you through the mud. You'd better steel yourself, and not give them any reason to focus on you,' she went on, squeezing his hand. 'If I were you, between now and the election, I wouldn't allow myself the slightest hint of an indiscretion. The past is past, a memory; let's bring down the curtain on it. From now on it's going to be different. No one will have the courage to pillory you.'

Walter listened quietly to Melanie's words. For a moment he felt ashamed of himself for what he had done last night; but he recovered quickly and started talking about his plans for the future.

'Tomorrow there'll be a press release about my candidacy. Cameron promised to include something positive about my family life. You'll see, everything will work out just fine.'

Yet, even as he spoke, he was rummaging through his memories of the past year for the incidents that might get him into trouble. He came to the conclusion that everything could be disregarded except his two-year-old relationship with Barbara.

Barbara's husband, Elmer Redwick, a well-known local businessman, was constantly on the road. He rarely spent a day under the same roof as his wife. If he weren't on his plane, then he would be on board his private yacht. Their marriage was more amicable than romantic, but in its own way, well adjusted.

Elmer and Barbara lived their separate lives. Barbara was devoted to the golf course, to her exercise routine (now in her thirties, she had a perfect, sport-honed figure), and to her single-engined Cessna that she used to fly on pleasure trips. Elmer spent his time building up and running financial conglomerates. According to experts in the field he had a fiendishly clever mind for everything that had to do with making money. He gave his wife the green light to do as she pleased so long as she didn't advertise her affairs. He never held her accountable for her movements, never had her traced, never looked into her activities and her associations. Elmer placed himself and his work above everything else.

Walter liked Barbara not only for her complete sense of freedom but also because she never made any wilful demands on him. They always met at their leisure, when neither of them had any other obligations. He didn't have to woo her, make up lies for her, play a role to her, or be anyone other than himself. She accepted life as it came to her. If it felt good, it was good, and she knew what was right for her, and how to get what she wanted. That was all she needed from life. She was a perfect partner.

When they first met, Walter had immediately come under her spell. He approached her that same day, but with caution – in the manner of an experienced hunter stalking his prey. He paid her little compliments, praised the beauty of her green eyes and curly auburn hair, and of course he lavished his smiles on her. Finally Barbara reacted to all this song and dance with her natural straightforwardness: 'If you want me, why wait? We can get together right now.' Walter was intrigued by this sudden decision, but he never had a chance to find out what triggered the instant attraction in her. At the beginning of their relationship he desperately wanted to know, but later, as they got closer to each other, the question faded away.

He also found it hard to believe that here was a human creature who was not only intent on receiving her share from life, but also on giving some back, who could reciprocate every good word, gesture, caress, in a natural and matter-of-fact manner. It puzzled him that in all that time they knew each other there was never a loud word between them. He ran into Elmer only once at a cocktail party. Barbara introduced Walter the way one usually presents a best friend.

The husband looked his rival over thoroughly from head to toe before nodding with the laconic remark: 'I always find my wife has good judgment when it comes to men.' And with that he gulped down a glass of champagne.

That evening Barbara didn't seek out Walter even once, and he didn't pursue her either. He too thought it more appropriate and reasonable to avoid hanging around with his girlfriend at a party where her husband was also a guest. He was satisfied with spotting her now and then among the other guests. He watched her from the corner of his eye. He was not without feelings of jealousy. Of the husband.

All the same, going home from the party he felt reasonably at peace with the world and with himself. 'This is the way it has to be,' he thought.

Chapter 10

MURDER IN HOTEL ODÉON
—IV—

MAYOR HUGO WAGNER got to know Viktor a year earlier in the Club as another discovery of Artur's. Since then, they had spent many happy hours together. Viktor was not only young but exceptionally handsome. After an evening spent with him Hugo always went home refreshed, fulfilled, and in a good mood. Nina even remarked once that he must have very good company to entertain him if he came away in such good cheer. Hugo only nodded absentmindedly.

He got together with Viktor in the Club twice a month. The last time, though, Valerian, the ever-popular clown of the Club, almost spoiled it for him, perhaps because Valerian was drunk. Without any provocation, he had started taunting Viktor. Hugo tried to stop it, but the flow of invective continued, and finally Valerian muttered something about Viktor being his acquisition and how it was obvious that the boy was in love with him, Valerian, alone. The phrase 'in love' pushed Hugo over the edge, and without any hesitation and with all the force he could muster, he punched Valerian in the chest. Staggered by the blow, the man went down on the floor. Like a tiger, Viktor immediately leapt into the fray and tried to revive his lover, desperately shouting for water and ice. He cast murderous looks at Hugo, who, having shocked himself by his unthinking act, sought to undo the damage.

Viktor did not show up at the next scheduled meeting with Hugo. Long weeks had passed when one night, fairly late, looking as innocent as a lamb, as if nothing had happened, Viktor appeared by Valerian's side on the lowermost steps of the cellar bar. Pressing his way farther in, he passed right by the Mayor without acknowledging his presence, as if passing a stranger. Hugo was sitting by himself at the bar, looking forlorn. That evening's company had broken up earlier than usual. Artur too had some urgent business to attend to. Hugo sought out his lover with his eyes, casting long looks in his direction, but could not bring himself to walk up to him. After all, he was thinking, it was Viktor who left me in the lurch and more than likely cheated on me. But why? This question had been bothering him ever since the day of the knockout punch. It seemed to him they had had a very intimate relationship in every respect; everything was on the level between them. They never argued about anything, never even raised their voices with each other. What had Valerian got that he hadn't? How did Valerian seduce the boy? Hugo was unable to stem the tide of jealousy that flooded his whole body. Losing Viktor came at the worst time; the Balzac Street tragedy was taking a heavy toll on him. Apart from worries about the ultimate outcome of the investigation, it had left him twice as busy as before. He rarely had a chance to relax. This emotional state caught him by surprise; he couldn't imagine love could be like that. When he had been courting Nina he never experienced such stabbing throbs of pain in an open wound in his chest. Or perhaps it had not been the real thing, not real love?

In the past he had lived in the belief that only in younger people could feelings cause such physical tortures. At a mature age people react differently. They're more rational. More understanding. More willing to compromise. They don't take chances, they don't expose their souls to all kinds of dangers. They can control themselves. Hugo marshalled whole rafts of rational argument in an effort to calm himself, but they failed to stop him from becoming more and more impatient and nervous. He had become unable to deal with opinions contrary to his own; he would get easily aroused, and ready, like a furious hound, to savage the offender.

And now here was his chance; he could walk up to Viktor, ask for an explanation and perhaps straighten things out between them. But he's not doing it.

He's just sitting there at the bar, staring straight ahead, totally paralysed. Hasn't he suffered enough in the past two weeks? Shouldn't he ask Viktor for some kind of explanation for his strange and hurtful behaviour? On his part, Hugo had done everything to make their relationship work; he had taken special pains to ensure that the social difference between them would not raise its head.

Their very first meeting actually preceded their formal introduction at the Club by two weeks. One morning Nina rather tartly reminded Hugo that he was seriously overdue for a haircut. She made him promise to go to the barber immediately. Getting into the mayoral limo parked in front, he asked the chauffeur to make a detour to his usual barbershop downtown.

It was a few minutes past eight when he stepped into the shop, and he was surprised to find only one barber on duty at this normally busy morning hour, and not the man he was accustomed to, Nandi. Hugo introduced himself to the new barber and inquired about Nandi. 'Nandi is on vacation,' said Viktor, the new barber, and he invited the customer to sit down, offering to cut his hair since he was already there. Hugo made himself comfortable in the revolving chair, and while he was fitted out with a clean sheet around his neck he explained what his requirements were: 'Short on the back and the sides and longer in front, parted almost in the middle but not quite.'

Viktor quickly got to work. As he listened to the clicking of the scissors Hugo casually scrutinized the barber. His hair was not only wavy but had ringlets in it in a feminine fashion. He had bushy eyebrows, black eyes, a lean, bony face, and a nose that was slightly bent. He was of average height, very slender, not muscular, rather all bones and sinew. Hugo thought him attractive, although he found his mannerisms definitely girlish. He held the comb between two fingers, his little finger sticking out as if he were trying to point to something with it. The deft employment of his busy hands, however, did not stop Viktor from telling Hugo all about himself. He had only moved to the city a year ago. He had been a manager of a barber shop in a village, but he had got fed up with that small place, which offered little in the way of entertainment except television. He really enjoyed living in a big city where he could go to the cinema and theatre. He was also finding new friends. And he didn't hesitate to reveal that he was already thirty-six but still unmarried even though he had had many opportunities in years past.

He dramatized his story with wide gestures. 'Every time someone proposed to me' – that's how he put it with a wink – 'I answered with a definite no. A family is a millstone around your neck, not to speak of the responsibility. I'm used to being alone.' When he was thirty, he had lost both his parents in quick succession. He had only an aunt left. 'And she lives at the other end of the country,' he said sadly, as he slowly circled the customer's head with a hand mirror and asked him how he liked the results.

Hugo smiled with satisfaction.

'Good job.'

Viktor helped him out of the seat, gave his clothes a quick once-over with a brush, and said with a grin: 'Thank you Sir, thank you Mister Mayor!'

Hugo looked at him in surprise. 'I only gave you my first name.'

Viktor grinned: 'I've seen your picture in the papers, not to mention the television news.'

Hugo nodded, 'Yes, of course. I tend to forget how often I'm interviewed on TV or just asked for comments. Almost every day, in fact.'

Two weeks later they met again in Eddy's Bar. Their relationship took off quickly.

Hugo still remembered when and where he had entrusted Artur with the job of doing a quiet but thorough background check on Viktor to make sure there was nothing in his past that could spell trouble.

A few days later Artur reported back that there were no problems as far as Viktor was concerned. He had always been very discreet about his relationships, and there was nothing in his past that could one day present a problem.

—*Chapter 11*—

FOR ZENO, the major expansion of the factory – the installation of the new poultry-processing assembly line – was an emotional challenge as well as a big job of work. He was conscious that it affected the welfare of a small community whose members counted on the expansion for their livelihood – for their future. The income from their jobs here provided them with houses, cars, furniture, vacations and entertainment, bank loans, and everything else that was important to them in life.

Of course, the plant, indeed the whole company, belonged exclusively to Sylvia; therefore, sacrificing a large portion of the profit, ploughing it back into the business did not seem like a personal burden to him. He could easily do without some of the showier expenditures. Maybe Sylvia had a little less to squander, but he could not think of any other drawbacks. The investment would not only pay for itself but would bring extra profit. He was sure of that.

Returning to his office, he found two stacks of mail towering on his desk. Dora had already sorted the outside mail from the house mail. He reached for the house mail first. He riffled through the envelopes quickly until he came upon the one from the marketing department. He immediately ripped it open. The envelope contained only business documents. He impatiently flipped them over one by one with shaking fingers. At the bottom of the last sheet there was a short line, scrawled in pencil:

I love you.
W.

He smiled, relishing the thought that Wanda could not

restrain herself. He closed his eyes. He could see the girl before him. The pixie nose in the round face. He took a sheet of blank paper and scribbled a few words as a quick response:

> I'm always with you. Even at a distance I'm taking care that no harm of any kind should ever come to you.
> You've become the meaning of my life.
> Z.

Before burying the note among the office documents he re-read it. He wondered where the words had come from. He was a fifty-year-old man. He hadn't written anything like this before. He sealed the envelope and put it with the others in the out-tray.

The next day Wanda's first letter arrived:

> I'm reading your letter and every portion of my body is throbbing. You are a marvel! I didn't imagine you could write like this. You are usually so businesslike, so careful, so precise.
> I was so happy when you offered me the job, because I wanted you. I wanted to see your body, feel your arms and taste your lips. I love you without limits, I'm all yours. I can hardly wait to see you.
> I'm trembling with expectation,
> W.

Staring at these words Zeno finally made up his mind to spend the weekend with Wanda, if it was at all possible. Their first encounter had been awkward, complicated, and self-conscious. He hadn't been able to give himself over to the situation – to the euphoria he had felt. The memory of that night was swirling around him; he could still feel the touch of the girl's body. Those passing moments now seemed unreal and yet he could not stop thinking about them.

On Tuesday Sylvia announced she was going on a

golfing outing on Saturday and Sunday. 'Team competition among us girls,' she said, smoothing her hair back with both hands. 'I told them there was nothing to hold me back; you're busy with the new installation and would understand if I join them. Do you mind?'

All Zeno could think about was the fickleness of fate, and how sometimes it offers opportunity on a platter.

*   *   *

He was a happy man when he stood up from his desk to go to the outer office to consult Dora about vacation resorts. But before reaching the door he turned back; there was no reason to involve the secretary in his plans for an illicit weekend. Instead, he checked out a guide for a suitable hideaway within a reasonable distance. He decided on Banff, a mountain resort only a hundred and thirty kilometres away, less than two hours by car on the Trans-Canada Highway. His one problem had been what story to tell Sylvia to justify the trip; but he had dismissed this minor detail – he would have plenty of time to come up with an alibi. If he put the problem aside, it would eventually take care of itself. And now that had happened: Sylvia was the one who had first announced her plans to take the weekend off, and all he had to do was adjust to her schedule with a believable story.

Thinking back about his life with Sylvia he had to admit she was never a burden to him, she never assailed him with suspicions about possible betrayals, and she was willing to overlook some of his passing adventures and treat them as jokes. He enjoyed total freedom with her.

Twenty years ago, when they got married, both had practical motives. Zeno, although he didn't necessarily want to admit it, had wanted a springboard for his ambitions.

Sylvia was only two years younger than Zeno. After graduation from college she set off on a trip around the world. She planned on travelling for a year, but more than two years had passed by the time she made her way home. She was not interested in any particular career. Her father was in failing health at that time and, being an only child, she was heir to a sizable fortune. She had lost her mother at an early age in childbirth complications that also claimed the life of the baby.

She felt she had to do something with her life. If nothing else, she could get married. For example, to Zeno who seemed to be both an attractive and sensible choice. She knew nothing about running the family business and the factory, even less of the technology of poultry processing and market strategy. Zeno on the other hand was burning with ambition and eagerness to prove himself in the world; he was the ideal person to take into the family business and perhaps to let him run it one day.

Three months into their marriage Sylvia's father suffered a sudden heart attack after dinner. He recovered consciousness just long enough to make a will.

After his death, all the burden of the business fell upon Zeno's shoulders. Sylvia didn't feel able to move a muscle; she didn't feel like getting out of the house or even seeing anyone. She sat by herself in the living room with the curtains drawn, listening to Chopin. She lived in this lethargy month after month while Zeno managed the meatpacking plant. He went to work early in the morning, returned home late, sometimes after midnight. He was well aware of Sylvia's condition, and it worried him that he could spend so little time with her. Once he got up in the middle of an important meeting and left the conference table to run home and check on her. On entering the house he found her in bed with an open tranquilliser bottle on the bedside table. He thought only a few pills were missing, not enough for a lethal dose. Nevertheless, he did not return to the plant but waited until she woke up. From that day on he hired a nurse to stay with her; he told Sylvia she was a maid.

They both wanted to have a child, but Sylvia's pregnancies ended in miscarriage and then depression. Zeno worked hard to bring her out of it. He arranged outings for her, and weekend parties with friends. After a while, she did begin to improve.

Twenty uneventful years passed, uneventful to the point of boredom. There were years when they did some travelling, but Zeno could not stay away from the plant for more than a week, and their trips were more hurried than leisurely; they could never enjoy a peaceful vacation. Eventually Sylvia occupied herself with charitable work and the socializing it involved. She was elected secretary of the local Red Cross, and threw herself into the work. Their relationship also benefited; they hardly ever argued about anything, partly because they spent so little time together.

Zeno was an attentive husband; from time to time he would surprise Sylvia with little presents and he never forgot their wedding anniversary; when they travelled he was always the one to fill out the visa applications, and unlike many husbands, he didn't have to ask his wife for her date of birth.

At the beginning of their marriage they did love each other, but over the years passion slowly gave way to strong, lasting friendship. It never occurred to Sylvia that Zeno might desert her some day. She found it amusing and exciting when Zeno started flirting with a cream puff, because she knew it would never threaten their own relationship.

*   *   *

The phone rang on Zeno's desk. It was the head of the processing department, asking what programme he should arrange for the director of the machine tool company arriving the following day. Zeno advised him to take the visitor to Canmore, a resort between Calgary and Banff, where he could join them on Sunday afternoon. But all that time he was thinking only of how fate was smiling yet again on his weekend with Wanda; now he could tell Sylvia he had a business obligation, an appointment with a supplier passing through the area. If they started back from Banff early enough, he should have plenty of time to exchange a few words with the VIP visitor. He could hardly believe his luck at this unexpected turn of events. He was thinking of having Wanda summoned to his office when the secretary announced the head of the local labour union who wanted to speak with him.

'Right now?' Zeno asked, unable to hide his annoyance.

'Yes, he says it's urgent.'

'Okay, bring him in please,' he sighed as he headed for the small conference table in the corner.

Marcel, a lean, intelligent-looking, balding man, spoke in a soothing tone of voice.

'Excuse me Chief, but I have something very urgent to put to you,' he said while shifting his weight from one foot to another.

'Why don't you sit down?' Zeno played host to the visitor. 'You look worried. What's the problem?'

'Chief, I know we've met several times in the past few days, but somehow I never got a chance to tell you how upset the women are,' he said, looking down at the table as if he had no intention of ever lifting his eyes again.

'Let's hear what it's about, Marcel.'

'Look, Chief, it's about the assembly line…'

'Okay, let's stop there; everyone knows that the installation of the new assembly line is only a matter of weeks away,' Zeno pointed out, annoyed.

'But that's exactly the problem! The women are worried about their jobs. The newly installed equipment will require fewer hands. We figure at least thirty people will be laid off, plus at least three maintenance workers. Nobody wants that. No one can afford the luxury of being unemployed.'

Zeno cut him short. 'And what is it the union expects from me?' he asked, struggling to keep his frazzled nerves under control.

It had hit home; he had just realized that in spite of all his efforts he could not make himself accepted as a friend of the labour union. All this time it had made no impression when he was telling his workers: 'In my facility there's no need for union protection, because I know exactly what you people need – money first, more money second, and even more money third, and ever better working conditions.' But now it looked like he really didn't know all that well what his workers needed.

Zeno looked at the man sitting in front of him.

'We want the management to guarantee full employment for all our members. We want no one laid off,' Marcel said with determination, undisturbed by the momentary silence.

'But that's impossible!' Zeno was drumming with his fingers on the table.

'In that case, Chief, we have no choice but go on strike in ten days.'

'Please stop calling me "Chief", my name is Zeno.' He spoke with rancour and strong emphasis to Marcel. 'And you picked the peak of the poultry season to lodge your grievance, didn't you? Didn't you people consider the consequences of your action? That we would not be able to deliver, that we lose orders. Not only that, but the customers, too, forever, because this is just what the competition is waiting for – an opportunity to get to our clientele. No, you didn't. And now you're willing to risk the very existence of this plant – this company!' he thundered.

Zeno could hardly restrain himself. He found the demands of the union totally irrational. His eyes kept shifting from the union leader to the blueprints on the table.

'You people asked for the new installation – you

said it would increase the company's productivity and economic strength, and you could work under cleaner, more hygienic conditions. I could go along with that. I satisfied your demands. But you were perfectly aware of the implications of a new production line, you knew that a cutback in workforce was part of the deal. So why are you attacking me now?'

'We're not attacking you, Zeno. We agree with everything you said. All we're asking is that you carry out your plans for the new facility without a reduction in the workforce.'

'And what am I going to do with the excess workforce? Am I to use them like extras in a film and have them stand around doing nothing?'

'No, not at all. What we had in mind was reassignment of the excess workers to the de-boning and quartering section, where the staff are now overworked. That is the hardest phase of the processing. It is impossible to keep up the pace in an eight-hour workday even with the scheduled breaks. With a bigger labour force we could turn out better quality products. If we take into account that the new equipment is designed to double production, then we can increase not only quantity but quality as well.'

'In effect, you guys want me to double the work force in the de-boning and quartering section of the production line?'

'Exactly.'

Zeno knew the proposal wasn't without merit, but it made the expansion a riskier venture. 'Give me a few days to consider your proposal,' he said to Marcel. 'A week from today you'll have my final answer.'

He got up from the conference table, signalling the end of meeting. In parting he offered his hand. Marcel's palm was somewhat moist, and he had a few beads of sweat coursing down his brow.

'The only thing that beats me is why you didn't come out with all this last week when I asked you if you had any problems or unresolved issues that needed to be dealt with,' Zeno said sharply at the end.

'I wasn't quite prepared, Zeno. Believe me, it's not easy for me. I had to come today, because there was no way of putting it off any more.' On his way out he gave his cap slight tug.

As soon as the door closed behind Marcel, Zeno slumped down into his leather armchair. I didn't need this now, he thought. Just to occupy himself, he started shuffling the papers strewn all over his desk.

He decided to have the chief accountant go over the labour costs involved and ask him to prepare another version of the budget with twenty-six employees added, which would leave only seven to be laid off. It was all problematic, but the issue had to be resolved before irreparable damage was caused.

He sat there for a time, slumped in his chair, his mind paralysed. And then he remembered that before Marcel showed up he was going to have Wanda summoned.

The girl appeared with a big bundle of files under one arm. She has found a perfect cover, Zeno thought looking at her slim figure. She looked even more beautiful to him than two days earlier when they had spent the evening together.

Wanda was ecstatic about the invitation for the weekend. They parted with the plan that Zeno would pick her up Saturday morning at her apartment.

Chapter 12

CHRISTINE WAS BUSY in the kitchen. She was thinking about Wanda. Her relationship with her daughter was not as easy these days as it used to be. Preparing supper, she didn't even hear her husband enter the house until Henrik showed up in his business suit in the door leading from the foyer.

He was late and stole a guilty glance at the clock on the wall over the breakfast nook.

Christine was tossing salad greens in a large wooden bowl. Henrik gave her a hug, wrapping his arms around her still slender waist, nearly reached by her long blond hair.

'I'm afraid I didn't have a very good day today,' he said.

'But wasn't it payday?'

'Yes.' Henrik paused while he parked his briefcase on the side table with a tired swing of his arm. 'That's what ruined the day for me. You know how much overtime I put in last week, even working Saturday and Sunday, and guess what? Today I look at my paycheck and I figure it's two hundred short. So I show it to my boss. He acts like he doesn't understand what it's about. And then I reminded him about the new computer program that I had to spend all that extra time on. "Yeah, yeah," he said, "Henrik, these are hard times we're living in." And that was it – he considered the matter settled. A little later he came by though and assured me the director was very pleased with my work, and next month my paycheck will reflect his gratitude.'

'We could have used that money now," Christine said. 'With the car giving so much trouble and the real estate tax going up, let alone that we haven't been able to go on a vacation for two years.' His wife was dishing out her complaints with the supper.

'I know,' said Henrik tiredly. 'It's hard to keep up. It's the same for everyone. You're seduced into buying houses and cars you can't afford, and by the time you wake up from the dream, you find yourself in debt up to your ears.' Henrik spread his arms in a dramatic gesture. 'So you run around, driving yourself ragged, hustling, working your hands to the bone, and then you don't even realize you've grown old, your life is over.'

'Eat your supper!' Christine broke into his tirade.

'Why? Isn't this the truth though? I work with figures all day in the bank, hammering at mathematical formulas, and what do I get out of it? No bonus, no money for the car payment, no money for the mortgage, no new furniture, no money even for small things, like books!'

'Henrik, please stop!' Christine pleaded. 'I've heard all this fifty million times. No one forced you to buy the house or anything else. You bought all those things with your eyes wide open.'

'Yes, I know, because we had to live somewhere, we had to get to work somehow, but...' Henrik gave a despairing wave of the hand and dipped his spoon into the soup.

'Where is Patrick?' he asked suddenly when he realized he hasn't seen his son since he had got home.

'He's with the neighbours, the kids are playing. This morning I took him with me to my language class. He behaved himself.'

'And are you making progress?'

'Not much. Half the class are beginners. Anyway, I can't get used to this country. I'm always homesick.'

'But it was you who wanted us to emigrate here!'

'Yes, but only for the sake of the children. I wanted a better life for them.'

'Some better life. Wage slavery!'

'Well, what was waiting for them at home? The Garden of Eden?'

'It was your choice.'

'I really can't understand you! I've had enough of this.' Christine put down her spoon and remained still with a cold look frozen on her face.

Henrik scooped up the last drops of soup, and forcing a smile on his face he shrugged his shoulders.

'You see, this is a game we should never engage in. We should never fight. What do we accomplish by that? Tell you what, if you want, we can go home for a visit next year. Maybe that will cure your homesickness for a few years. How about that?' He stroked his wife's arm in a gesture of reconciliation and leaned back in his seat before he spoke again. 'Did you speak with Wanda today?'

'Only yesterday. I called her today in her office but she was away from her desk. I expect she's doing fine. She says she enjoys doing the work, and her co-workers are very nice to her.' Christine put the roast and the salad in front Henrik.

'That job she got is like winning the lottery. It was a lucky break for her out of the blue. If I hadn't gone to Walter's campaign rally, we'd have a big problem on our hands. It's frightening how hard it is nowadays to find a job.'

Neither of them said anything for a while. Henrik became aware of the silence and removed himself to the living room without another word. He took a book off the shelf. He read for a while, and then dozed off.

—*Chapter 13*—

Murder in Hotel Odéon
—V—

H UGO AND VIKTOR usually met in one of the apartments maintained by the city for visiting dignitaries. Hugo appreciated that his lover showed no signs of wanting to abuse his confidence. Viktor remained very polite, always soft-spoken, and their relationship developed into true friendship. He had an interest in literature, which surprised Hugo. He became aware of it the second or third time they were together. While Hugo was rummaging for something to drink in the kitchen Viktor picked up from the lower shelf of the coffee table a Hemingway novel that Hugo thought little of: *Across the River and into the Trees*. Its cover showed a military officer and a lady in a vaguely Venetian setting. When Hugo saw the book, he declared as he lowered himself with a sigh into an armchair across the table, 'That happens to be Hemingway's worst novel.'

It was then that Victor surprised him with a story he hadn't heard before, about Hemingway and Ezra Pound.

'Did you know Hemingway probably saved Ezra Pound's life after the second World War when Pound might have been executed as a war criminal for making fascist propaganda broadcasts from Italy?'

'Pound was crazy.'

'I don't know. Officially, he was declared crazy after the war, and put in a psychiatric hospital, but Hemingway may have been responsible for that. Otherwise Pound might have been hanged as a traitor. Hemingway suggested to the poet MacLeish, who was head of the Library of Congress, that Pound's friends should defend

67

him on the basis that the broadcasts were just craziness. That Pound was looney. Hemingway said it was obvious when Pound was writing his *Cantos* that his mind had been going. So Pound's lawyers did defend him on the basis that he was crazy, and it worked.'

'So where did you learn all this?' Now as the Mayor was looking at Viktor, his face was more relaxed and less critical.

'I read it somewhere.'

'I didn't realize you were so interested in literature,' Hugo said, going over went to Viktor and stroking his luxuriant head of hair. 'I used to think barbers were only interested in sports.'

This off-hand remark felt like a jab in the stomach to Viktor. So far he had assumed Hugo had seen him as an equal partner, a flesh-and-blood, thinking person, and not only a sex object to help act out his sexual fantasies. He had grown to love Hugo, and not just for the sexual pleasure of their relationship, but simply because he enjoyed his friend's company. He had found a true friend in Hugo. Hugo exuded confidence, and it was something new to Viktor who had never felt so well protected. Should anything happen to him, now he had someone to turn to for help and advice. In Hugo's company he felt shielded from the barbs and vagaries of the world. It was the first time in his life that he had this reassuring feeling, and he enjoyed it without analysing it too much.

And then one evening something inexplicable happened to him.

*   *   *

It was just before closing time as Valerian walked through the door of the barbershop. Viktor greeted him like an old and valued customer even though he knew him only by reputation as a famous attorney. A woman living next door often sang his praises. Dr Valerian Lang had represented her in a lawsuit against a government agency, with unexpected victory for her.

'He's an extraordinary orator. He knows everything,' she went around telling everyone at that time, perhaps trying to repay Valerian for the success.

It was common knowledge that to win a lawsuit was not easy, but to win against an arm of the government was nearly impossible.

The attorney was gaunt, tall, and well-dressed, with a ramrod posture that gave him a look of determination. He always wore a bow tie, and there was an exotic kind of elegance about him. His appearance suggested an artist more than an attorney, but his greyish-green eyes spoke of a fearless personality.

'Dear Viktor,' he began grandiloquently, 'I hope you can accommodate the request of a modest man like myself before you shut down your shop for the night. In a word, can you give me a haircut now, or should I come back tomorrow?'

'No problem, not for you, Counsellor, of course I can…but please, take this seat.' Viktor pointed at a chair, the first one in the row. 'I'll get to work in a moment.'

'That's very accommodating of you indeed,' the lawyer said, in a voice that reminded Viktor of an actor performing on a stage. That impression deepened when Valerian continued, 'If you had told me to come back tomorrow, I would have recited the following few lines –' before intoning in a stentorian voice on his way to the chair:

> '*Qui finem quaeris amoris,*
> *(Cedit amor rebus) res age …*'

With the last words echoing in the shop, Valerian sat down. 'In case you've forgotten your Latin, that means: "If you wish to put an end to love, attend to your job – love defers to business".'

Viktor was startled, but also curious. He had done

Latin at school. 'What's that from?' he asked, looking at the lawyer with curiosity, while trying to remember. 'I came across those lines before, but I can't remember where.'

'That's all right, take your time. If it doesn't come to you by the time you finish, I'll give you a hint. But if you want I can recite it again for you.' Then Valerian started over.

By the time Viktor was through with his work, however, the owner of the establishment had returned to close up for the day. He had his daughter with him, and the verse had gone from everybody's mind.

On his way home, the lines came back to Viktor, but he couldn't think where they came from. Deep in thought, he was unaware at first that a car was pulling closer to the curb and slowing down beside him. Then he heard a familiar voice.

'*Cedit amor rebus* – it's Ovid. Do you remember it now?'

Valerian was chuckling behind the steering wheel. 'If you're on your way home, Victor, how about a drink? I have no one waiting for me. I'm at liberty.'

'No one's waiting for me either.' Viktor slid into the passenger seat.

'Have you ever been to Eddy's Bar?' Valerian asked his passenger after he secured his seat belt.

'A few times.'

'Do you know anyone there?'

'Yes. Artur.'

'Anyone else?'

'Yes. There's also Hugo.'

'The Mayor?'

'Yes.'

They were both silent for a while. Viktor was worrying about having named the people he knew. Maybe it was a mistake. Indeed, did Valerian even know about the private parties? Dammit, how could he be so irresponsible? When Valerian said nothing, Victor wondered if he might also be a member of the Club. But Viktor had never seen him at these events. So why was he remaining silent?

Valerian was sitting behind the steering wheel in a state of bewilderment and had to pretend he was concentrating only on his driving. Well, it certainly looked like Viktor too belonged to the city's inner circle. He felt compelled to take another look at his passenger. Artur had teased Valerian at the time when he introduced him to the Club with the remark – pretentious, it seemed to Valerian – that the élite of the city were drawn to the place. Since then whenever the Club came up in conversation between them there was a derisive grin on Valerian's face, and he put a sneer into the word élite. He had not been to the parties at the Club for over a year now. He found most of the members boring. In his opinion, the true aristocracy of any time should be well-educated, the supporters of progressive ideas, combative, and disputatious. But, to his sorrow, he had had to conclude that the Club rarely offered a kindred spirit.

The only exception was Artur. They had met during his years at the university. They were actually classmates. Artur was intellectually alert, sparkling with humour and ideas, all the things Valerian was seeking in a friend. Their debates remained like intellectual fireworks in his memory. The other students seemed lackadaisical sheep next to his friend.

Artur was the only one who noticed his absence from the Club, and even questioned him about it. He advised Valerian to grow up at last and accept the world as it was. Stop making waves, stop being eternally dissatisfied. Leave the confrontation to others and start seeing life as it is, not as a dream.

'That's settled then, we're going to Eddy's Bar unless you have strong objections,' said Valerian finally, breaking the silence that had built up between them. 'I guess you're no stranger to the place.'

Viktor nodded without saying anything. He was leaning back and listening to the soft jazz on the radio. He cast a few surreptitious glances toward Valerian. He found the attorney pleasant, well-groomed, and even attractive. A strange feeling began to settle over his soul, the realization that he liked this man. Maybe more: maybe he desired him.

His glance now slipped to Valerian's hands on the steering wheel. The long fingers were crowned with carefully manicured fingernails. He liked clean nails. As a schoolchild, a biology teacher had impressed on him the importance of clean fingernails. She used to bring a tennis-ball-size magnifying glass to class and called the students one by one to the podium so that she could examine the condition of their nails.

Both men were in a good mood getting out of the car outside Eddy's Bar, Valerian even rubbing his hands together with a smile.

Instead of sitting down at the bar, Valerian steered his guest to a small table in a corner. 'Will you join me in a single malt Scotch?' he asked, and ordered Lagavulin and mineral water for them both.

The waiter brought the drinks at lightning speed. They raised their glasses for a toast. Valerian looked Viktor in the eye and reached for his hand. Viktor let his look linger on his new companion, but then he averted his eyes and pulled back his hand as if ashamed of himself.

Hugo's smooth and friendly face appeared to him. The one-year-old story of their quiet and intimate belonging to each other played itself out in front of his mind's eye. He was suddenly afraid, and wanted to back away from the thought of a challenge looming ahead: would he have to choose between Valerian and Hugo? But who says I have to choose? Valerian doesn't come to the Club much, and the chance of the two of them running into each other is negligible. There's no reason either of them should find out about the other. Except that this is cheating. The realization stabbed his soul.

No, I don't have to rush into a decision right now. I'll just sit back and let things happen.

Valerian, as if he were aware of Viktor's dilemma, asked him up to his apartment.

Viktor was unsure what to do. He kept his eyes on the table, away from the yearning of Valerian's glances, trying to avoid having to face a decision. But then something happened, something that he could not later either explain or justify. He quickly drained his glass and jumped to his feet waving to Valerian: 'Fine, but then let's get going at once. In another minute, who knows, I might change my mind.'

—*Chapter 14*—

THE WIDER REPERCUSSIONS of Zeno's conversation with Marcel had already come back to him through the grapevine. Zeno found he had no choice but to consider the union leader's proposal. If he laid off the thirty-three employees, the union would call for a strike, and that would be the end of everything. The competition would pry away the steady customers, and the expensive new production line would be wasted. Apparently everyone was waiting for his decision.

Getting to work with his calculator, he divided the day into two eight-hour shifts. The design of the production line in the de-boning section called for twenty-eight workers. If he were to increase that number by fourteen for each shift then each worker would have more time to de-bone the chicken parts, leaving less meat on the bones and adding to the total weight of the final product. But how much? He continued calculating and came up finally with a figure of 985.6 kilograms a month, which was not enough to cover the monthly salary of twenty-eight employees. However, this section is the bottleneck, he thought; the productivity of the whole plant depends on this one section. That should justify the employment of twenty-eight extra employees. In addition, the job of de-boning and slicing would be done in a better, more efficient manner, and the resulting product could command a higher price in the market. The big question was whether he would be able to cut himself a larger market share. There was a chance it could be done. He rang his secretary and asked for the head of the marketing division.

While waiting he stretched out in his swivel chair and picked up the mail of the day. In the bundle a light blue envelope stood out, a press release about Walter's campaign. The leaflet inside had two photos, one of them showing Walter staring through his glasses and the other with Walter and Melanie cheek to cheek – the picture of marital bliss. Looks like they managed to make peace, Zeno observed with satisfaction. He ignored the rest of the outside mail and began looking at the house mail. It took him a few seconds to find the envelope he was interested in, which was small, plain white, and sealed. He turned it over twice but could not find any writing on it. He slit it open with the letter opener. Wanda's letter fell out. Leaning back in his chair, he began reading it.

> My Dearest, my love, I don't know what's come over me, but today I can't help thinking about you. And what it will be like tomorrow on our trip.
> I am counting the minutes as they pass by at snail's pace. I can hardly wait for you to take me in your arms again and spoil me like no one ever has.
> With kisses and more kisses on your tender lips,
> W.

Zeno could not understand what was happening to him. What business did a fifty-year-old man have with a twenty-something girl, he kept asking himself over and over again. Did he have it in him to offer the kind of excitement a girl of her age was likely to expect? It'll work out somehow, he reassured himself. After all, this was not his first extramarital affair. Still, none of them ever affected him this way, not to the point where he was considering the break-up of his marriage to Sylvia.

He genuinely surprised himself by even thinking of divorce: how could it ever have entered his mind? Maybe I should skip that trip tomorrow. I should think of a good excuse. I'll call Wanda in the evening and tell her I'm profoundly sorry, but something important has come up – an emergency meeting with the president of the company that's providing the new production facility. That's even true, he thought, but what if it plunged the girl into despair? What if it caused her to do something they both would forever regret?

In the end he came to an agreement with himself: he would go ahead with the trip the next day, but would try to convince Wanda just to enjoy their time together now, without investing her hopes in the future.

I'll have to get her to understand that, no matter how great it is for me to be with her, this is not a long-term relationship. He had plenty of reasons to muster: he was too old for her; he was in a happy marriage which he had no intention of wrecking. They could go on seeing each other, of course, but Wanda had to remember he was spoken for. Besides, Wanda should not be distracted from her studies.

He was roused from his thoughts by the ringing of the phone. The secretary announced Vince, the head of the marketing department.

'You called me, Chief,' Vince said, busily trying to put his pen back in his pocket while also accepting the hand Zeno was extending toward him.

'How many times have I asked you to skip this business about "Chief"? Zeno happens to be my honest given name,' the Chief protested.

'Right you are, Chief...I mean Zeno,' he corrected himself, smiling.

'I'll tell you why I asked you here. This afternoon I made some calculations. You've probably heard about the strike threat if we lay off any union member after the installation of the new equipment. The jobs of thirty-three workers are involved. The capacity of the upgraded plant is eight thousand chickens. According to my new calculations, if I increase the labour force in the de-boning section by fifty percent it will be possible to process four thousand extra chickens.'

'You mean in two shifts,' said Vince, echoing Zeno's scheme.

'Yes, that's right. And of course that means we're talking about a fifty percent increase in production. We have contract customers for the processing of eight thousand birds, so what I want to know is, what are our chances of finding a market for the extra production we're contemplating?'

The question hung in the air for a minute. The development had caught Vince unprepared.

'I don't see much chance of that at present. The market is too competitive.'

'What if we were to invest in two extra large-capacity refrigerator trucks and start delivering our product to markets farther afield? What would you say to that?' Zeno asked.

'Well, in that case, we can target all possible clients within a three-hundred-kilometre radius,' Vince answered. 'And that would give us a realistic chance. But before anything else we need to survey the market carefully. In the meantime I'd like you to give me a week's grace. I need time to assess the outlying markets, and then I'll report back to you.'

'That's fine by me,' said Zeno getting up and holding out a hand over the desk to say goodbye, before escorting Vince towards the outer office.

Zeno felt more hopeful. He had one other matter to settle, which concerned Sander Wilson, the head engineer of the new production line: to set the time and place for their meeting the coming weekend. Their plan was for Sander to meet Ned Koch, the president of the manufacturing company, in the town of Canmore, and for Zeno to join them on Sunday afternoon to negotiate any points that might have eluded the other two.

Sander showed up a few minutes later. A short man, he wore a white butcher's coat, and always got to the point without wasting time on pleasantries and formalities.

Zeno trusted him implicitly, for his personal integrity as well as for his expertise.

'I booked a room in the same hotel where Mr Koch is staying, but only for Saturday night, because Ned wants to head for home on Sunday afternoon. I hope this won't be a problem?'

'I was planning on joining you two for lunch on Sunday. Unfortunately, something has come up, and I too will have to take an unexpected overnight trip,' said Zeno briskly. 'But I'll be in the hotel by three o'clock latest, and we can attend to any unresolved issues right then and there.'

As soon as he blurted this out he regretted it.

I should not have said anything about taking an overnight trip. Sylvia knows him, they exchange a word or two now and then, and he might mention it. Zeno realized how careless he had been; he really must watch his tongue.

No, nothing to worry about, he went on, calming himself. Sander is not that kind of a man, not a tattletale. In any case, I've never heard Sylvia talk company business; I've never had any work-related news coming back to me through her. I can rely on Sander's loyalty a hundred percent.

Sander was already long gone when, still sitting behind his desk, Zeno kept going over every word of their conversation, searching for one that might come back to haunt him. Then his eyes fell upon the un-addressed white envelope on the desk; he retrieved Wanda's letter from it and read it again. And again.

Wanda's full of drive, determined to get everything she can out of life, he concluded. New questions flooded his mind. Why did he think even for a minute that he might want to change his life, leave Sylvia, and run into the arms of this flirtatious young girl? The very idea seemed to him now bizarre, attributable perhaps to an unfamiliar, reckless side of himself – one that was emerging now for the first time.

Chapter 15

SYLVIA WAS ALREADY PACKING for her golf outing when Zeno woke. After she slipped back into the bedroom, his first reaction was to close his eyes, pretending to be still asleep. She made her way to the chest quietly and started sliding drawers in and out.

Obviously looking for something, Zeno smiled to himself. Women, he thought, are always passionate about looking for some mislaid item, something they are convinced was there the day before; the only thing they are not sure about is where that 'there' is.

'Looking for something my dear?' Zeno opened his eyes.

'Sorry, didn't mean to disturb your sleep,' Sylvia murmured. 'I can't imagine where my white suede gloves have got to. Only last week I saw them in one of these drawers, but now they're gone as if the earth's swallowed them up.'

Zeno could not help chuckling about the scene, thinking how right he had been in his assessment.

Later on, when Sylvia had given up the search for the gloves and decided to buy a new pair, Zeno asked her, 'Are you planning to spend the night in the hotel by the golf course?'

'Yes, Susan and I decided it didn't make sense for us to drive all the way home when we will have to be on the course again early in the morning. By the way, when are you planning to get home?' She turned to her husband with an absent-minded expression. Her face showed that in her mind she was still searching for the lost pair of gloves.

'I'll be home by tomorrow evening. Ned insists that he has to get back to his family that afternoon.'

After Sylvia left, Zeno crawled out of bed. He drew back the curtains and looked outside. A bright summer morning faced him.

Sylvia called out goodbye and he could hear the rumbling noise of the garage door that sounded like a coffee grinder as it went up and then lowered itself with a thud. He hurried with his own bag to the garage.

Although an inner voice was urging caution and common sense, he answered it with only a shrug.

He pushed the buzzer at the front door of Wanda's high-rise. There was no greeting from the intercom, only a buzz from the lock. Wanda had an apartment on the second floor, so he could take the stairs. Her door was open a crack. As soon as he entered, Wanda rushed up to him and threw her arms around him enthusiastically.

Can I make you some tea? Come on, take a rest for a while.

They sat down in the tiny kitchen, but only for a moment. Zeno urged the girl to hurry so they could get ahead of the weekend traffic.

Soon the silver Mercedes sedan was whizzing them noiselessly through the empty downtown streets. Wanda reached over the gear shift to touch Zeno's hand. She didn't want to think about the past or the future. She was interested only in the present. She was all set to devote the next day and a half to Zeno.

*   *   *

That morning, she had awakened with a stiff back. Paul had not slept at her place that night. The evening before, she had got rid of him saying she was not in the mood for company. She needed her own space, the freedom to move about. He was not to come near her place till Monday night.

Paul was barely eighteen. Both his parents worked in

the oil industry and spent the better part of their lives in the shadow of oil derricks. They rarely came home.

As an only child and left to himself, Paul was lonely, and loneliness eventually made him a loner.

He had nearly finished his first semester, but in his studies he could not find what he was looking for. He was still attending his classes, more or less, but he skipped most of the exams. He was obsessed with video games.

That was how they met – in a video-game arcade. That evening Wanda took him up to her apartment and robbed him of his virginity. From then on he started hanging out in her apartment, because somehow he felt at home there, and he absented himself only after their frequent spats, which arose nearly always from Paul's unwillingness to pitch in with housework. He spent most of his time either sleeping or playing with his electronic puzzles. When challenged to do more he angrily announced that, like it or not, he had no energy for other effort. This in turn sent Wanda into a rage, and she kicked him out in spite of her continuing sympathy for the ineffectual, incompetent boy – as she thought of him. 'My house is not a luxury hotel for idlers! Come back only when you decide to change and you're willing to clean up at least the mess you make,' she shouted at him every time before she slammed the door on him.

After a few days Paul would saunter back to Wanda, promising to shape up, do some cleaning, and even wash the dishes if it were absolutely necessary.

At times like this Wanda's heart would melt. She would take him in her arms like a child, cuddle him, kissing his lips, and while rocking him in her embrace, promise never to throw him out again, but it would really make her happy if he changed and started doing some work.

In the wake of such dramatic scenes, peace and quiet would reign again; a fragile order would return. Wanda often wondered just why she loved him so much, why she kept nurturing that good-for-nothing brat, but she could come up with only one reason: he does everything I tell him in bed. With that she considered the case closed.

This morning, before remembering she had kicked him out, she reached out to touch Paul. She felt a new pain shooting through her body from the move. Just when I could really use a good massage, she thought to herself wistfully on finding his side vacant.

She crawled out of bed without much enthusiasm and staggered to the kitchen, bending and stretching several times, but the numbness did not show any signs of abating. She started up the coffee maker and then ran a bath, sprinkling in a generous portion of bath salts.

She lay in the water for several minutes with her eyes closed, feeling the pain slowly dissipate from her back.

She pictured Zeno in front of her, thinking to herself, he's good-looking, wealthy, intelligent, but the fact remains: he's fifty! Old! On top of that, he's married. Whatever made me pick him? I must be out of my mind! And this game may not be without its dangers, she thought, periodically lifting a leg out of the water in order to make sure the pain was gone from her back.

Who cares, dangerous or not, it's a game, and I am going to live for it for the next two days and put everything else out of my mind. After all, I'll be vacationing with a real live big-shot industrialist. So, let it rip! Refreshed, she stepped out of the tub almost completely free of pain, with a liberated soul and a clear conscience.

—*Chapter 16*—

THE DRIVE to the five-star hotel in the mountain resort took just an hour and a half. At the impressive entrance a doorman wearing a top hat and white gloves helped Wanda out of the car with a flourish and then began unloading the trunk. Zeno took hold of the girl's hand and started leading her to the reception desk. There was another pair of white gloves along the way to point the direction in the lobby.

He stepped up to the dark hardwood counter, full of happy expectations. But as he stood there for a second or two it occurred to him the place might be fully booked, it being a weekend. He should have made a reservation ahead of time.

The woman behind the counter must have sensed Zeno's momentary hesitation, because she greeted him with extra warmth.

'I'd like to have a room with a double bed for one night,' Zeno blurted out quickly. Then, to make himself clear, he added: 'For two.'

There was a quick, piercing look from behind the counter at Wanda, who kept shifting her weight from one leg to the other as she feasted her eyes on the soaring walls of the pagan temple she found herself in.

The receptionist's experienced eyes immediately took in the situation. A tone of sour irony entered her voice.

'If you can give me just a minute,' she said, giving another look to the gaping girl, 'I'll check and see if we have a late cancellation.'

She moved down the counter and started playing on a keyboard with great concentration, giving the appearance she was doing her best for the guests. Then she stepped back to face Zeno and announced apologetically:

'It's the weekend, as you know, and all our rooms are booked for the night. But on the third floor we have a special suite. If you're interested I can show it to you. The rate for a night is twelve hundred.'

When she got to the figure in her spiel she looked Zeno directly in the eye, as if challenging the man: Well, mister, the night of love you're planning, will it be worth that much to you?

'Fine, let's take a look,' Zeno agreed without hesitation.

The receptionist started walking toward the elevator with slow, deliberate steps beckoning with a raised hand to her guests to follow her.

The spacious elevator, appointed with mahogany, slowly made its ascent to the heights. The receptionist stared at the floor while Wanda's eyes were on Zeno. On the third floor there was a tiny tinkling noise, the elevator carriage gave a slight jolt, and the doors silently opened. They both followed in the receptionist's tracks, though she turned back a few times to make sure she had not lost them.

The hallways of the hotel were covered with coffee-brown tapestry, all outlined by walnut mouldings. Along the walls, at leisurely intervals, were Victorian carved oak side tables and small commodes. The receptionist led them to a massive oak double door and turned her key in the lock with a ritualistic gesture. As they strolled into the suite she kept flipping more and more light switches. The sunlight was muted by the heavy crimson drapery on the windows. Wanda, entranced by the spectacle, looked around with undisguised astonishment.

'I must beg your indulgence,' the receptionist said, pointing at a pair of single beds, and shifting her gaze from Zeno to Wanda and back again. 'Unfortunately the suite is furnished only with this sleeping arrangement.'

'It will do perfectly well,' Zeno snapped back, looking at Wanda, whose face telegraphed her agreement.

'Well then, would you like to take the suite?'

'Yes, we'll take it,' Zeno spoke definitively but he gave

the place another final, sweeping look as if to confirm his decision to himself.

While waiting for their bags, Zeno went downstairs to sign the register and Wanda checked out the apartment one feature at a time. The first thing she opened was the heavy armoire; inside wide-shouldered, lacquered wooden clothes hangers lined up in two sizes, male and female. On top of the rococo, bowfront chest of drawers was a delicate porcelain dish gilded at the rim and glazed in various shades of blue, as well as a tall, slender glass vase. Between them stood a barely audible antique ormolu clock, its case decorated with inlaid curlicues. The living room was taken up mostly by a coffee table on delicately carved cabriolet legs, surrounded by comfortable armchairs upholstered with empire-style striped silk. Over the table hung an elaborate and enormous Venetian-style crystal chandelier. Each room had a picture window with heavy velvet drapery fluted at the sides, ready to be drawn for complete darkness if required. The heavy fabric of the bed-covers was woven with gold threads snaking in and out.

Wanda touched all of these pieces, ran a hand over the polished surfaces of the furniture, picked up the decorative accessories; she was overwhelmed by their richness. The bathroom held even more impressive surprises for her. The walls were covered with white-veined, meter-long slabs of marble and the floor was black granite. The white-marbled shower cubicle was equipped with a gilded, rain-producing shower head the size of a top hat, the kind she had only seen in films. The long counter containing a double basin was filled with so many potions that it would have taken all day to try each item.

So this is what the world of the rich is like. This is how they live, those who can shell out twelve hundred for a single night without batting an eyelid, she thought. She had been the guest at some swanky places in her life, but nothing nearly as luxurious.

The bell rang in the entrance foyer. It was the bellhop with the luggage on a cart with a pair of shiny brass rods arched over it. Zeno immediately applied himself to the task of finding the right place for the bags. He pressed a ten-dollar bill in the departing bellhop's hand and then locked the door.

'Well, will this suit you?' he asked, giving Wanda a hug. 'It's kind of cosy, isn't it?'

'It's divine.' She was bubbling over.

Her eyes were drawn to the wrought-iron railing of a balcony beyond the tulle curtains of the windows, and she wasted no time swinging the glass door open to what turned out to be a large terrace, furnished with wicker armchairs. The panorama took her breath away. On the foothills, snow sparkled on the branches of pine trees.

'Now! I want you right now,' Wanda whispered, and pulled the man to the bedroom.

Sometime later, as he lay on his back under an opiate cloud of gratification, Zeno could concentrate only on the slow ebbing of pleasure. Calm was slowly seeping back into his body with the passing minutes. Hours?

Wanda too sank into reveries for a time, and then got out of bed with a light leap. She stopped to survey Zeno's naked body. Her gaze lingered over the crotch area, wandered around the muscles of his thighs. 'Your body's beautiful,' she told him.

Zeno did not seem to hear her; he looked to be sleeping, his chest slowly heaving.

Wanda turned around and headed for the bathroom. While rummaging among the colourful assortment of shampoos and liquid body soaps in green and yellow ampoules she continued thinking about Zeno's body. She wasn't lying when she complimented him, although she would have lied if necessary. Even though he was fifty, his body still looked good.

They changed and went down to the hotel lobby. Zeno put an arm around Wanda's shoulders and let go only while passing the massive carved-wood reception counter. He stole a glance in that direction, but now there was no one standing behind it.

The two-storey-high ceiling echoed a soft melody. The music was arresting, silky, seeping from a hidden source into the vast space like fog. It was a while before they saw its source – a gilded harp being played by a platinum blonde, her long fingers gliding over the strings. She barely touched the instrument. She and the harp seemed to form a pair of playmates engaged in a private game of their own. At times she flexed her wrists to the beat, flipping them up high and letting them drop almost in servile submission.

Zeno stopped in his tracks, mesmerized.

Wanda stood hesitantly by his side until she too came under the spell of the melody.

The two of them walked out the front door of the hotel as if stepping out of a dream. There was a trail skirting the forest, and they wandered along it. When they stopped, they embraced.

At one of these stops, sitting on a log, Zeno turned silent, deep in thought.

'Is anything bothering you?' Wanda asked tenderly. 'You look like you have worries.'

'They're my flesh and blood,' Zeno answered, laughing. All the same, he was glad to talk about his problems at the plant, the upcoming strike now planned by the union, the trouble with the installation of the new production line, and finally he even sketched out a brief account of the fickle market conditions of processed meat.

'But never mind,' he said with a wave of his hand. 'We're here to forget about all that and relax. We'd better get back if we want something to eat.'

By the time they got back to the hotel they found the white tuxedoed waiters and busboys busy setting the tables for the next meal in the dining hall. They gave questioning looks at the entering guests. One of them finally decided to pay attention to them; he slowly walked up to Zeno and Wanda to tell them with almost offensively deliberate calmness that mealtime was over, the dining room was closed.

Sensing rage brewing in Zeno, Wanda saved the situation by slipping an arm around his and suggesting they go back to the room and call for something that they could enjoy on their private terrace. It would surely be more fun and cosier than to sit in a big dining hall with the walls echoing emptiness. The girl's warm voice, the gentleness of her eyes, quenched Zeno's rage as fast as it had erupted. Squeezing Wanda's shoulder, he cast a contemptuous glance after the retreating figure of the waiter who had thrown them out of the restaurant.

The terrace of their suite was bathed in early afternoon sunshine which put Zeno in a better mood; by the time he had plucked a bottle of champagne from the mini bar and uncorked it with a loud pop, he had forgotten his earlier aggravation. Everything intoxicated him: the sunshine, the white mountain peaks, the pine trees shuffling under them, Wanda's smile, her slender figure.

The meal served to them was faultless, and they lingered contentedly in the company of the champagne bottle and the coffee pot. Neither of them felt like talking. Zeno was enjoying the quiet, schedule-free afternoon: doing nothing was exactly what he felt like.

Wanda was flipping through a glossy travel directory she had found on the coffee table of the sitting room. The title on the cover said it all: *Luxury Hotels of the World*. She smiled seeing some of the pictures and then went on flipping the pages. She looked at the colourful world depicted on these pages as if dreaming and yet trying to convince herself she was awake.

Zeno lay curled up on the bed, at peace. But not for long. Without any conscious thought, without either of them initiating it, they soon found themselves in each other's arms again. The champagne, the resumption of sex, and the peace of the faraway mountains filtering through the curtains left them in a state of pleasant lassitude.

Zeno woke to find the girl was no longer by his side. He got up and went in search of her all over the apartment. He stepped out into the entrance foyer that had another door to the sprawling bathroom and it was open. His eyes came to rest on the girl standing in front of a full-length mirror that covered the whole wall and was powerfully illuminated. She was completely naked and apparently engaged in a thorough examination or admiration of her body, caressing her breasts and hips, lifting her buttocks to get a better view, first from the left and then from the right. Contentment was glowing on her face as she stopped for a minute before she leaned closer to the mirror to smooth out her eyebrows, nose, lips, and then she started coddling her breasts in the gentle basket of her fingertips as if trying to make sure of their beauty and suppleness. Zeno lost himself in the spectacle for a while, he didn't know how long, before noiselessly creeping back to bed. In his imagination he replayed the scene he had just witnessed. It shocked him in a way, but at the same time, it delighted him. He could see in it something beyond the frivolity, beyond the girl's act of body worship; he could see the desperate search for certainty and the joyful discovery of being there.

That night they made love twice more, both times glued to each other's lips as if it was for the last time, the last embrace before an impending disaster was soon to strike them down.

In the morning, spots of light breaking through the curtain flickered up and down the lacquered parquet floor like the sparkling scales of a fish. Zeno spent some time watching them while turning over in his mind the problem of this new relationship. It was clear to him that he had to put an end to it as soon as possible. Yes, I love her, I worship her, he was thinking, but we don't belong together. He especially thought about the age difference;

he argued with himself, but all the other arguments against the relationship somehow lost their clarity the more he thought about them. He had to admit defeat. He was hopelessly in love.

They skipped breakfast, and went for a walk instead, but at noon they were among the first guests for lunch and got the best table in the dining room, by a window overlooking the park and the mountains beyond. They each ordered a glass of champagne, but Zeno barely sipped his, using it only to toast Wanda.

The waiter serving them was a twenty-something lean and tall young man with a black moustache. He jumped to fulfil any request with an almost derisively obsequious flourish. The girl's eyes followed his every move with undisguised interest. Several times she looked at him with an expression that reflected admiration, beaming secret signals toward him with a little smile from the corners of her mouth. At first Zeno watched the girl's barely disguised game in silence and without emotion, but as it continued all through the meal he eventually found it insulting to him.

'I'd like you to stop flirting with the waiter,' he said to Wanda sharply, taking advantage of the young man's brief absence. 'I'm sorry but I find it brazen of you to start winking at someone else while you're still with me, and doing it so provocatively that it would drive the gentlest of men to reach for a knife,' he whispered into the girl's ear, sputtering with rage.

Wanda stared back at him with innocence in her eyes as if to ask him what this was all about: have you taken leave of your senses? Instead of protesting or demanding an apology she turned her head toward the mountains without a word.

In the meantime the waiter returned, fussed with the table, poured more mineral water and red wine for the girl.

'Ready for the check please. Charge the lunch to our room, number 301.'

Before he left, the waiter directed a half-smile at the girl, who had had her head turned away obviously under stress; Zeno took that smile as another obnoxious provocation.

'Shall we go?'

The girl rose from her chair moodily. Her face was unhappy, and her eyes were sending lightning bolts at her lover.

As they were leaving the restaurant, he thought he heard the waiter talking about them to another member of staff. He caught the words 'old fart' and 'sugar daddy' and had a suspicion he was intended to hear them. Zeno missed the rest of it, but that was enough. Sick at heart and his soul in tatters, he strode to the elevator with the girl by his side.

Back in the suite they started packing without any further talk. They looked at each other only when they were finished and had nothing else to look at. Wanda put on a conciliatory expression for Zeno whose face still carried the marks of an emotional upheaval: male pride badly mangled. They were already seated in the car and slowly inching their way out of the parking lot when Zeno reached for Wanda's hand, held it tenderly and informed her that on the way home they would have to make a stop for a brief business meeting.

'It won't take long, you'll see. At most an hour. I'll try to get it over with as fast as I can. I hope we'll be home by six in the evening,' he said softly.

Wanda agreed with a wordless nod.

They remained silent all the way to Canmore.

*   *   *

When they arrived at the hotel in Canmore, Zeno asked the girl not to stray too far from the car because there was a good chance the meeting would be short. Again Wanda nodded but said nothing.

Zeno ran into Sander and Mr Koch in the hotel lobby, and Sander steered the three of them to the café.

Although he was years younger than Zeno, Ned Koch had deep wrinkles in his dark face, but his body exuded energy and flexibility. The three of them found a booth before the waiter hurried over. Sander did not waste time getting down to business.

'First of all, let me say we've had a very productive weekend,' he said launching into his report. 'I've had plenty of time to clear up a lot of details with Ned. As it stands now he will be delivering some parts of the new production line in three weeks. There's one hitch though – he has a problem with the scalding equipment: the parts for that come from a factory where the workers have been on strike for the past two weeks. But Ned figures it's bound to end next week and then it'll be only a question of days before he gets the parts he needs. And there's another problem: the installation team scheduled for this job is working fifteen hundred kilometres from here at present, installing and starting up a similar facility. The estimated time for that is about four weeks. But all in all, according to my calculations, that team should be ready for us by the time we have all the equipment for our new production line.'

'The only thing I'd like to add,' Ned interrupted, breaking into Sander's report, 'is that we do have four installation teams, but three of them are committed for at least four months, and only the one my friend here mentioned is available.'

'Are you saying you're not sure you can stick to the schedule and the deadlines specified in the contract?' asked Zeno, shifting his gaze to Ned Koch.

'That's about it,' answered Sander with some hesitation, seeing the visitor's lips remaining firmly shut. 'That's what

Ned says. We can expect a delay of about two or three weeks.'

'That's the worst-case scenario,' added the head of the tool and die company. 'Only in the worst case.'

This turn of events came as an unpleasant surprise to Zeno. He had expected everything to work out according to plan. He had allowed three weeks for the installation and start-up. If in the meantime Vince managed to drum up more business there could be a real problem fulfilling those new contracts. He knew all too well the inexorable principle of the market: you've got to deliver the merchandise on time and with quality guaranteed; otherwise you lose the newly conquered territory – immediately and forever. These thoughts were turning over in Zeno's mind while the other two continued discussing other minor points.

'Once and for all, I'd like to make one thing clear: the contract made with my company is binding not only on me but on you, Ned. If you fail to live up to it, I expect you to compensate us for lost revenue, or else I'll take you to court for damages,' said Zeno somberly. 'I hope with all my heart it will never come to that.'

Ned Koch looked at Sander and then bowed his head as if admitting guilt.

The sudden silence of embarrassment was broken by Zeno.

'I have to get back to the city,' he said, standing up, and then turned to Ned. 'And I also want to add I'm taking my leave in a hopeful spirit and I trust the whole job will proceed according to our agreement.'

Zeno shook hands with both of them. He waved an at-ease sign to Sander who was about to leap to his feet, ready to walk the boss to his car. There was no need for further formalities.

In the parking lot he found Wanda still sitting in the silver Mercedes. Her look was unhappy and unfocused. She pretended to be listening to the loud music from the radio, but her thoughts were elsewhere. She was still under the influence of the events in the restaurant. She was saddened and annoyed by Zeno's inability to understand that she had to gain the approval and admiration of everyone, not only of her lover.

Yes, indeed, she enjoyed flirting. Any place she went her first order of business was to make herself noticed. She had to shine constantly in the limelight, to be the centre of attention at all times. She could not accept Zeno's objection to this inner need of hers. Why did it irritate him that she wanted to be liked by everyone? Her being pleasant to everyone was totally innocent, it meant nothing. She had learned from experience that her provocative demeanour always created a better atmosphere, lightened up the mood of any room. True, in some cases there were people who misinterpreted her signals and rudely demanded a follow-up, but she always managed to put them in their place.

'This is a day of surprises,' said Zeno, settling down behind the wheel in a manner that showed he was trying to relax and get over his earlier tension.

Veering out of the parking lot he kept glancing at Wanda. She still looked out of sorts, dispirited. He was suddenly seized by the idea of making up to her, and he forced a smile on his face.

'Well now, that wasn't so bad, was it?' he asked with a hint of apology. 'I just learned the plant expansion may be delayed, that's what the contractor just told me. The head honcho. I'll have to think of some way of getting around this problem,' said Zeno with a sigh and then aimed his eyes at the highway.

By the time they reached the city, there was a thaw between them. Wanda was talking about her approaching exams and about her father – the way he broke his back working at the bank from dawn to dusk and was getting nothing out of it except a sour personality.

'He's only been like this since he started working for

that fucked-up bank,' she kept repeating with considerable emotion. 'Before that he used to be different person, a happy man; he used to take us on outings, and he was always kind to mother. But now...'

While listening to her, Zeno was again occupied with his own problems in his mind, even as he tried to pay attention to the girl and to comment on some of her complaints.

The parking spaces in front of Wanda's apartment building were all taken, and they had to drive to the parking lot behind. The girl had regained her usual high spirits as she started to take her luggage from the depths of the trunk.

'Why don't you come up,' she suggested to Zeno, looking at him not only with entreaty but desire in her eyes. 'I'll put on some tea and we can talk some more.'

Zeno was unmoved. Without emotion he slammed down the lid of the trunk, but took hold of the suitcase and followed the girl. In the dim light of the staircase, Wanda suddenly came to a halt on a landing. She put down her pocketbook and threw her arms around him.

'I want your lips, right now,' she whispered, clinging to Zeno. He let himself be carried along.

Excited, Wanda had to struggle to unlock the door to the apartment with a nervously shaking hand. Once inside, she tossed her jacket on an armchair in the living room, took the suitcase away from Zeno, and then dragged him into the bedroom.

They were about to fall into bed when they both noticed at the same time that the bed was already occupied by a naked young man sleeping there, turned toward the wall. Wanda's arm stiffened and fell to her side as she stood there next to Zeno, frozen in shock.

'He's...he's...' but that was all she could force from her throat.

—*Chapter 17*—

PAUL HAD ENOUGH of nights spent in crowded, noisy, and smelly dormitories and decided, come what may, he would go back to Wanda's private hideaway. As a scholarship student, she was lucky enough to have one of the apartments the university was renting in her building for the overflow from the dorms, and even luckier with her roommate who had quit without notice, leaving Wanda to luxuriate in privacy.

Paul was already on his way when he suddenly remembered that the girl had thrown him out with the warning that he was not to return before Monday night under any circumstances. What the hell, he thought, what's one day here or there? Wanda was sure to make peace with him and take him back. While waiting for the bus he noticed an ordinary-looking bar on the corner, and he had an idea. He would go there and have a cup of coffee or perhaps a drink to gather strength for the confrontation ahead.

Stepping into a dimly-lit place that felt more like the inside of a fish bowl, he immediately realized he was not in just any old watering hole, especially when he was stopped from going farther in by a young, well-built skinhead who examined Paul from every side and asked for ID. Paul automatically reached into his pocket to produce his student card to the bouncer. The skinhead took the card, turned it over several times, compared the picture with its bearer, shook his head slowly from side to side like he still had his doubts about the guest, but then with a sudden gesture handed the card back. 'Okay,' he nodded, waving him in through a short passage.

There were more shadows than light inside. A stage, looking very much like a boxing ring without the ropes,

was in the middle. The revolving light fixture above let
patches of colour sweep the whole place. A central square
column was covered with mirrors, and there were more
mirrors on the walls, flooding the place with a cavalcade
of reflected coloured light and mysterious shadows.

The only things clearly visible were the stage and the
naked girl dancing on it. She was sliding and slithering
on a metal pole in front of the mirrors, to the thumping
rhythm of music from strategically placed loudspeakers.
The waves of her heaving body undulated to the beat.
Paul felt intoxicated by the unexpected sight, and fairly
collapsed into a chair. A waitress with a white ribbon in
her hair soon appeared in front of him. He ordered a beer
keeping his eyes glued to the girl dancing on the stage.

The waitress immediately returned with the bottle. He
had to look through all his pockets to scrape together the
price of the beer which was three times higher than in an
ordinary bar. He told himself to take small sips to make
the beer last; he had no money left for a second drink.
Paul rarely visited striptease bars. And never alone, always
in a group, when he and his companions felt free to play
the debonair playboys while making deprecating remarks
about the dancers, although at the end they would all
admit the show was arousing.

Having been recently initiated in the art of carnal love
by Wanda, now Paul looked at the show from a different
vantage point. He was able to scrutinize the dancer's wide
open thighs calmly and with objectivity. While he was
grazing the landscape of the girl's bare skin with his eyes,
he was thinking about the pleasures he had experienced
with Wanda. He recognized some of the same lines in
the dancer's limbs, and the slight fuzz on her thighs as
it glistened in the spotlight, and he had the impression
that he was discovering the infinity of the universe in the
shaved crotch thrust in the face of the shadowy patrons.
He was fascinated by what he saw, but now in the way

a man of the world, a connoisseur, usually speaks of a special night at the opera or a delicate object of art.

Paul was getting physically aroused. The sight of the girl's graceful body and fine lines of her labia fired him up. He was trying to fight it off, telling himself to take it easy, because what he was seeing had no reality.

He was so engrossed in the show and in his thoughts that he did not notice when he finished the last sip of beer. The next thing he knew the nearly naked and nearly flat-chested girl with the white ribbon in her hair was standing beside him, placing a fresh bottle on the table and snatching the empty away in one deft motion of her hand. Then she kept standing there, waiting for Paul to pay for the new order.

The boy looked at her in panic.

'I have no more money.' The words came squeaking out of him – he was stricken with horror.

'Listen buster, you're going to pay for it one way or another. You've been sitting here for an hour nursing one measly bottle. This is not a welfare agency! People who come in here have to order something!' The girl screamed back at him and then ran off like a wind-up toy when the spring goes into action.

In seconds the bouncer gorilla appeared at the table and with his huge paw he grabbed the boy by the scruff of his neck and dragged him out to the sidewalk. Before letting him go, he smacked him on the face with his other paw. The boy received a second blow when he hit the pavement with his nose bleeding profusely.

Tormented more by humiliation than by pain he lay in the middle of the sidewalk, unable to move. The passersby had to walk carefully around him, as if they were stepping around dog-do.

It took him a few minutes to get back on his feet. His shirt was covered with patches of blood. He tried hiding them with his jacket as much as he could, but he still looked a mess.

Wanda's apartment was four bus stops away. He had his student pass with him in his pocket, but he decided to walk.

It was Sunday, dusk was settling down, and the streets were quiet. Inside Paul, however, screams of fear, rage and humiliation were reverberating.

Paul had always had a problem saying what he felt, which was a reason he searched for solitude in the noisy dormitory building. Sometimes he would lock himself in his room in the dorm, not wanting to see anyone. If someone was not familiar with his peculiar ways and wanted to contact him for some reason, he would find no admittance to his room. Recently, in order to avoid any misunderstanding, he posted a big sign on his door with the following message: OUT OF ORDER. CLOSED!!!

One time his father, home unexpectedly from his oil wells, dropped by to see Paul, and was surprised to see the notice posted on the door of his room. He was home for two days, but he did not have a chance to speak with his son. It was days later before he was able to reach him by telephone. He asked his son what was his problem; he could not understand what it was all about.

Paul felt a surge of relief at the sight of Wanda's apartment house. He had with him the keys to the girl's apartment. It was pleasantly warm in the entrance foyer. He kicked off his shoes, but did not bother putting on the slippers assigned to him. He considered them superfluous aristocratic frills.

'Slippers are for those who live in bygone days,' he remarked once to Wanda when she asked him not to walk around in his socks.

Now he walked into the apartment barefoot. He stripped off his clothes, tossed them on an armchair, and then went into the bathroom to turn on the hot water faucet to draw a bath.

He caught himself nodding off in the tub. The warm water was soothing, caressing his skin. He washed his face repeatedly, especially where the blow had landed. He could see he had a black eye when he looked into the mirror. He went to bed naked. The cool touch of the bed sheets was relaxing, and he stared at the ceiling for a while. He was thinking about Wanda, trying to sort out his feelings for her. The girl was like a mother to him, the way she coddled him, kissing his eyes; it was like when he was a tiny child and his mother was still around for him.

He woke up with Wanda standing over the bed, pulling the comforter off him and battering him with a stream of filthy words. For a moment he didn't even know where he was. His whole body was sore, not only his face.

'Get out!' she screamed, beside herself with rage. 'Get out of here at once! You've wrecked my life. You wretch! What did I tell you? Not to show your face before Monday night! Isn't that what I said? Here, take your rags and get out.' She ran out to the living room, gathered Paul's clothes, and dumped them on the bed.

Paul sat up in bed, rubbing his sore eye. He could see Wanda coming back to the bedroom, hear her scream at him, but could not understand why.

'Forgive me for coming back a day early, I got a bad beating,' he answered in a faint, barely audible voice without thinking about it. 'That's why I came to you.'

Wanda looked surprised. She turned on the reading lamp on the night table, leaned over the bed, searching the boy's face with her eyes. She could not miss the sizable swelling developing on the boy's cheek.

'My god, what happened to you? Who beat you up? Where did it happen?' The girl's voice sounded gentler.

'You won't believe it.' Paul slowly launched into his story: 'Somehow I drifted into a strip joint. All I wanted was a beer, and it was only later I realized where I was.'

'A strip joint?' She was screaming again. 'What the hell were you doing in a strip joint? Don't I strip for you often enough? Don't I let you stick it in any time you feel like it, in any position you want?' Wanda renewed her attack.

'I told you it was by accident. Don't you understand? It was an accident,' he pleaded by way of atonement.

'Yeah, you men, you're all the same!' Wanda snapped back, letting her slender fingers wander over the boy's face. 'My god, what did they do to you? And did you put some antiseptic on it?' Horrified, she was already on her way to the bathroom without waiting for an answer.

'I found a cream in the medicine cabinet and I put some on the bruise,' said the boy proudly, finally able to point to some accomplishment of his own without Wanda's help.

'That's good. That should help.' The girl came back to the bed and sat down on its edge.

Then she drew closer to the boy.

'If you only knew what you did to me by coming back sooner than you were supposed to,' she whispered gently stroking Paul's head.

She went on stroking it tenderly and with feeling. Then she bent down to kiss him. Not once but over and over again.

The night came upon them sleeping together, naked in each other's arms. They had made love twice before falling asleep.

Chapter 18

MURDER IN HOTEL ODÉON
—VI—

WHILE DRIVING to the country house Hugo was thinking about Lidia. He wished she wouldn't phone him at home. There was no unfinished business between them.

After their first introduction, they met again two or three times. Every time it was implied that it was for the last time and they always parted on that note, expecting their paths to take them in different directions. On top of that, Hugo was often bothered by pangs of conscience whenever he thought of his lover, Viktor. He could not avoid thinking he was sneakily cheating on his true love with the hermaphrodite Lidia.

Viktor is the person I really need, he's enough for me; he makes me feel safe. I don't have to worry about unpleasant surprises if I stick with him. It's a comfortable relationship. Viktor never makes demands. Never makes any fuss or creates tension. And he was always available whenever Hugo could take a break from his busy schedule to meet with him.

Lidia was a different story. She – her preferred gender identity – was always making demands. She ordered a special brand of Champagne and one bottle was never enough for her – she wanted at least three. Although they never actually had a loud argument, the makings of a clash were always hovering over their heads like a storm cloud. On top of that Lidia was a heavy smoker, which Hugo found hard to put up with. After their time in bed she was usually past her second bottle and unable to hold a conversation. She just sat in an armchair with unfocused, drunken eyes, lighting up one cigarette after another. It was impossible to air the room, but Hugo found that the act of opening windows at least gave him a way of controlling his growing nervousness. He could not read in the thick smoke swirling through the whole room, and he had no hope of relaxing. This was the limit, the point at which he felt he could stand it no longer. He felt like throwing her out. Yet Lidia just calmly sat there, following him with her somnolent, unfocused eyes as he paced up and down, and smiling quietly to herself without saying a word. That too irritated Hugo. What the hell is she smiling about? Is she trying to make a fool of me?

Their interaction took on a different mood when they ran into each other in the corridors or meeting rooms of City Hall. Lidia was always enchantingly attentive. In the presence of other city employees she acted deferentially toward Hugo, with the respect due to his office. There was no trace of the shrew in her behaviour. She was a pleasant sight that turned heads; her wardrobe was chic and often provocative. She wore the latest fashion from expensive boutiques. Hugo even wondered once how a city employee could afford such a fashion show. His curiosity was, however, quickly satisfied. The most reliable operators of the rumour mill informed him of Lidia's love life in lurid details. According to them Lidia counted a rich industrialist among her admirers. Artur, too, confirmed the information when Hugo questioned him on the subject.

The country house was only fifty kilometres from the city, located in a hilly area, ideal for growing grapes. The small vineyard behind the house was leased to Péter, a neighbour, in return for fifty bottles of wine every year. But not just any kind of wine. It had to be the best quality, the *grand vin* of the estate; if it happened to be a bad year for growing grapes, the fifty bottles of red were to be supplied from a better vintage. The old man, Péter, took pride in his art of wine making and was eager to show the fancy city folk that he did not pursue it merely for profit.

There were two ways to enter the house. One was through the garage and the other through the front gate. The big double gate could be operated by remote control, but Hugo considered the use of it unnecessary ostentation, and they always entered through the garage. The middle of the yard was taken up by an oversized swimming pool. Although it was fed by a natural hot water spring and built for year-round use, they only kept it open in summer when they often had house parties. Sometimes they had visiting dignitaries from the capital, and the pool was reserved for them exclusively as a special favour. The wine maker next door had a helper who made sure the pool was always ready for the enjoyment of the guests. When the pool was newly built Nina went bathing in it every weekend. But then something happened that forever afterwards made Nina feel faint every time she looked at the pool.

There had been an incident that left a stain – literally – on the pool. On that occasion the VIP guest was a member of the government, a minister from Bucharest and a keen swimmer. The minister arrived with his family, a wife and two children, but he seemed to forget about them as soon as he saw the pool. He hurried off to change into a swimsuit.

As always, Nina, the helpful hostess, was busy arranging for the luggage to be delivered to the rest of the family. Péter too was lending a hand; he had come over as soon as he heard they had arrived. He was itching to see a real government minister up close.

All the guests were already settled in their rooms when from an upstairs window Nina caught a glimpse of the minister as he was getting ready to dive into the shallow pool, only a meter and a half even at the deep end. Something awful was about to happen, she was sure;

she held her breath in fright, unable to get a squeal out of her throat, but even if she could have, it was too late. Head first, the minister disappeared with a big splash beneath the surface of the pool.

At long last he reappeared, painting a wide, crimson streak in the water. Blood was gushing from his head.

Fortunately the wound was only skin deep. It was stitched up in no time at the emergency ward of the local clinic, and the whole house breathed a collective sigh of relief on seeing the guest back again with his head swaddled in bandages. Since that incident, however, Nina could not look at the pool without getting a feeling of queasiness. The unfortunate accident also prompted the posting of five conspicuously placed 'DANGER' signs warning against diving into the pool from any direction; it was to be entered only by the decorative steps at one end.

Shortly after they arrived and started unloading the suitcases from the car, Péter appeared from next door in the opening cut into the shared fence. He greeted them with his usual big smile under his walrus moustache. He held his tall, gaunt figure straight, but bent his head slightly in a sign of respect. He insisted on addressing Hugo always as 'Mister Mayor', pronouncing the words reverently.

Hugo found it irritating that after so many years of being neighbours, the old man remained so obsequious instead of behaving naturally. He had repeatedly asked the old man to call him by his name and the old man promised to comply, but the next time they met it was back to Mister Mayor.

Now, once again, the old busybody was trying to make himself indispensable to the city folk, asking humbly if they found the place in order and everything to their liking before Hugo and Nina had even set foot inside.

Hugo listened patiently to the old man, giving him

the respect he deserved. Without him, who would have
kept an eye on their villa in their absence? Who would
have cared for it with so much devotion?

The old man gave a detailed report on the events of
the past week in the village. He complained about the
mail carrier who was drinking too much and not doing
everything the job required; for example he would not
take orders for newspaper subscriptions.

'And the dogs?' Nina interrupted the faithfully
rendered report. 'How are the dogs?'

'Oh, the dogs?' The old man repeated the question.
'Doing fine, just fine. They're eating well and running
around a lot. Don't you worry; I don't give them more
than what they need. You can see them in a minute, I'll
bring them out,' said the old man and, putting a suitcase
down on the threshold of the front entrance, he set out
in the direction of the dog kennels in the back of the
property.

In short order he was back with the two Vizsla dogs
on leash. Catching sight of Nina they wanted to leap
happily on her. But Péter held on firmly to the leashes
so that they had to wait for Nina to get there before she
could stroke their heads.

It had been Nina's idea to have the two dogs. At first
Hugo wouldn't hear of it.

'Buying two dogs is the same as getting two new
family members. They're going to give you a lot of
trouble.'

He wasn't entirely wrong. After the vet visits for
inoculations and de-worming, they had to find a trainer.
And since the trainer did not make house calls, they
had to deliver the dogs and pick them up four times a
week. All that required money, time, energy. 'It would
have been better to adopt a child from the foundling
home. We could have done better,' thundered Hugo on
one occasion.

The mention of children disturbed Nina deeply. It

was a serious mistake. Hugo could see that at once, but it was too late to try and stuff back into his mouth the word that had slipped out unintentionally.

He did not have happy memories about that period in their life together when they kept going from one doctor to the next in hopes of having a child. They tried everything from homeopathy to whatever else seemed promising, but they had no success. Finally it was Nina who threw in the towel, casually announcing one night at dinner: 'So we couldn't manage to have a child. We're not the first, and unfortunately not the last.'

It took months for Nina to recover from her despondency and depression. During this period, the subject of children was never mentioned.

Now Hugo looked at the pale brown dogs with irritation. Seeing this, Nina told her husband he didn't deserve the dogs, and swept off with them on their taut leashes.

The evening came upon the hilly land stealthily while Hugo unpacked the suitcases one by one. He could not help wondering why in the world they had to pack all that stuff for two nights away from home, and then take it all back again, when most of the stuff they transported would never be used. He added this unnecessary operation to his wife's tab. Luckily, while engaged with it, he gradually lost his irritation. By the time Nina came back to the house everything was put away in its place. Appreciating that her husband, instead of watching television in her absence, had made himself useful, she threw her arms around him in the kitchen and planted a big kiss on his forehead.

Nina was an exceptional housewife. If she had the ingredients to hand, she could whip up a meal in minutes. Péter had brought over a dozen bottles of red, and handed them over to Hugo with a beaming face and the comment, 'These are the best.'

Finally left alone, they lit three candles before dinner.

'What's bothering you?' Nina asked, not looking up from her plate as she spoke. 'I've been noticing for days that there's something wrong.'

Leaving the question hanging in the air, Hugo raised his wine glass to his lips and took two sips from it.

'It's that building collapse,' he said at last. 'I can't stop thinking about it. But you know, now I'm beginning to think you were right all along. I've no reason to blame myself.'

—Chapter 19—

ENO FOUND HIMSELF in his car without knowing
how he got there from Wanda's apartment;
the scene there had blinded him as if someone
had splashed a bucket of blood in his face. Then the pain
of humiliation gave way to fury. His hand was shaking
with rage as he reached into his pocket for the car keys.

Wanda had run out of the apartment after Zeno and
tried to explain in the staircase that she was the victim
of a terrible misunderstanding. It was just her nephew
who used to visit her sometimes, he too was a student
at the city's university, please, wait...but she couldn't
convince Zeno. He didn't even stop to listen to her but
kept clattering down the stairs.

The girl looked after him in despair.

How did I get myself into this mess, Zeno wondered
as he drove away from Wanda's apartment. How gullible
could I have been? A deceitful, disgraceful creature is
all she is. My God, what have I done to deserve this
humiliation? Her lover, a young man, lying naked in her
bed. A cousin indeed! Who'd fall for that?

I asked for it! I'm an easy mark, a target, that's what
I am; he drummed it out on the steering wheel with
his fingers. I knew this would happen! I knew her type!
Shame on me!

Wanda now seemed alien to him, someone very far
away, someone from whom he desperately wanted to
escape.

What kind of a fool does she think I am? No question,
I've got to break off this relationship. Tomorrow I'll have
her come to my office and give her the sack. Without
further delay. Yes, immediately, he went on fuming.

But the next moment he heard another voice:

Why fire her? With that you'd only prove yourself no better than she is.

What's this thirst for revenge? Get over it!

If she cheated on you, so what? Case closed. Do you have any more business with her?

No, you don't.

Then why would you make such a ruckus?

But the hitch is I am in love with her…I fell in love with her more deeply than with anyone else before…

So what? You'll forget her. You've been in love before, haven't you? And you've been disappointed before, haven't you?

This is different; nothing like this has never happened to me before. I used to think when you turn fifty you become immune to such things as passionate love. Suddenly there she was in front of me, giving herself to me in a way no one has ever done before. Certainly not Sylvia!

It makes no sense, no sense at all! At your age…

What age? Are you telling me at this age one is already…

Come on, take it easy, relax. That's all I'm saying. Tomorrow, act like nothing happened…

That's what I'm going to do!

He felt disgusted with himself walking into his own house. He was glad to see his wife was not yet home. He didn't bother to take off his shoes as he usually did. Just as he was, he collapsed into a stuffed chair and turned on the TV. He peered out at the screen from behind a forest of his thoughts, but nothing registered in his mind.

Sylvia woke him up. She kissed his forehead gently.

'Have you been home long?' she asked, but then without waiting for an answer she hurried to unpack his bags.

Zeno was groggy getting up, so he dropped back again into the chair.

'How did it go?' Sylvia asked looking into her husband's fog-bound face.

'All right. Pretty well, in fact,' muttered Zeno, haunted again by Wanda's face appearing from nowhere. 'These business meetings seem to have got more tiring lately. Maybe it's a sign of old age creeping up on me,' he sighed and headed for the bathroom.

'Come now, Zeno! Old age? From you, who can still move mountains?'

'You know, I don't feel like moving them any longer.' He waved his hand in resignation. 'Much better to leave them where they are.'

*   *   *

'Your tea's getting cold!' Zeno heard his wife from the kitchen.

'Coming!' cried Zeno, wrapping himself tightly in his bathrobe.

Sylvia was holding a magazine in one hand and her breakfast coffee mug in the other.

'Listen to this, it's very interesting.' And she started reading from the magazine: ' "It is unnatural for a woman to limit herself to one man during the short period of her highest fertility, during the prime of her life. She's expected to reserve for one man what he cannot fully utilise but other men would love to have, and as a result of her self-denial she misses out on those other men. So it seems that men are philanderers for the first half of their lives, and live the other half as cuckolded husbands." '

'Who wrote this?'

'The writer of the article took the quote from an essay Arthur Schopenhauer wrote around 1850, *The Metaphysics of Sexual Love*.'

'I don't quite follow you. I mean I understand what it says, what I don't see is how it relates to anything,' Zeno stuttered in confusion, as Wanda came to his mind.

For a woman to limit herself to one man during the short period of her highest fertility, during the prime of her life, it is unnatural...The words echoed inside him.

That fits Wanda to a T, all right, he thought bitterly. She wants to use her beauty, her seductive powers, the perfection of her body, now, at her peak. After that, what's left for her? Her brood to take care of. Perhaps Schopenhauer was right.

The foul mood of last night came back to him.

Love, if it's true love, should be limited to a cast of two. There's no room for other characters in it. I'll have to look up this Schopenhauer, he made a mental note to himself.

'I just find it interesting, that's all.' Sylvia dropped the magazine on the table. 'The last two days have worn me out too. Zsuzsa isn't pleasant company any more. She's complaining all the time and she's never satisfied with anything although she gets everything she wants from her husband: money, love, freedom, everything. But she doesn't know what to do with herself.'

'She gets everything handed to her on a platter,' said Zeno, 'that's her problem. If she had to work for a living and put up with a cantankerous boss, she'd be more grateful for what she has. But as it is, running around in mink coats, in expensive cars, decked out like a Christmas tree with the creations of the best jewellers, she doesn't know what she wants. Those who have too much money never have enough to buy happiness.'

'Wait a minute Zeno! What's got into you?'

'Nothing. I have no patience for those who are wallowing in luxury while others...'

'Are you by any chance talking about me?' Sylvia gave her husband a piercing look.

'Sorry. Obviously that didn't come out the way I meant it. Of course I wouldn't put you among the so-called idle rich. You have your charity work, you do a lot for those in need. But Zsuzsa? What does she ever do? But let's drop this now, I am looking forward to some tough times this week,' Zeno sighed and gave his wife a peck on the cheek for goodbye.

On his way out his eyes fell upon the open magazine on the table.

'Can I take this with me?' he asked, and without waiting for an answer, he grabbed the glossy magazine and tucked it under his arm.

Chapter 20

MURDER IN HOTEL ODÉON
—VII—

Hugo was at work when he first read the report of Viktor's murder. He remembered that day vividly. Every small detail was etched in his memory.

He remembered he had awakened in a bad mood. Nina was already pottering in the kitchen, complaining about the cleaning lady, saying she was doing more damage than good. She dusted only the surfaces that were always in plain view. The library was a mess even though the cleaning lady had clear and repeated orders to straighten out the place. 'Yes, missus,' she kept saying, 'as soon as I can make the time I'll move all the books around. Don't you worry about it, you don't have to show me, I know exactly how you like it done, just leave it to me.' That's all Nina was able to get out of her, but somehow the cleaning lady could never manage to 'make the time' to get the work done. 'But in the kitchen she always follows me around. I don't have a moment to myself. I can't understand why and how I got stuck with this woman. The day she started working here I could tell from the way she handled herself that she would not work out, and I even told you so,' moaned Nina.

Hugo just sat there in silence, occupied with his own thoughts, sipping the mint tea set out before him. He had no wish to argue with his wife over an issue that he felt had been unjustly dropped in his lap. He had nothing to do with the hiring of the cleaning woman. There had been three applicants for the job advertised in the paper. Nina interviewed them all and made her own decision.

He remembered the details of the business ahead of him that day. There was a visit by a foreign delegation on the schedule. The town council had requested new buses: the various proposals had to be evaluated and voted on – usually that involved hours of debate before a majority decision could be reached. And there was an afternoon meeting with the district Prefect.

He remembered how, after drinking up his tea and collecting his papers and documents, he embraced Nina before he took off for work.

His limo was waiting as usual, in front of the house. He got into the back seat with an official smile on his face. The temperature of the car was already adjusted. He was finding the world dull that day, so low in spirits that he hardly noticed when the chauffeur brought the car to a halt in front of the main entrance of City Hall.

A mug of freshly brewed linden tea was waiting for him on his desk, as well as the morning reports. He riffled through them without much interest and then picked up the daily papers. One of them had a banner headline: 'The Mayor Promises But Never Accomplishes.'

Finally awake, he started to read the story. It was about the new buses; the gist of the story was that the Mayor had promised to deliver them before the end of last year, but nothing had materialized yet, because the Mayor himself was interfering with the decision-making. '...Who knows what the personal financial interests of the Mayor are in this issue?' was the conclusion of the lead article.

That too stuck in his memory, along with the state of nerves that came over him after reading the article. He guessed the story had been commissioned by the opposition on the City Council so that they could corner him at the next meeting and force him into accepting a tender that was not the best one. People without principles, Hugo thought, fuming. He felt the taste for battle rising in him and was ready to turn the page when he spotted another headline in bold print: 'MURDER IN HOTEL ODÉON.' He started to scan the story with a view to its implications for local tourism, something crime reporters never thought about. The ominous news item started out with the familiar clichés:

> Yesterday morning a chambermaid at Hotel Odéon failed after repeated attempts to enter a guest room on the second floor. As she explained to the members of the crime investigation unit, when she could not unlock the door with her own passkey she alerted the hotel manager and the maintenance crew. After a mechanic managed to jimmy the lock, she and other hotel staff entered the room. They were met by a gruesome sight. On the bed lay the dead body of a man, in a pool of blood. The police were instantly called, followed by teams of detectives and CSI personnel. Two doctors had determined that the victim had been drained of blood after his penis had been severed completely. The police from the local precinct identified the corpse as belonging to a thirty-six-year-old barber by the name of Viktor Faludi. A widespread hunt for the perpetrator is now under way.

Hugo was shaken to the core when he saw Viktor's name. He could not believe his eyes. He had to read the news story again, word by word.

He still couldn't believe the victim was the same Viktor he knew. It had to be a mistake; he had seen the man only the day before in Valerian's company, and the freshness of the experience of running into Victor made it difficult for him to believe that he could be the victim.

Before he knew it, his hand automatically pushed the paper aside.

He opened the folder containing the reports of the day and flipped through the contents with trembling fingers, looking for the police report. The first item addressed Viktor's murder.

He would never forget reading it; he had sat at his desk feeling mentally and spiritually broken.

Finally he decided to call the Chief of Police and ask him to give a detailed report on the circumstances surrounding the murder. A moment later though, he changed his mind. Maybe I'd better get into the car and drive to police headquarters, he whispered to the desk.

He started to make his way to the door when he suddenly froze.

My God, this business has wiped everything from my mind. He stood there for a minute, but then stepped out the door and asked the secretary if she had heard from the visiting foreign dignitaries.

'I was just going to talk to you about that,' she responded quickly in her sing-song office voice. 'They phoned a few minutes ago; they're stuck in traffic and will be delayed at least an hour. The Prefect, however, sent a note confirming the afternoon meeting, and mentioned he might look in when the foreign delegation arrived.'

Hugo looked at his watch. It said nine o'clock.

'I'm going to see the chief of police, I'll be back shortly,' he announced and headed for the corridor while the secretary was already turning her attention to her hair.

Police Headquarters was a ten-minute ride from City Hall. While the limo was meandering through the morning rush hour traffic there was plenty of time for various new thoughts to stir up Hugo's mind. He began to doubt the wisdom of his questioning the chief of police about the murder. He had never asked him about a case before. Maybe he would be tempting fate, exposing himself to suspicions, if he attributed such importance to the death of a barber? The barber was no relation, nor a friend of his.

But he was my usual barber, and there's nothing wrong with that. Why, some people harass the police on account of a cat stuck on a tree branch, so what's so unusual about my inquiring about my unfortunate barber? Why should that arouse suspicion?

On the other hand, would it have been better if I called first to make sure the Chief was available? I shouldn't barge in like this, I should simply call him and pass the time of day first and then just as an afterthought bring up the murder, considering that it's no run-of-the-mill murder we're talking about. His hands couldn't stay still, he kept clicking and relocking an empty briefcase left on the seat.

After all, why shouldn't I have a chat with Chief Jonas Balog? He's a good friend of mine, and I was the one who nominated him for the job and lobbied for him with the Council members.

And then suddenly Viktor's face intruded into his thoughts. With his mind's eye he could see the morgue; he had visited the place a few times before, but now it was Viktor laid out in a refrigerated drawer with a huge open wound in his mangled crotch. The image made him shiver. His heart began to beat uncontrollably. He knew he would fall victim to a panic attack unless he could drive away the images invading his consciousness.

'Here we are, Sir,' the driver said. He turned to the Mayor, but seeing his distraught expression and that he was not moving, he added in a worried tone of voice: 'Anything wrong? Sir, are you feeling all right?'

'Oh, I didn't realize, sorry about that. Yes, yes, here we are,' Hugo stuttered in confusion, seeing they were already parked in front of Police Headquarters. 'You know what?' The Mayor changed his tone to that of irritation as if he had been insulted, and now he must recover his dignity with a harsh comeback, 'I've changed my mind. Let's go back to the office,' he ordered sinking back with relief into the soft seat of the limo.

The driver shrugged. A few more times he glanced back at his boss in the rear-view mirror, trying to make sure there was nothing wrong with the old man except he'd just got up on the wrong side of the bed this morning.

By the time they got back to the Mayor's office the Prefect was already there, engaged in banter with the office workers in the anteroom.

*   *   *

'Have the authorities started giving you trouble again about the collapsed building?' Nina asked her husband a week later.

'No,' said Hugo, surprised. 'Why do you ask?'

'I saw something in the paper about a police detective dropping in to see you. Detective Fabian Mueller, I think that was his name.'

Hugo nodded. 'Yes, that's his name, but it wasn't the building he was interested in. At first he was talking about this and that, and the collapsed tenement, but then he ended up asking me about a barber called Viktor, wanting to know if I knew him.'

'The barber you go to – isn't he called Viktor?'

Startled, Hugo nodded. 'Yes, of course, you were in the shop once, weren't you, when we were on the way to…'

'Isn't he the young man who was murdered in a hotel in such a gruesome way?' asked Nina in a low voice tinged with dread. 'Remember, it was on all the front pages about a week ago. We were talking about it at the market. It was the butchery that was so horrible. Didn't they cut off his penis?' asked Nina, visibly disturbed.

Hugo was shaken by this questioning about a subject

which privately had been occupying all his thoughts, but about which he thought Nina knew nothing.

Then, without waiting for an answer, she plied her husband with another question: 'And why did the detective go to you? I heard that a suspect was already in custody. At the market, they were saying that a good-looking attorney with a big reputation had been arrested.'

'Yes, that's true. Three days after the murder, Valerian Lang was arrested and held in custody pending investigation. The detective's visit to me was routine. I only saw him in the outer office for a minute or so. He just wanted to know if I was acquainted with the barber and if I had had any dealings with Valerian.'

'And had you?' Nina asked, without a pause.

'Yes, of course. I'd run into him sometimes at Eddy's Bar. He was a classmate of Artur Liptak's in law school. Artur introduced him to me. Apart from that, I had never had any other dealings with him. Not even city business.'

'The papers say the attorney was the victim's lover. And that he...what's his name again?'

'Valerian.'

'Yes, Valerian killed his lover out of jealousy.'

'Where did you get this idea of lovers?'

'It's in the papers.'

'Oh, those newspapermen scribble all kinds of nonsense.'

'So you say they were not lovers?'

'How would I know? I wasn't there, was I?

—*Chapter 21*—

THE PRESS CLUB was located on the first floor of the farthest wing of the *Monitor* Building in Calgary, out of the hustle and bustle. Its mahogany-panelled walls and ceiling and leather-covered chairs and sofas gave the impression of a pleasantly quiet drawing room, in spite of the room's large size. The inch-thick wall-to-wall carpeting had a liana-like decorative pattern on an olive-green background. Round and square tables alternated, each with a thick sheet of glass on top. The lighting was subdued, coming from brass sconces with coloured cut-glass shades.

Walter staked out a far corner as his favourite hangout. From there he had a good view of the whole place. He could remain undisturbed by the traffic flow and yet see who came in, who was leaving, and who was meeting whom. He could wave a friendly hello to colleagues taking a break from work or stopping by for a quick one before going home. This location had strategic importance; it was a stage. And that was where he was headed on entering the club that late afternoon. He dropped onto a cool leather sofa.

A waitress with boredom written all over her face, especially in her grey eyes, dragged herself toward the table. Walter amused himself by trying to guess why a young and apparently healthy woman would go around with a world-weary expression in a place devoted to jollity and relaxation. Either an aspiring writer or actress, except the latter would have put on a better performance. But he refrained from asking, and ordered a Scotch on the rocks with soda on the side.

He had just got up from his desk, having completed his column for the day with his commentary on the state of the nation. At such times he always felt like someone who had just won a battle. Leaning back with satisfaction on the sofa, he was ready to reward himself with a 'cigar break' to air out his head, and let all the leftover thoughts fly away.

It had to be an invisible cigar now, but he even felt it in his hand, rolled it between his fingers, while he let his gaze wander around the great hall, the way generals survey the field. If he wrote something to his own satisfaction, it felt to him as if it had already appeared in print, and everybody knew about it. He craved and demanded instant praise and recognition from everyone in the building even if his column was to appear only in the next day's issue.

The world-weary waitress placed the glass on the empty table in a leisurely manner. While she was pouring the soda water from a bottle, she spilled some of it on the glass table-top. Not letting it stop her, she continued pouring, taking her time but without much care – preoccupied with her novel-in-progress, Walter thought to himself.

A minute or two later, Joseph Singer, an associate editor-in-chief, pushed his low-hung pot-belly through the swing door of the Press Club, and as soon as he spotted Walter, he headed for his table.

Joseph Singer came from a poor family. His university scholarship had been considered and approved by a committee consisting of the pillars of the community of a small provincial town. They had not been unfriendly – their demeanour was that of eminent citizens who possess souls as well as money and power, and who tried to help those in need. They had displayed no arrogance, nor the pompous gestures of aristocracy. They were doing what they felt was their moral duty.

Joseph usually wore an open-neck shirt, a sweater, and blue jeans to work, with his hair combed smoothly back. In contrast to his belly, he had a lean face with a pair of burning black eyes. He was a member of the small clique at the paper that kept an eye on the ideological integrity of their publication. They kept a watch over all the writers lest they deviate from the unstated but vigorously enforced party line. He liked to present himself as a liberal, open-minded editor who was always ready for a debate but never prepared to come out a loser.

'I've just read your latest,' he said to Walter as he sat down beside him. He pulled a pipe out of his pocket. For him now the pipe served the same purpose as Walter's imaginary cigar – it was more of a symbol of something than the instrument of a bad habit. He would have given his soul for a good smoke, but he didn't indulge. He satisfied his craving by sticking the thing in his mouth and sucking air through it a couple of times to see it wasn't plugged up.

'So what do you think of it?' Walter asked, as Emil Bouchard, another colleague, came to sit with them. Walter nodded to Emil by way of a greeting.

'Well, I read it several times,' said Joseph, 'and one thing puzzles me. What are you doing among conservatives – how come you are not a liberal?'

'You make it sound like there's some difference between them,' put in Emil, '– as if the whole political scene were more than just a stage production.'

Walter shifted restlessly, wanting to bring the conversation back to his column. He had written about the effects of the revolution in technology. 'It made man forget what it means to be a human,' he said. 'Today all he does after work is turn on the television, watch the news and fall asleep during the movie that follows.'

'And don't forget about computers,' Emil put in, 'the harm they're doing. In the old days, tracking down a book was an exciting venture, now it's nothing. Now the whole universe is at our fingertips. We can study the sky through super-size telescopes in space; we can explore faraway invisible regions and map new galaxies by the radio waves they emit. And then you pose the question about modern man finding his place in the universe. Let them read poetry, Byron, Whitman, Goethe, Blake. Or else the philosophers like Kant, Schopenhauer, Sartre, Heidegger. It's only through intellectual pursuit of happiness that man can regain the human qualities of old. That's the only escape route from the treadmill, from boredom, from spiritual torpor.'

'Go and tell that to Zeno's meatpacking workers,' said Walter laughing, 'For them, the number one activity is making money, as much as they can, so as to pay off the mortgage on the apartment, make monthly car payments, send the children to school, and maybe take a holiday once a year. This is what they consider important in their lives – not the works of Homer, Virgil, Dante, Stendhal, and Updike.'

After a while, Emil got up looking at his watch and made his apologies for having to leave. He had promised to meet his wife at the mall. Walter and Joseph too gathered themselves up from the depths of the sofa, calling the waitress. 'Gentlemen, you were my guests today,' Joseph announced with an air of magnanimity, using his own credit card to cover the check.

Although it was a summer evening there was a cool breeze outside. Walter was shivering by the time he got to his car, especially when he realized he was going to be late getting home, and Melanie would not be happy about that.

*   *   *

Walter let his gaze rest on Barbara as she lay next to him, watching his lover's ribcage, her generous breasts rising and falling with every breath. He felt overcome by a pleasant fatigue, a perfect state of relaxation. I am well-prepared, I have sly contingency plans for every eventuality.

Walter had never aspired to being good.

In the past few days, Walter and Melanie had been

living together on good terms. Both arrived home late
in the afternoon or early evening. Almost every evening
Walter readily took it upon himself to prepare dinner, but
before doing anything else he got wine glasses ready. He
brought up a bottle or two of *pinot noir* from the cellar. He
would fill the glasses and then keep refilling them while
cooking. Always twice as much in his glass. It was an
essential ritual for him to slosh a little wine into whatever
he was sautéing. In the meantime Melanie would catch
up with other housework. Caroline was usually talking to
her friends on the phone.

Lying here with Barbara, Walter found that scene
projecting itself on his mind. He grew tense thinking that
Melanie was probably getting impatient waiting for him
at home while he was with Barbara. He looked at the
clock: it was only six-thirty. He gave the woman a gentle
hug, felt her breasts and kissed them. Then he got out of
bed and started dressing.

Barbara quickly turned over, looking at him with
sleepy eyes.

'What's happened? Where are you going?' she
whispered as if there were others in the apartment.

'Got to get home, Barbara,' he answered with
determination.

'You said you were staying.'

'Yes, but I've changed my mind.'

'Why?'

'I wish you'd understand. I've just got back together
with Melanie. I cannot do that to her, staying out so soon.'

'So how long have you been feeling this way?'

'Barbara, you know how it is. I'm facing an election
campaign. It's likely I'm already getting phone calls at
home from election headquarters. And what is Melanie
to say? Where am I?'

'But it's good when we're together.' Barbara was
stretching as if trying to hold on to the post-coital
pleasure.

'I know, Barbara. It's great for me too. 'But once this election circus is over we will have some good times again. You'll see!'

'When will I see you again?'

'I hope as soon as Monday. You promised to take me for a ride in your new flying machine.'

'Not next week, but the following week for sure. Ted claims he has to take it on a shakedown flight – a waste of time I think – and only then can he hand over the plane to me. And he also wanted me to put in a couple of hours of fly time with him so I can get used to the controls.'

'He's right,' he agreed. 'I'm sure it takes time to get to know a new plane and feel comfortable with it.'

They said goodbye as if he was about to set out on a long journey. Barbara wrapped her arms around his neck and let go of him only after a long hot kiss.

The traffic was still heavy in the city. The road on which he was driving – a major thoroughfare lined with glittering shop windows and sidewalks crowded with people – had three lanes in each direction and also had streetcars running down the middle. Inevitable roadwork narrowed the road to two lanes, and the traffic lights caused more delays. Although it hadn't started raining yet, it was in the air. Walter drove without thinking about anything, his mind overwhelmed by the day's events. He was unable to entertain another thought except getting home as soon as possible.

When he arrived, Melanie came to the door.

'My poor darling, they are making you work so hard at that newspaper,' she said tenderly, stroking her husband's face.

'I'm not coming from there. I stopped in at the Press Club, I had some details to sort out with Cameron, the campaign chairman,' he answered in the most natural tone he could muster.

'But just a few minutes ago Cameron was asking

me where you were. He said he had important news to discuss with you.'

Walter was just slipping out of his coat. His arm stayed up in the air for a few seconds. He dropped it quietly before answering.

'But dear, that was not Cameron Fowler. More likely, it was Cam O'Hara looking for me, the head of security. That's a Cameron, too,' he improvised on the spot, feeling his stomach suddenly twisting into a knot.

'I see,' said Melanie with a shrug. 'Well, I can't know them all.'

'You will,' he said quietly. 'Was he ringing from home, or did he leave a phone number where I can reach him?'

'The number's on the pad by the phone.'

Good thing I came home when I did, thought Walter. This could've caused a scandal. Well, at least I can say my danger-sensing antennae are still in good working order and still tell me when it's time to run and where. He hurried to the phone, and dialled. Cameron picked up.

'I was beginning to worry I might not reach you today,' he said with some resentment.

'I just got home.' Walter's voice was soothing.

'We're in trouble, old boy!' Cameron went on without any of the usual pleasantries.

'What's wrong?'

'Looks like not everyone likes you at your newspaper. But that's not the problem. The problem is one of your hot-headed colleagues decided to teach you a lesson. Ever since you announced you had settled your family affairs and went back to Melanie, he took it upon himself to tail you after work. Today he asked to see me. At our meeting he presented me with compromising photos and a diary he kept of your dates with Elmer's wife: times, places, everything.'

'With Barbara?' Walter asked, swallowing hard.

'Yes. His camera caught you with her in various locations and various poses. He informed me in no uncertain terms that if we can't convince you to withdraw from the parliamentary race, he would pass all this material evidence to a rival daily paper in town.'

Walter hung on to every word he was hearing from Cameron. At first he thought he didn't hear it right, but slowly everything became clear, like the image of a monster stepping out of the fog.

'Hello, are you still there? Still on the phone? Hello!' Cameron's words seemed like they were coming from the world hereafter.

'Yes, I'm still here,' he whispered with an effort.

'Tomorrow we must get together about this. I called in the members of the nominating committee. I know it's Saturday. But when I explained to them what this was about they all agreed to convene.'

'You've told them already?' Walter was surprised.

'Why, what would you have done in my place? This is an emergency. Your young colleague set a deadline, and we must hammer out a decision and fast.'

'Deadline?'

'Next week, Wednesday evening.'

'Would you reveal the name of this co-worker of mine?'

'Tomorrow when we meet. Until then rest up for this confrontation. Try to relax, if you can.' And with that Cameron ended the conversation.

Walter turned pale, seeing the receiver shake when he replaced it. He buried his trembling hands in his pockets and forced himself to produce a smile as he stepped into the kitchen.

Melanie gave him a searching look. The signs of distress on his face were only made deeper by his effort at hiding them.

'Anything wrong?' she asked anxiously.

'Nothing…Nothing more than the usual pre-election campaign issues. Cameron passed on a message that we're all to meet at ten tomorrow morning. The members of the committee have already been summoned.'

'In that case, it must be serious.'

'In a way yes, and yet no. Let me keep this issue to myself for the time being. I'll tell you all about it tomorrow when I come back from the meeting.' Walter was anxious to find a way out of the dilemma.

During their marriage Melanie had got used to being satisfied with such information as her husband shared with her. And now, especially since they had got back together, she would not have wanted to hurt him or bother him with persistent curiosity.

'But what would you say,' said Walter, 'to a good beef stew? Cooked in red wine?' He clapped his hands together in a show of good cheer. 'Yesterday I got a beautiful piece of beef from the butcher.'

—*Chapter 22*—

ORNING FELL ON WALTER like a sack of cement. He woke with a hangover, a pain in his shoulder, and a crick in his neck as if he had spent all night wrestling with invisible forces.

The ten o'clock meeting came back to his mind. The thought of it immediately caused his stomach to tense up. He could not get up from the bed. He waited a while for the spasm to abate. Melanie was lying on his right, still asleep.

He crawled out of bed gingerly.

The clock on the wall showed eight.

He stumbled out to the kitchen and started to busy himself, although he didn't really accomplish much. He stacked and re-stacked the dishes and plates from last night's dinner. It took him another few minutes to decide to place them in the dishwasher.

The Saturday morning traffic was light. Only a few cars were on the road, mostly people doing their weekly shopping.

On the way to the meeting Walter did a lot of thinking. The more he considered how he would deal with the nominating committee, the firmer his decision became not to give up, but to fight. After all, their job was to help him and not to judge him.

No, I'm not going to back down.

Yes, I'll admit I made a mistake. But who doesn't sometimes? Anyway, it was their idea for me to make peace with Melanie.

They must help me neutralize this crisis.

I wonder who the piece of garbage is who's behind this?

The election campaign office was located on the vacant

ground floor of a new high-rise apartment building. As
soon as he opened the door he became aware of people
talking inside; some committee members must have arrived
early. He steeled himself to look confident as he stepped
into the conference room. Suddenly silence descended.
Cameron, catching sight of Walter, immediately came to
greet him.

'It seems the urgency of the situation brought us in
early,' Cameron explained briskly as he shook hands with
Walter. 'Come and sit here up front with me.'

From a side door Miriam's plump figure appeared
holding a big tray in her hands. Steam rose from the six
cups of coffee on the tray. The smell made Walter feel
queasy again, and he quickly moved away in the opposite
direction. Cameron rose to speak, taking a file from his
briefcase on the table.

'Last night I called Walter and informed him of the
bare facts. We have the photos here and the photocopies
of the surveillance diary,' he said, passing the fat folder to
Ralph.

Ralph opened the folder with a sigh. The slight tremor
of his hand seemed to give greater significance to each
item he turned over. He lingered over some of the photos,
then went on to the next, alternately nodding and shaking
his head, and when he was done he passed it to the person
sitting next to him.

Walter was the last in the chain, the last one to hold
the whole mess in his hands. He read all the diary notes,
line by line, but he gave the photos only a cursory glance
before handing the package back to Cameron.

'What can I say? It's all true,' Walter said leaning back
in his chair. The colour pictures showed him with Barbara.
In the first one they were entering a café, arm in arm. In
another one they were embracing, and in the third they
were kissing goodbye in front of his car. The notebook
gave the dates, times, and places of assignations.   He

turned to Cameron. 'Don't you think it's time you tell us who's behind all this, who followed me everywhere?'

'Could I ask you to be patient a little longer; everything in its time,' said Cameron, who was looking at the committee members expectantly.

Miriam was the first one to break the heavy silence of the room.

'I see only one solution. There's no question but that Walter must withdraw from the race and turn down the nomination. If this person, whatever his name, makes this stuff public, there'll be no power in heaven or hell that could possibly wash the mud off him.'

'I can't understand it. What were you thinking?' Mark stared at Walter. 'You knew that a responsibility came with the nomination. You owe something to the party. You can't pretend to be so naïve that you didn't realize that the minute it was known you were the candidate, you became a public figure, someone whose every move, every step would be carefully scrutinized.'

'Or simply watched as a matter of routine, as the material in the folder proves,' added Miriam.

'Look, we're not here to excoriate Walter. I imagine he's had time to take stock of the situation,' Cameron said, trying to change the tone of the debate. 'Instead, we should try to figure out how to go on from here, if we are going on at all.'

'There's no point trying to defy social convention and ossified habits. The voters give their vote to a candidate who personifies all the qualities they lack,' said Miriam, still holding the coffee mug in her hand.

'I have to agree with Miriam,' said Ralph, whose small, dark eyes glowed with intelligence. 'The majority of the electorate does expect a paragon – moral, intelligent, incorruptible, a faithful husband, a good father – and even a keeper of campaign promises.'

Walter took advantage of a moment's silence. 'Obviously, I'm in a difficult situation,' he said. 'When the nomination process was under way I didn't come to you as a total stranger, but as someone who lives in the heart of the public arena, someone who is around every day with his writing, someone whose political and social views have a significant influence over public opinion. It's true that after my marriage soured I started a relationship with another woman. But I didn't steal, I didn't kill, I didn't commit any crime. This relationship is my private business. It doesn't force me to do less or more for the electorate, doesn't conflict with the interests of the voters, doesn't waste public funds, and I don't think it damages public morality. It's my private tragedy that I cannot get along with my wife, but that does not mean I torment her, batter her, or, God forbid, shoot her. Instead we fit in with each other, we work out a way of life that allows us to live together in peace as long as it benefits both of us. We are talking about a decision, a mutual agreement, between two independent human beings. The way Barbara and her husband, Elmer, work this out between themselves does not concern the voting citizens either.'

'I beg your pardon,' Miriam snorted, upset. Her husband had left her only months before to live with her best friend, of all people. 'But a man in a responsible position cannot afford to say "Well, I'll sleep a little bit with this woman and then a little bit with another".'

'You've got it wrong, it's not the way it works!' Alfred cut in sharply. 'In politics, if necessary, everybody sleeps with everybody else.'

A roar of laughter broke the hushed tone of the room. Cameron was laughing so hard that tears came to his eyes.

'I have a suggestion.' Alfred leaned back in his chair. 'Let's negotiate with this gentleman, although he could hardly be called one. What's his name?'

'Bradley Northrup,' Cameron replied without hesitation.

Walter was startled to hear the name.

Bradley's office was next door to Walter's. He had a pleasant manner, a cheerful disposition, and was friendly with everyone. There was never a dispute or a harsh word between them. He often sought Walter's advice. Walter was now shocked to realize that this pleasant young man was preparing to carry out his political assassination.

'I can't imagine him doing this on his own accord,' he said. 'There must be somebody behind him. Maybe someone bribed him, to drag me through the mud. Maybe someone from the opposition.'

'You mean you know him?' Alfred turned to Walter.

'His office is right next to mine.'

'I see.'

'A young guy, maybe thirty, quiet, polite. He doesn't exactly write masterpieces. He used to bring me news items for my financial column.'

'Would you have considered him capable of this?'

'No. I wouldn't have expected it.'

'Forget him, he's not the subject of our discussion,' Cameron stopped them impatiently.

'But he is. We're discussing the character of the person who's trying to blackmail us,' Alfred shot back. 'We'd better know everything we can about him. If we don't know whose service he's in, how can we possibly fight him?'

'I've already spoken to our security man. He'll have the low-down on this jerk in a day or two. But for now, time is of the essence, and I'd like to walk out of this meeting with some kind of solution to this problem,' said Cameron, scanning the faces of the committee members.

'Listen. We have two choices. One, Walter withdraws. I hope you realize this is a choice we just can't afford at this moment; we have already invested too much in his candidacy. The second would be an authorization for Cameron to negotiate with Northrup and, if necessary, buy the compromising material from him,' argued Alfred.

'I support the latter solution,' said Ralph raising his hand.

'And I'll join you,' nodded Mark in approval.

'And you?' Cameron turned to Miriam.

'I abstain.'

Cameron sighed with relief. 'I accept the majority decision. And the job you've given me. I'll make sure our security man gets the low-down on Northrup as soon as possible. Let's agree to meet here again Monday evening at six.'

The meeting broke up, only Cameron and Walter lingering in the room. Walter was deep in thought, lost to his surroundings.

'I'm relieved,' Cameron said to Walter. 'I was afraid Miriam would do anything to turn the committee against you, and I was most worried about was Ralph.'

'So was I.' Walter's debate with Ralph for the party's nomination was still vivid in his memory.

Ralph had tried to convince the members of the committee that he was a better-qualified candidate than Walter. He made the point that although his rival and colleague was a much-respected heavyweight in the media, and had more virtues than vices, his marital status left him vulnerable.

'Are you saying a divorced man can't represent the community?' Walter had responded scornfully.

'Yes, that's exactly what I'm saying,' Ralph had said.

'It's not piety voters are looking for in a candidate,' Walter had retorted. 'It's the willingness and ability to do battle.'

Remembering that discussion, Walter knew he had been right.

'Anyway,' continued Cameron when he and Walter were left alone, 'I still think we can fight off this thing. If I hear anything new I'll let you know at once.'

They both headed for the coat rack. As they were leaving, Cameron said abruptly: 'Just one thing bothers me. The campaign has barely got under way, and right at the start, this has happened. I wonder what other problems are waiting for us down the road?'

—*Chapter 23*—

T AMAS RATED the airline dinner a gourmet treat. Perhaps there was even too much of it, he thought, but still managed to polish off the raspberry-laced dessert. He had not eaten so well in a very long time. After his tray was collected, he reached for his manuscript; it fell open at the place held by the red pen.

MURDER IN HOTEL ODÉON
—VIII—

I N THE SECOND-FLOOR CAFÉ of the newspaper office Markus Frankel was oblivious to the world, engrossed in correcting Vilmos's manuscript, a piece on the emotional toll the Balzac Street disaster was taking on the city.

Markus was a short-tempered man with little patience for others, especially writers. In the upper left-hand pocket of his coat he always carried the stub of a pencil, sharpened to a point and ready for use. Whenever Vilmos handed him a manuscript Markus automatically reached for his pencil, and instead of reading through the piece before correcting it, he immediately fell upon the first sentence and started fixing it. Between corrections he would pause briefly. Raising his eyes he would launch into a debate with Vilmos. He questioned words and whole sentences; he either rewrote them or just crossed them out. This nerve-racking, pompous rigmarole inevitably enraged Vilmos. He turned beet-red and tried to wrest his piece from the would-be teacher's hands, but the other would not let go. The ensuing scuffle usually ended, however, with Markus suddenly changing his tune to soothe the other's ruffled nerves. He gently grabbed the would-be author by the shoulders like a teacher might a naughty brat caught red-handed at some mischief. But no matter how conciliatory his tone became, his judgment was final, and he insisted on doing the rewrite then and there. His voice hardened again against any objection, and in long convoluted sentences he tortured Vilmos with questions: Why did he use this or that word? Did he know the actual meaning of this word or that? Finally he would cross out the lines at issue and write his version of them in his meticulous longhand.

Every encounter between them degenerated into a circus act. Vilmos promised himself a thousand times never to go to Markus again for an opinion, but in the last minute he seemed to forget the offensive arguments, and almost as if driven by a masochistic compulsion, he kept returning to the editor with his newly penned writings. The truth was he didn't have a direct access to the city editor; his entrée to the newspaper was through Markus.

On this occasion though, before things could get out of hand, Markus's arduous and unrewarding work was interrupted by Dr Artur Liptak. The attorney was a familiar face in the editorial rooms of the paper. Now, however, he stopped in the doorway as if not quite sure he was in the right place. Seconds passed, and he remained there, frozen to the spot, looking at Vilmos and company as if without seeing them before he made up his mind to amble over to their table.

He slumped down into an empty chair with a worried look. For a while he listened to Markus's tart objections concerning Vilmos's manuscript. The stickler was holding up the word 'immanent' for a critical look like a fisherman who had caught the big one.

'My boy, this word has no place in this context, this is not philosophy,' he said glaring at Vilmos with annoyance. 'The reports in a daily newspaper must be accessible, expressive, and should not require any of the readers to reach for a dictionary to find out what a word like "immanent" means. Most likely, they'll confuse it with "imminent", a more common word.'

The attorney looked on with a mixture of pique and disbelief.

'Excuse me, but why shouldn't this young man use the word "immanent"?' he thundered. 'Just because Uncle Joe doesn't understand it doesn't mean Vilmos has to erase it from his vocabulary, or run away from it, like the French did from rats during the plague.'

Vilmos recognised the reference to Camus's *La Peste*; smugly, he wondered if Markus did too.

Markus looked deflated but maintained the appearance of someone immersed in thought. He turned back to the manuscript, but was again interrupted.

'I am completely beside myself,' the attorney was saying, bending his shoulders forward. 'I can't believe what has happened. I've just come from the city jail. You recall Dr Valerian Lang, that gaunt, thin man who used to come here with me? We were in the same class at the university. As you've probably heard, he's been arrested for the Hotel Odéon murder. You can understand how the news of his arrest affected me. It happened two weeks ago, but I only heard about it the day before yesterday, when it made to papers. Rumours were circulating in town, but I paid no attention.

'And then it came out…' and here the attorney's voice took on the tone of someone with inside information about the story, 'that our friend was gay, well-known to the authorities; he frequented clubs of dubious repute and had suspicious contacts. You know what the authorities are like – they immediately focused on him and others like him. They want to saddle him with the murder of the barber, another gay boy. The prominent leaders of the city don't like to see someone like him strolling through their ranks and supposedly having connections in high places with political power brokers. I strongly suspect they wanted to get him out of the way, and that's why he was arrested. And the poor fellow maintains he's innocent to anyone who has a chance to listen. He's fighting tooth and nail what he sees as a trumped-up charge.'

Vilmos was giving Artur all his attention, although Markus continued to work on the manuscript as he listened.

'So I decided,' continued the lawyer, 'that it was time for me to get to the bottom of this affair. Early this morning I went to see my unfortunate friend in prison. It was not an uplifting experience, I can tell you. Just getting past the prison gates was an adventure. At my first attempt I was rebuffed out of hand. But I still have some connections in the justice system; so I made a few phone calls. To cut a long story short – as you know, impossible is not in my vocabulary – I got inside. My escort took me to a tiny, barely furnished waiting room. I had to wait another half an hour before Valerian appeared. During that time I had a chance to look over the charges against him.

'The story is that two months ago Valerian came into intimate contact with this boy, who was fifteen years his junior. My friend says it was merely a fleeting fancy. He claims he could never get along with the victim because he was very obstinate, sometimes demanding and aggressive. According to our friend they met only four or five times. The big problem is that, on the eve of the barber's murder, they happened to run into each other at Eddy's Bar where they had a few drinks together before parting. The following morning a young man, soon identified as the barber, was found murdered in a room of a local hotel, as you have probably read in the papers. His genitalia had been cut off with a sharp knife or perhaps a straight razor, and he simply bled to death.

The investigators on the scene came to the conclusion that Valerian was the perpetrator since he was the last one seen with the boy. The doorman of the hotel categorically states, and is willing to swear to it, that the lawyer left toward dawn. The curious thing though – and it's something that adds spice to the story – is that those working at the hotel desk did not see Valerian that night; but they did two days earlier, when he had taken a room in the hotel and occupied it the whole night. The investigators have so far failed to throw light on the contradiction presented by the doorman, who is adamant that Valerian was there on the night of the murder and yet no one else saw him. Clearly, my friend has been framed,' Artur said worriedly, 'but it seems that no one can help him prove his innocence.'

—*Chapter 24*—

A T LAST Tamas saw the roofs of a large city as the plane descended towards Toronto. He put his notebook in his bag.

At passport control, at least ten lines formed if not more. Following the example of the others, Tamas took out his documents – the residence permit, and the brown passport valid only for thirty days.

When his turn came, the immigration officer looked at his documents without comment. He attached the residence permit to the passport with a paper clip, looked Tamas in the face, and wished him a good evening.

Tamas felt he could breathe easier now that he was through with the immigration process. It was only later that he was to learn that this was just the prelude to the real thing.

Beyond the gates of passport control, there was a wooden podium in the middle of the exit corridor. Another uniformed man asked for his papers again. Without opening the passport he waved to his left.

Tamas turned left. The corridor led to an enormous hall. About three-quarters of the space was taken up by rows and rows of chairs. He sat down. After a few minutes he observed that those entering the hall first went to a cylindrical apparatus and tore off a small stub from it. Curiosity prompted him to explore. On closer scrutiny, he discovered that the gadget was dispensing numbers for the line. He took one too and sat down again. He began to wonder if there was another flight to Calgary; he was sure to miss the one he had tickets for.

Gradually, almost imperceptibly, the hall filled up.

While more and more people gathered, Tamas was looking for familiar faces among them. It took him a while to spot in the far corner the two unruly kids with their young parents. Seeing these fellow refugees made him feel a little less lonely.

Along one wall of the hall there was a row of six counters. From behind them clerks were calling the travellers by number.

Two hours must have passed before his turn came.

A chubby young lady went over his papers. She scrutinized each one with a tired expression. Finally, she informed him that he had missed his connecting flight, and it was too late to catch another that day, so he would have to spend the night in a local hotel. At the same time she assured him that the airline company would cover the costs and take care of transportation to the hotel and back to the airport the next day. In a leisurely manner she stuffed all the papers back into the manila envelope which she handed to Tamas, telling him to report to room number 17 off the large waiting area of the airport.

When he got there, he found a small group already gathered in front of it.

Joining them, he awaited further developments.

All of them were groggy from the flight, tired of carrying their bags, and disheartened by all this having to wait.

Suddenly the door opened. A tallish, middle-aged, bespectacled woman with dark, short hair appeared. She was wearing a uniform-like outfit that enhanced her authority in spite of the light overcoat slung over one shoulder. As she stepped outside she seemed to be surprised by the crowd waiting for her. She had a list in her hand. She read off ten names.

She counted those who stepped forward and beckoned to them to follow.

The small group of lucky ones broke off from the stranded crowd like a chunk breaking off from an imperceptibly moving glacier.

The rest remained standing in front of the closed door.

They continued waiting.

Tamas looked sadly at those who were on their way. He thought about Iren and his two boys left behind, someplace far away, someplace he used to call home. He was painfully aware of the distance between him and his loved ones, but since he had landed, his anxiety over them was mixed with hope.

Now all I have to do is be patient. Patient, he repeated to himself. Patient.

He didn't even notice when the official returned to the group of the stranded. She called ten more names. Tamas was not among them.

Now there were only eight of them still waiting.

The woman official came back for them with a twinkle in her eyes. But she still checked their names. And then beckoned again.

She led them out into the air. A fresh, unfamiliar, robust wind hit them in the face. Tamas unconsciously tried to pull his sports coat tighter on his chest, but it was still just a sports coat. They were to board a van that would take them to the hotel. After dinner everyone was free until the morning. By eight-thirty the next day all eight of them were to be ready to take the same van back to the airport. The tickets were already re-issued for the flight in the morning. The gate indicated on the old ticket would again be the one to go to. If anyone had any questions this was the time to ask.

No one spoke up.

They were standing in the wind-buffeted evening. Automobiles passed by, braking and then speeding up again. Limousines were gliding past them like random dreams. Joyous laughter drifted over from one of the pedestrian islands. People rushed past with carts loaded down with luggage. Taxis lined up, and then pulled away one by one; honking was heard, engines roared and faded away, the doors of automobiles slammed. All these five-second dramatic scenes were etching themselves into an evening of goose bumps. Entranced by them, Tamas watched the turmoil, the chaotic stage that, nevertheless, had everything in its right place, as if directed by an invisible hand toward redeeming order.

In the van it was warm and quiet. At least two passengers fell asleep with their heads dropped to one side. The others were busy shifting their gaze at the varied features of the landscape passing by, the freeway flooded by light.

The hotel clerk handed out keys and gave them directions to the dining room in sign language, using his hands and feet. It was still crowded is spite of the late hour when Tamas made his way there after leaving his bag in his room. He sat down at the only unoccupied table, and placed the dinner voucher on it.

When the black tuxedoed waiter with the bow tie saw the voucher the smile froze on his face. He turned around and returned with a plastic pitcher, filled the glass with water and ice cubes, and then vanished.

Tamas looked around. Seated at the dimly lit tables were men and women gesticulating, speaking sometimes softly, sometimes loudly, filling the place with the noise of a jet engine. In one corner there was a young couple holding hands.

Plates, napkins, silverware, a steaming bowl of soup, noise, butter, bread, freshly cooked vegetable garnish, laughter, the red streak produced by a cut through the meat, hands raised and dropped reaching for the salt shaker, doors slamming, voices whispering, squealing, shouting, laughing…A blindingly white plate. Words creeping in from here and there.

'Is it the way you like it?'

'Is the meat tender enough?'

Can I get you anything else?'

'No, it's a prepaid dinner voucher.'

'Then don't bother with him, leave him alone.'

'Go to the other corner, the couple there look like they have money.'

'Did they start with champagne?'
'I dropped a tray, and all the glasses smashed.'
'Sweep it up!'
'Why not call the busboy?'
'Did everything on the tray break?'
'Yeah.'
'That will come out of your pay check.'
'Sniff out the serious tippers!'
Tamas dropped into bed like a stone into a dried-up but still muddy well.

*   *   *

When he was a child, the restful oblivion of sleep often eluded Tamas. Instead, often fearsome, ghostlike shadows appeared to him in spite of the pitch dark night blanketing the room.

One night, when he lay awake in bed tortured by images of the latest fairy tale, he became aware of his father's voice. He had just returned home in an angry mood from the evening shift. Tamas could hear him clearly as he was relating a story to his mother in the kitchen: how he had taken Tamas's broken sled to the shop for welding, but when he wanted to bring it back home, the night watchman did not believe it was his own, brought for fixing. The man immediately confiscated it and even threatened to report the incident to the management. When Tamas's father saw how serious the situation was becoming, he tried to appeal to the better feelings of the watchman, speaking heart-breakingly of Tamas and how much the repaired sled would mean to the child. These gentle words did not miss their mark and the old man relented. 'My story brought tears to his eyes.' His father's voice carried from the kitchen through the thin wall. 'Finally he let me drag the sled home.'

Hearing the story Tamas leaped out of bed, and the next minute he was in the kitchen to greet his Dad, but seeing his parents' surprise at his sudden appearance when he was thought to be fast asleep, he automatically changed his expression to that of sorrow. At that time his face was like a fine instrument sensitive to the slightest disapproval. Without saying a word his father pulled a coat on Tamas, wound a scarf around his neck, put a cap on his head, buried his feet in boots, and then, holding his hand, he started out for the backyard to show him the sled, right there. When Tamas realized he was to be taken out into the pitch dark outside he began to weep piteously. His mother warned his father: 'The boy is afraid of the dark, don't take him out there now.' Whereupon the man exploded. 'What? You're telling me my son is afraid of the dark? That's impossible! What do you mean afraid? Well, let me teach him to be afraid!' he yelled and started dragging the bawling boy out to the courtyard.

The late-night pandemonium soon attracted the shoemaker from the apartment next door. He tried to reason with the furious father, asking him to let go of the boy before he went out of his mind with fear. But it did no good. Next day the shoemaker went to the local police precinct and reported Tamas's father for abusing the child.

There was a thorough investigation of the incident. Tamas still remembered the family court, the fine. And the smouldering rage. The father did not speak to Tamas for a long time afterwards.

It was a different story with his grandparents in the country. Tamas was allowed to be afraid there. Grandma never sent him alone into the dark apartment, not even when it was hard for her to hoist herself out of the kitchen chair because she was overweight and it caused constant pain in her feet. If need be, she escorted him all the way to his room, and never left him alone before she clicked on the small light on the night table. As an adult Tamas was still a bit afraid to be alone in the dark, but not unbearably so. He just didn't like it.

*   *   *

On awakening, Tamas did not remember what had happened the night before. He was looking at his foot which was sticking out from under the blanket while he became aware of a strange rattle, screams, loud crashes, and music.

It's the TV, of course. I didn't turn it off, he remembered, solving the riddle of the strange sounds. But the sights that greeted him were equally alien. There was nothing familiar in the new surroundings. His eyes wandered around the strange, dim room. It seemed an unfriendly environment in which he woke.

Tamas leapt out of bed, but then stopped in the middle of the room. He surveyed the landscape. In the meantime the explosions of incoming rocket fire continued and the engines of helicopters were roaring away. He finally turned off the TV. He sat down on the bed.

I've arrived, he thought.

He was in room 601. He discovered the number on the small plastic disc attached to the key as he was heading out into the corridor. By the time he turned back to take a last look, the heavy door had slammed shut and locked itself with a loud click. He dropped the key into his pocket and started walking down the corridor until he came to the elevator. After a time, it stopped with a ring, and the door opened.

He was already in the lobby when it suddenly came back to him that at 8:30 A.M. he was supposed to report at the entrance, ready to return to the airport. He nervously glanced at his wrist but there was no watch on it. He must have left it in the room.

On the wall above the concierge, there was not one but a total of six wall clocks. The first one showed the local time − 8:28.

He ran back upstairs and then down again. His legs were still shaking from the sprint when he climbed into the airport bus. Watching the alien cityscape from the safe vantage point of his seat on the bus he was able finally to relax. He surveyed the fleeting sights as if they had already become a pleasant memory.

Soon after, he was looking out the window of an airplane. They climbed quickly to cruising altitude. The flight time to his destination was about four hours. He made himself comfortable in the manner of an experienced traveller. He declined both milk and lemon when his tea was poured out for him. But then he changed his mind. The pretty stewardess gave him a withering look for rejecting her earlier offer of milk in the little plastic containers. This time she put a double portion on Tamas's small fold-down table so that she wouldn't have to make another trip.

Looking out the window he found the sky an unreal shade of blue. Tamas had never seen it like that before, not at 10 km up in the air. Just before landing, the plane flew over the crest of a long mountain range, turned an almost complete circle in the air, and then softly, almost unnoticeably glided onto the runway.

In the arrival hall he came upon a middle-aged lady wearing a poppy-red jacket and holding a small cardboard sign with 'Immigration Office' written on it.

'I am Tamas...' he said, hesitantly approaching her.

'Welcome! Welcome!' she repeated several times. 'On behalf of every administrator working in the Immigration Office I am pleased to welcome you to Calgary,' she said loudly and slowly, almost syllable by syllable. 'I am Linda,' she introduced herself while taking a measure of the newcomer. 'Do you have all your bags?' she asked, seeing Tamas nervously looking around.

Noting her look of enquiry, he answered, 'Everything is fine,' blushing slightly. That was the sum total of his knowledge of the English language spoken around him, and after saying it he remained silent.

On the other hand, words came pouring out of the

lady like water from a broken pipe. With a big smile she explained that she was almost late because she had to take her child to the doctor. Her husband was away on business, and she was not on good terms with her mother-in-law, and so she had to take care of everything herself.

Tamas could understand only a word here and there. He was unable to make out what she was saying. So he just nodded politely whenever Linda paused to take a breath. Finally, Linda stopped, looked at him, and went back to talking one syllable at a time.

'Am I talking too fast for you?'

Tamas gave a smile. Fast, that was one thing he understood. He continued nodding.

They got into Linda's car. Forgetting Tamas's limited command of the language, the administrator plunged into the role of a tourist guide. Resuming her quickly rolling sentences, she pointed out the various parts of the city as they were passing through them, as well as telling him about the important sights – which was famous for what, why it was a tourist attraction, where festivals were arranged on weekends, and what artists appeared there, and so on.

They were soon whizzing through the streets of the central business district. Tamas was awestruck by the almost infinitely tall office towers and the waves of humanity flooding the sidewalks. The city was laid out in a geometric pattern of straight avenues and streets; there were no curves in any of the thoroughfares, and only the thick forest of traffic lights slowed down the traffic.

Eventually they stopped in front of an older corner building that was only a few storeys high. As she got out, Linda explained to Tamas that this was the hotel where he was to stay. At least for a few days, until the Office found him a more permanent apartment. Before taking her leave, she pressed an envelope in his hand containing the address of the Immigration Office and the name of the administrator he was to visit the next morning. Then she led him into the hotel and left him in the care of the concierge who gave Tamas the room key with an icy look of suspicion. Linda's job was over, and she offered her hand in farewell.

'Once more, welcome! Have a nice day! See you again soon.' And she hurried back to her car.

Tamas gathered his possessions and set off for the elevator when he heard the voice of the concierge behind him: 'Keep in mind the Immigration Office will not pay for the use of the telephone or the minibar.'

Tamas turned back and looked at the representative of the hotel with obvious incomprehension. But the latter just shook his head in resignation. 'These immigrants – zombies,' he muttered to himself.

—Chapter 25—

Tamas's room was on the fourth floor, no. 413. He went over in his mind the sounds of the concierge's words of warning, and he was able to make out some of the words: telephone, minibar, not. From these he deduced that these two things were not to be touched.

But a telephone was what he needed now. First of all, he wanted to call Iren and give her the good news. He was out at last – he was safe.

Besides Iren, he was to call a local journalist by the name of Walter Wallmeyer, whose name had been given to him by a friendly official back in the transit camp, a person with connections in the outside world. That official promised to write a letter to Walter about Tamas, asking him to help the new immigrant settle in.

'Look, it'll be a strange city, an alien environment and you'll need a friendly contact. Walter is an outstanding man, he speaks our language, and even if you're lucky and don't need his help, at least there'll be one person you'll know and you won't be totally alone.'

Now he was looking for room 413. He already had the key in the lock when he was struck by the number – 413 – and his arm froze.

That 13 is a bad omen. If I start my new life here, what lies ahead for me?

The room was not inviting. The air was stale and smelled of mildew. The window was covered by a heavy plain canvas curtain. Everything about the place was unwelcoming.

He quickly drew back the canvas curtain and opened the window. Immediately, fresh, fragrant summer air filled the room, but there wasn't enough of it, and he opened the door too in order to create a draft. He unpacked his tiny suitcase, taking out his one and only suit, bought in a second-hand store while he was in the transit camp. He tried smoothing out his two wrinkled shirts to no avail, so he gave up and hung them on wire hangers he found in the closet. Then he collected his toiletries and put them in the bathroom. With that he was finished.

He became aware of people passing by his door. One man stopped to peek into the room with curiosity; another man, whom he didn't like the look of, with long unkempt hair, even lingered in front of the open door, glaring persistently at Tamas who felt all his gumption drain out of him. As soon as the onlooker finally moved on he ran to the door, shut it, and locked it too.

For a desk there was a wide shelf on the wall with various advertisements and a hotel directory. Leafing through it he soon came upon a price list of phone calls to various locations. He needed to know how much it would cost to call home, but his country was not listed. Finally an asterisk led him to a footnote that said it would cost a minimum of nine dollars of his new bank notes to call Iren. He was horrified. From an inside pocket he produced all his riches. Like someone believing in miracles, perhaps even in the bank notes being able to reproduce and multiply in the interim, he counted his money again. He found two ten-dollar bills and two fives. That was all he had. Calling Iren would cost one third of the cash he had.

He racked his brains about what to do. Finally, he decided to make the call. But to be sure he was doing it right, he would ask the concierge for help.

Once out in the corridor he turned back because he wasn't sure if he had locked his door. He hadn't. The door opened.

The elevator made a stop just one floor below. Two scantily-clad young women entered laughing loudly and easily, in the company of a man. The sharp smell of perfume filled the confined space at once. One of the women was so generously endowed up front that the yellow silk blouse barely covered her. It was obvious she did not bother with a bra. The brown circles around her nipples were clearly visible through the flimsy fabric. Her midriff and navel were not covered at all. She was wearing a white miniskirt that barely reached the bottom fold of her buttocks. Her girlfriend was dressed the same, except her breasts were smaller.

Tamas eyed the loud, jabbering, laughing trio. His first thought was that they were leaving a party on the third floor, and it was only later that evening that he found out that there was a striptease bar in the hotel basement. What the third floor rooms were used for was open to speculation, but Tamas was in no mood to speculate.

The concierge looked with indifference bordering on hostility at the piece of paper with the phone number and the ten-dollar bill next to it that Tamas placed on the counter. He examined the number and the bank note and gestured to Tamas to go up to his room where the call would be transferred.

Tamas set off for the elevator with mixed emotions; he even wondered whether he had written the right number on the paper. Did the hotel clerk understand that the numeral 3 below meant that he wanted a 3-minute call? And that the call had to be transferred to room 413?

Well, I'll see what happens, the die is cast, he decided pushing the button for the elevator.

Stepping out on the fourth floor it hit him that perhaps the call had gone through in the meantime, and he was ambling along leisurely as if he had all the time in the world. Immediately he broke into a trot to his room and unlocked the door with shaking hands.

No, there was no need for alarm. The telephone was sitting silently on the night table. He let out a great sigh of relief. He went over to the window and closed it halfway to muffle the street noise that might otherwise prevent him from hearing the phone ring.

He sat down in the one chair in the room and waited. Minutes went by at snail's pace while the mute telephone sat silent as a sphinx. Tamas tried hypnotizing it, willing it to speak up.

Half an hour passed like this while he was just sitting, listening to his pounding heart and waiting for the phone to ring. Nothing. Still nothing. He considered running downstairs and asking the clerk about the delay with the connection.

Yes, I've got to do something, but what if the call comes through when I am on my way down? Or up? He resisted the temptation to do something foolish.

Well, then I have no choice but to get hold of that phone and ask the man downstairs what's the hold-up. He convinced himself that was the best solution to the problem. Mustering his meagre command of the language, he tried to compose the question. He tried several versions, but they all sounded incoherent and stupid. Now he bitterly regretted not having used the time in the transit camp to study the language of his future homeland instead of taking on odd jobs to make money.

But Iren depended on the packages I was sending. I simply had to work and earn some money, he reminded himself.

A sharp ring cut into his thoughts.

He leapt at the phone, his heart pounding wildly. He wrenched the receiver off the hook and shouted into it.

'Hello, hello, Iren, my dear, is that you?'

From far away, as if coming from some cavity in the ground, there was a weak voice.

'Tamas, it's me – Iren. Hello!'

He was not sure if he heard it right. He asked again.

'Iren my dear, is that you?'

'Yes, yes, now I can hear you much better. My God, Tamas, did you get there all right?'

'Yes, my dear, I've finally arrived. I'm fine, no problems.'

'But you were supposed to get there yesterday. I was so worried that something had happened to you.'

'I missed my connecting flight yesterday, and so I had to wait for another one until this morning, but I'm here now in Calgary, safe and sound.'

Iren was sobbing softly at the other end of the line.

'Don't, please, my dear, don't be silly, don't cry. Everything is fine. I'm here, I've arrived. Don't worry, it won't take too long before you and the kids will be here with me, you'll see.'

Tamas suddenly remembered that he had paid only for three minutes. And he had neglected to check the time on the red digital clock at the bottom of the TV screen when he picked up the receiver. He was in a panic and hurried to finish the conversation.

'Iren my dear, we're running out of time, and I don't have money for more. But I'll write to you, today. We have to hang up soon. Just one more thing,' he added quickly, 'how are the kids? Tell them I love them very much and you too, my dear. Now I have to hang up. As soon as I make some money, I'll call you.' He rattled off the words as fast as he could and slammed down the receiver.

His heart was throbbing in his throat. He sat down in the chair again. He tried to breathe slowly and evenly, because he felt he was about to faint.

I cannot let anything bad happen to me now; he was determined to get hold of himself.

Minutes went by while he stayed like this, staring into nothing. Then he felt strong enough to stand up and search the room for the room key. When he found it he went down to the hotel desk. The clerk looked at him inquiringly as if trying to read his face, as if to say:

Well, what about it, big hero? Did you speak to your little woman?

Clumsily Tamas composed the question: 'Minute, how

many?' The clerk answered curtly, almost unwillingly, 'The call lasted less than a full minute.'

Tamas returned to his room feeling considerably calmer.

So far so good. What's next on the agenda? he asked himself.

Yes, next I'll have to call Walter Wallmeyer, it came back to him.

From his pocket he fished out his small address book.

*   *   *

Walter was engaged in a conversation with Emil Bouchard, his colleague, when the telephone rang on his desk.

'Wallmeyer,' he barked into phone.

'How do you do,' he heard a nervous voice say. My name is Tamas... You don't know me. I got your phone number from your friend Pascal Orbán, he told me to call you as soon as I got here.'

On hearing the name Pascal Orbán, Walter's voice immediately mellowed.

'So you are Tamas? Yes, I remember now. Pascal wrote me a few weeks ago and said you would look me up.' Walter sounded friendly and spirited now.

'When did you arrive?'

'My plane landed a few hours ago.

'Is everything all right with you? You have a place to stay?'

'For the time being I am at the Warwick Hotel, but tomorrow I have to go to the Immigration Office. I am to see an official by the name of Mr Bertold Thompson.' Tamas dropped down on the bed, feeling all the strength draining out of him. He needed a firm place to rest.

'What time are you expected there?'

'Any time before noon.'

'Well, then let me suggest the following. At ten o'clock I have an appointment in the same building. I'll pick you up at the hotel. Actually I happen to know Bertold. I'll put in a good word for you. Wait for me in the hotel lobby at nine-thirty. Now then, welcome, Tamas. And I'll see you tomorrow.' Walter replaced the receiver.

'Forgive me for carrying on a conversation in your presence in a foreign language.' He turned to Emil, 'but I was talking to a newly arrived immigrant, a young man. Can you imagine where these newcomers are housed by that liberal government? I give you one guess.'

'At the Warwick,' Emil answered without hesitation.

'Exactly. In that fleabag. And don't ask me how much it's costing the taxpayer. You see, that's another reason why I must win the upcoming election.' Walter restlessly paced his office.

'So you're telling me the owner of Warwick will not be able to convince you Conservatives to put up the newly arrived immigrants in his hotel if you win the election?'

'That's exactly what I'm telling you. We are not for sale, we can't be bought.'

'Fine, fine, but the Conservatives need money too. Don't forget election time rolls around every four years, and money always has to be raised for the next campaign. Lots of money,' Emil remarked bitterly as he turned to face Walter.

'You're right, of course, but we still shouldn't solicit contributions from businessmen of the Warwick calibre. And we shouldn't accept a penny from them.'

'Let's talk about that after you win the election,' replied Emil sceptically holding out his hand by way of farewell.

*   *   *

After this telephone conversation, Tamas was filled with elation, a welcome sensation after the last few days.

That's the kind of welcome my weary soul needed. Thank you, Pascal, thank you, he thought. He no longer felt alone, no longer one against the world! Suddenly he found the room too small to contain his newly rekindled spirit.

I've got to get out of here, out to the street! He grabbed his jacket and stepped out of the hotel lobby onto the sidewalk, interested now in this new world, and with the feeling of a job well done.

Two hours later he returned to his hotel room with picture postcards and stamps in his hand.

He wrote his postcards, then stretched out on the bed and picked up his notebook, starting to read where he had left off when his plane was about to land.

—*Chapter 26*—

MURDER IN HOTEL ODÉON
—IX—

ARTUR WOULD NEVER FORGET his visit to Valerian
in the prison. He was reading the charges when
his friend was brought in. Artur was shocked by his
appearance. He looked almost like a total stranger. His
cheeks were hollow from starvation and he had let his
beard grow. When he saw Artur however, he acted like
he was on a stage. He spread his arms wide and greeted
his visitor by reciting lines from a Latin poem:

> '*Alfene immemor atque unanimis false sodalibus,*
> *iam te nil miseret, dure, tui dulcis amiculi?*'

'Catullus?'

'Right you are, Artur. Do you remember in college
when we used to quote from works of literature and
the other had to guess the author?' Artur wondered if
there was significance in the lines Valerian had chosen –
*...is there now no pity in you, hard of heart, for your sweet
loving friend?*

After a pause, Valerian went on: 'In the past few days
I've also had Boëthius on my mind, because I wanted
to feel free even in this miserable jail. What was it
Professor Calvasin kept telling us? Imagination is man's
most dependable weapon. With its help one can knock
down walls, traverse borders, and defeat fear, the beast
that invades the soul.'

Each scanned the other's face. Valerian was obviously
thinking that if Artur had an ounce of honour and
gumption, he'd take a stand on behalf of his innocence

159

and start a campaign in the local papers for his liberation. And Artur wondered what the hell he was doing there in this dingy prison waiting room when he had better things to do, such as enjoying Lidia, the object of his attentions in the past few weeks and someone who had shared previously unknown pleasures with him. True, her delusions of grandeur could be irritating, but who is without faults nowadays? Lidia had beautiful features, a generous bosom and a seductively slender waist.

'Light is flooding the window, and yet I languish in darkness,' Valerian looked his guest in the face. 'Like the practitioners of Kabbalah I've been racking my brains in order to create a deity who could pay attention to me and lend me a helping hand.'

'You should concentrate on those who put you in here. They have the power to grant you something no deity is capable of. Where are your friends?' Artur was nervously drumming with his fingers while looking into his colleague's eyes. 'I should be fighting a battle of motives, fingerprints and forensic evidence. Reason and good friends are the key to your liberation.'

' "My good friend, I have no friends." That's another quote. Actually, I used to be blessed with good company, but now I seem to suffer from an infectious disease, and everyone pulls back, avoids me, and runs away from me. I am sitting here in the lowest circle of hell, invoking God.' Valerian put his hands together to demonstrate his way of trying to escape his predicament.

'Listen Valerian, stop playing the fool. Why preach to the converted? Have you lost your senses? What's got into you? All you have to say is where you were on that particular night.'

'You think it'll help?'

'I don't just think so, I know so, for sure. Don't be so naïve, Valerian, come out with it. Where the hell were you if not in the hotel? It's that simple.' Artur was looking at his friend. He felt overwhelmed, close to being unable to control himself.

The facts made no sense to him. He could not believe someone in trouble would rather hide something than extricate himself from the situation by coming clean about his whereabouts. His anger was fed by his inability to do anything, other than to look at Valerian quizzically. It was exhausting him to wait for his friend to answer.

'I am not free to divulge that. But I can state categorically that on that particular night I was not in the hotel. Believe me, it's a question of life and death that prevents me from proving my alibi.'

'Whose life and death? What could be more important than your freedom?' said Artur as he nervously crumpled a corner of the folder in front of him. 'Wake up Valerian!' he shouted and slammed his open palm down on the table.

Valerian remained motionless sitting across the table.

His serenity is infectious, Artur was thinking to himself, and he too remained silent. For a moment he had the feeling he was not in a room of the local prison but outdoors somewhere. Valerian's hands were fiddling with a piece of paper while his eyes were focused on the blank wall before him.

'It bothers me to discover you're of no more help than the others,' Valerian said uneasily. His tone made it obvious that further conversation would be a burden to him.

'In that case you have no one to blame but yourself,' Artur said, frustrated. His hand, which had lain idle in his lap like a stunned bird, now suddenly came alive, and he offered it by way of farewell and started to get ready to depart. After a while he got up from the chair.

Valerian's eyes were hanging on his friend, expecting a verdict of acquittal. 'But Artur, you do believe me, don't you?'

*   *   *

'You can understand I had nothing to offer for encouragement,' Artur said, continuing his story to the two journalists. 'All in all, I was completely devastated by the surroundings, the atmosphere, and Valerian's behaviour. He blames the authorities for his miserable situation, even though if he could prove he was not at the scene of the crime, nobody would bother him. He could walk free,' he sighed again as if suffering Valerian's hopeless fate. 'I don't want to paint you a detailed picture of prison life, I'll leave it to your imagination. And your investigative skills. You are journalists. I really think you ought to start a campaign to free him. Isn't that your job?' he concluded somberly, adding more weight to the gravity of his prison story.

'But what makes you think he is innocent?' asked Markus, apparently having given up on pruning Vilmos's manuscript.

'My dear fellow, have you ever heard from anyone that civil liberties are respected in this country? Valerian was arrested on the evidence of one witness, who, by the way, has an IQ of 85. Don't forget we're talking about a hotel, a public place where lots of people move through every day. But in spite of all that, the detective branch of the prosecutor's office is no longer pursuing the matter; it is satisfied with the testimony of one simple-minded witness.'

Markus sat silently staring at the table. Vilmos swept up his defaced manuscript, folded it carefully and slipped it in his pocket. He had no further business there. There was little chance of Markus assigning the Valerian story to him.

—*Chapter 27*—

WHEN ZENO ARRIVED at the factory, the first worker he ran into was Dora. She greeted him warmly and with a pleasant smile.

Dora was thirty-nine, tall with a slender figure that she emphasized by always wearing a low-cut neckline, even though her short bleached blonde hair and bright black eyes were enough to make her look very attractive. Male visitors to Zeno's office never failed to comment on her good looks.

'Not that I want to seem forward or anything,' many of them remarked, 'but you have a very pretty secretary.'

Zeno acknowledged the observation even while he was trying hard to banish from his mind a whole series of memories connected to Dora.

Those memories dated from the time he was taking over the firm.

In those days they spent a lot of time together. The secretary was married to an engineer whose work took him away from home for long periods. Dora raised their little boy virtually alone. She often complained of loneliness, taking every opportunity to bring up the subject. Zeno was warned by his father-in-law before his death that, if and when the time came for him to take over, he should learn all he could from Dora but without ever becoming personally involved with her, no matter how attractive and desirable she was. 'I can tell you from experience,' he whispered, 'it leads to no good when the boss, especially the owner of the business, jumps into bed with an employee. First of all he'll lose her respect and then he cannot give her tasks as a boss but must ask her to perform favours as a sex partner – and the two roles are very different.'

The old man was right; Zeno found an invaluable friend in Dora whose business experience, technical know-how, and willingness to work were invaluable to him in the first few months.

Unfortunately, Zeno did not follow the second part of the old man's advice.

Fresh at the job as the new boss, Zeno was working very closely with Dora. The woman seemed reticent and modest in the beginning, but as time went by she became more and more forthcoming, and the cleavage of her dresses deeper and deeper. She had shapely, round, velvety breasts. Every time she bent closer to Zeno, either accidentally or by design, she practically put them on open display.

One evening, when they were about to leave the office after working late, Dora leaned closer to him and planted a light goodnight kiss on his lips.

At first the gesture seemed so natural to Zeno, that he paid little attention to it, his mind still on the work on hand. But when he realised what was happening, he pulled her back to him, took her into his arms and started kissing her with uninhibited passion. Dora did not resist; she let him grab her, do with her as he pleased, even reciprocating the erotic exploration, helping him press his body against hers. They parted with a date set for the afternoon of the following day, which was a Saturday.

The firm maintained an apartment on the grounds for visiting business associates. Fitted with modern furniture, it was pleasant, informal, anonymous – the perfect love nest.

Zeno arrived there a half an hour before the appointed time. He had a huge bouquet of red roses.

To be on the safe side, he drew the curtains and turned on the lights in every room except the bedroom where he experimented with various combinations of lights until he decided to leave only the wall sconces on; their indirect light gave the room an intimate air without being too dim.

He was bemused by his almost school-boyish preparations, clicking switches on and off, running out of the bedroom to the hallway to observe the effect.

He had a problem with the roses, too. He could not find the right place for them. First he had to find a vase large enough to hold the bouquet, and then to run all over the apartment trying various spots, until he finally decided to leave it on top of the chest of drawers in the bedroom, where it would stand out and could been seen even from the bed.

While waiting for Dora he restlessly paced the apartment. He turned on the TV, watched a part of the news. They were to meet at one, and it was already four minutes past when the doorbell rang. He hurried to the door. Dora, like a teenage girl sneaking into a forbidden place, slipped quickly and unobtrusively inside the apartment.

All this was a long time ago. He no longer remembered the taste of the kisses. Somehow the passage of time had washed them away. But the outlines of Dora's slender body were still clearly etched in his memory. She undressed in the bathroom and by the time Zeno stepped into the bedroom she was already under the blanket. He took his time to lift it as if unwrapping a special present, and went on a tour of discovery over her body. He observed to his sorrow that Dora's otherwise shapely breasts were beginning to sag, but otherwise it was faultless.

Later they met many more times. Their sex was uninhibited. They abandoned themselves with wildness to the demands of the body.

Zeno was glad to see that Dora never abused the special relationship between them. She continued to act as his secretary in a professional and respectful manner, and he was glad that in this one respect his father-in-law turned out to be wrong.

As years went by, their relationship did not mature into anything more than pleasant memories. Dora got divorced, and married the manager of a service garage at an automobile dealership. To Zeno she seemed to have at last found the perfect partner. After her second marriage she never complained of loneliness. Their working relationship remained not only intact but better than ever. He could always rely on Dora, even at weekends, if necessary. She continued to behave like a good and special friend.

*   *   *

As soon as Zeno entered the office he instructed his secretary to ask Vince to report to him. Vince was head of the marketing department and also had responsibility for the purchasing of fowl.

'How's the boss doing today?' Vince asked Dora when he appeared in her office.

'Why, how should he be?' Dora eyed him suspiciously.

'I heard from Sander that he had a meeting with Ned Koch who had some bad news for him.'

Vince put on a happy face stepping into Zeno's office. 'I have nothing but good news!' he announced.

'Glad to hear it,' said Zeno, pointing to a chair.

'I heard it directly from some of our customers that they were approached by two of our competitors who offered new contracts for delivery in light of the labour problems here that they heard about. I don't have to tell you how glad I was to hear from both of these buyers that no matter what happened they weren't going to sign up with any other meat packing firm; they're going to stick with us through these difficulties. You see Zeno, there are still a few honest businessmen in this world!' he added with a beaming face.

'But Vince, you have to take into account that we have

to deal with the buyers of thirty-eight food retailers, and if the other thirty-six see things differently, that'll be the end of us.'

Vince did not respond.

'Well, we'll see. It'll work out somehow,' Zeno concluded, smiling at Vince. 'There was something else I wanted to discuss with you. I wanted to remind you of the job I asked you to do for me not too long ago.'

Vince nodded, and his expression made it clear he did not have to be told twice; he understood the first time.

'I know you always have the acquisitions diary with you, Vince. How do we stand on that score?'

Vince speedily produced the little notebook from his pocket, opened it and reported.

'We have contracts for the steady supply of eight thousand live fowls till the end of this year. In addition, I've made sure that in case some of our farms are not able to comply with the schedule of deliveries we have at least two other possible sources in reserve. So we will not be caught off guard.'

Dora came on to say that there was a phone call. Walter was on the line.

'Put him through, please,' Zeno answered, as Vince left the office.

'I hope you had a nice weekend,' said Walter, his voice upbeat as usual.

'Unfortunately, it was a working weekend,' he replied a little too quickly. He disliked lying to a friend.

'I'm calling to invite you to appear on my TV show next week. I don't know if you've ever seen any of my programmes. I report mostly business news, but also comment on the state of the economy in general, sometimes in the form of an interview. I wondered if you'd like to be my guest on my next show,' said Walter.

'When is the next show?'

'Don't worry, it's not carried live. We record it Thursday, and it'll be shown Friday.'

'Thursday would be good. What time?'

'We could meet at four in the afternoon in the lobby of the Chamber of Commerce.'

'Fine, I'll make a note of it. And how are things going for you?'

'For the time being I'm taking my campaign to rallies organized by voting districts. It's a new experience for me to meet so many people. Have you seen my press releases?'

'Yes, I was glad to hear you and Melanie have made peace.'

'Well, we really never had a falling out,' Walter protested.

'Yes, I know it's for the sake of the image, but…'

'You can imagine how glad I was when we got back together again. It'll make a difference for Caroline too – so everything is looking up.' Walter sounded too much like he was making a campaign speech.

'And how about Barbara?'

'Barbara understands. Somehow we have to get through these difficult times.'

'I wonder how you manage,' sighed Zeno, again thinking about Wanda.

'Okay, see you at four P.M. Thursday.' They said goodbye.

'Somehow we have to get through these difficult times…' Walter's words echoed in Zeno's ears. After all, it's no small matter to cut out of my life a woman as if we had never known each other. Sylvia came to his mind, and the quote: 'Men are philanderers for the first half of their lives and live the other half as cuckolded husbands.'

I wonder how Elmer feels about that. Then he wondered why Elmer came to his mind; they hardly ever saw each other, perhaps once a year and only by accident.

A sickening feeling of anxiety took hold of him.

'I've thrown away everything,' he was thinking. 'There's nothing left, nothing I can take comfort in.'

Zeno was wondering what had happened to his love

for Sylvia. It seemed to have evaporated into thin air, almost as if he had never experienced even affection for her. Now he was regarding their love like an old piece of furniture one might come upon in the basement, something no longer used, and waiting to be shipped off to charity at the next big spring cleaning.

Taking stock of everything he had, including family, work, friends, and success, he found nothing among them that gave him much satisfaction.

Maybe it's just a passing mood, he told himself. Things can change for the better. I'll start up the new plant, I'll keep all the employees. I'll take Sylvia on a cruise to the Islands. I've been promising this for years and years. And it would do me good to go to the fitness centre a few times a week. And as far as Wanda is concerned, I'll have to forget her, no matter how much it hurts.

Soon though, Wanda's face was crowding out everyone else again.

No, he had no intention of ever seeing her again. This morning he had made a firm resolution to forget her. Finding a naked young man in her bed last night was the end of everything.

Still, he reached anxiously for the mail of the day, picking out an inter-office envelope from the marketing department.

Chapter 28

Murder in Hotel Odéon
—X—

THE BUILDING was well over a hundred years old. It was intended as an administrative office building. Later, after some historical changes, it was turned into a prison.

Valerian was put up in a room designed for eight, not quite eighteen square meters in size. Even though the beds were bunk-style, the four bunks took up most of the floor space, leaving little room for the residents to move about.

Most of his fellow inmates had already been sentenced. Salomon got four-and-a-half years for sexual assault, Jakob a year and a half for fraud, Dani two years for indecent exposure, while Janos, the youngest in this unhappy crew, had his verdict handed to him only that week: six years for embezzlement. Valerian and two other cell mates were being held in pre-trial detention.

At the beginning peace and quiet ruled over the cell, unusual among those confined in a cramped space. This was largely due to the close friendship between Jakob and Dani, which had a calming influence over the others.

Then David, serving three years for theft, arrived – transferred from another cell for incompatibility.

For a few days he kept to himself, but then he began to make trouble. If Jakob and Dani were competing in calisthenics, he did not cheer them on but instead, he tried to set them against one another. His aggression seemed a deep-rooted, integral part of him.

After the conversation with Artur, Valerian went back to his cell in a foul mood, more despondent than ever. It appeared to him that Artur was more interested in finding out what Valerian had said to the detective about the members of the Club and their affairs, than he was in achieving Valerian's freedom.

I just want to get the whole thing over with, I want to stamp it paid. As long as it's unresolved, the papers will keep writing about it and I won't have a moment's peace, thought Valerian, while walking alongside a guard in an endless corridor.

Now, however, he was afraid of his thoughts. He was terrified by the idea of having to face that stranger and explain to him who killed Viktor. No, it was not he, Valerian, who had done it, but that weird person who's been doing everything in his power to convince him that he was not alone that night in Viktor's room, and he saw exactly just what happened.

He saw Viktor's face racked with pain, the blood, the severed part of his body lying there, his mute, voiceless shouts, the brutality, the loathing, the horror crying out to Heaven. But who is this stranger who keeps contradicting him? What enables him to have a better idea of the truth?

'I can see your face!' whispered Valerian to himself, not realizing how loud it was.

The guard walking next to him perked up.

'Speaking to me?'

The clanging of the footfalls echoed evenly, rhythmically on the stone floor.

They were marching side by side. The two of them.

Valerian went straight to his bunk, which was the third from the door. He had the lower bunk, and he dropped down on it as soon as he got there. The fog was slowly lifting from his mind and was replaced by an aching sensation of missing something.

He was no longer searching for anything and seeing only the graffiti-covered walls of the cell, the loathsome cave drawings of modern-day Neanderthals, all interspersed by suspiciously brown smudges.

Jakob and Dani were doing their usual evening calisthenics. There was barely enough room for the two of them side by side. Salomon was lying on the first bed, staring into space with a frozen expression. Janos, also was lying in his bed, with David standing above him. A vitriolic tirade was coming out of his mouth, like an open sewer of vulgarities, describing the victim's supposed personal habits. Then suddenly David loosened his pants, took out his limp but thick penis and tried forcing it into Janos's mouth.

'Here it is, take it in, you no-account little shit, you fucked-up mother-killer. Come on, go ahead, have a little fun. I'll show you who you are, you thief, you miserable worm...'

With nausea written all over his face Janos did his best to push David away, his eyes desperately searching the room, hoping for someone to come to the rescue.

But help was not forthcoming. No one moved. Salomon, Valerian, and the rest were keeping silent, as if nothing was happening. Jakob and Dani barely turned their eyes toward the source of the clamour, and did not let it interfere with their evening calisthenics.

David, seeing no one about to stop him, seemed to work himself into a frenzy as he started massaging himself with powerful, convulsive movements, and he finally pressed his hugely swollen erection against Janos's face whom he had laid flat on his bed and held captive by sitting on his chest.

That was when Valerian finally jumped up from his bed, ran to the scene of commotion, and started kicking and punching David with all the strength he could muster.

Janos took the opportunity to free his hands and slipped out of the brutal confrontation, seeking refuge with the workout team.

It didn't take long for the athletically built David to subdue his unexpected but much weaker attacker, the scrawny Valerian, and to twist his arms behind him in a stranglehold.

'Now, mister attorney, I'll show you,' he hissed with rage, 'I'll show you who's your lord and master!'

He laid Valerian prone on the bed, front forward, and with his free hand he delivered a powerful punch to his victim's face. It seemed the blow knocked Valerian unconscious; his body went into a convulsion, but then the next minute he shook his head as if getting his second wind, and tried to free himself. But he could not wiggle out of the steely grip of David's huge hand; every time he tried to move, David gave his arm another twist – and then, letting out animal-like growls, he peeled off Valerian's pants and thrust his enormous erection into Valerian's bare buttocks.

But by then Jakob and Dani had risen from the floor. They fell upon David, and after a brief but brutal struggle they succeeded in freeing Valerian from his hands.

'You've gone mad, you wretched jerk!' They kept punching the rapist all over his body.

The noise of the commotion and the loud imprecations soon attracted two guards to the bars.

'What's the matter with you jailbirds?' bellowed one of the guards. 'You guys want me to bring out the strait jackets? What's got into you, you creeps?' He went on bellowing with his gaze scanning the room.

Silence had descended on the cell suddenly, except for the quiet groaning of Valerian who was still lying prone on the bed.

None of the residents of the cell answered the guard.

'Any of you hurt?' shouted a taller, mustachioed guard.

'Nothing special, no problem, everything is fine, it's just that we had a little difference of opinion. You know, the usual stuff,' Janos said, hastening to fill the pause, before climbing back into his bunk.

—Chapter 29—

ZENO HARDLY BELIEVED HIS EYES when he read the first letter Wanda wrote to him after his discovery of the young man in her bed.

My Dear Love,

I realize our relationship is very new, you have not had a chance to get to know me.

My apologies for the misunderstanding yesterday. Trust me, believe me. I wouldn't want to cause you grief or hurt you for anything in the world. The love I feel for you is true and sincere. Appearances are deceiving! I am yours alone! I belong to you alone!

Thank you, my dear, for the unforgettable weekend.

I'm waiting for you to write back to me, to take me in your arms and kiss me like no one else has ever done before.

With everlasting love,
W.

She thinks I'm an ass, he said to himself, and a blind one at that. The evidence is right in front of me, and she denies what I can clearly see. Not a chance, my dear, no more of this. It's all over! You get that? Over!

And yet!

Images leaped into his mind. The white, tight skin of the girl's body, her moist, soft lips, her caresses, her warm embraces.

He pulled out a fresh sheet of paper from a drawer and started writing:

My Dear Wanda,

Never would I have done to you what you did to me.

There was no need for you to deceive me. Why didn't you just tell me you were not alone, that you had a friend? I would have understood.

Why didn't you warn me in advance?

I am angry with you, not because you have someone else, but because you were deceitful about it.

Z.

He looked for an envelope, but could not find a suitable one.

He called out to Dora for more envelopes. And then asked her to dispatch the mail of the marketing department as soon as possible, and directly to Wanda.

He avoided meeting Wanda that day. He gave himself until tomorrow to sort out his thoughts and arrive at a decision.

The next morning, he came to the plant determined to break off all correspondence with the girl. He felt strong. I know she's playing with me, making a fool of me, humiliating me. If there was a note from Wanda, he would not dignify it with a reply.

Barely saying good morning to Dora, he tore into his office, and headed straight for the stand holding the mail of the day. His fingers trembling, he ransacked the pile for the manila mailing folder with the white elastic band from the marketing department. When he found it, he emptied its contents on the desktop. He picked out the sealed white envelope, ripped it open, and then he let his eyes race over the note, taking in every word with intoxicated impatience.

My Dear, my Love,

Forgive me for besieging you all the time and for not wanting to let you go. But I simply cannot because in the last few days I could think of nothing but us always being together, just you and me, and our children, in love with each other forever. I am unpredictable, selfish, and

self-centred, yet I love you immensely. Let us make each
other happy. While we can.

Waiting for you, but in the meantime write to me.
W.

Without stopping to think Zeno reached for a sheet of
paper and began to write.

My Darling,
I feel exactly the way you do. I cannot stop thinking
about you. Trust yourself to me, stay with me, be mine.
Entirely mine.

To me, you are life itself. I love you, I love you, I
love you!
Z.

He went over his words again. He was on the verge
of crumpling the note for the wastebasket, but in the
last second he changed his mind. He slipped it into an
envelope, and hid the envelope in the larger document
holder that he placed in the folder of the marketing
department.

I've gone too far to stop now. I am helpless. She's got
the better of me. I'll deserve my retribution when it's
meted out to me, he was thinking as he asked Dora into
his office.

The secretary gave her boss a searching look. He was
bent over his desk.

'Has something happened?' she asked in the neutral
tone of someone anxious not to intrude or put herself
forward.

Zeno stared blankly back at her for a moment before
he could restore his business-like expression.

'Walter is planning to do an interview with me. I'll
have to bone up on the main topic. I'll need statistical
data about the meat-processing industry, because he might
ask questions involving facts and figures I should have at

my fingertips. Please, could you gather all the information that may be relevant?'

'You'll have it on your desk by this afternoon,' she answered, but then stayed in the office as if waiting for something more.

'That's all I had in mind just now. I'm going down to the new processing plant to see how far they've progressed with the installation.'

He felt calmer now, after sending that response to Wanda. He no longer had himself to fight, only Wanda. He would put off their meeting until the afternoon.

He forced himself to wait until Dora stepped out before he dialled the extension of the marketing department. It rang at least five or six times before it was answered by a male voice unfamiliar to Zeno. He turned out to belong to one of the drivers of the trucks that transported the live animals; at the moment he was the only one in the office. All the others were busy checking the newly arrived stock, but they were expected back soon. Zeno asked him to tell Wanda that the company president, Mr Langdon, wanted her in his office.

When she arrived, he was immersed in the report about the state of the food industry, and he didn't even notice the door opening. She entered as quietly as the next moment enters one's life. Only the soft click of the door closing behind her made Zeno raise his head from the bunch of papers in his hand. The girl looked depressed and disturbed, certainly uncomfortable. Her eyes however, were glistening, their deep turquoise colour emphasised.

Zeno did not get up to greet her. Instead, he leaned back in his swivel chair to make himself comfortable with his legs crossed. Wanda seemed at a loss as to what to do next. She stopped in front of the desk with her hands leaning on the back of the chair in front of it.

'Why don't you sit down,' he invited her.

The girl pulled the chair back cautiously, but without

taking her eyes off him for a moment. It was as if she feared he might tear her apart.

She's playing with me, pretending repentance. Why did I write those letters to her if I don't want her any longer? But I do! I do want her! It's only that I am letting her run herself ragged, wear herself out. It's my turn to play with her.

He'd crush me under his foot like a cigarette butt, or stone me to death, if he had half a chance. I'd better be the dear beloved who's hopelessly in love with him. I want him to want me! These were the thoughts running through her mind.

'I have a confession to make. Paul is no nephew of mine. He's a leftover from an earlier relationship.'

That was how she said it, an earlier relationship, while she was twiddling her thumbs in her lap, not having the courage to meet Zeno's eyes. She said it repentantly, in all sincerity. She showed no trace of deviousness, playacting, or of any attempt to lead him on.

'I guessed as much. Actually, I knew it.'

'I'm sorry about it, I truly am. I have given a lot of thought to just what to do. Paul is inept and helpless. He grew up without the benefit of parents – they were never around. They're crazy. They've wasted their whole lives among oil rigs. I am the only person Paul can rely on.' She paused to look at Zeno, but he remained silent.

'You on the other hand, you're important to me, very important; for your sake, yesterday morning I kicked him out. Yes, he did have a key to my apartment, but I told him not to come back. I told him to leave me in peace, stop clinging to me, stop dragging me down with his helplessness, acting like a helpless baby. That's not the kind of man I need. I said I had someone else, that I was in love with you, and I want only you. I told him we'd made love, not once but many times, told him I wanted to be only yours, I didn't need him. I told him to get that through his thick skull and leave me alone, I couldn't...

I couldn't go on like that. Zeno, my one and only, please help me. Trust me!'

Such momentum, such power, such irresistible all-encompassing passion radiated from her words that they brought a twinkle to Zeno's eyes.

Sylvia has never done anything like this; she's never hurt me, never lied to me, never had the need to beseech me.

Passion soon won the day. They made peace when Zeno, forgetting all his earlier doubts and resolutions, found himself in Wanda's arms, whispering: 'You're my life's greatest love. I've never loved anyone else like this, and that's why I can't help but forgive you.'

Zeno could not stem the tide of apprehensions but neither could he extricate himself. I'm a pawn in the hands of a destiny called Wanda.

Chapter 30

MURDER IN HOTEL ODÉON
—XI—

'DID YOU SLEEP BADLY last night?' Nina asked when her husband came into the kitchen of the country house.

Hugo's head felt heavy after three bottles of red, and his expression was hangdog, but he wondered about her question.

'It's just that I heard moaning and groaning while I was fixing breakfast,' Nina explained.

Hugo had no idea she had heard him. 'Just a dream,' he mumbled. 'Sorry about that.'

Nina put a platter of toasts, scrambled eggs, and fried sausages on the table. They ate without exchanging another word, but the woman's eyes were glowing with warmth.

After breakfast Nina suggested they go for a walk, saying that nothing was as relaxing as a country walk. Stepping out to the road they ran into Péter. He looked like he had been hanging around for a while but without any particular chore to attend to. Catching sight of him Hugo thought the old man had been hoping for the chance for another chat.

'I've been looking at this hedge. It could use a good trim. As soon as it turns a little warmer, the weeds will take over straight away. Before you know it, you won't be able to take a step without getting tangled up in them,' Péter said, launching into a hurried explanation.

'Péter, you're too ambitious. You're always finding yourself another job to do.'

'Well, I don't spend the time twiddling my thumbs,

that's for sure. Boredom is a stranger to me. But I've been wondering about the wine I brought over on your last visit here. Have you had a chance to taste it yet?' The old man looked from one to the other.

Just how long has that old boy been hanging around only to ask us how we liked his wine? The thought flashed across Hugo's mind. Well, then he deserves to be rewarded for his efforts. 'If I were to tell you we finished off three bottles just last night, would that be sufficient praise for your wine-making skills?' Hugo asked him.

'Not really sufficient, no, but if you drank so much of it, it could not have been all that bad,' he said smiling, apparently satisfied with what he had in fact expected to hear. 'You have to give wine its due – in fact more: it needs our soul too, so that its body has spirit,' he remarked, not very successfully disguising his joy.

His mission successfully accomplished, he said goodbye.

'You've been driving yourself too hard, living under too much stress,' Nina said to her husband then.

In fact, Hugo had awakened with a feeling of pressure on his chest. It had happened before – anxiety, he had been told – but this time it was more painful, verging on a spasm. The dead Victor's face appeared to him. So this is what it's all about. The power of the soul over the body. But why is he haunting me?

'It seems to me that something's bothering you that you're not willing to talk about,' Nina persisted.

His wife was right. Hugo was thinking about Viktor. He wondered what footprints Viktor had left behind in his carelessly meandering path.

—*Chapter 31*—

TAMAS LOOKED THROUGH the newspapers in the hotel lobby while he waited for Walter. Although he understood very little of the text, he had resolved to spend at least an hour every day reading the papers. This was the advice the language teacher in the transit camp gave to the prospective immigrants. He believed that the daily papers were the most faithful reflection of the living language, and told the students of the class to read them as often as possible, preferably saying every word out loud, even if the text was still incomprehensible.

The day before, he had written two postcards to Iren and the children. Since his arrival he missed them even more. In the camp, especially on rainy Sunday afternoons, the separation from his family used to feel like a physical pain in the chest. Now that the prospect of a firm base – a country where he could be safe and settle down – was almost in his grasp, his longing for his family began to flare up inside him more and more often.

Walter arrived six minutes early. Tamas immediately recognized him from Pascal's description, by the thick glasses and the neatly trimmed beard. With a face beaming with anticipation he hurried over to Walter and extended a hand. 'Sir, I'm Tamas. You are Mr Walter Wallmeyer, aren't you?'

'Just Walter to you.' Walter squeezed the hand extended to him. 'Once more, welcome here, my boy! Are you learning the language?'

'I want to. So far I have just been reading the newspapers.'

'That's good. For you, learning the language has to be the number one priority. Concentrate all your efforts now on that one thing. The next step, when you can speak the language at least on a minimal level, is finding a job. And then you can have the yoke of your family around your neck again.' Walter laughed at his little joke, but then turned more serious. 'I know, of course it's not a yoke, and I can understand how much you must miss them.

'You'll adjust before you know it,' Walter went on. 'You'll get to know the city gradually, and soon you'll find new friends here. In fact, you already have the first one,' he said, pointing to himself.

During their drive through the city, Walter told Tamas about himself, revealing that he had been chosen by his party as candidate in the upcoming parliamentary election. He also talked about his personal life, how he recently got back together with his wife, Melanie, after two years of separation. He mentioned nothing of the troubles that had suddenly cropped up in the past few days.

Tamas too kept back information, saying nothing of the real reason behind his sudden flight from the country. He spoke about the months he had spent in the refugee camp, how defenceless and vulnerable he felt there. The help he had received from Pascal, however, gave him new hope and restored his self-confidence. Pascal even got him a temporary job there with a construction company.

Soon they reached their destination.

When Walter had parked his car under the eight-storey office building which housed the Immigration Office, Tamas felt his stomach contorting into knots. Every time he had to visit an official bureau now he found it hard to breathe.

Walter dashed forward with long and energetic steps, radiating the image of a man with a purpose and a heavy schedule of appointments he had to keep.

They got out of the elevator on the third floor and stepped into a narrow corridor. Chairs were lined up along the walls. Doors opened to the left and right. They took the second door on the right and found themselves in a small waiting room.

Walter asked Tamas to sit down and wait while he found out if Bertold was ready to see them. Tamas picked up a few of the small brochures from the plexiglass holders on the wall and tried to decipher them.

In the meantime a couple arrived with two children in tow. The little boy and girl immediately started chasing each other, making such a racket that Tamas found it impossible to concentrate on his reading. The mother made no effort to control the children; she seemed sleepy and listless, sitting apart from the man.

'We've been here a year and a half,' she said with a yawn, 'and we still haven't found a job. I'm tired of this whole thing. It was a crazy idea to drag us here, to the end of the world where I can do nothing but feel lonely all the time. We have no friends. We come here to see these officials once a week like common beggars and beg for another week's delay. We have nothing to offer but the hope that maybe some miracle will happen.'

The man looked just as bored listening to the woman's words. Tamas had little interest in them until he recognized that the language they were speaking was familiar. The woman stopped talking then, and only the screams of the frolicking children could be heard.

Walter appeared in the opening of the inner door and beckoned with his head for Tamas to follow him.

Bertold was short and wiry, with a balding head and a jovial smile. Walter took on the role of the interpreter. His obvious long acquaintance with the official gave Tamas confidence, too.

'Linda reported your arrival to me this morning.' The official began without any preamble, turning to Tamas and offering him his hand over the desk. 'I don't know how much of our city you've seen in the short time since you arrived, but you may have noticed that although it's a small city, it's undergoing dynamic development. True enough,

at the present time we're facing an economic downturn…'
He paused here as if to get confirmation from Walter
who remained silent, and then went on to complete the
sentence he had started, 'but we hope it's not going to last
long, and the economy will pick up again, and jobs will be
easier to come by. You are still young, you have your life
ahead of you; your chances of adapting to our world are
very good, once your command of the language improves.
I realize you would like to have your family follow you
here as soon as possible, but I and all of us here consider
it important that you first consolidate your situation and
then, step by step, that will be addressed.'

'Yes, sir, you're perfectly right.' Tamas kept nodding
with determination, 'these are the priorities I set myself.
Learning the language is very important to me.'

'Tamas, let me tell you what you'll have to do. You'll
report to me here once a week. Wednesday is the best
day for me, so I ask you to keep that in mind. The rest
of the week it can be a madhouse here. Every week you
report to me on the progress of your job search and
your language studies. At the same time I will disburse
the weekly allowance which now amounts to thirty-five
dollars.'

'That's all?' cut in Walter, looking at the official,
astonished.

'It was less than three months ago that the government
increased this aid for single individuals from twenty-seven
to thirty five, and a little more for families,' said Bertold
indignantly.

'But this is less than the current welfare payment,'
remonstrated Walter.

'You politicians have the power to decide how much we
spend on what. We anonymous little grey public servants
only execute the policies you make,' replied the official,
and then, to cut the debate short, he quickly turned back
to Tamas. 'Let me continue then. I've tried to speed up
the process of getting you settled in your own apartment.

I hope by the end of the week you'll be able to leave the hotel. You'll see the whole world will look different from a home of your own.'

Tamas paid close attention to Bertold's every word, as if standing before a judge, waiting for a verdict. He was trying to match the words of Walter's translation to what he had heard from the administrator.

'I am very grateful,' he said. 'But can you tell me when I can start a language course? Can I sign up tomorrow?'

'The Immigration Office has its own language school. But all the courses are now well underway. However, I know some churches operate such courses, especially for beginners, and these are short, maximum eight weeks long. Perhaps you should look into that. Walter can probably help you there.' Bertold looked at his journalist friend. 'If you cannot come up with anything by next Wednesday, I might gather some more information, and we will work out something.'

Bertold stopped to catch his breath. He shuffled some papers on his desk. Eventually he picked up a pen and wrote out what looked like a cheque, and signed it at the bottom. When he was finished he handed the piece of paper to Tamas.

'This is your weekly allowance. When we're finished here, you'll find the cashier's office at the third door down the hall. They will cash this for you at once. Show them your passport. But I have not mentioned the most important part. Your rent will be paid by the Immigration Office for the first three months, and then we'll have to reconsider your situation if you still don't have a regular job and income. We can extend the rent payments for another few months. According to the statistics only those who don't want to work are unable to find a job within six months.'

'Considering the current economic conditions, Tamas is not going to have an easy time of it,' Walter again remonstrated, as if defending his own personal interest.

'Yes, I know, it takes quite a bit of ingenuity to find a job nowadays,' the official agreed, and then looked at Tamas again. 'What kind of work would you like to do to start with?'

'I'll accept anything!' Tamas answered firmly and clearly.

'Anything?'

'Yes! I decided that until I acquire at least the rudiments of the language I'll accept any kind of a job. In the camp, too, I did every kind of work from cleaning, sweeping, chopping wood, serving as a busboy, to plastering walls.' Tamas decided to make no mention of his minor journalism experience.

'In that case you can be sure you'll find a job in no time at all,' said the official with a satisfied smile. 'And it will also help you learn the language.'

'I'd like to immerse myself in the language for a couple of weeks, if possible,' Tamas added, looking at the two others with hope in his eyes.

'I see no problem with that.' The official looked at Walter and then continued: 'So that's everything, I think? You have the weekly allowance, the apartment search is in progress. Also the apartment will come furnished. It will not be a royal suite, but it will have a table, a bed, chairs, and even an easy chair, and we will provide some cooking equipment and utensils. The kitchen will be fully equipped and stocked. Not bad, is it?' He winked at Tamas. 'I left out pillows and bed linen. That too will be provided,' added the official triumphantly.

Tamas listened in silence. He kept nodding in approval, although he was not really interested in the bed, the forks and spoons, the chairs and the bed linen; what he wanted most passionately was to get going. His impatience was getting unbearable. He felt like waving goodbye to Walter and running home to read and study.

Afterwards, he wondered what Walter thought of him. And of course, Bertold, too. Did he succeed in convincing the official of his commitment to his future and of his eagerness to start working as soon as possible? Did he make it plain he did not want to be a burden on his host society? Tamas recalled the official's words when he was escorting his visitors out. 'This is a living example of total failure, the nightmare of the Immigration Office,' Bertold had said, pointing at the family camping in the waiting room, keeping his voice to a whisper so the offenders could not hear him. 'They've been living here a year-and-a-half now at the taxpayers' expense and have no intention of working.' Tamas couldn't help worrying that the official meant this remark for him as a fair warning for the future. But why would the official do that when he, Tamas, did everything in his power to prove he was ready to get to work? It's impossible that the official would have misunderstood his intention to spend the next few weeks on learning the language. What use would I be if I can't communicate? Like someone waking up from a dream he looked around himself in the street, trying to figure out where he was.

Before they parted, Walter had explained how he could find his way back to his hotel. Now Tamas thought he recognized a landmark from his earlier forays into the city. And then another. In a few minutes he knew exactly which way to go.

—*Chapter 32*—

COMING IN from the parking lot at the newspaper office, Walter ran into Bradley Northrup.
'Good morning,' he called out.
'And good morning to you.' The younger colleague nodded. 'At least so far this summer hasn't been too hot,' he added, holding the entrance door open for Walter.

Walter, looking at him, was tempted to sit down with Bradley and talk this whole business over with him, rather than just leave the mess to Cameron. On the other hand, he was afraid he might just ruin everything.

Getting out of the elevator on the same floor, Bradley turned right and Walter to the left. They parted with a nod, without saying anything further.

Walter's mind though was racing. He wandered from one shelf to another, rearranging stacks of journals, putting stray newspaper clippings away in a folder. Then he sat down behind his desk. For some time he kept twirling his fountain pen between his fingers, unscrewing and replacing the cap with the white star at its top.

He stared at the monitor of his word processor without an idea, without even knowing what he was looking at. He felt removed from the world. Although he had promised Joseph to deliver his column on time, words were escaping him. He pulled down a volume of Dostoevsky's works and read a few pages from *Crime and Punishment*, landing on a line of Pytor Petrovich that 'a man should not be indebted to his wife, but it is better for a wife to look upon her husband as her benefactor...' Engrossed in his reading he was startled when Joseph Singer's voice rang out in the background.

'I'm glad to see you in so early this morning. My sources tell me you're doing an interview with Zeno –

about his meat plant for your TV programme. I thought I'd suggest the paper could run a story on this subject from you.'

'Good idea. The interview will be aired Friday, so we could have a preliminary report and analysis in Thursday's issue.'

'That will be fine. I have to admit though it's not the reason for my visit,' he continued. 'I've been told that Bradley Northrup is blackmailing you.'

Joseph paused, watching Walter's face for any little tremor or other sign of reaction.

'I was told about it late evening the day before yesterday,' Walter said, trying to take the edge off the significance of the news.

'I thought that in my twenty-five years in this business I've seen everything, but I've never run into such a low-down trick.'

'Thanks for saying that,' said Walter. 'My fellow party members yesterday handed down their indictment: it seems I am a moral wreck – my behaviour is unconscionable. I admit I made a mistake, and I should have ended my relationship with Barbara long ago. But...' He paused to draw a breath. 'Maybe you can understand. Before I made up with Melanie, I asked Barbara what she thought about it. She thought it was a terrific idea. But she didn't think we should break up.'

He paused again as if trying to decide whether to go on. Should he really bare his soul? Eventually the words started tumbling out of him.

'Joseph,' he began, but first he had to clear his throat. 'I swear I did try to bring common sense to bear on the issue. I explained to Barbara that it was only for a short time, until election day, both of us could deal with it. But she didn't want things to change and I suppose I didn't either. Yes, I know I behaved like a teenager! You know the saying: Logic is always right and yet can't get the better of those who want to live in opposition to it.'

Joseph felt embarrassed, but at the same time he could not help being touched by Walter's openness. When he had first heard the news of the blackmail, he was mainly worried about the adverse publicity for his newspaper, about the damage such a public accusation could cause even if it was baseless. At the same time it was perfectly clear to him that in Walter's case the 'base' was not likely to be lacking. The owners of the company might even ask him to fire the immoral journalist; then what was he going to do? Walter would be losing his job and at the same time his candidacy. He was expecting the worst.

'Yesterday I was put on the carpet by the nominating committee.'

'And what was the outcome?'

'Cameron Fowler, the chairman – you probably know him – assured me they were going to do everything in their power to neutralize this threat. He's planning to meet with Bradley. As I understand it, he's going to try and come to some kind of an agreement with him.'

'And what if he fails, if the person behind Bradley is not interested in money but in your destruction?'

'The thought has occurred to me, yes. One or two names have crossed my mind.'

'For example?'

'You'll laugh, but Elmer Redwick, Barbara's husband, was the first one I thought of. But I immediately rejected it. The man's a gentleman. He has known about the relationship between me and Barbara, and he has never even hinted at the subject to his wife.'

'Very cosy! On the other hand I cannot see anyone among the possible Conservative hopefuls who could benefit by getting you out of the way, because your election district has always gone to the liberals. Tough territory. Can you think of anyone wanting to take away the nomination from you that badly?' Joseph pressed.

'I'd put my money on Ralph...He's a member of the committee and he was also counting on the nomination.

I got the impression he was always jealous. He thinks I'm a better orator and have better rapport with people. I suspect he's even jealous of me for knowing the people I know.'

'I hope you understand.' Joseph took a deep breath before he spoke again, 'I'm not going to kick Bradley Northrup out until you settle your affairs. But after that he'll have to go at once!'

His voice carried the weight of sincere sympathy for his friend. He felt an ache in his heart thinking about the possibility that their ways might very soon have to part.

—*Chapter 33*—

I N HIS EAGERNESS to learn the language, Tamas made
up his mind to leave the TV set on all the time. He
hoped that by watching and listening, especially to
programmes with a lot of dialogue, he could slowly get his
ear adapted to the rhythm of the new language and adopt
to its flow and its unexpected sounds; but his inability to
understand any of the talk he heard put a damper on his
ambitions. He decided he would go on watching even if
the words were to demolish him. He lay back in bed and
surrendered himself to the programme that was playing.

He woke up seeing dusk setting in, the sky turning
grey outside, and on the TV a Western movie with John
Wayne. It bothered his conscience that he had fallen
asleep during the talk show that had been on earlier.
His lapse made him feel restless. He thought of writing
another letter to Iren, but he found himself too befuddled
for the task. Then he thought of taking a walk. He had
not yet seen the city at night, and maybe fresh air would
restore his equilibrium.

The street was awash with a flood of light, and full
of high-spirited people rushing by; they all had some
place to go. The muffled roar of automobile engines was
vibrating in the air from left and right.

I'll just walk to the corner, look around, and turn back,
he decided. He felt too vulnerable to venture farther. The
first thing he observed was a bristle-faced, shabby man
staggering across the sidewalk in front of him. He was
careful to go around the unsteady figure in a wide arc to
avoid bumping into him.

The cool breeze of the evening stole into his short
jacket. Shivering, he turned around, giving up on his
energetic plans to explore the night-time city; shadowy

side streets and boulevard lights would just have to wait, he decided.

Back to his room, he found the message light blinking on his telephone. He picked up the receiver and pressed the button. It was Walter: 'Hello, hello, my friend, I thought I'd find you in your room. I'll try again in a half an hour.'

Hell and damnation, as soon as I step outside for a minute there's a call for me. He switched on the TV and was about to flop down on the bed when the phone rang again. 'You got back home pretty fast,' Walter observed at the other end. Unless you have something else on your plate tonight, I'd like to take you to a wake. What do you say?'

Tamas wasn't sure he understood correctly what he'd heard. But not wanting to offend his newly acquired friend and mentor, he only hesitated for a second before blurting out that he was free and ready for anything.

'Be in the lobby in fifteen minutes. I'll come by to pick you up.' Without waiting for an answer, Walter hung up.

A wake? Tamas was trying to digest Walter's words. We just got acquainted, and he wants to introduce me to a dead man?

Quickly, he undressed, changed his shirt, put on a dark tie, and then slipped into his one and only suit. It was grey.

When he stepped out of the hotel he saw Walter's car waiting by the curb. He dashed over to open the passenger door.

'I thought I'd show you a little more of this world. It's too bad that it happens to be a sad occasion, but I wanted you to get to know the Baroness before we consign her earthly remains to the ground,' said Walter almost apologetically. 'The old Baroness was ninety-seven when she passed away yesterday. I learned about it only last night.

'Once we're there you'll see why I am doing this.' The

journalist allowed himself a sly smile. 'Many of my friends will be there and some of them are influential people who might be useful to you, including my friend, Zeno, who is an industrialist. Also two clergymen will be celebrating the service. It's to your advantage to get to know them. You never know when you might need the help of these church organizations.'

'And who was this Baroness?' asked Tamas, now getting curious.

'She was an interesting woman, a colourful figure. Her husband, Baron Pellegrini, was an influential politician. He had enormous inherited wealth. Old money. He and his wife paved the way for the immigration of a lot of refugees from the war. He was the permanent President of two of the largest charities. The Baron's been dead for ten years, but still commands the respect of many who talk about him as if he were alive and active. Baroness Pellegrini continued her husband's charity work after his death. She did a lot for our community, too. She was a deeply religious and sensitive woman, very much devoted to the arts. She was good to me. She treated me like a son, and she supported my political career with all the power and influence she had.' Tamas thought he saw Walter wiping away a tear. 'You can imagine how I feel now that she's no longer with us.'

His curiosity piqued, Tamas now listened to Walter's words with greater attention. He tried to conjure up the Baron Pellegrini's figure. A tall, gaunt man with a monocle appeared in his mind's eye. That was how he always imagined an aristocrat. He smiled to himself at this cartoon creature of his fantasy.

They parked by a house that looked like a small mansion, but in that wealthy neighbourhood of huge Victorian residences it did not seem ostentatious. Parking was not easy, even though the parking ban in the area had been lifted for the occasion. The side streets were lined solid with parked cars from end to end, but eventually they were fortunate to spot a sports car pulling out in front of them.

They entered the place through a two-storey entranceway decorated with marble columns. They walked on gold-edged tiles of the mosaic floor in the hall. Tamas had never seen anything like that in his life. A heavy gilded crystal chandelier hung from the two-storey-high ceiling. The whole place was flooded with light. The murmur of softly spoken, subdued whispers seeped in from every direction.

A gaunt man dressed in black and wearing a mourning tie was there to receive them. He greeted Walter as an old acquaintance, and then with a few soft words and a ritual gesture, he directed them to the second-floor salon where the body of the Baroness lay in state in an open casket.

Tamas observed his surroundings with awe. He thanked his lucky stars that he had changed clothes at the last minute. He followed in Walter's tracks up the red-veined marble stairs. The salon to where they were directed by the man who greeted them looked more like a small ballroom. It had six floor-to-ceiling windows facing the street, covered by dark red velvet drapes. Against the walls there was a row of gilded chairs, upholstered with empire-green plush. In the middle of the hall, in a hand-carved oak casket on a bier, lay Baroness Pellegrini. At each of the four corners of the black-draped bier stood a black-uniformed guardsman. On the right side of the bier, the portrait of the Baroness was displayed in a deep blue frame.

They both stopped in front of the casket and said a short prayer with hands raised in the proper prayerful pose. After making the sign of the cross, they bowed to the earthly remains of the Baroness. Walter stepped closer to the casket. Tears rose to his eyes as he looked at the face under the thin veil; he waved his hand in a gesture of a goodbye kiss, and then with long strides he hurried out of the hall. Tamas followed him, moved by what he had seen. He found Walter on a terrace, and he touched his friend on the arm as a sign of condolence. Walter took off his thick glasses again, and wiped them with his handkerchief.

The reception room next to the funeral salon was already crowded with mourners. When Walter and his friend entered, some of the guests already there turned to greet them. One of them was Zeno, who seemed to have arrived just ahead of them and was still lingering at the fringes of the crowd of mourners. 'He immigrated here yesterday afternoon,' Walter explained after he introduced Tamas.

'It's very hard to make a new start any time,' Zeno said, shaking his hand firmly, 'but to make one in an entirely unknown foreign world is a serious challenge. I wish you success.'

While they were talking Walter got permission from the house's caretaker to bring his two friends on a guided tour. 'This may be my last chance to stroll through this little palace. I'd like to do it once more just for old time's sake.'

As the three of them started down the main stairway, old memories were awakened in Walter's mind, from the time Baron Pellegrini was still in his prime, still in command of his faculties. Afternoon tea was often served in the small salon they now entered. Walter spoke of the style of the antique furniture, and Zeno's attention was attracted to a baroque chest of drawers with veined marble top. Between two Meissen porcelain figurines there was a small black casket with exotic gilt decoration on it. Zeno reached for it with idle curiosity, and opened it.

'Zeno, please don't mess with that,' Walter said suddenly in alarm. 'Put it back where you found it, and don't touch anything.'

'But what's this inside?'

Walter took the box from him and opened the top. A small glass ampoule was hidden in the red-velvet-lined interior. He flipped the cover shut again and put the casket back in its place.

'That little ampoule contains cyanide. These things were made and used during the Nazi terror. Baron Pellegrini received it as a souvenir from one of his grateful refugees. That man was so happy to have escaped from the concentration camps and death by gas that he presented this to the Baron as a reminder of that hellish time. The Baron was very proud of his achievements in helping so many enemies of Naziism to emigrate to this country.'

The tour continued from room to room. Walter explained in great detail what he knew about each piece and what memories he had relating to it, whether it was a piece of furniture, a painting, or even a music box. There was so much to see that Tamas hardly knew which way to turn.

At the end of the tour Walter stepped forward to greet a priest, pulling Tamas with him. 'Father Garnini, let me introduce Tamas who just recently arrived in this country as a new immigrant. We've paid our last respects to Baroness Pellegrini.'

The reverend greeted Tamas kindly, his greyish hair glistening in the light of the chandeliers. Then he took a card from his pocket and wrote the name 'Evelyn' on it along with some other notes, and handed it to Tamas. 'That's the name of an administrator in the Immigration Office. We've been supporting each other's causes; don't hesitate to look her up. She'll surely help you with the immigration of your wife and children.'

Then he turned back to Walter. 'Bring your friend to Sunday Mass,' he said, 'I'd like to get to know him.'

'We'll be there, Father,' Walter answered readily. In fact he was already thinking of inviting Tamas to his house that weekend. Melanie would surely take to him. He could spend some time with them.

—*Chapter 34*—

Murder in Hotel Odéon
—XII—

Sluggish with exhaustion, Artur Liptak was sitting in a far corner of Eddy's Bar, in a despondent state of mind. He had come to this place with the clear intention of getting seriously drunk. He started the process by ordering a double vodka and a pitcher of beer.

He had spent the afternoon with Detective Fabian Mueller, a pudgy gentleman in his late fifties. The detective's clean-shaven face was dominated by a straight nose of intimidating size. He wore his thinning hair combed straight back. He dressed with care but without extravagance. Under his navy-blue blazer he wore a shirt of a dusty-rose shade. He seemed to walk with an effort, and yet at times he pounced out of his chair with great vigour only to pace his tiny office with a slow limp. At first, he expressed his hope in a conversational tone that Artur could help him clear up the murder case on hand and tie up some loose ends. Their afternoon interview kept coming back to Artur.

'This week I repeatedly interrogated Dr Valerian Lang, the attorney – the distinguished attorney. I reminded him several times that if he hadn't committed the crime, all he had to do was to provide an alibi – a plausible and verifiable alibi. That was the only condition of his release.'

'I told him the same thing,' Artur said as he leaned back in his chair, still studying the detective with an attorney's eye. 'And more, I practically begged him. For some reason he is being very obstinate. But why? After all, his life hangs in the balance. At a minimum his freedom is at stake.'

'I've uncovered evidence of someone else visiting Viktor in his hotel room about the same time as Dr Lang. The identity of the other visitor is still unknown to me, and it's not clear which one of them left first. If I could pin a name on the second visitor I'd have a much easier time. But I already know one thing: that person was a woman.' Fabian rose suddenly from his seat, tossing on the desk the ballpoint pen he had been twirling between his fingers. 'Dr Liptak, that's where you come in. Can you help me find that mystery visitor?' He nailed the question directly at the lawyer's chest, looking at him with expectation mixed with suspicion.

'How can I possibly help you? You keep talking to me as if I had some information I was reluctant to share with you. That's far from the case; I have no intention of withholding any evidence from you. After all, I want the best for Valerian; he's my friend. We were in the same class at the university. For five years we were together, through thick and thin. We were like brothers, almost.'

'I realize that, but what I'd like to know now is whether Viktor belonged to your circle of friends.' The detective here stopped his pacing right in front of his suspect, closely watching every tremor on his face.

'No, he did not belong to my circle of friends. If that is your information, it is incorrect,' protested Artur. 'Yes, I admit I saw Viktor a couple of times at Eddy's Bar, but as you well know –' and here he returned the detective's stern gaze, 'that bar is a public place. Anyone can walk in there. Even you, for instance.'

'But not when you people close the place for a private function! Or am I ill-informed on that subject, too?'

'Well, yes, it can happen sometimes that we have a friendly get-together by invitation only.'

Artur began to feel like a wanted criminal, with a noose waiting for him or at least a long prison sentence.

He wondered just how much the detective knew about his circle of friends. The detective clearly knew something, but from whom and how? How much? Artur was the unofficial security officer of their little assembly; it was impossible for any information to leak out suddenly without his knowing about it.

He searched his memory. No, he could not come up with anything that should give cause for worry.

But then all of a sudden Valerian's face popped into his mind. What if he had blabbed something to Fabian? Maybe not intentionally, but he could have let something slip, Artur concluded.

For now the best strategy for him seemed to be to let the detective do the talking, to let him expound his theories. Perhaps he could even learn something helpful from the policeman.

'According to the information I have…' and Fabian sat down again behind his desk, 'Viktor was indeed very much a member of this – what do you call it – fraternal association.'

'Look, Inspector,' the lawyer said, putting his palms together on his chest in a gesture designed to demonstrate his ease of mind, thinking that addressing the detective as 'Inspector' would also curry favour with him. 'As in any association, or society, this particular group too has, and will continue to have, its regulars. But just because somebody shows up once in a while as the guest of a member or at some particular event or other, it doesn't make him a regular participating member of that group.'

Fabian crossed his legs and nodded benevolently, not once but twice.

'I happen to agree with you. However, I have it from reliable sources that Viktor was indeed a regular, participating member of your secret society, if I may call it that.'

Artur was flabbergasted to hear this from Mueller. The conviction was growing inside him that it was

Valerian who had let his mouth work overtime. Otherwise, how else could the detective come up with a phrase like 'secret society'?

Very well – Artur pursued the thought – if indeed Valerian broke his oath of secrecy, what and how much did he blab? On the other hand, if he was not the perpetrator of the crime as he claims, then what was the purpose of spilling information that could get others into trouble? Artur was torn by these thoughts, but he decided to let the detective go on rolling the dice and see what turned up.

'Viktor was most definitely not a bona fide member of our group,' declared Artur with as much conviction as he could muster.

'And how about Mr Hugo Wagner, our esteemed Mayor?'

—Chapter 35—

THE ELECTION NEWS in a fax from Ottawa gave Cameron Fowler new heart early in the morning. According to the poll conducted the previous week the Conservative party was leading by a comfortable 15% margin. Walter's going to be happy with that, he thought.

He had made an appointment with Bradley Northrup to meet at ten in a downtown café. Held up by the bumper-to-bumper traffic, he was seven minutes late and found Bradley already stirring his coffee. They eyed each other coldly as Cameron sat down across the table.

Bradley, looking preoccupied, took his time to start talking.

'It may sound strange to you, but this whole business is even more distasteful to me than it must be to you.'

'I'd like you to be totally candid with me and tell it the way it is,' Cameron said. 'Obviously, there's someone behind you, someone who put you up to this, someone who probably blackmailed you, otherwise I can't imagine you capable of something so dirty. I came here to see if there's a way I can bargain with you. And if there is, we have to agree on a price. I can't believe you've done this just because you hate Wallmeyer's guts, or because you think you're saving the electorate from another immoral politician.'

Bradley was still silent. Cameron's straightforward approach seemed to have confused him. When he finally started to speak, it was in a barely audible whisper.

'No, it's nothing personal.'

'Then what's it about?'

'I'm in debt. I owe a lot of money.' The words came out of him with a groan, as if squeezed out of him.

'So it's all about money?' sighed Cameron with great relief. 'Just how much do you owe? I will not ask to whom.'

'Unfortunately my creditor is not after the money. Instead, this person wants Walter's head on a platter.'

'Are we talking about a politician?' Cameron snapped back.

'No, there's no politics involved at all.'

'But what's the motive then?'

'I believe it's personal.'

'Is Elmer Redwick, Barbara's husband, involved in this?'

'No.' Bradley was quite firm. 'Let me assure you it does not involve Elmer.'

'Then it doesn't make sense to me! The person behind you is not a politician, not Elmer, then who is it we're talking about?'

'I'm not at liberty to reveal that,' Bradley said, staring at the table with a disconsolate expression. 'Suffice it to say that the person who commissioned me is not interested in money, only in Walter's head.'

They were both silent for a while. The spectre of impending disaster hovered between them.

Again it was Cameron who broke the silence.

'Tell me at least, how much do you owe?'

'A lot.'

'Well, give me a figure.' Cameron tried being businesslike.

'I'm in debt for a huge sum of money,' Bradley repeated with an effort,

'Okay, let's have it!'

'With interest, it comes to almost a hundred thousand,' he blurted out.

'I realize it's not my business, but may I ask how you've spent such an enormous sum of money? After all, your job as a journalist brings in a comfortable income.'

'Gambling.'

Cameron was flabbergasted. He just sat there, unable

to respond. Gambling, he kept repeating it to himself, as if he had seen a thing of horror.

'That much money? My God, did you gamble away that much money? And how long did it take you to lose so much?' Cameron asked impulsively.

'Not much longer than six months.'

'Okay, well, the origin of your debt and its repayment are none of my business, I agree. But let me ask you another question. How do you think we can solve the present crisis? Have you considered any alternatives at all? Do you have any suggestions on that score?'

'No, unfortunately I don't.' Bradley, his eyes tortured, finally looked at Cameron.

'Who's financing this whole enterprise? Who paid the private detectives who must have taken and developed those pictures?'

'No one. I did all the work.'

'Are you that depraved?' Cameron exclaimed.

'No, it's just that I am cornered, and I'm not in a position to say no.'

'Okay, you're right, let's drop that aspect of it. But if we have no choice why did you agree to meet with me?'

'Because I wanted to ease my conscience. And perhaps, also because...' he looked down again pensively, 'I was hoping the two of us together could work out some kind of a compromise.'

'What can we work out? If it's not money the blackmailer wants, if he just wants Walter? If I had more time to think...' He stopped mid-sentence, wondering if there was any chance he could arrange some sort of stall.

'Have you handed over the material to this person yet?' he asked Bradley.

'No. Not yet. I need to be sure about the money before I do that.'

'If you give me sixty days, we might be able to get you some money. Can you stall the blackmailer for that long?'

Even as he spoke, Cameron was calculating. Today's

poll results were predicting a Conservative victory with a large majority. If the day of reckoning could be put off for two months, there would be only three weeks of the campaign left before election day. If in the meantime Walter had managed to refrain from seeing Barbara even once during that time, there was a chance the evidence of the photograph would not influence public opinion, because the affair would be past history, not one that was ongoing.

'Look, will you see if you can stall him for that long?'

Bradley said nothing.

'You know, you are making a powerful enemy with this blackmail,' Cameron said in a different tone. 'Not just Walter. The entire Conservative Party. It's in your interest to give us more time.'

Bradley's look remained glacial, but after a moment he said, 'Sure, I'll do it, why not?'

'Does he know you were meeting me today?'

'Yes, the boss knows. I'm to report back this afternoon.'

'In person?'

'No, by telephone.'

Cameron had been hoping that he could have someone tail Bradley and learn the identity of the instigator. He was not surprised, however, that the people behind the scheme would have foreseen that danger.

'After I deliver your proposition I'll call you back immediately,' said Bradley with little encouragement in his tone.

'I'll be in my office till five today, and I'll be at home this evening. Let me give you my home phone number.' Cameron fished out a name card from his pocket and handed it over.

He picked up the tab to take it to the cashier on his way out. Out on the sidewalk he was overcome suddenly by doubt as he made his way to the garage to get his car. With hindsight, his proposition seemed infantile.

Why would anyone keep silent about those photographs

for sixty days if the purpose is to destroy Walter right now? Waiting for the traffic light to change, he sank back into despair. No, there's no magic potion, no silver bullet, it's all over.

It would be best to convince Walter to announce that he was dropping out of the race that same day. True, they had already spent two hundred thousand on his campaign alone, but there was no shortage of grassroots donations, they were rolling in at a rate never seen before. And not just piddling sums. They could put Ralph in Walter's place. If they put Ralph in Walter's place everything would continue smoothly and without a hitch, he assured himself, but then he thought about it more.

The only problem with that solution was Ralph – he was a bad candidate. He was not in the same class as Walter. He lacked Walter's intellect and his good rapport with people. In fact, he was a shadow of Walter, Cameron concluded with a bitter taste in his mouth. I'd better wait till the evening to get a consensus about how we proceed. I'll have to call on the committee members one by one and report on that meeting with Bradley Northrup.

*   *   *

Bradley roamed the streets all afternoon.

The offices of the Gambling Addicts' Mutual Aid Society were located on the ground floor of a low, two-storey commercial building. Before he had hit bottom and got himself hopelessly in debt, Bradley often turned to them for advice, even attending self-help group sessions. Now that he unexpectedly found himself in front of this building, he felt a desire awakening in him to talk to someone inside. In the therapy sessions and the group meetings he had made a few friends, but he had lost touch with them, even though he often wondered how they had fared.

Bradley thought back to the days when he was still

hoping he could recover from his addiction. At these meetings, he could clearly see the dangerous traps lying ahead, but out in the world on his own he could not pass a gambling casino without entering it as if entranced.

The next thing he knew he would be tossing a hundred-dollar chip on the red. The rest would follow like a lava flow. He would wake up from this euphoria when he was again out in the sidewalk with his pockets empty, trying to figure out how much he had lost. As one evening in the casino followed another, his deficit mounted up. In a matter of a few months he was in hock for eighty thousand. Plus interest.

He was still standing in front of the simple, nondescript building when it occurred to him that he had promised to call his creditor that afternoon. He looked around for a public phone, but there was none in the neighbourhood. He walked more quickly, and two streets down he finally spotted one on a wall.

It took some time before his call was answered.

'Bradley here. Good afternoon, ma'am,' he said

'You kept me waiting long enough for the call. Well, what's the decision?'

'The thing is, there isn't one really...' he stuttered. 'Mr Fowler asked for more time.'

'Did he say why?'

'He says he's assuming it's Walter we want to hurt, not the party. He says the party needs time to make arrangements.'

'That's the party's problem.'

'He says they'll make a lot of trouble for me.'

'I can make a lot of trouble for you. I bought your debts from some dangerous people.'

'They just want two months. And they say they'll pay half my debt.'

'How magnanimous of them! Well, it's a clever ploy.'

'I promised to call Cameron as soon as I talked to you.'

'All right, tell them they can have a one-month

extension of the deadline, but they have to pay off all your gambling debts. At once. If they accept this counter-offer, call me back.'

The line went silent with a click.

Bradley too hung up. He took a paper tissue from his pocket and wiped his sweaty palms. He felt desolate and helpless there by the telephone on the sidewalk, trying to gather strength for the next step.

He dialled again. Cameron's voice was on the line.

'Tell me, did they agree?'

'No...well, in a way...yes.'

'What do you mean?'

'They offered a one-month extension, but only if you cover all my debts, not just half,' he blurted out and swallowed hard at the end.

Cameron stared ahead, thinking it over. He clutched the receiver nervously in his left hand.

'In that case I am not ready to give an answer. To make that decision I'll have to call a meeting of the campaign committee. I'll give you our answer by tomorrow noon. Good night,' he said curtly and hung up.

A few minutes later he called Walter with the news, asking him to be at campaign headquarters by ten o'clock next morning; he was going to call for another emergency meeting of the committee to discuss the new developments.

Cameron faced his task without a clue. If the blackmailer is not interested in money, then why the demand for that enormous sum? Why only half of the extension? He could not find any rhyme or reason to it. He sighed, deciding it was time to go home. He had had enough for that day.

Chapter 36

T AMAS STILL WAS UNABLE to read the newspapers. He did find Walter's column in the *Monitor*, but could understand almost none of it, even after reading and re-reading it several times. Frustrated, he decided to take a break and go for a walk in the neighbourhood.

The sun was blindingly bright. He diverted himself by looking at billboard advertisements and signs on shop windows, reading each one and trying to understand the message. He spent an hour and a half rambling through the main thoroughfares and then he went back to his room. He turned on the TV and sprawled out on the bed. In a few minutes he dozed off.

The ringing of the telephone woke him. It was Walter, who told Tamas to get paper and pen ready, he was going to dictate the address and phone number of the central welfare office of the diocese. He made Tamas promise to visit the office that day and look for someone by the name of Eugene Mazur, an administrator.

'In that office they'll put your name on a list of the unemployed looking for work, and while you're there, ask them when they are going to start the next language course for beginners. I spoke to Bertold in the Immigration Office, and he assured me that in two or three days you'll be able to move out of the hotel, they've already found an apartment for you. So what do you say to that? Things are working out for you, aren't they?' He blurted this out in his rapid-fire style, all in one breath.

Tamas was on his way in a few minutes. He was already out in the street when he wanted to check the slip of paper for the address again. Stopping in his tracks, he went through all his pockets looking for it, but he could not find it. In a panic, he backtracked his way to the hotel in the hope of finding that critical piece of paper. If he had dropped it in his excitement only minutes earlier, he had a good chance of finding it somewhere, either on the sidewalk or in the hotel. Finally, on checking the inside pocket of his sports coat again, he came upon the lost treasure, the critical little page torn from a notebook. He wiped the perspiration from his forehead with a deep sigh of relief.

The Pastoral Centre for Welfare Services was housed in such an imposing nineteenth-century structure that Tamas hesitated to climb the steps to enter it. But once inside, he liked the place, especially how busy it was; in the whirl of people running up and down no one noticed his embarrassing helplessness. Walter had even given him the room number of Mr Eugene Mazur's office. His knock on the door was not answered, so he timidly opened the door. He found himself facing a personable young man with curly red hair. Tamas recited carefully chosen and well-rehearsed phrases. The young official gave a friendly smile but no sign of comprehension. Nevertheless, he offered his client a seat, almost inviting him to feel at ease. Best of all he spoke slowly, pronouncing every word almost syllable by syllable in order to make himself more easily understood. Tamas got the gist of it and took it to mean: 'Sit down, stop worrying, patience.' Getting this far in learning the language made him feel better.

Without further delay he produced the ill-fated slip of paper; Walter's instructions were recorded on it with poor spelling, but Eugene's name and location were on it in addition to the purpose of the call. The young man nodded and started questioning Tamas for his personal data – his name, address, and phone number. Tamas more or less understood the questions and supplied the requested information eagerly but also haltingly and with a heavy accent. His limited command of English and the transient nature of his accommodations seemed to trouble the official. He put another, much longer question to Tamas who concluded it was about a more permanent address. Tamas was only too happy to supply the answer: 'Apartment, yes days, only few,' he said proudly. Eugene responded by asking him to come back as soon as he had his own place, so that it could be entered in his records. In the meantime a middle-aged but slender lady with long blond hair, wearing blue jeans, entered the office. Apologizing for the interruption she turned to Eugene. From her accent Tamas judged her too to be of foreign background. Eugene called her Mrs Christine Karady and whispered something in her ear. The lady turned to Tamas and asked him in his own language if she could be of any help.

As Tamas left the grand building, his face was beaming. Christine had taken care of all his problems. With her help he was able to communicate to Mr Mazur that he was ready and willing to do any kind of work although he had been in the country for only a few days.

Eugene entered the new information with great satisfaction into his records; he regarded the case as an easy one, and he held out the possibility of a job in the next few days. As far as learning the language was concerned, there was a course scheduled to start the following week for beginners and advanced students combined. I could not have wished for more in my wildest dreams, Tamas thought. On top of that, Christine gave him her home phone number, telling him not to hesitate to call her if he ever needed her help.

Things are moving forward, yes, they are, Tamas thought happily to himself, out on the sidewalk. Now he was able to take in the bright sunshine and bask in it. Even the traffic fumes that were hanging heavy in the air, he breathed in with contentment.

—*Chapter 37*—

MURDER IN HOTEL ODÉON
—XIII—

A NOTHER WEEKEND IN THE COUNTRY and too much
fresh air had worn out Hugo.

Showering on Monday morning, he thought about
Lidia, how he enjoyed her body and making love to it. If
only he could put up with her bad habits.

He found Nina in the kitchen, looking through the
morning paper. She cast a quick glance at Hugo and
then went back to her reading.

'Anything sensational in the paper?' Hugo inquired,
sitting down to the breakfast already waiting for him at
the other end of the table. He spread butter on his toast
as he looked expectantly at his wife. But no answer was
forthcoming.

'I take it from your silence the answer is no,' he said
finally.

'Nothing noteworthy,' Nina replied flatly, raising
her eyes from the newspaper. 'That is, unless you are
interested in the statement made by a Detective Fabian
Mueller assigned to the murder of that barber in Hotel
Odéon.'

'Why? What new information did the detective make
public?' The news struck Hugo like a lightning bolt.

'Detective Mueller,' began Nina, reading the news
item from the paper, 'assigned to the case of Viktor
Faludi, who had been murdered in a particularly cruel
manner in Hotel Odéon, made the following statement
to our reporter: "Although a suspect – Dr Valerian Lang,
a prominent attorney – has been arrested, the case is far
from being closed. We have uncovered new information,
new pieces of the puzzle, but I cannot comment on

these. One thing I can report, however, is that, on that tragic night, the victim had several visitors. Among them, according to reliable witnesses, there was a woman." That was the statement, but our paper will continue to keep its readers informed of all new developments.' Nina finished reciting the short paragraph from the paper and shifted her gaze to her husband.

For a few seconds she kept her eyes on his face. Then her eyelids dropped. But it was almost visible that her eyeballs were rolling at a furious pace behind their lids.

'What's the matter? Aren't you feeling well?' asked Hugo hurrying to her side to hold her hand.

'Nothing, nothing to worry about,' she said opening her eyes, but only to stare at the wall. 'It's just that I got a chill reading those words "particularly cruel manner." The way that poor barber was murdered!'

Hugo listened to her without a word. Eventually he picked up the piece of toast, listlessly finishing it.

'This case has been on my mind lately,' continued Nina, 'and I had to ask myself what it was that man had done to deserve this kind of end to his life. I remember the day after the murder the newspapers said the victim was gay, and speculated about jealousy as the attorney's motive. You remember now, Hugo? It would never have occurred to me that the attorney was a homosexual. Nothing about his gestures, nothing about his behaviour would have led me to suspect he was. Wouldn't you think there would be some kind of sign or habit that would let you know?' asked Nina with a frightening frigidity.

There was sorrow in her ebony eyes, even while they were throwing sparks.

'Did you know this about the barber? That he was gay?' she asked; and then as if fed up with the newspaper, she folded it and dropped it on the table.

'No, of course not, how could I have known?' Hugo blurted out. So he wouldn't have to say anything more, he stuffed the remains of the toast into his mouth.

Nina busied herself with the Monday morning mail. She was sorting the envelopes according to size.

'Anyway it's not as if homosexuality is considered abnormal any more,' he continued as if talking to himself. 'Obviously it's very fashionable in some circles.'

'Have you ever been in love with a man?' asked the woman with unaccustomed, almost preternatural, calm.

'No, although in my younger days at college, the idea interested me, but in reality...'

'Did you know Valerian Lang, the attorney?' Nina kept up the assault on her husband with an impatience she had never shown before.

'What's the point of this?' he asked nervously.

'Artur tells me that Valerian, too, is a member of your little society.'

'What society?' Hugo was getting more and more irritated, fidgeting uncomfortably on his kitchen stool; what was Nina doing talking to Artur?

'The society you attend two or three times a week, and from where you come home in an unusually good mood. I would say you return from there flying high on happiness. Isn't this true? Isn't this how you get home?'

'Nina! You're imagining things. Yes, I am in the habit of stopping at Eddy's Bar, but only for a moment of relaxation to clear my mind of city business. That's all, that's what it's all about. I don't know what Artur told you, but let me assure you nothing exotic ever takes place in that bar.'

Hugo slipped off the stool visibly shaken and eager to go. He took a few steps to the flower-pot in the corner of the kitchen, sticking a finger into the soil to see if it was still moist or maybe needed watering.

'No, nothing exotic ever takes place there,' Nina repeated the sentence. 'Nothing at all out of the ordinary.'

'If you have any reservations about this, then please spell them out in understandable terms and not in puzzles,' Hugo said, slowly allowing his voice rise to its usual, confident level. He wiped his mouth with a napkin and then made his way to Nina in small, measured steps. He took her in his arms, and kissed her forehead before leaving the house and walking out to the waiting limousine.

—Chapter 38—

S YLVIA WOULD NOT be back until late that evening. She had called Zeno to tell him she would be tied up with a Red Cross meeting until after dinner, but that the maid had prepared a cold supper for him which would be in the refrigerator. If he wanted a hot meal, he could probably get one at the Club on 13th Avenue. Zeno assured her he would take care of himself and would also return home late.

In the house mail from the marketing department he found a short note.

> My Love !
> I'll be waiting for you tonight with every part of me.
> I'll have a delicious dinner ready. If you can, please come
> by seven.
> With kisses,
>   W.

Zeno found the entrance to Wanda's apartment house unlocked. A terse warning note on the glass door explained the situation: THE BUZZER SYSTEM OF THE MAIN ENTRANCE IS TEMPORARILY OUT OF ORDER. YOUR COOPERATION WILL BE APPRECIATED.

Ignoring the elevator he ran up the stairs, taking two steps at a time. He stopped at the door of the girl's apartment, waited a few seconds, and only then did he ring the bell.

Wanda tumbled into his arms like a fragrant beach ball. He found her joy and childlike eagerness to please so sincere that he forgot his earlier worries. In the small entrance foyer he stepped into slippers, because she begged him to take off his shoes.

'This way you'll feel completely at home.' She gave him a conspiratorial smile.

They went into the kitchen. Only the light over the stove was on. The pale shadows seemed to expand the cramped place in the dim light. On the table the flame of a green candle quivered.

There were place settings for two, silverware and crimson napkins had been carefully arranged. Pots simmered on the stove.

'Let's have a drink. What would you like?' The girl embraced him again.

'Do you have cognac?'

They sat down facing each other. They clinked their glasses and started sipping.

'We'll have a gourmet supper.' She pointed to the pots and pans. 'I heard from your secretary that you only have a hot meal in the evening, so I made a cream of vegetable soup and for the main course a roast rabbit tenderloin with steamed potatoes.'

'That was nice of you, but the way I feel today I'm not sure if I am all that hungry,' said Zeno. He tried to hide his embarrassment then with a dry little laugh.

It was Wanda's exaggerated pleasantness that threw him off balance; so far he had marshalled only accusations against her in his mind, and it was hard to reconcile these with all the attention she was lavishing on him.

Wanda began to serve the dinner. Nimbly, and with quick, graceful movements of her wrists, she ladled out the cream soup into bowls. He dipped his spoon in it and stirred it up, letting it cool a little, but when the girl assured him it was not too hot, he ate it with gusto.

They were already working on the second course when the doorbell rang. Wanda hurried to the door and peered out through the spy hole, not once but several times. Then she quietly crept back.

'Just imagine, Paul is back again,' she whispered with a mixture of fright and surprise on her face. 'And I told him it was all over between us, and yet here he is, lurking around the place, wanting to come in… My God, what should I do?' The girl wrung her hands helplessly.

'This after you told him not to bother you? You said you'd given him his marching orders, so what's going on now?' Zeno asked, genuinely confused.

'The poor thing is so helpless, he's alone in the world!' Wanda lamented.

Zeno could not understand any part of the situation. It had not been his intention to push Paul out and take his place. When he met Wanda he didn't even know of the boy's existence.

Does this girl have any idea of what she wants? If she's so sorry for him, she must still be in love with him. Then what am I doing here? Why should I make life miserable for these young lovers? He stared at the table, profoundly confused.

Then something even more confusing happened. The girl suddenly jumped up from the table, ran over to the apartment door, and opened it. She stepped out into the hallway, with Zeno following her.

The hallway and the staircase were empty. Not a soul anywhere.

They both turned around, heading back to the apartment, when the girl glimpsed a small bouquet of white lilacs on the floor, just right of the threshold.

'Look, he's brought me flowers!' she cried out despondently. 'Never before did he bring me flowers! Oh, my poor little bastard!'

Zeno sat down at the table again with his stomach churning and his spirit extinguished. He had no appetite at all.

He asked for another shot of cognac.

'I don't understand why you asked me here tonight if you're still in love with Paul,' he asked harshly.

'No, I'm not in love with him, only…' whispered the girl as if to herself, 'I just feel sorry for him. He's a little wimp, that's all. You can understand that, can't you?' she looked at Zeno, entreatingly.

She got up and stood beside him, stroking his arm, his face, and then she squeezed herself between the chair and the table to sit in Zeno's lap. Nestled in his arms, she dropped her head on his chest as she went on gently nuzzling him.

'Please, don't be angry with me, my dear, I didn't intend to hurt you. I sincerely asked Paul to leave me alone, because I love only you, and no one else, my one and only, my love, please believe me.' She stood up and took Zeno's hand. 'Come on, I'll prove it to you,' she said, and led him into the bedroom.

*   *   *

It was past midnight when Zeno parked his car in the driveway in front of his two-storey colonial house. He didn't want to open the garage door in case he disturbed Silvia if she had already gone to sleep. He was right; the burglar alarm system was already activated. What if she has changed the code on me? The thought flashed across his guilty mind, but the digits he punched in worked.

He had mixed feelings about the evening. On the one hand he had experienced pleasures that he had never sampled before, but at the same time he was finding Wanda's claims of loving him with sincerity and abandon not easy to believe.

At every turn he was suspecting playacting, simulation, artifice. He tried to compare how he had felt tonight with the way he had felt after earlier sessions, but he could not get very far. In spite of everything that happened he still felt the enormous fire of love blazing inside him.

In the bedroom the light on the night table was still on. He was met by Sylvia's questioning look.

'Where have you been all this time?' she asked in a cold voice Zeno had never heard before.

'In the Club. Didn't you suggest that if I wanted something hot I should get it there?'

'That's one place you didn't go!' his wife hissed at him. 'The council meeting broke up at ten and I thought I'd stop there, and if I found you, I'd have a bite to eat. But you were nowhere near the place this evening. No one had seen you there! Would you like to tell me where you were?'

Sylvia spoke with such emotion that Zeno found himself defenceless.

'I was at another club,' he said on his way to the dressing room to get undressed.

'And who was with you?' His wife went on with the questioning in a sharp tone.

'I was alone. There was no one with me. I thought I was going to meet with Walter to discuss tomorrow's television interview, but I could not find him anywhere,' said Zeno quietly like someone who had nothing to hide, and started undressing.

Sylvia wasn't buying any of this. Her eyes coldly reflected the reading lamp.

'You've been cheating on me, haven't you?' she asked in the matter-of-fact voice of a polite stranger.

'Yes, as a matter of fact, I have, but let's talk about that tomorrow if you don't mind. I'm extremely tired tonight,' he said flatly, slipping under the covers.

Chapter 39

MURDER IN HOTEL ODÉON
—XIV—

O N THE DRIVE to the office, Hugo's mind kept returning to the disturbing conversation with his wife at breakfast.

The reference to Artur had been the most striking. It was a big surprise to him that Artur had talks with Nina that neither of them had ever mentioned. Nor their meetings in person.

I'll have to ask Artur about that. After all, it was he who wanted to see me about something. It'll be a good opportunity to clear up a few things.

But what business could he possibly have had with my wife? What reason did he have to keep quiet about it? The questions gave him a strange pang of pain.

He was so lost in thought that he was unaware the journey had ended until the door on the right opened and he saw Miklos, the driver, standing outside, waiting for him to step out. As he did so, he was struck by the noise of the city, which sounded louder to him than usual, almost as if it were blaring through loudspeakers. A sudden gust of wind lifted the flaps of his open coat and he needed both hands to pull them close around him. He climbed the stairs quickly to his suite of offices.

'Good morning, Elsa,' he said to the young office assistant, as he swung the door shut and tried on a half-hearted smile. 'Have you any good news for me today?'

But he rushed on to his own office without waiting for an answer.

Elsa followed him in before he had a chance to shut the door behind him.

'The Prefect is sending his thanks for last week's

appointment. He wants to know if you, Sir, would like to lunch with him today. He wants to invite you to the restaurant of Hotel Odéon, at one in the afternoon. What shall I tell him?'

'Tell him,' he said turning to Elsa and placing his patent leather attaché case beside his desk, 'tell him I'd be glad to accept the invitation, and I'll be there at one on the dot. But before you do, could you please make sure I don't have any other appointments for noon today?'

'I've already checked,' Elsa hurried to answer. 'Fortunately you don't. Not until three this afternoon when Dr Artur Liptak, the attorney, is supposed to meet with you. He says this was an appointment made last week.'

'Yes, yes, that's right.'

'I've already placed today's reports and the daily papers on your desk,' said the secretary before finally leaving the office.

Hugo's attention was elsewhere. He stepped over to his desk. He riffled through the file folder containing the day's reports, but then put them down again. There was a message that he was to ring Lidia.

He picked up the phone and asked Elsa to dial the Publicity Department. In a few seconds Lidia's voice rang out on the line.

'I have a few free minutes now to go over the projects for the upcoming quarter. I assume that was why you were looking for me.' Hugo rattled off the words. 'I suggest, if you can spare the time now, that we meet in the cafeteria, let's say in five minutes.'

The City Hall cafeteria was the one place where all the news, rumours, and hearsay of the city came together.

At coffee breaks news spread like wildfire. There was nothing going on in the city – no worthwhile event taking place – that one could not find out about in the cafeteria if one put one's mind to it.

The place was always jam-packed, especially at this time of the day, in the morning.

On entering, Hugo looked around the place, scanning the faces of those sitting at the tables until he spotted Lidia.

As he made his way across the large room he was greeted from left and right. Hugo graciously acknowledged each greeting with a nod and a smile. He thought to himself: everyone wants to know who it is I am to meet here and what I say. If they could, the whole horde would crowd around.

Lidia had already ordered her coffee. For Hugo she asked for linden tea.

'Nice to see you again,' she said, turning a smiling face toward the Mayor.

'What's up?' Hugo asked, lowering his voice to a barely audible level. 'Has something happened?'

'Something indeed!'

'I'm listening,' Hugo said curtly.

'Imagine that. Well you'll find this interesting: on Friday they asked me to come down to police headquarters,' said Lidia, launching into her story. 'It was a command performance for a gentleman by the name of Fabian Mueller in his office. He expressed a wish to have a chat with me. At first he did some small talk to warm me up, and then he got down to business. Among other things, he wanted to know where I was at the time of Viktor's murder, specifically on the night of April third, and the early morning of April fourth. He assured me that this was just part of a routine police investigation, questions they had to cover. There was nothing pointing in my direction as a suspect. But he had to insist on questioning me, because apparently one of the janitors at Hotel Odéon reported having seen a woman resembling me going up to the victim's room on the night of the crime.'

'And? Were you there or not?' asked Hugo, his voice turning tremulous in surprise.

'Yes, as a matter of fact, I was.'

—Chapter 40—

TAMAS WAS MOVING. The Immigration Office had rented an apartment for him. Linda phoned to tell him about it, saying he could pack up because she would be collecting him at ten o'clock tomorrow to bring him to it.

Then he had a call from Walter, reminding him of the Thursday afternoon television interview with Zeno, whom Tamas had met at the Baroness's wake. He thought Tamas would find it an interesting experience. They agreed to meet in the lobby of the Chamber of Commerce that afternoon at three.

Things were looking up, Tamas thought to himself. He pulled out the card Father Garnini had given him at the wake, turning it around in his hand, looking at it like a talisman, and the name Evelyn as his saviour.

As soon as he got into the new apartment he could start working. He would have to go back to Eugene, the employment agent in the church welfare centre, with his permanent address and phone number. And he also thought of Christine with gratitude; not only was she nice to him but also very helpful. Now, while he was thinking of her, he sought out her card in his pocket and entered the phone number in his address book with every other important number there. At the top of the list was Walter.

*   *   *

Walter's campaign manager was not feeling hopeful. Cameron had met the party's executive council earlier that morning. 'It's not going to be easy to get them to pay off Bradley's gambling debts,' Cameron told Walter.

'Mark and Miriam will almost certainly vote against it. I've talked to them already, and they're pretty fed up as it is. As soon as I have news for you, I'll let you know,' Cameron had added.

When Barbara rang a few minutes later, Walter was in a rotten mood. Just the person I need in my life right now, he thought to himself on hearing his lover's voice on the phone. Barbara sounded anxious. She said she'd missed him and wanted to see him.

'Ted, my airplane mechanic, promised I could test-fly my new Cessna. This weekend, if you have time, I could take you on the pleasure flight I promised you,' she said cheerfully, but her voice trailed off when Walter came on the line sounding nervous and preoccupied.

Walter was in no mood to go flying, and he knew he should not leave Melanie alone for the three-day weekend, but he found himself unable to refuse when Barbara proposed the flight.

Anyway, what was Barbara proposing, he reassured himself. It was only a short flight, not a night of sex. I'll work it out somehow, he thought. If I time things carefully, I can take care of everything. But I should eliminate Barbara from the picture after this last flight. She's caused me enough trouble already, so what am I doing still fooling around with her?

He had not written a line that morning. He had neither the inspiration nor the mood. Nor a theme. Nothing.

I'm burnt out. There's no point denying it. Still, I mustn't lose my head, he thought.

He read over some of the questions he was going to ask during the TV interview. He was not satisfied with any of them. He took out a fresh sheet of paper and started rephrasing the questions he would put to Zeno.

*   *   *

Zeno was wondering how much Sylvia knew. *You've been*

cheating on me, haven't you? she had said the night before. It's like she knows about Wanda and me. But what does she know, and how much?

He had no time though to find out; he had to decide now. Should he make a clean breast of it and ask for her forgiveness, admit he had made a huge mistake, had brought Sylvia grief she did not deserve, try to steal his way back into her heart, and perhaps make her forget this misstep?

But then there was Wanda. Did he really love that girl or was it a passing madness, a spell of the moment? Wanda was the challenge: pain personified, but also the fount of euphoria, the bittersweet fruit of flaming temptations, and a rejuvenating sense of rebellion.

Lingering in bed, he weighed the pros and cons. With Sylvia he had steadiness, security, and a well-balanced life. With Wanda came constant anxiety, torture to his soul, humiliation, but at the same time lust and fulfilment of the body he had never experienced before. Paul came to his mind; Wanda was going to bed with both of them, changing from one to the other like she changed her underwear, and without any sign of remorse. How can anyone live like that? He felt his fists tighten in fury and pain. Sylvia may be lacking the fiery passion that rages in Wanda, but loving her causes me no pain. Loving Wanda, however, is an ongoing Calvary.

Still undecided, Zeno got up and went to the kitchen, where he found Sylvia looking out the window, so deep in thought that she didn't notice him at first. It was the shuffle of his slippers that made her turn round. A smile spread over her face. She found her husband's pained expression funny.

'You look like a schoolboy the teacher orders to come up to his desk and explain why he hasn't done his homework.'

'Are you serious about what you asked last night?'

'Deadly serious,' she replied as she took a big, crackling

bite out of her toast. Her light brown eyes flashed like embers when a breeze passes over them. 'Well, where were you last night?'

Zeno felt his mind freeze. He was not prepared for direct confrontation. I'll have to come out with the whole story, he thought, and he nervously cleared his throat. He wanted to speak, but no sound came out. His wife continued the conversation for him.

'Zeno, stop acting like a child. Every time you cheated on me I knew about it. You can't hide anything, you always play with your cards on the table. Ironically it was your sincerity that made me fall in love with you in the first place.' She looked at her husband with a challenge but also with sadness.

She was wondering if she should cancel the promise she had made to herself the night before, and not go through with the divorce.

My God, why am I so weak? she thought then. I need to stand up for myself. That would be impossible living with Zeno.

'I've made up my mind,' she said almost at a whisper, and then she repeated it more loudly and with more determination. 'I've made up my mind to divorce you, Zeno. At the beginning it was very nice with you, I was in love with you and thought you too loved me.'

Sylvia searched her husband's face, looking for a clue to his thoughts. But it was no good, she found nothing. He just sat there in the kitchen chair looking at her.

I don't think it has penetrated his consciousness that I am asking for a divorce. He can't even comprehend it. Of course, the moment I reached this decision it struck me, too, as incomprehensible, Sylvia was thinking.

'I'll get going with the formalities this morning,' she said suddenly. 'I'll go and see my lawyer.' She walked out of the kitchen, leaving Zeno alone with his thoughts, his eyes lost somewhere beyond the walls.

*   *   *

When Linda arrived to pick him up, Tamas asked her to check his bill. He was worried about extra charges. He had already looked at it closely himself, but just to make sure, he enlisted Linda's help. After thorough scrutiny she confirmed that Tamas had not incurred any extra charges. 'It's okay,' she said. 'It's okay.' Tamas was deeply relieved, on top of the world in fact, getting in Linda's car.

'We're almost there,' she said, turning to Tamas when they left the main thoroughfare and entered a small side street. The area was built up with neat little single-family homes on small lawn-covered lots, most of them only one-storey high but some of them with a second floor added; these didn't stand out but completed the pattern of a residential community.

'It's a quiet area, you'll see,' Linda said smiling at the young man, but all he understood was 'quiet'.

They parked at the end of the street in front of a two-storey apartment house. The lower floor was left unfinished and used as a garage for cars parked between concrete pillars that supported the building above.

Not far from the building, not more than ten metres away, was a small creek, its banks overgrown with lush green grass. Tamas looked in delight at the park-like setting.

'Nice, isn't it?' Linda looked at his beaming face and waved to him to follow.

The staircase led into a long, narrow, and dimly-lit corridor where they passed five doors on both sides, each located to face the one opposite. At the sixth on the left, Linda stopped, unlocked the door, and they entered the apartment.

They found themselves in a sizable living room and kitchen combined into one, the kitchen alcove fully equipped with wall cabinets, a refrigerator and an electric stove. The living room was more sparsely furnished, having only a small dining table with four chairs and a tiny desk with an armchair in front of it. Tamas, however, looked around with satisfaction. He quickly turned his attention to the box they carried in with them; it contained all kinds of useful items, including eating utensils, cooking pots, bed sheets, and even an alarm clock.

'It's not very much, but you'll find the necessities,' Linda said, as Tamas eagerly looked over the kitchenware and other treasures of his new household. A sheet of paper contained an inventory of the items received, and Linda asked Tamas to sign it where it was marked with an 'x' if he found everything listed there. Tamas gave Linda a chastened look; he didn't understand what was expected of him. When he realized the document was about the bounty he had just received, he took out his pen and produced a carefully calligraphed signature.

'Thank you, thank you,' he said, almost overcome with emotion.

On her way out, Linda opened another door that led into the bedroom.

'I almost forgot about this room.' She turned back toward Tamas after taking a quick look at the only piece of furniture in the place, the bed. 'The night table and a lamp will be delivered tomorrow,' she said, but he was only able to catch the word 'lamp'.

'The next time you see Bertold Thompson he'll give you some cash so that you can buy a clock radio and a telephone. The monthly subscription rate is relatively low, but you have to watch out for those long-distance calls, they can add up very fast. Well, good luck with your new apartment.' She extended her hand toward Tamas. 'Making a new start in life is difficult and worrisome, but you'll see, perseverance, diligence, and patience will pay off in the long run.' She recited the words carefully and closed the apartment door behind her.

Tamas registered only the Bertold Thompson name

and concluded he'd better pay him a visit the next day, perhaps in the morning.

Left alone in his apartment, Tamas got to work unpacking his few items of clothing and hung them up in the closet in the bedroom. He placed his single book, Goethe's *Faust*, and his notebook on the small end-table. He flopped down into the armchair and took a deep breath.

Chapter 41

S YLVIA HAD MADE an appointment with her lawyer. Deep inside, she was not sure that she really wanted to divorce Zeno. All she wanted was his attention, the realization from him that the years spent together meant something, that the habit of togetherness may have lacked the grand storms of passion but could not be erased at a stroke of the pen.

At the start of his affair with Wanda, she was convinced that it too would pass soon, like the others. Those earlier affairs had caused her pain, but she had regarded this as a kind of atonement for her failure to produce children. The affair with Wanda was different. The more she learned about it, the more she realised, to her despair, that this one was seriously affecting Zeno.

So now she found herself sitting in the reception room of the law office, looking over the magazines on the coffee table. She felt her decision had to be final, unalterable. The deeper the nostalgia for the past sank into her soul, the more she fought against it, trying to fend off all doubt.

Mr Conrad Bergson's secretary, sitting behind a desk, was busy shuffling papers, but her eyes were on Sylvia and alive with curiosity. She used to know Sylvia in high school and was eager to know what problem had brought her to this office. Sylvia became aware of the secretary's intrusive looks, and she tried to bury her face in a magazine she had casually opened. But she didn't have to stay in hiding long; soon Mr Bergson's tall figure appeared at the end of the hallway.

He greeted her with a bright smile. 'It's been too long,' the lawyer said, as he escorted her to a small conference room.

Conrad was an old family acquaintance; he was the

executor of the will he had prepared for Sylvia's father. He was well past seventy, but it didn't show. He had an athletic physique and his face was surprisingly wrinkle-free.

Sylvia was fiddling with her white pocketbook as if for a minute she had forgotten where she was and why.

'I'm sorry I barged into your office in such a hurry.' She was taking comfort in talking to the lawyer as an old friend in the midst of a social call rather than a business meeting. 'But I felt if I put it off any longer my resolve might weaken and I mightn't have the strength to go through with what I need to do.'

The lawyer was all curiosity. He even raised an eyebrow slightly as if he had a feeling he was going to hear something totally unexpected.

'The thing is...' Sylvia lifted her gaze from the pocketbook, 'I want to get a divorce. From Zeno.'

While slowly dragging the words out of herself she was searching the man's face, watching how it was affected, what kind of judgment it showed, disapproval or encouragement.

Conrad's expression became impassive, changing from social to professional. Only his eyes opened a little wider, but hardly noticeably.

'Tell me all about it. What happened?' he asked softly, apologetically, as if talking about some trivial matter that needed attention.

'Nothing unusual. Or we might say the usual. Men like young girls. To get to the heart of the matter, Zeno has fallen madly in love with a college girl, and although he has not yet come out with it, he seems to be contemplating divorce. This was the impression I got reading the letters that passed between the two of them.'

'So you have evidence of infidelity?'

'A lot. I have copies of their complete correspondence. In addition, I have the testimony of two hotel employees, one the hotel receptionist and the other a waiter Zeno had a run in with because the waiter refused to serve him and his lady after hours.'

'Any other evidence?'

'A few photos I took myself when they were dining together, after which they adjourned to the girl's apartment.'

Sylvia gave her account haltingly, obviously in distress. She was actually ashamed of herself for displaying the dirty laundry of her family to an old acquaintance at the first meeting after many years. What bothered her more than anything was having to talk about her husband's peccadilloes; it made her feel ashamed for the husband she still loved at that minute. Every word she came out with pained her.

And then she fell silent, waiting for the lawyer to ask his questions.

'Excuse me, but please refresh my memory – do you have any children from this marriage?'

'No.' Sylvia shook her head, again twisting the handle of her purse between her fingers.

'And if I remember correctly you are the sole heir to the company your father established, aren't you?'

'Yes, you remember correctly,' she answered softly.

The lawyer fell silent for a minute while rearranging the documents in a folder on the table, and then he shifted his gaze to Sylvia.

'We've known each other for a long, long time, and I would like you to consider my advice as that of an old friend. Give yourself a few days to think this over. And if you still feel the same way after that time, I'll prepare and file the divorce papers.'

Based on his years of experience, Conrad was hoping his client would accept his suggestion thus giving him some time in which to contact Zeno. In the meantime, Sylvia might question her decision and may be agreeable to a reconciliatory meeting with Zeno on neutral ground in the lawyer's office.

'No, that's out of the question.' Sylvia, suddenly electrified, leapt to her feet. 'I told you before I asked for this appointment that I had struggled with this decision for weeks. I had already weighed every aspect of this case, all the pros and cons. My decision is final. I want to start divorce proceedings now. So please, I beg of you not to try to dissuade me again.'

Sylvia sounded irritated, not just agitated. The anger that had suddenly flared up blazed from her eyes. Conrad could no longer recognize the happy young woman he used to know.

After seeing her out he immediately asked his secretary to call Mr Zeno Langdon, the chief executive of Farm Fresh poultry processing company. But then he changed his mind.

'Sorry, forget it,' he said in a more businesslike tone and closed the door of his office behind him.

—Chapter 42—

Murder in Hotel Odéon
—XV—

I T WAS A BOMBSHELL Artur was completely unprepared for – that the detective knew about the Mayor's membership of the Eddy's Bar Club. He could feel goose bumps popping up on his back. Things were taking a serious turn. He took his time though with his answer.

'Yes, Hugo may come around more often, but he's not officially a charter member either!'

'And unofficially?' The word flew out of Mueller's mouth like a bullet from a gun.

'Neither officially, nor unofficially. Not in any shape or form. You may have heard some rumours about Hugo, but trust me, you were grossly misinformed,' answered Artur with a great show of indignation.

Must not rush into this, he told himself, trying to calm down. I must convince this policeman that Hugo had nothing to do with our little society.

'Take it easy, counsellor; this is not for the record, it's not an official questioning under caution, only a little friendly conversation, no need to get so worked up,' said Fabian Mueller with a smile, sensing that Artur was about to go on the attack.

'In that case, Inspector, I'd like to ask you,' he went on, emphasizing this mode of address, seeing that it seemed to have the intended favourable affect, 'would you be so kind and tell me what you actually have on your mind?'

Artur's eyes came to rest on a painting, most likely a reproduction, decorating the wall behind his interlocutor. It depicted a young peasant woman dressed in folk costume, her golden braids twisted into a bun on the back of her head, sitting at a spinning wheel and with an outstretched arm guiding the yarn being spun. In the background there was the whitewashed wall of a cottage and its thatched roof with a small cloud looking down from the bright blue sky. The picture radiated tranquillity, Artur thought wistfully.

'I'd like you to fill in the empty boxes in my crossword puzzle,' said the detective, giving a slightly deprecating smile.

'My life is an open book.' The lawyer returned the detective's cliché with one of his own, spreading his arms out as if to let the other read his chest. 'I have nothing to hide. Why wouldn't I want to help my friend get out of jail, especially as you claim that somehow I have it in my power to do so? And, by implication, why wouldn't I want to help you?'

Now they were both taking the measure of each other, each trying to read the other's face.

'The question has occurred to me, too. Indeed, why wouldn't you want to lend your support to my investigation? Perhaps there's a reason, like you want to cover up something that's more important to you than your friend's freedom.'

'Are you saying you doubt my word?' Artur's indignation was not courtroom theatrics.

'Do you see now what I was trying to get at earlier? Hold it, Counsellor, I'm still in charge here.'

Suddenly inspiration struck Artur.

'You know what? How about you giving me a little time, a little reprieve, and let's see if I can't produce that woman for you, that second visitor Viktor had, just before his demise. Your sources provided the gender already. What do you say to that?'

The detective busied himself with the ballpoint pen. 'I think that's a good idea. It would certainly get the ball rolling. If we could lay our hands on that second visitor, it's quite possible that we could eliminate Valerian as a suspect and let him go. Provided we find sufficient evidence to support the theory that the second visitor entered Viktor's room not before but after Valerian. Even then we'd still be left with an unanswered question. What if Valerian left the room only temporarily while the second visitor lingered there, and then he returned shortly afterwards?'

'Yes, in that case Valerian would still need to come up with an alibi. He'd have to prove what time he arrived at the hotel and what time he left and where he went from the hotel.' Artur was spinning the thread of the same thought.

'Correct. Your logic, dear colleague, is impeccable,' the detective said smiling. 'We'd still need an alibi from Valerian. On the other hand, you're right in pointing out that when we find that second visitor we'll be able to gain a lot more information on things that could lead to the eventual solution. We both agree on that point.' The detective nodded several times as if to express agreement with his own observations. 'I shall keep you no longer from your normal business. You're a gentleman and a scholar. You know how to bear up under difficult circumstances. You don't get overly upset, only slightly rattled, when you try to foil my questions with lies… Or excuse me…' the detective caught himself being somewhat too blunt and stopped to search for a less blunt word, 'that is, even when your answers fall short of the whole truth. Otherwise you're a pleasant and polite person to talk to, a perfect conversationalist.' Fabian piled on the pleasantries, perhaps in exchange for the 'inspector' moniker.

Artur was not in a great hurry to rise from his chair. He sensed that the battle between them was far from over, and he was faced by a formidable foe, who, seemingly to confuse the issue, had just assured him of his goodwill. That was not quite enough to allay Artur's worries. He had no idea where to turn next, whom to seek out for help, how to ferret out who was the second visitor so he could make good on his promise to the detective.

'Very well, let's just leave it at that. I'll contact you as soon as I learn anything,' Artur said finally, holding out his hand.

They parted like two good friends. Although neither of them said so, it was obvious to both that their conversation had yielded nothing concrete. On the contrary, it opened up more new questions than it answered.

Later on that afternoon Artur found himself pretty much alone sitting in Eddy's Bar. He was consuming his vodka in tiny sips, taking his time. But even so the first few drops had warmed up his empty stomach. The beer chaser also did its bit to help him get pleasantly woozy. He had skipped lunch that day, and his breakfast too had been skimpy. He thought of ordering a cheese sandwich, but the waiter was nowhere to be found.

While raising his glass to his lips for the umpteenth time it occurred to him he'd better start sorting out his thoughts about the afternoon's encounter. One thing was clear: he had to alert Hugo about his name being involved in the investigation, about Fabian – the hound dog on their trail. He had not seen the Mayor for several days, and he would have to get in touch with him the next day at the latest and give him a detailed report on his interview at the police station.

Besides, Hugo had to know something.

He kept idly circling the rim of his glass with the tip of his forefinger.

Thoughts were racing through his mind one after another, but the one question that kept coming back to him was: who could have been the woman who dropped in on Viktor at the hotel in the middle of the night?

Chapter 43

ENO WONDERED SUDDENLY if he was in danger of ending up destitute. A divorce from Sylvia would also mean a divorce from the firm that had been a great part of his life. It all depended on how the divorce court went. I've been reinvesting all my savings in the company, and now the family home and two cars are the only property we have in common.

Thinking about the prospect, he froze. He was going to be out of a job, too. How would it look for him to come to work as another employee, and that was only if Sylvia was willing to keep him on as hired help, the manager of the company?

I wonder what evidence Sylvia has against me? The question seemed the nearest thing to a life preserver. If she's in possession of the letters – which is quite possible – she has very good grounds for divorce. But what if I sought reconciliation? Another life preserver, but it was out of reach as soon as he came upon it.

He knew his wife's temperament; once she made up her mind about something she would not budge.

The fact is, he concluded, I'm finished.

He had a shower, and decided to go into work as usual.

Dora was waiting for him, full of news and looking cheerful. The machinery for the new processing line had arrived. Some parts had already been lifted into place. Clusters of workers were busying themselves among the enormous transport trailers; the whole community of the plant was abuzz with enthusiasm.

'A secretary from Mr Conrad Bergson's law office called, but then she said the lawyer changed his mind and would call again if he needed to talk to you.' Dora opened the door for Zeno into his office.

He was in no mood for any of this. A yearning for peace was overpowering him, as if he were seeking solace for the loss of his soul, seeking the forgiveness of his sins. His eyes scanned the office. He could have described each piece of furniture with his eyes closed, each curve in the woodwork as if he had lovingly dusted the place with a soft rag every day.

Are these the last minutes I am to spend in their company? Is this the end, the unfulfilled dream? He thought of Wanda again; even though he loved her so much that he would have given his life for her, he realized that the girl was unpredictable both in her mind and her heart. One moment, Wanda confessed to intoxicating, all-encompassing love for him, beaming with sincerity and conviction; the next minute she was capable of acting in direct contradiction of everything she had said. She did that to him and to Paul alike.

Is this the girl I want to tie myself to, the one with whom I imagine my new life? As a pauper without a job? What is she going to say to that?

He dismissed the questions from his frazzled mind. I want her body, her lips, her eyes, her face, her kisses, the fiery nest of her lap, her smile, her sin-filled soul! I'll face whatever lies ahead.

*   *   *

Walter was reviewing his list of questions for the TV interview when he had the idea of asking Zeno over for cocktails Sunday evening, and telling him to bring Sylvia along too; women are always more at ease and contribute more to the conversation when there are other women around. He had a small cocktail party in mind that perhaps Cameron and his wife also could attend. He was taken with the idea, and was already rubbing his hands in anticipation when it occurred to him that Barbara also wanted him to spend Sunday with her.

I'll have to tell her it's impossible now, the Saturday excursion flight will take at least an hour and a half, I'll have to be back for lunch, then riding in the afternoon, so I'll be free for the evening. I'll have to tell Barbara I can't stay with her after the flight, I need to be at home. Walter went on finalizing his plans, but he was stopped in his tracks when he remembered Barbara had become more demanding lately, more obstinate and less accommodating, to the point that he found it hard to put up with her outbursts. She had as little rationality as a sultry, frustrated teenager.

I'll have to have a word with her, approach her carefully and try to reason with her, make her understand that it would be better for both of us if we met less often or not at all during this election campaign period. The flight should be nothing more than a flight, and even that should be cut short and considered the last contact for the time being.

Walter's thoughts were interrupted by the telephone ringing on his desk. He grabbed the receiver like a life preserver. It was Cameron at the other end.

'I have good news for you,' Cameron said in a dry but calm tone that intimated something important in the air. 'The committee unanimously decided to meet Bradley's terms and pay off his gambling debts. We could benefit from the one-month delay, and if you stop providing the opposition with further ammunition against yourself, we think we can counteract the mud the opposition is sure to sling at us. So now I am asking you to watch your step for the immediate future. Keep in mind that you are under constant surveillance, constantly tailed and watched.'

Cameron said goodbye without waiting for an answer. Walter remembered about Sunday's cocktail party when it was too late. But he let the receiver drop back in its cradle. I'll talk to him about that later, he thought, while letting himself enjoy the good news.

Yes sir, yes sir, I'll show them I am capable of winning.

I'll show them Walter cannot be simply written off. Even his loathing for Bradley lost some of its edge. That miserable worm gambled away not only his mind and his fortune but his good name as well. The thoughts followed one another in happy succession.

Finally something good is happening to me for a change! Now I am back on top, riding the crest of the wave again. Weather-beaten and with sails in shreds, but unstoppable.

He could not sit still in his office. He gathered his notes, stuffed them into a cardboard folder and hurried out to be under the blue sky.

Chapter 44

N OW HAVING TO FEND FOR HIMSELF, Tamas found his first experience of a supermarket almost too much for him. The day before, Linda had pointed out a shopping centre on the main road, just before they turned into the side street of his apartment complex.

When he ventured into that huge brightly-lit building, he found the plentitude of merchandise and the number of aisles mind-boggling. He jumped from one item to the next, comparing the prices of various kinds of bread; he could not believe the price of cold cuts and cheese, they were so frighteningly high. Same thing with butter. The salamis and sausages dangling on display were priced close to their weight in gold, gram for gram. He didn't like the price stickers on the boxed milk, and the ones on bottled mineral water made his heart skip a beat. He didn't know what to do. He replaced the empty shopping basket on the stack by the cashier and walked out of the cavernous store. He was almost at the corner when he realized with a shock what he had done.

Well, that won't do, he thought to himself. He had to go back. His new refrigerator was empty and he was hungry. He hadn't eaten anything since lunch time the day before. I've got to go back and try finding something I can afford, he decided. He made another turnabout and hurried back to the store.

Ten minutes later he emerged with two plastic bags in his hands. There was hardly any money left of the weekly food allowance, and he had only put bread, eggs, butter, cold cuts, milk, and a small bag of coffee in his basket. On the way home he tried to keep up his hope that as soon as he had a job he would be able to afford more.

Once he had his family with him he wouldn't be able to keep them in bread and water unless he got a job.

He put the groceries away in the refrigerator and left the apartment. He didn't want to admit it, but his first shopping experience had completely worn him out. While he was living in the hotel he could not really appreciate the prices of various items of food, because he didn't have to pay for any of it. Now that he was standing on his own feet, necessity was bringing him closer to the everyday life.

I've got to find a job, the sooner the better. I'm a jack-of-all-trades. I'll take any job I'm offered. It was a gleam of hope. He was sure his luck would soon change.

Deeply preoccupied with these thoughts, he was walking with his head down. His gaze shifted for a fraction of a second to the shoulder of the roadway. He stopped abruptly. That crumpled piece of paper between those two parked cars, didn't it look like a bank note? The question flashed through his mind as the momentum of his steps carried him forward, so that he had to turn around and retrace his steps. In seconds he was back at the spot. He bent down and picked up the intriguing piece of paper. As soon as he had it between his fingers he could feel from its weight – it was not one, but a small bundle of bank notes, folded in two. He was overcome by excitement; he felt his heart pumping as he unfolded the small wad of money at the creases. Yes, sure enough, it was money, the currency of the land, a packet of several bank notes stuck together. Suddenly, as if caught at some kind of a mischief, he raised his head from the hoard and looked around to see if anyone was watching. But the street was empty as usual, pedestrians being a rare species in the outskirts of town, especially in a side street.

He began to feel almost feverish. With shaking fingers he separated the bank notes and started counting them. He felt like a professional poker player picking the hand just dealt to him. He was on a treasure hunt. This one is a twenty-dollar bill, and here's another, and another twenty

followed by yet another; he had trouble controlling his
fingers in his excitement. He was close to fainting. It
seemed to him the next bank note took something like
eternity to show itself. It was a five-dollar bill.

The five was followed by a similar one, and then
another one, and when he glanced at the last one in the
pack he felt a pain grip his heart and tasted bitterness
in his mouth at the thought that it, too, was only a five-
dollar bill and there were no more. No more surprises.

Regaining his composure he cast his eyes up and down
the street. Nothing was moving, not even the leaves of a
maple nearby.

They add up to a hundred dollars, whichever way I
count them, he observed, and then suddenly he was struck
by uncertainty. He didn't know whether to laugh or cry. I
must return this found money to its rightful owner; the
thought pierced him to the quick. What a loss it must be
to someone reaching into his pocket for it and finding
nothing! He felt the pain as if he had himself lost that
wad of money. And what if the person who lost it is as
poor as I am? He went on torturing himself. The wife
who probably sent him to do the shopping is waiting for
him at home with two hungry children. What am I to
do? The question tore his conscience. Yes, yes, but there's
no one around I can ask: Pardon me Sir, but did you
happen to lose a wad of money?

He had no idea how much longer he would have stood
there by the curb of that empty sidewalk if a car had not
passed by whose driver gave him a curious, inquiring look.
Pedestrians looked suspicious in this strange new world.

Tamas quickly put aside his wrenching scruples and
slipped the money in his pocket. Slowly, almost stumbling,
he continued on his way to the bus stop. I'll use this
money to call Iren and the kids, he decided, and the idea
made him feel happier. His pangs of conscience ceased,
and he felt relieved, lighter, freer, and unsullied by sin.

In the central office of the telephone company he

spent a long time just standing around and gaping without anyone taking notice of him. Finally he ventured up to one of the windows on the long counter, and using mostly body language, he communicated his needs to the smiling lady there. She asked for all kinds of documents and identification papers. Luckily, since he was also going to visit Evelyn in the Immigration Office, he had all his papers with him, including the brown temporary passport with the immigration permit tacked to it by a paper clip. That seemed to satisfy the official requirements. The smiling lady photocopied these documents and handed them back to Tamas. She even filled in the questionnaire for him. At first, he was peeved at this; she probably thinks I am illiterate just because I don't speak English. But when she pushed the form in front of him for his signature he had to admit it was a good thing his language skills had not allowed him to express his peevishness, because he would have stood helpless till the following morning if he'd been left on his own to face the endless questions and quantities of information in that confounded form.

And then came the unpleasant surprises: he had to pay the first month's basic charge and the rent of the telephone set, all of which seemed modest enough, but then they added the fee for having the line connected. After examining the total bill he fell into a moment of panic, searching all his pockets, until he remembered which one had the wad he had found that morning. He fished it out and carefully picked out the required amount: twenty-five dollars. He still felt guilty about that money, but he wondered now what on earth he would have done if he hadn't been lucky enough to find it.

The telephone number assigned to him included the digits 911. Almost the same as the fire department, he observed.

She promised to have the line connected by the early part of the following week. He did not have to stay home to wait for the linemen; they could do their job without him.

He walked out of the telephone centre's offices with the satisfied feeling of a job well done and headed toward his next destination – the Immigration Office. He had to take the streetcar again, as the government offices were all located in the heart of the city.

The congestion in the city streets was already reaching its peak. Wherever he looked he could see endless lines of cars, practically grown together, forming one long steel chain. Tamas was horrified by the sight.

In the streetcar, he started wondering if he should drop by to see Eugene first; it was to be a brief visit, as he only had to give him his permanent address and phone number. He spread the city map that had all the important points marked – all the places he had to deal with. After studying it, he came to the conclusion that if, instead of getting off at the third stop, he went to the fifth, got off, and walked three blocks at a right angle, he would end up at the welfare services of the central pastoral office. Then he changed his mind again and decided to go seek out that Evelyn first.

According to Father Garnini's card, her office was on the second floor of the tall glass and steel structures, so he took the escalator. The office he wanted was marked with such huge letters that even the blind could not have missed it.

He had to enter through a double door into a waiting room big enough to hold at least a hundred people. The centre part was taken up by chairs arranged in neat rows, most of them already occupied. Some people were reading newspapers, holding a book or a magazine; some were twiddling their thumbs, some just staring into space with a vacant expression. In the left corner there were two kids making a racket on a well-worn rug. One of them had a toy truck in his hand and the other a clay clown.

The chairs faced a long counter, running from one

wall to the other. Behind it there were at least ten clerks receiving clients. The conversations were subdued. Only scraps of words wafted in the direction of Tamas, and he understood very little. He looked around in vain for an usher, or at least for a sign to tell him what to do, until he noticed that the new arrivals, people who came in after him, went to a small machine and tore a slip of paper from it. He did the same. His chit had the number 233 printed on it. Looking toward the counter again he noticed an electronic number display above every clerk. Number 167 was being served.

I have a long wait ahead of me, he thought. I should have gone to see Eugene first. By the time I get through here, he'll have left his office. He was getting worried. His eyes wandered to the clock on the wall. Well, it's only two-thirty now, he observed, trying to stay calm. He eased himself into a nearby chair.

Over a half an hour later the numbers were slowly climbing higher on the digital displays. He was annoyed with himself for not bringing something to read. And then a lightning bolt out of the sky: it occurred to him that he had promised to meet Walter in the lobby of the Chamber of Commerce. He felt heat rising inside his body. Beads of perspiration formed on his forehead. Well, I screwed that up, he told himself. It's too late, I'd never get there in time. And it's more important for me to see Eugene. I'll tell Walter the truth and he'll forgive me. I have a lot of urgent business to take care of, and he'll understand.

When he woke from his reverie he noticed they were already at number 232. Then suddenly his number came up.

A young man with auburn hair and a thin moustache was the next available agent. Tamas took out Father Gardini's card with Evelyn Kinney's name on the back and placed it on the counter.

'I'd like to speak to this lady,' he stuttered, pointing at the back of the card.

The young man turned around and disappeared among the other administrators with the card in his hand. After a short interval he returned with a blond lady in a trim white blouse and blue skirt.

'I am Evelyn Kinney, how can I help you?' she asked in a soft voice.

Tamas kept nervously shifting his weight from one foot to the other.

'Father Garnini sent me here,' he blurted out, but then he had to stop, because even the few words he had rehearsed were suddenly gone.

'Oh, yes,' she mumbled. 'Father Garnini. Oh yes. In other words, you need an interpreter,' she concluded in a tone that was turning increasingly dry.

She turned back to the young man with the thin moustache. He went off and then in another short interval that seemed like eternity to Tamas, he returned in the company of a younger lady. The girl smiled encouragingly at Tamas, who immediately relaxed. He returned the girl's smile.

'Today I'll be your interpreter,' she said softly with a warm glow in her eyes.

'I came here on the recommendation of Father Garnini. I would like to file an application for my family's immigration.' He turned to Evelyn while the girl fluently interpreted.

'Yes, indeed.' Evelyn stopped to clear her throat. 'Reverend Garnini called me asking for my help, but I had to explain to him that this is a State-run agency, and everybody is supposed to be treated equally. No one gets special consideration,' she intoned in a colourless, official tone.

'But I'm not asking for anything outside of the normal channels or anything that may conflict with official procedures.' Tamas tried to force a smile on his face as he looked hopefully at the administrator. 'I was only hoping that the recommendation might speed up the paperwork.'

'In other words you were looking for special treatment,' said Evelyn, furrowing her brow in a display of displeasure. 'What do you call this, if not seeking special treatment? There's no room for such things in this office.'

Tamas wished the earth would swallow him up. He had come prepared for everything except this. 'I wanted nothing but to have my wife and children with me as soon as possible.' He spoke before he had time to think. His throat tightened up again. He wanted to elaborate, but Evelyn was the first to speak.

'Let's see your papers. What documents do you have with you?'

'Here's my passport.' He pulled out the brown passport and opened it where the permanent residence permit was attached.

The official took the package from him, leafed through the passport, and unfolded the residence permit. She seemed to scrutinize every entry with great attention.

'This is all in order.' She placed the documents on the counter, and from a drawer below she produced an application form. She was still flanked by the young man and the interpreter. She started filling out the form.

'You have an apartment?'

'Yes,' Tamas answered readily and showed the address written out on a page of his note pad.

'Telephone number?'

He pointed it out.

'Your employer's name and address?'

'I have not yet found... I'm going today to the employment agent of the welfare services of the church,' Tamas said and swallowed hard.

'So you're unemployed?' she asked, raising her voice suddenly so that everyone was looking at her. 'Under the existing regulations, if you have no job, you cannot file for the immigration of your family.'

Tamas felt a lump in his throat and perspiration in the palm of his hands.

'You've got to understand, once and for all, that no one here is entitled to special treatment. A person, who has no job, no regular income, cannot bring his family here. Period.' She picked up the papers and handed them to Tamas.

'Come back again when you've found a job. Goodbye.'

She had barely finished the last word when she turned on her heels and waved to the interpreter to follow her.

Tamas stood before the counter, devastated. The young man spread his hands with a sour grin of sympathy, indicating that the audience was over; Tamas was free to leave.

He was in a daze as he made his way out of the crowded office. Close to sobbing and his hands clenched into fists, he could scarcely see or hear as he trudged back to the escalators.

He halted there and stood motionless for a time. People were rushing past him; some of them even had to bump into him to get on the moving stairs. He took no notice of any of that, as if turned to stone, with his gaze lost in the distance.

He came to himself slowly and stepped on the escalator. There were tears in his eyes then, not just one, but almost a stream that made two deep furrows on his face. He clenched his hands again. I'll show these bureaucrats. I will have a job inside a week, he whispered.

With the city map spread out in front of him, he looked for the 'X' marking the welfare office, and then he headed for the streetcar stop.

He found his way to Eugene Mazur's office without any problem. In the ornate lobby of the already familiar, venerable old building he had to knock twice before getting any response. Opening the door he found himself confronted by Eugene's always-cheerful face. The

administrator politely rose from his desk and leaned over
to greet Tamas like an old friend.

'I'm glad to see you again. Just today I spoke about you
to Christine; you remember the lady you met here before.
But what am I talking about – why don't I just ask her to
join us and translate.'

He grabbed the phone and dialled.

'She'll be with us a in a second,' said Eugene rubbing
his hands with satisfaction and sat down again behind his
desk.

In less than a minute Christine's slender figure slipped
into the room.

Tamas got up and accepted the hand she extended
toward him. It was soft and warm.

They both sat down on a bench against the wall.

'What can we do for you today?' asked Eugene with
friendly concern.

'I have good news,' said Tamas taking some papers
out of his pocket. 'Yesterday I moved into my apartment,
and today I ordered the telephone to be connected,' he
continued, fishing out the folded copy of the contract and
handing it to Eugene.

The administrator took a glance at the papers, and
then entered the address and phone number into a ledger
in front of him.

Christine and Tamas waited for him in silence to
finish writing.

'Well, we're all set.' Eugene looked at the young man,
'I have all your data on file.'

Tamas's jaw dropped in disappointment.

'And what about a job?' he asked.

'Oh, yes. All in good time. As you can see the
country's whole economy is in recession, and our region
is particularly affected. I think I brought this up at our
earlier meeting.' He looked at the interpreter to emphasize
his point. 'There are very few openings available.'

'Yes, but I thought I understood that as soon as I had

an address and a phone number I could get a job,' Tamas said with desperation muffling his voice.

Christine seemed to understand Tamas's feelings as she watched the scene. She hastened to expand on her colleague's assessment of the situation. 'Perhaps what he said at the time didn't quite sink in,' she said to Tamas, and to soften the blow she put a hand on his shoulder.

Observing the drama in progress in front of him, Eugene took a questionnaire from a desk drawer.

'Let's just see what kind of work you can do. Do you have a trade?'

'Anything!' Tamas blurted out, looking at Eugene defiantly.

'You can't possibly have experience in every field,' the official said, smiling.

'Hands-on experience in every phase of construction, and the past few years I've been in a supervisory position. But here I know I'll have start all over again. Besides, construction is at a standstill. So what I am saying is, I'm willing to accept any kind of work in the meantime.'

'Janitorial work, too? Cleaning rest rooms?' Eugene looked up from his notes.

'Yes, anything. There's no line of work I would refuse, as long as it's a regular full-time job with regular pay.'

In his mind's eye he could see Evelyn's expressionless face as she shrugged her shoulders and intoned icily: 'No one gets special treatment here; if you don't have a job, a regular monthly or weekly income, you cannot file for the immigration of your family.' He got cold shivers now. His shirt got soaking wet from perspiration.

Christine noticed the change in the young man.

'Is anything wrong? Are you feeling all right?' she asked with concern.

'No, nothing.' Tamas shook his head, 'I am all right really, it's just that I worry a lot when I think about my family. I have not seen them for a year, and today in the Immigration Office they told me that I cannot apply for their immigration before I get a full-time job. If I can't even set my application in motion, who knows how long it will take. I'm afraid it may be years before they can join me here.'

'On the other hand, I do have some good news for you,' Eugene said trying to reduce the tension suddenly taking over the room. 'Monday there'll be a new language course starting here in this centre. You could enrol now. The cost is minimal, only fifty dollars for the whole course, which covers the educational materials involved; the teachers are volunteers,' he said smiling again at Christine as if expecting an answer from her.

Tamas immediately perked up.

'That's terrific, something I wasn't even counting on.' He looked hopeful again.

But then a new thought clouded his face.

'And how is it scheduled? In the morning or the afternoon?' he asked anxiously.

'It's an intensive course, offered daily from nine to twelve.'

'But what if I get a job in the meantime? In that case...' his voice lost its momentum, '...in that case, I will not be able to attend classes?' He gave Eugene a piercing look even though he was pretty certain the administrator had nothing to do with the scheduling of classes.

'In that case, no, it would not work for you,' said Eugene wearily. 'But new classes are starting at the centre all the time, including afternoon and evening classes for those who already have a job. I suggest you sign up for this class now, and if you get lucky and get a job before the course ends, you can always transfer to another class. Eventually everything will work out, you'll see. Time will solve every problem.' He nodded encouragingly toward Tamas. 'Let me assure you I'll do all I can to put you to work, because I've never met another man as determined to succeed as you are, my friend.' And with that he got up from his desk, holding a hand out toward Tamas.

Tamas said goodbye to both of them a little too quickly, and he was already halfway out the door when Christine told him to wait for her in the hallway, she had something to say.

'Eugene's become very fond of you. You can be sure your future is in good hands,' she said when she joined Tamas a few minutes later. 'Among our employment agents he has the highest success rate and the widest circle of friends among potential employers. Monday, you can start that language course; it's a step in the right direction. Don't worry yourself about anything except moving forward – one step at a time. One step at a time.'

Tamas listened to her politely and heard what she said, but he was in no mood to work through what it all meant in reality.

'Anyway,' she added, her face smoothing into a smile, 'I want to invite you to our home for dinner. How would Sunday suit you? I am good in the kitchen, even if I say so myself. It must be a long time since you've tasted good home cooking. I'll cook chicken soup and beef goulash, and for desert, floating islands. What do you say to that?'

'My favourites! How did you know I like all three of those dishes so much?'

'Just a lucky guess. You'll have a good time with us. I have a little boy, Patrick, and a daughter, Wanda, who's at the university. A very nice person, you'll see.'

WALTER FELT he was back on top of the world after hearing Cameron's news about the opinion polls. He remembered Melanie saying to him that his life was guided by one ideology alone, the ideology of battle. 'I've never met anyone who was so ready to fight over everything,' his wife often remarked.

He expected to find Tamas waiting for him in the lobby before his interview with Zeno. Something must have happened, he thought with irritation, and he left a message with the desk at the entrance telling Tamas where he should look for the studio, just in case he showed up.

In the third floor studio, he greeted Zeno hurriedly in the busy crowd. The stagehands were bringing in a table and two swivel chairs, and the two friends paid little attention to each other until they were already seated facing the glaring studio lights. Walter was shocked by the care-worn expression on Zeno's face that he saw on the small control monitor.

'Anything wrong?' he whispered when they were past the microphone test.

'No, no problem,' Zeno answered softly, adjusting his yellow tie.

The director waved, holding the fingers of his left hand aloft. The signature tune of the show started, then three fingers, two, one, and Walter was on.

'Welcome to this week's edition of *The Walter Wallmeyer Show*. Our guest today is Mr Zeno Langdon, the chief executive officer of the local Farm-Fresh poultry processing company, a family-owned but sizable enterprise.'

Walter began with introductory remarks, and a few general questions about the meatpacking industry, moving on to questions about the future plans and expansion strategy of Zeno's company.

'Are you planning any layoffs?' Walter asked unexpectedly.

'I'm happy to say we're not,' Zeno answered. 'There were fears for a time that we might have to downsize the workforce by 33 to 36 employees, but thanks to the efforts of our engineers and marketing department, and the leadership of the local labour union, we are not contemplating any layoffs as of this year.'

Once out of the glare of the studio lights, Walter invited Zeno for a glass of beer, and led the way to the studio's cafe on the other side of the hallway.

'You did well.' Walter patted his friend on the shoulder. 'The union leaders should be pleased.'

'I've already let them know the time of the broadcast.'

'Just before the recording you didn't look so well. You looked like a chicken facing the slaughterhouse of the Farm-Fresh company.'

'Oh, it's nothing, I'm just tired,' Zeno answered apologetically and then took a large swig of his beer.

'Are you sure?' Walter looked his friend in the eye. 'I've never seen you like this.'

'Sylvia wants a divorce, that's all.'

'I don't get it.'

'It's not complicated. She wants a divorce, and that's that,' Zeno said, looking away, visibly upset by the subject.

'You messed up, did you?'

Zeno was silent for a few minutes.

'I can't understand it myself, Walter,' he said then. 'You know, I've had affairs once in a while. But now something strange has happened to me. Just over a month ago I met a girl. Still in college. You were there – it was at your nomination session.'

'I'm sorry, there were so many people there, I don't remember anyone in particular.'

'I gave her a summer job at the plant's sales department.

And then she started flirting with me, or maybe it was me who started it; it's hard to tell now. The fact is I fell for her. Passionately, like a teenager.'

'And Sylvia found out?'

'She must have, because this morning she said she'd had enough of me, she wanted a new life and decided to get a divorce.'

'If I remember correctly, she's the sole owner of the company.'

'Yes.'

'So where does that leave you? More than two decades of your life and labour gone?'

'Maybe I'll get a job somewhere. I know this business inside out, someone's bound to offer me a job.'

Deep in thought, Walter kept turning his beer glass on the wet counter. The news came as a surprise to him. A shock. He searched his mind for words of encouragement and advice, but couldn't come up anything meaningful to say. Somewhere in his soul he saw a shipwreck looming ahead of him, too.

'Perhaps there's a chance you can make up with Sylvia,' he said somberly.

'Too late. And I don't really want to either.'

A server walked into the almost empty bar, apparently to check the place. She looked over the customers, the status of their drinks, and then left again. She was in her early twenties, in a light blue skirt. Her long, braided pigtail was swinging like the pendulum of a grandfather clock. The two men's vacant eyes followed her every move.

'I feel completely drained,' Zeno said. I was waiting for a miracle all this time, but I don't see one coming to my rescue. Today I had to make up my mind.'

They finished off their beer. Zeno was the first to stand up. He went to the bar and paid the tab. 'And how are things with you?' he asked on their way out.

'You don't want to know.' Walter waved a hand in

resignation. 'Barely keeping my head above water. Or only up for one more breath.'

'Melanie?'

'She's fine, no problem. She's been really good to me lately, kinder than ever, very supportive.'

On parting at the entrance, they shook hands, each trying to search the other's face. Neither of them could see through the tangle of troubles that clouded both their faces.

*   *   *

'How did it go?' Dora asked, when Zeno returned to the office. 'The interview.'

'Okay, I think.'

She looked at her boss with a worried expression, apparently aware of the strain he was under. 'More of the machinery arrived this afternoon,' she reported.

Unexpectedly, he felt very close to Dora again. Almost as close as when they used to meet to make love in the company apartment.

'Sylvia wants a divorce,' he said in voice drained of all emotion.

'What did you do?'

As logical as it was, the question came to him as a surprise. He tried to read her face, looking for a smile or a frown. But she turned away, seemingly to examine the potted plants in the corner.

'Well?'

'It's happened before, a little fling, now and then. Weeks and months later, it was always all in the past and forgotten.'

'And now? Isn't Wanda one of those?'

'If you know all about it, why ask?'

It must have hurt Dora when she had become aware of the Wanda affair. She was jealous as usual whenever someone got too close to Zeno, including Sylvia.

'Is it serious? I mean this relationship with Wanda?'

'Yes, I am afraid so. I think it's an obsession. In my sober moments I tell myself it's madness, but the next minute my mind goes blank again. The age difference between us is huge, and yet the attraction is fatal.'

'What you need is rehab for sex addicts.'

'Maybe. But I wonder why she wants a divorce now after all these years.'

'Maybe you didn't give Sylvia much of a choice.'

'In my own way, I've been a good husband. I've been working dawn to dusk to build her firm. Because it *is* her firm. It's all hers. I don't own even a fraction of it. Not even a paper clip.'

His face transformed, reflecting more sorrow than resentment. He looked at Dora, wanting to say something kind in return for her sincere concern. He could see her once again in his arms, hear himself whisper sweet nothings like in the old days, but the image soon became fuzzy, and then his mind again a clean slate – wiped clean of the romantic memories. He knew they could never be restored.

'Sit down with her and talk it over,' Dora said, shattering the brittle silence. 'You could ask her for more time, so that both of you could think it over. This should not be her decision alone, not when it comes to a question concerning both of you.'

She stepped over to the window. She idly drew the curtains, and looked out at the company parking lot. A car pulled in to the part reserved for visitors, and a woman jumped out of the car. She started running away, but then she changed course and turned back to the car. In the meantime, a man sprang from the driver's seat and shouted something to the woman, who in turn charged at him, hitting him with a briefcase in her hand. The man held his arms over his head in defence.

'Don't make a hasty decision,' said Dora. She walked away from the window and left her boss alone in his office.

—*Chapter 46*—

TAMAS ALREADY HAD THE KEY in the door of his apartment when the door across the hallway opened. A bushy-haired, lean boy in his early twenties was standing there. His black eyes seemed unfocused. Tamas took one look at him and turned away, even though his first reaction was to say hello.

'Gaspar. Hi!' The neighbour boy held a hand out to Tamas. 'Linda told me to look you up. I've been keeping an eye out for you for hours. Sure looks like you've been out all day,' he said, speaking Tamas's native language, swinging his arms nervously.

Tamas looked at the fellow reluctantly. Nevertheless, he accepted the hand held out to him. It was soft and moist with perspiration.

'Linda suggested I go to you for help with anything, because she thinks you've had more experience, and I feel kind of lost here,' the boy said, shifting the weight from one foot to the other to the rhythm of his arms as if shuffling in one place. 'I told Linda I want to go home, I can't make it here, I can't stand it here, this world is too alien to me.'

'In that case, why did you bother coming here?' Tamas asked with irritation, not knowing what to make of him.

He unlocked his door, and beckoned with his head to the boy. Gaspar followed in an almost servile manner into the apartment. He left the door ajar.

'Go back and shut the door, will you?' Tamas said without much enthusiasm, and put his bag on the kitchen counter. Then he led the way into the living room, and sat down in the armchair.

The boy stuck his unkempt head through the doorway. 'Can I come in?' he asked quietly.

'Sure, sure.' Tamas was impatient. He was in no mood for company, especially that of an uninvited stranger.

The boy stood stock still in the middle of the room. He had dirty blue jeans and a well-worn, wrinkled plaid shirt.

'Pull up a chair,' Tamas growled, and the boy followed his instructions like a robot.

'Okay, tell me what's up?'

'Well, I figured...' the boy started and stopped, and then he started again, 'I kind of figured if I came here, I'd be all set, things would work out for me.'

'And who was going to make them work out for you?' Tamas wanted to end this conversation, or at least put it off till next morning.

'Well, in a new...what I mean...in a new country I'd be okay. That's what everyone said.'

'Were you homeless back home?'

'No, not really...just sort of...yes.'

'What do you say we continue this conversation tomorrow? I've had a very long and very tiring day.'

'That's fine with me. Tomorrow will do me fine.' Gaspar shrugged his shoulders as he headed for the door.

'Please put the chair back where you found it!' Tamas reminded the boy irritably.

Gaspar turned back, casting an uncertain look toward Tamas. He picked up the chair and put it back by the table.

That evening the world did not bother Tamas again.

He was awakened in the morning by thunderous banging on his apartment door. He glanced at the alarm clock. It showed ten thirty. He could not believe his eyes. He hurried to the door and opened it, forgetting that he was still in his pyjamas. He found himself confronted by two hefty policemen. Uniformed and armed. He looked at them in panic. So after all this time he was going to be arrested and brought back home. He cursed himself for not having looked through the spy hole. He had got too confident too quickly here. He hadn't even checked the window of the apartment for an escape route. He had no idea what to do now.

Not a word passed his lips as he stood there motionless.

Then he caught a glimpse of Gaspar's messy mane behind the policemen. Finally, giving way to their body language more than to their words, Tamas opened the door wide and let all three of them in his apartment.

One of the officers of the law went straight for the armchair and took it over. The other one went through the apartment, looking into every nook and cranny, and then he sat down in one of the chairs by the table. Gaspar seemed stuck, standing in the middle of the room. He looked like a badly executed piece of sculpture representing the personification of catastrophe.

Tamas stared at him. 'What's this about?' he asked, trying not to sound too frightened.

'I was only hungry,' the boy mumbled.

Tamas was bewildered

'I went into the store, but there was no…'

'What are you talking about?'

'There was no money left in my pocket.'

'But what does that have to do with me? Why are you here?

'Well, the store said I stole something, so they called the police, and then I called Walter's office. He talked to the police. He told them to come to your place, and wait for him here.'

'Walter Wallmeyer? How do you know Walter?'

'He was with that Bertold character.'

'In the Immigration Office?'

'Uh-huh…'

'So you stole something from a shop – that's why you're here.' The relief Tamas felt was overwhelming. 'This is just about some shoplifting you did?' The sense of immediate terror left Tamas, but all the same, he kept looking from Gaspar to the policemen and back. He could not fathom a reason for Walter sending the police to his apartment instead of to Gaspar's. Was there any chance that Walter had connections to the Eddy's Bar set, and knew the real reason Tamas had to flee his home? The silence of the policemen worried him. He was at a loss.

The uneasy impasse was broken when suddenly the door burst open and Walter came in.

'Good morning, everyone!' he greeted the silent group and then turned to Tamas. 'I'll tell you all about it, but first I'll have to talk to the police.'

Without pausing he switched languages as he addressed the men in uniform. One of them handed him the police report about the shoplifting episode. He read it carefully before returning it.

'Fine,' he said to the policeman. 'Can I have a copy of this?' The policeman nodded.

'My boy,' he turned to Gaspar's murky eyes, 'you'll have to go with the police, down to the precinct. But I've talked to the shopkeeper, and he agreed to drop his complaint against you. By the time you get to the precinct I'll be there and I'll bring the owner of the store too.

'I'll see you gentlemen later,' he said to the police, and then turned to Tamas. 'And I'd be grateful if you'd wait here; please don't go anywhere until we get back.'

The policemen got to their feet and muttered something resembling a goodbye. They hauled a cowering Gaspar off with them.

When everyone was gone from the apartment, Tamas set off for the bathroom. He stepped into the shower and turned on the cold water tap full blast, hoping to regain his equilibrium under the cool stream of water. It helped a little, but not enough to stop him panicking a few minutes later when there was another knock on the door. This time he took no chances; he peered through the spy hole. Walter was standing outside.

'Very unpleasant situation. Lucky thing I happen to know the owner of the store. I featured him and his store in my column once in the paper I work for. Ever since, he can't stop thanking me,' said the journalist coming into the apartment. 'I saw Gaspar home just now.'

Tamas closed the door behind him, showed Walter into the living room, and offered him a seat.

'Hard to imagine why such an aimless, unmotivated person was ever brought to this country,' Walter sighed as he took the easy chair. He volunteered no explanation of why he had told the police to bring Gaspar to Tamas's apartment, and Tamas thought better of asking.

He explained how the case was continuing in the police precinct. Even though the shopkeeper was willing to drop charges, the culprit could not just be allowed to go free. The judicial process still had to take its course. He looked around the apartment.

Tamas followed his eyes.

'I have nothing to offer you except instant coffee. Can I make you a cup?' asked Tamas, and turned immediately to the kitchen cabinet.

'Thank you, I think I'll have a cup. I see you are settling in. You've got a cosy place here; Spartan, of course, but it's a home. I suppose when your family joins you, you'll be looking for a bigger place.'

The word 'family' rattled Tamas again. He could see Evelyn's face as she intoned icily: An immigrant who doesn't have a job and a regular income cannot apply for the immigration of his family.

He made coffee for them both and sat down at the table.

'Anything wrong?' Walter inquired.

'Not really. Maybe things have not been going my way lately.' He said nothing about the fright the visit from the police had given to him, but he described the shock he experienced in the supermarket and how he would not be allowed to start the process of bringing his family in until he had a job.

'Don't worry, all in due time. By the way, I had my TV show taped yesterday. Why weren't you there?'

Tamas told him how long he had to wait for his interview at the Immigration Office, and then he had to go and see Eugene, the employment agent at the pastoral welfare agency. It had all taken so long that he had missed the recording of the TV show.

'And did Eugene enter your name on the list of those actively seeking employment?'

'Oh, yes, he did, that's all done, but the problem is there are so few job openings.'

'Yes, yes, I know you're impatient. But give it time, and you'll see everything will work out,' Walter assured him, as he stood up from the table. 'This weekend I'm going to be very busy, but the following weekend we'll have you over for dinner. I've already cleared it with my wife, Melanie. So get to work, start studying the language, because Melanie is a professional, a language teacher, and she'll give you a test.' Walter smiled at his threat.

'Today I signed up for a language course. I'm starting Monday.'

'I was sure from the beginning that you were not one to stay idle.'

—Chapter 47—

Murder in Hotel Odéon
—XVI—

'So are you going to tell me what you were doing in Victor's hotel room the night he was murdered?' Hugo asked Lidia finally.

'Viktor called me before midnight asking me to go up to his room, because he'd had a spat with Valerian and he was in need of moral support. A shoulder to lean on. When I entered the room Valerian was already gone; he must have left only minutes before. According to Viktor the argument was about something trivial; apparently Valerian had been acting strangely. Every little thing gave him an attack of the nerves. They say he's been behaving like that ever since that fight you two had over Viktor.' Lidia stopped to take a breath. She was obviously enjoying herself, reliving the excitement of the story. 'It must have been two in the morning when I left him. I think I was quite successful in consoling him. As you well know I have a trick or two up my sleeve. What happened afterwards is beyond my imagination.'

'Where did you go from the hotel?' asked Hugo at once, without waiting for Lidia to finish her story.

'Where? Strange question. Where did you think I went? I went home. Where else would I have gone? Don't I have to make an appearance every morning at my place of employment? I do have to get some rest.' She was looking at the Mayor angrily.

'Can you prove you were at home by two in the morning?' asked Hugo brusquely.

'What's got into you, Hugo? Have you changed jobs with Detective Mueller? I didn't think this was Police

Headquarters.' Lidia's voice was attracting curious looks from tables nearby.

'Forgive me, I went too far,' Hugo said, toning down his voice. 'I got a little carried away. This unfortunate business has worn me out, too. I really liked Viktor, liked him a lot, and perhaps that's why I overreacted.'

'Don't worry about it. That's all right, I can understand you.' Lidia looked at Hugo with sadness. 'Yes, I can prove I got home about two A.M. I found I didn't have my key to the front door of the apartment house with me, so I had to wake up the building superintendent, who, needless to say, treated me like a potential housebreaker. On top of that, he created such a scene that every tenant in the building was woken up. But that's another story.'

Hugo was sitting bent over, deep in thought. He took a few sips of his tea and then shifted his gaze back at Lidia's face.

According to her story it was not Valerian who killed Viktor but someone else. But what if Valerian later changed his mind and went back to the hotel? Hugo was mulling over what he had heard. It was a good thing Artur had asked for an appointment for this afternoon; maybe he could throw some light on the mystery.

He turned to Lidia. 'What else did the detective ask about?'

'All he said he was going to let me know if he needed me again.'

'What would he need you for? Didn't you demand to know?'

'Why should I care? It's enough for me to know I am not connected with the crime. The rest is up to the investigator, it's his business.'

'His business, his business, but...'

'Why shouldn't I cooperate if I can?' She made a gesture of helplessness as she looked at the man. 'Do you have some objection?'

'Come on Lidia, what are you talking about? Why

should I have an objection? For my part, I also hope our investigator friend…' he pronounced the word 'friend' in such a tone as to make it clear he meant the opposite, 'will soon be able to close the case.'

'Who knows? Maybe yes, maybe no. He cannot be having an easy time of it.'

'Did Detective Mueller ask about our Club?' Hugo looked up unexpectedly like a hunter ambushing his quarry.

'Yes, most definitely. He asked a lot about Eddy's Bar. He wanted to know what kind of clientèle frequent the place, how many, what they have in common, what ties them together, what the special events are, and did I know Viktor? And of course he asked about you and Artur.'

'And what did you say?'

'Just generalities.'

'What do you mean by "generalities"?' He again raised his voice. 'What generalities? What did you actually say?'

'Just that we had a circle of friends who liked to get together and pass the time relaxing. That's all, nothing else.'

'Did you name names?'

'There was no need. Mueller had his own membership list.'

'Membership list?'

'Yes. Membership list. He had it in front of him in a folder on the desk. He was reading out some of the names from it.'

'Would I know any of them?'

'I suppose so. It's not often that strangers visit us.'

'That's not what I meant.'

'You mean the prominent citizens among them?'

'Yes, of course.'

'Hugo, really, you're so full of yourself!' Lidia burst out laughing, and her tinkling trills again raised a few eyebrows at the neighbouring tables.

'Please, keep it down, you're attracting attention!' He tried to restrain her.

'Sorry, but I could not help myself. What's done is done. All right, I'll be quiet from now on.' The girl put on a serious face again.

'And what did you say the Club members had in common?' Hugo tried to steer the conversation back to business.

'Look, if you insist on going on like this, I am not willing to say another word. Please, I beg of you, stop interrogating me. Why are you like this to me? If you really want to know: I did not give away anything concrete, any bare facts. After all, Mueller's business is to get the murderer and not sniff around the life of our friendly circle.'

Lidia was slowly tearing her napkin into tiny pieces. Every question Hugo put to her resulted in a nervous tremor on her face. She was not her usual self in spite of her efforts to pretend she was.

'And now it's really time for me to get back to work!' She leaped to her feet, making ready to go with or without Hugo.

'All right, just one more thing,' insisted Hugo. 'Did you tell the detective that you too visited Viktor on the night of his death?'

'No, I didn't,' sighed Lidia quietly and took a step away from the table. 'If anything happens, I'll get in touch with you immediately,' she whispered, waving goodbye to the Mayor.

Hugo stayed behind at the café table. He poured out more tea from the porcelain pot. Chances are Valerian did not go back to Viktor on that terrible night, he thought still stirring the tea in his cup.

Lidia could not have committed the murder because, according to the pathologist's report, death occurred between five thirty and six in the morning, about sixty minutes after the amputation of the sex organ. If Lidia got home by two that night, and she has witnesses to prove it... No, it doesn't make sense.

Hugo was struck by the realization that, in that case, Valerian had to be the perpetrator.

Chapter 48

THEY WERE TO MEET at nine A.M. in the parking lot of the city's largest shopping mall. It was Walter's idea; he thought it safer if they went from there in Barbara's car to the small airport where she kept her plane. At this early hour the huge parking lot was practically empty and easy to survey from every direction. If anyone was following them it could be readily detected from a distance. He told Melanie he was going to the fitness centre and then to the tennis court, so she should not expect him back before dinner. Caroline, as soon as she heard about her father's plans, announced she wanted to go along. Walter had a hard time talking her out of it. His daughter made a face and even let slip a swear word that shocked him, but he pretended not to have heard.

They were already in Barbara's car, on their way to the airport, when the morning's scene came back to him.

'Caroline can't stand it if you ask her to do something she doesn't feel like doing. And she swears like a trooper, my little girl...'

'Didn't you know? Girls can get into a towering rage that will outdo anything a boy can produce.'

'I won't disagree with you.'

'Don't even try,' Barbara said, letting out a long laugh. She reached over and stroked Walter's hair. 'Hey, loosen up, be happy. Soon we'll be flying free of these earthbound cares. You're going to like my new flying machine. I think it's fantastic. So far I've flown it only on break-in flights with Ted, our mechanic. He's impressed by its engine power, and by the way it manoeuvres in the air. So forget everything else, enjoy the flight and the bright blue sky.'

But Walter could not relax. He could not shake off the tension and anxiety that had been building up inside him during the past week and was slowly taking over his whole being. Even Barbara's good mood irritated him. He would have liked nothing better now than for the day to end, for it to be evening already, to be at the dinner table with Melanie and his daughter.

'Are you going to make love to me up there?' said Barbara suddenly, grabbing his hand.

'Make love? What on earth are you talking about? A plane in the air is not like a car parked on a lonely road!'

The image popped into his mind, because indeed it was in a car that they had first had sex.

'I'll show you how it can be done. I bet you've never made love in mid-air before.'

'Actually, no, I haven't,' he answered with something close to irritation; he had no interest in sex at the moment.

'Don't be so stuffy!' Barbara was trying to cheer him up. 'You look as if I were leading you to the guillotine.'

She was laughing at her own joke, making Walter's nerves feel even more raw.

For a while they drove in silence. Not a cloud in the sky. It was an especially lovely summer day. The air was clear, so clear that the snow-capped mountains could be seen a hundred kilometres away.

'Cameron called me a couple of days ago.' Walter broke the silence while adjusting the safety belt on his shoulder.

'I was just about to ask you how your problems were working out,' Barbara said, throwing him a quick side-glance.

'He came to an agreement with Bradley Northrup.'

'Right.'

'They will pay his debts. In return, the blackmailer will give us a month's delay.'

'Yes, I know. What else is new?'

Walter became alert. 'How did you know?'

'Didn't you tell me about this agreement?'

'When did I tell you?' asked Walter.

'The last time we met,' she said without hesitation and

without looking at him, concentrating all her attention on the road.

'But the last time we met was before this whole business started,' Walter remarked pensively, searching his memory for any occasion when he could have discussed Bradley Northrup's blackmail proposal with her.

'You mentioned it on the phone. Just think about it.'

'Ever since they started tailing me, and perhaps even tapping my phone, I have not talked about these matters outside the election committee,' said Walter, annoyed. He was trying to figure who could have been Barbara's source of information, but he could not come up with a satisfactory explanation. Maybe she's right, he conceded in his mind, I've been so harassed lately, it's getting to the point I don't know what I'm saying.

The small airport for commuter airlines and private planes was more than half an hour from the city, but as it was Saturday, the highway had very little traffic.

When they got to Hangar 8, Ted was already waiting for them, impatiently pacing by the plane outside.

'Good morning Mrs Redwick, and good morning Assemblyman. I was hoping you'd get here earlier,' he said almost brusquely, as if in a hurry to be somewhere else. But then, turning to Walter he added in a friendlier tone, 'It's my son's birthday today, and I am supposed to take him to the amusement park.'

'One minute, and we'll be done,' she assured him.

'I've checked out the plane again. All set to go. Filled up both fuel tanks, all the way. I wrote down all the radio frequencies you need. The note is on the instrument panel.'

'What else should I know, Ted?' Barbara, too, was getting impatient.

'The side wind from the south is strong today. Remember that on takeoff. That's all. I've got to get moving. When you come back, roll the plane back into the hangar. Happy landings!' Ted added by way of farewell and then hurried off.

Barbara and Walter walked a full circle around the plane. The bottom half was cream-coloured and the top brown with two white streaks in between. Barbara ran a hand over each of the rubber tyres of the landing gear. She opened the door and climbed into the pilot's seat. Walter followed her in from the other side. Barbara looked around in the cabin before she placed the headset on her head. First she turned on the electricity, then switched on the two-way radio. She took out a clipboard with Ted's radio frequency list fastened to it. She set the two-way radio to the required frequency and told Walter to put on his earphones as well, saying that was the only way they could communicate. In the earphones the airport's weather report came on. The WHI ten o'clock report: Runway 16 assigned to takeoff, the direction of the wind, temperature, the height of the sparse cloud cover.

'This is wonderful weather,' she added through the headphones.

Walter nodded.

After Barbara got the plane ready for takeoff, she switched the radio to the frequency of the airport ground traffic control.

'Fox Echo Bravo to Control.'

'Tower to Fox Echo Bravo.'

'Fox Echo Bravo at Hangar 8, two persons aboard, WHI report acknowledged, preparing for an excursion flight at 6,000 feet altitude, touching Ban Point and back according to flight plan filed yesterday, requesting permission to taxi to Runway 16.'

'Fox Echo Bravo permitted to taxi to Runway 16.'

'Received, Fox Echo Bravo.'

The last plane landing was still on the runway ahead of them. Barbara waited for it to get out of the way before she pulled the speed control. The engine responded with a roar and the plane lunged forward, rapidly gaining speed. She watched the speedometer and slowly pulled the control stick toward her. The plane rose slowly, smoothly.

With her right foot, she pressed down on the directional control pedal, adjusting to the drift of the wind.

At a thousand feet she let up on the gas, watching the RPM of the engine, the altimeter, and the compass. In the meantime she got in touch with the tower to notify them of her intention to switch to radar frequency but report back when she reached Ban Point. They continued their ascent. At six thousand feet she turned on the autopilot. Underneath them, a map of geometrically arranged farmlands was taking shape.

'Having fun?' Barbara turned to Walter, putting a hand on his shoulder.

Walter was sitting stiffly in his seat with the headset still on.

'You can take that off now,' Barbara urged him, laughing again. 'I'll take care of everything that happens up here. Well now, are ready to make love to me?'

'I thought you were kidding.' Walter looked at her, taken aback.

'Come on, kiss me!' She leaned over.

Walter didn't make a move.

'Are you afraid?'

'Yes, a little.'

'What do you mean by a little? One's either afraid or not,' said Barbara.

'In that case, you can say I'm afraid.'

'I told you not to worry. This plane is ultra safe. Don't be silly, come and kiss me.'

Walter let her kiss him. But he didn't feel anything. Except perhaps indifference.

He didn't resist at first when she reached into his pants and started playing with him.

Then, with a shiver, he pushed Barbara away.

'Leave it alone,' he said sharply.

The plane was moving smoothly through the air, encountering no turbulence. The engine was purring evenly. They could have been standing still.

Barbara, visibly hurt, withdrew to her seat.

'It's been bothering me ever since this morning how you knew about the agreement between Cameron Fowler and Bradley Northrup,' he said, looking at her with suspicion.

'I knew, that's all.'

'Through Cameron?'

'No, I've not talked to him. I'm trying to understand why you're so uptight and unbearable. Tell me, do you love me at all?' Barbara was sounding querulous.

Walter was silent for a time. As if he had run out of words.

'I was thinking it would be best for both of us to end this relationship,' he said finally, looking out the right window. 'It's getting more and more troublesome.'

'Walter, you've gone crazy. Why break up now? Why? Don't I love you enough? Now that I've devoted years of my life to you, you've decided to give it all up, now you want to dump me?' Unusually, Barbara kept raising her voice; in it rebellion was mixed with desperation.

'I'm afraid your love has become something of a burden!' said Walter.

'A burden? For Heaven's sake, I sacrificed my marriage to be with you. You're a horrible beast, that's what you are!' Barbara, furious, was screaming at the top of her voice now. 'Well then, you might as well know who I am, you wretched nobody, you freak!'

With a sudden move Barbara turned off the auto pilot and grabbed hold of the control stick.

'If you really want to know: yes, it was I who hired that Mr Northrup, I and I alone! Did you hear that?' Her voice was a furious screech. 'I don't want you to move to Ottawa, and so you shall not. – You dance to my tune, Walter!'

The whole world suddenly turned dark before Walter, he could no longer hear or see. He grabbed Barbara's throat and started squeezing it. The woman fought back, desperately struggling to free herself from Walter's stranglehold.

—Chapter 49—

I T WAS SATURDAY, and Tamas had no agenda for the day. No bureaucrats to deal with. It seemed like a good day for him to catch his breath. He considered walking down to the creek and stretching out on the grass. Thoughts criss-crossed his mind, but an hour later he found himself still inside, still sitting in the easy chair with the empty coffee mug in his hands, gazing into the distance. He was back home, talking with Iren about everyday problems, and then he went outside with the boys to play in the yard, under the huge linden tree. He could see the old neighbours, the engineer couple whispering into his ear that he was in serious trouble.

A knock on the door roused him from his reveries. He jumped to his feet frightened, remembering the police visit of yesterday. He caught a glimpse of Gaspar's unkempt mane through the spy hole.

Reluctantly he opened the door, giving the boy a questioning look. Gaspar remained standing there without a word.

'Well, all right, come in,' said Tamas finally, nodding in the direction of the living room.

Gaspar stopped in the middle of the room and waited for Tamas to lock the door.

'I hope you haven't got yourself into more trouble.' He tried to decipher the boy's face.

Gaspar kept his silence, frozen to the spot.

'Why don't you sit down?' Tamas said, trying to hide his irritation.

Gaspar sat down by the table. He dropped both hands in his lap but seemed unable to open his mouth.

'Can I help you with something?'

No answer.

'If you don't talk I'll never find out what your problem is!' Tamas urged.

'I need money,' the boy said finally.

'You need money? Didn't you get some from Bertold?'

'Yes, I did.'

'And? What happened to it?'

'I've spent it.'

'On what? Food?'

'No.'

'Tell me for God's sake what you've spent it on!' Tamas was running out of patience.

'I bought grass.'

'Grass?'

'Yes.'

'You mean drugs?'

'Umm, yeah.'

'Are you crazy? You have nothing to eat, but you go and buy grass?'

'It wasn't any good.'

'So you got taken for a ride as well?'

The boy was silent again.

'And now, what do you need the money for? For more drugs?'

'No.'

'Then what for?'

'I'm hungry.'

'Of course you are, if you've wasted all your money on grass. Is that why you tried to steal? Because you were hungry?'

'Not today, I didn't want to steal. I promised Walter that I wouldn't steal any more. Not here,' he added in a low voice.

'You've brought enough attention on us already.' Tamas was bitter. He was trying to think of a way to help this helpless, hapless fellow. He barely had enough to eat himself. And he had only twenty-five in cash – all that was left of the money he found.

'I'm selling my easy chair,' Gaspar volunteered, this time without prodding.

'Your easy chair? So what are going to sit on?'

'I have two chairs, they'll do,' the boy was mumbling.

'And how much are you asking?'

'Ten will do.'

Tamas did not take him up on the offer.

'Not too much, is it?' Now it was the boy's turn to speak.

'And what can you get for that, to fill you up?'

'Milk and bread. It'll be enough for that.'

This seemed reasonable to Tamas. Not only that, but he saw the possibilities of having a second easy chair. But not this way! Not through the helplessness and misery of a poor fellow immigrant. He looked at Gaspar thoughtfully.

'Okay, bring it over.'

It didn't take a minute, and the boy was there with the easy chair.

'Put it next to the other one,' Tamas directed the boy.

Indeed, the two easy chairs looked much better together on either side of the coffee table; they made the place look like a home.

'Here you go, ten bucks.' Tamas ransacked his pockets for the bank note and then handed it to Gaspar. Then he suddenly pulled out another ten-dollar bill and added it to the first one.

'Take it, another ten,' he said quickly, 'before I change my mind.'

'But that makes it twenty,' mumbled the boy in confusion.

'Yes, twenty. Put it away. But take care how you spend it, because I have no food in the house and no money left either, so don't expect any more.'

As soon as Gaspar left, Tamas sat down in the newly purchased easy chair with a heavy soul. He found it just as comfortable as his own. It had the same style and colour, too. In his mind's eye he could see the boy gulping down the bread and washing it down with milk.

The easy chair bargain though gave him a pang of conscience. He felt he had taken advantage of Gaspar and robbed him of his rightful possession. It was only later the thought struck him that the chair might not even have been Gaspar's to sell.

He was on the verge of running across the hall with the wretched easy chair. But then he compromised with himself. I can think of it as a loan. I can sell the chair back for the same price, any time he wants it.

In the end he carried out his earlier plan and went out to the creek. He felt homesick and sad.

Chapter 50

Tᴇᴅ ᴛᴏᴏᴋ ʜɪs sᴏɴ to the amusement park and didn't get back until late afternoon. His wife was waiting for him in a flurry of excitement. There was a phone call earlier that afternoon about Mrs Redwick's plane. It was missing with two people on board.

Ted ran to the phone and called the airport control tower.

His call was redirected twice before he could talk to a controller.

'Yes, this is Ted Rider, the aviation mechanic from Hangar 8.'

'Tower Supervisor Roger Olson. Are you the one who got Mrs Redwick's plane ready for her flight this morning?' His voice was sombre.

'Yes, it was me. I checked it out and refuelled it. Why do you ask?'

'The plane disappeared from the radar screen forty-two minutes after takeoff and lost radio contact at the same time. It did not report back from Ban Point where it was planning to turn back.'

'What if they saw a nice pasture and decided to land?'

'She filed a flight plan for an excursion flight. The plane is not on its planned course. As far as we know it has disappeared.'

'That's impossible,' answered Ted, feeling his throat going dry. 'The plane is brand new. I've taken it personally on a total of twenty hours of shakedown flights. I checked out every part of it, every instrument. Are you sure it's Mrs Redwick's plane that's gone off the radar?'

'Absolutely,' said the supervisor.

'I don't understand,' Ted stuttered. 'I checked out everything. Everything was in perfect working order when

I handed the plane over to Mrs Redwick this morning.
I even warned her about the southerly wind, that she
should take it into account on takeoff.'

'Do you know who her passenger was?'

'Sure, I even said hello to him when they arrived.
Assemblyman Walter Wallmeyer, that's who he was. They
had flown together before in the old plane.'

'Are you sure?' the voice insisted.

'Dead sure.'

'The chief wants you to get in your car right away and
come out to the airport.'

'Yes sir, right away. I'll be there as soon as I can.'

There was a deadly pallor on his face when Ted
replaced the receiver.

'I've got to go out to the airport at once. I've got to get
out there at once,' he kept repeating to his wife and son.

'But what about my birthday?' His son burst into tears.
'You promised a surprise, a surprise present.'

'All right, all right, as soon as I get back home you'll
have your surprise. You'll see. And you'll never guess what
it is,' said Ted trying to console the boy. 'When I finish
there, I'll come straight home,' he said by way of goodbye,
and without a backward glance he stepped out the front
door.

At the airport Ted headed straight for the office of
the security chief. He had had some minor business there
before. He knocked on the door.

Albert Reed was about fifty, a completely bald, big,
heavy-set man. At first sight he made a threatening
impression because of his bulk, and anyone who didn't
know him was inclined to stay out of his way.

'Ted, sit down,' he instructed, pointing to a small desk
in the corner, 'and write a full report. Write down how
you prepared Mrs Redwick's plane for this morning's
flight. Include everything to the smallest detail, giving a
full account of your activities yesterday and during the
night...'

'I did nothing during the night,' Ted interrupted. 'I slept.'

'That's all right Ted, put it all down on paper, and don't forget this morning, what you were doing before you handed the key over to Barbara. And then describe Mrs Redwick's state of mind as you observed it. Was she excited? Nervous? Did you notice anything different about her?'

'No, Sir, she was her usual self, friendly and cheerful, like always.'

'Fine, Ted, put that down, too. Furthermore...' the chief paused here as if undecided on the next point.

'Name the man who accompanied Mrs Redwick...'

'Walter Wallmeyer, the national assemblyman, Sir.' Ted cut the question short again.

'Not assemblyman, only a candidate for the assembly,' Albert Reed corrected the mechanic. 'How did you know him?'

'I've often seen him on TV. Some time last year he flew with Mrs Redwick in her previous plane.'

'Fine, Ted, put that all down on paper without omitting the smallest detail. When you're done, you can leave.'

'But is it true they can't find Mrs Redwick's plane?'

'I'm afraid so. It disappeared from the radar screen without sending out any distress signals. And she did not follow the flight plan she had filed. Okay, now get to work,' Albert said, nodding toward the small desk.

When he eventually received the report, he went over it, asking additional questions and confirmations, and then summarized his judgment, 'Good work, Ted. Thanks a lot!'

'No problem, Sir,' answered Ted. 'Tomorrow is Sunday, my day off. So how can I inquire about Mrs Redwick's plane, if it should turn up?'

'Just call me directly,' said Albert, producing a name card and dismissing the mechanic.

Ted was feeling deeply disturbed when he got into his car. He didn't let it cross his mind that he might never again see Barbara and Walter alive; but when he got home and gave his wife a hug, his hands were still shaking from the strain of the day. He gave evasive answers to his little boy when he tried to question his father about the missing plane.

'Maybe, my boy, we're worrying about nothing, and everything will turn out fine in the end,' he said, stroking the boy's head.

—Chapter 51—

Murder in Hotel Odéon
—XVII—

WHAT COULD HAVE BROUGHT Viktor to the Hotel Odéon the night he was murdered ? Hugo was wondering. Viktor was not in the habit of frequenting hotels. He always had his dates in private apartments. Never in motels or hotels, or any other place used by the public. He must have had a date with someone who did not have an apartment and didn't want to be seen at Viktor's place. It must have been the murderer who convinced him to take a room at the Odéon. Yes, this is what must have happened, the only possible explanation, the Mayor decided.

The more he weighed the possibility, the more complicated the case seemed. Suddenly he glanced at his watch. He had been sitting in the café for a whole hour.

Elsa was waiting for him with the news that he had missed a lot of calls. She had a list of those whose business could not be put off.

When Hugo glanced at the list, he could see that Detective Fabian Mueller was one of the names on it.

So the investigator thinks the time is ripe for a more thorough questioning, he mused, and then lingered over the echo of the word 'questioning'.

Lidia's account of the murder came back to him, and this time it made him think about it in personal terms. Let me see, it took place very late on the night of April third, but more like the morning of April fourth.

Where was I that night?

He reached for his appointment calendar. It was not to hand on the desk. He looked through the drawers. Nothing.

He panicked.

I must find that diary at once! The desperate words rumbled through his mind in dismay.

He renewed the search, this time feverishly. He searched every drawer, every nook and cranny, but he couldn't find it even on the bookshelves. The failure ratcheted his nervous tension.

As he stood, frozen with helplessness, in a corner of his spacious office, he suddenly had an idea: maybe Elsa had the diary. It was she who always entered the appointments.

He immediately called her in.

The secretary entered without delay and with a business smile on her face.

Hugo's eyes latched on to the grey cover of the diary in her hand. He did not refer to it, but instead made a comment about the Prefect as he walked up to Elsa and quite matter-of-factly and without a word took the notebook from her hand.

As soon as he was alone, Hugo fell upon the appointment diary with a vigour he didn't know he had.

He concentrated his attention on events recorded a few weeks earlier. He surprised himself with the eagerness of his curiosity and the nervous energy it generated.

I'm acting like I was about to discover in this notebook the answer to the big question: who murdered Viktor? he upbraided himself.

No, he whispered.

But yes, but yes! Yes, I've been out of my mind with despair and painful disappointment, and yes, I'd wished Viktor's death. He ran his trembling hand over the clean surface of his desk as if seeking to calm himself with that gesture.

Oh, my God, How could I be his killer? I who can't even hurt a fly! he cried out voicelessly.

He completely surrendered himself to the accelerating

rhythm of the words tumbling through his mind. His heart too adjusted to the out-of-control pulsation.

What kind of a manic feeling, what kind of unknown instinct is at work inside me? – he was questioning himself, infuriated.

With shaking fingers he kept turning the pages of the notebook in front of him.

It was a secret, a deep, dark secret he was after.

There was bad blood between the two of them. He was angry with Viktor for having left him for Valerian. For jilting him.

He left me! He left me! He let the syllables drop one by one, the words that had such a horrible meaning for him, something beyond belief.

And I loved him so much! he whimpered, almost without noticing. He kept turning the heavy pages of the diary faster and faster, with obsessive, crazed effort. His hand suddenly came to a halt in mid-air and slowly went limp, as a bird falls when hit by a shot in flight.

He looked up.

Like someone waking from deep sleep, he slowly let his gaze wander around his office room. His hands were no longer shaking. From the depths of his soul an ache was gushing up in a thick, black stream.

April the third.

The diary markings for the day took up a half a page.

At eleven A.M. he was at a meeting of the City Council. Lunch in the afternoon, from one to two. Then an open office period till three-thirty. Followed by a meeting with the members of the committee investigating the building collapse. Consultation in the Prefect's office at six P.M. At seven-thirty an evening at the theatre. *The Physicists* by Dürrenmatt. He read the last line again.

No, that couldn't be right! He had absolutely no

recollection of seeing that drama, or of attending a performance of any kind at the theatre in recent weeks.

But then, where was I?

Where was I? Where? He kept repeating the question with the desperation of someone who already knows the answer but refuses to accept it.

—*Chapter 52*—

S YLVIA WAS NOWHERE to be seen when Zeno got home from the plant on Friday night.

Her car is in the garage, so where could she have gone, he was wondering, as he went through the house looking for her. He finally found her in the downstairs darkened suite, with the shutters closed. She was lying in bed. The place was illuminated only by a few rays of streetlight that managed to sneak in through the gaps between the slats of the shutters. He barged in with so much noise that he was sure he must have awakened her. Her silence, however, was unbroken when he stood still for a while. He also became aware of Sylvia's gentle snoring. He retreated on tiptoe, very carefully.

The scene made him feel bitter again. Even if the flames of youthful love between them had died down some time ago, he was used to her company; she was always around. He knew every little gesture of hers, how she reacted in a given situation, what she was going to say, how she would lick her lips with the tip of her tongue when she was nervous. It even occurred to him that he should check the sleeping pills; if anything happened to her, he would feel responsible. But no, her life was now in her own hands; she wanted nothing to do with him.

She's no longer willing to share a bed with me. She's moved out of the master bedroom. This is another way she wants to humiliate me, to show her moral superiority, to put me in my place.

He would have been shocked if he had listened to himself under normal circumstances, but these weren't normal circumstances, and he had wounds to lick.

Although he was hungry, he did not bother with supper. Tired and depressed, he returned to the bedroom.

As he undressed he tried to decide how to spend the weekend, two full days that he had free, because Wanda could not be with him. She had been assigned the job of shepherding visiting students from the University of British Columbia and she would be busy till Monday night.

Before turning off the reading lamp by the bed he was thinking he would go back to work Saturday, spend the day there doing various chores, and on Sunday he might be able to think more productively.

The next morning, he woke earlier than usual. He walked out to the kitchen to make himself breakfast. He found Sylvia already there. She was setting the table. There were two of everything, from which he guessed that his wife was not entirely spurning him. She greeted him with indifference.

'You gave me quite a scare last night,' Zeno complained. 'I searched the whole house for you. You might have told me you were taking refuge in the guest room. I hadn't expected that.'

'I can't understand what stuff men are made of. It always surprises me that every time you men do something unforgivable, you act the part of the injured party.'

'You're right, of course. If we're to get a divorce there's no reason for us to sleep in the same bed,' conceded Zeno, buttering his toast.

Sylvia placed a tomato on her plate, but before quartering it with her knife she looked at her husband.

'Do you have any idea, Zeno, what it means to truly love someone? What it means to want that person body and soul, every minute of every day, wanting to breathe as one with that person, to look for his every glance, to desire his caresses, the touch of the skin, the lips, to imagine the world together, to plan a life together? Do you know what it's like to wait for the loved one night after night, to anticipate what goes on in the mind of the other, how to make that loved one only yours, while you hope you can surrender yourself to your lover? To think of the one you love as the most important thing in your life, without which you simply cannot exist?'

Sylvia took a long, emotional look in front of her. In her words, the tone of resignation, the loneliness of facing unknown future, and the pain of the present blended together.

'I've read your letters to Wanda,' she said abruptly.

Zeno stopped eating, unable to meet Sylvia's gaze. He was shocked. So someone hated him enough to turn over copies of his letters to Wanda. Who was it? Who could have done it? The question kept torturing him.

'What you wrote in those letters, how you feel about someone else – how can you expect me to live with that?' she went on bitterly. 'No, I don't have to carry on as if nothing had happened and live with this misery,' she said, now choking in tears.

He looked at her in surprise. He understood the words his wife was saying only too well, but he was unable to feel or respond to her emotion.

'Yes, Sylvia, I love her. Why should I deny it? I love her with my whole being, and I can't explain why. She's much younger than me, a thoughtless flirt, you'd probably say she's a slut. But she has a hold over me, she radiates an irresistible attractive force with such intensity that, in spite of my better judgment, I can't tear myself away from her. I know this makes no sense to you, and I find it hard to explain it to myself. She's there with me wherever I go, in my mind, and I'm incapable of banishing her, eradicating her, or pretending she didn't happen. I can't help it. I'm sorry. You can tear me to shreds, burn me, and flush my ashes down the toilet, but I'll still be saying that I love her.'

Sylvia got up, pulled the lapels of her bathrobe tighter, and left the kitchen without giving Zeno another look. Later, much later, he too rose from the kitchen stool, gathered the dirty dishes, put them in the dishwasher, and pushed the start button.

All the way to the plant he was racking his brain over the question: who could have been that wretched scum who had spied on him and presented his wife with the incriminating love letters?

—*Chapter 53*—

B Y THAT AFTERNOON the media were beginning to report the bare facts of the missing private plane, starkly stating that earlier that morning Barbara Redwick, the wife of the multimillionaire Elmer Redwick, had taken off in her single-engine Cessna and in less than an hour, her plane had disappeared into thin air. Some of the newscasts mentioned one other person aboard, and according to unofficial rumours that person was none other than Walter Wallmeyer, the well-known journalist for the local daily *Monitor*, and a candidate for the National Assembly in the upcoming elections.

Melanie was so immersed in the lesson plan for Monday's classes that at first she didn't pay attention to the details of the announcement.

But on catching Walter's name her ears pricked up. Her initial impression was that perhaps she had misunderstood the names in the news item or else someone was pulling a practical joke on her husband.

She called Caroline down to the living room and asked her if she had heard the news on the radio.

Caroline was listening to a heavy metal band. 'Me? The news on the radio?'

'All right, princess, I was only asking,' said Melanie, shaking her head in resignation.

She tried to think of someone to call, someone who might have heard the news. Cameron probably keeps a tab on everything that's going on, she was thinking, as she looked for his number. A woman's voice answered at the other end.

'This is Melanie, Mrs Wallmeyer. I'd like to speak to Mr Cameron Fowler,' she explained.

'One moment please, I'll get him for you,' answered the voice.

'Hello, Fowler here.'

'Sorry to bother you on a Saturday, but I heard a strange item on the radio news, and I don't know what to make of it. They said...'

'I know,' he interrupted Melanie. 'I know about it.'

'Is this true, or some bad joke?'

Cameron had been notified hours earlier about the disappearance of the plane with Walter aboard. He could not believe it either. He had to check and recheck several times to make sure what he had heard was true. And then the phone started ringing off the hook, the members of the election committee were calling, one after another, all anxious about the news. They unanimously decided not to convene until Barbara's missing Cessna was found.

'The situation is as follows...' Cameron launched into a long-winded explanation, but Melanie, knowing what was coming, interrupted him.

'Is it true or not that Barbara and Walter are missing in an airplane?'

'Yes, it is,' Cameron groaned, but could not continue with his speech.

'How long have you known?'

'Now look...' The man tried to regain his authoritative tone, 'That's not how these things work. Just because the airport report says they cannot find the plane, it doesn't necessarily mean we have to assume the worst possibility. It's conceivable they had to make an emergency landing. Anything could have happened. During the afternoon they sent out several police helicopters to search the area for the plane. Forty-two minutes is not such a long time, they could not have flown very far, and they'll be found soon now. In other words...' But his words were only echoed by silence from the other end. 'Melanie, are you still there?'

'Yes.' The answer came in a whisper which slowly amplified into sobs.

'Melanie, you'll see, there's no reason to imagine the worst, and they'll turn up yet all right. Let's keep our hopes up.'

'Yes, yes, you're right, but…' she answered, choking on her own words. 'You know even if they do turn up all right, I can't stop thinking of him choosing to be up there flying with Barbara now, and…'

'I've warned Walter often enough that he should break up with Barbara, but…I'm really sorry, Melanie, I've done everything in my power. Believe me, Melanie, I did. Melanie, are you still there?'

'Melanie, Melanie?' he asked again.

'Yes.' There was a faint voice.

'As soon as I hear anything from the police I'll give you a call. And now, you just try to relax and take it easy,' he said, without conviction.

'Thanks.' Melanie's voice fluttered through just before the phone went dead.

The conversation left Cameron more upset than before, as if infected by Melanie's despair. He couldn't sit still for a minute; he kept pacing his apartment, not knowing what to do with himself.

Long minutes crept by before he managed to call the police air traffic safety unit. He asked them to hold back notifying Walter's family until they knew something definite – that is, until they found the missing plane.

He knew it was a pointless effort to gain time. He regretted making the call as soon as he hung up. Melanie obviously had a right to know what had happened to her husband. He opened the liquor cabinet. His hand hovered nervously over the bottles, looking for something strong to put his mind in a fog. While he was pouring himself a cognac he heard the phone ring next door. He picked up his glass and hurried to answer the call.

'Hello, yes, go ahead, this is Cameron Fowler speaking.'

'The captain of the aviation safety unit would like to speak to you,' a female voice said. 'Please hold on.'

'This is Captain Rudolph Sorensen speaking, the captain of the air traffic safety unit. I was asked by one of my colleagues to call you first before contacting the family of the victims.'

'What do you mean by victims?' Cameron responded without thinking.

'Almost an hour ago we found the missing aircraft. Unfortunately the pilot and her passenger had lost their lives. The plane crashed into a barn.'

'Good God,' Cameron said, feeling his knees about to give way. Then he pulled himself together and continued. 'Captain, can I ask you a favour?' he said hesitantly.

'Sure, go ahead.'

'I would like to ask you to choose your words carefully when you talk to Mrs Wallmeyer. She's a very sensitive and fragile soul. Sorry to bring this up, maybe it's stupid of me, you people are more experienced in such matters… You know how to deal with the situation.'

'Yes, I understand, Sir. Good talking to you.' The voice died away almost on the dot punctuated by the click at the other end.

Cameron continued standing there, frozen to the spot with the receiver still in his hand. He couldn't seem to put it down.

*   *   *

Caroline peeled the earphones off her head and set off toward the kitchen in search of something to eat. On her way she was distracted by the sound of throat-choking sobs.

At first she could not decide where the noise was coming from. She tried a few rooms, and then in the master bedroom, found Melanie lying flat on the large bed. The sight froze her to the spot. She ran to her stepmother, grabbing her hand, and talking in a soothing tone.

'What's wrong? Please tell me what's wrong? What's happened to you?' she kept asking. It was more an entreaty than an expression of curiosity. She had never seen her stepmother cry before, and she automatically reached out to console her, to give her a hug, to stop her sobs.

'Your father,' came the disjointed words finally from the woman's chest.

'What about my father?' the girl asked, feeling Melanie's hysteria affecting her nerves, too.

'I don't quite know, not quite sure, apparently...'

'Tell me, Melanie, please. What are you trying to say?' She held Melanie's hand and stroked her brow.

'It's missing, they can't find it...'

'What's missing?'

'The plane...'

'Melanie, please, I beg of you, what is it they can't find?'

Melanie's eyes were red from crying when she looked up, and then she broke into sobs again. Caroline knelt down by the bed and touched Melanie's hair with a soothing hand. Then she remembered Melanie asking her about a news item on the radio just half an hour earlier. She leaped to her feet and ran downstairs to turn on the TV. There was a lengthy documentary on the usual news channel. She switched to the next, going up and down the channels, punching the buttons on the remote. One of them flashed her father's picture but since the sound was turned down she couldn't hear a word of the report. By the time she raised the volume the picture was gone and another news item came on. She kept playing the remote control like a keyboard until she finally came to a local channel that was just starting its news hour. She stopped and listened intently. The anchorman's voice was sombre –

'...We have to start with a news bulletin about a shocking tragedy. This morning a four-seat Cessna private aircraft bearing the markings FEB, with two passengers on board, disappeared from the radar less than an hour

after takeoff. The small private plane was piloted by Mrs
Barbara Redwick, the wife of Mr Elmer Redwick, the
well-known entrepreneur. Her passenger was Walter
Wallmeyer, a contributing editor of the local daily, the
Monitor, and the Conservative candidate for the National
Assembly. Around noon the police instituted a search by
sending out two helicopters. A few hours later one of
them found the missing plane. For reasons still under
investigation the single-engine Cessna crashed into a
remote farm building and exploded on impact. The two
people on board did not survive. The commander of the
special air traffic safety unit informed us that the plane
was in the air for an excursion tour and expected back
at the same airport. More details of the accident will be
coming up later in this broadcast...'

The news item ended with Barbara's and then Walter's
publicity photo flashed upon the screen.

Caroline, with the remote in her hand, remained
standing as if turned to stone. Suddenly the various events
of the day fell into a pattern she could understand.

—*Chapter 54*—

T HE EXISTING ABATTOIR FACILITIES were undergoing maintenance work during this weekend downtime. The first person Zeno ran into in the corridor was Marcel, the leader of the union local.

'We saw you, boss, and heard you in yesterday's television broadcast. We liked everything you said. I mean, as far as this plant and its upgrading is concerned.' The union man was careful with his words.

Zeno felt more like a fellow employee when he patted him on the back and turned to move on.

Little does he suspect what's in store for them if indeed I have to take a hike; if he could read my mind right now, even that measly little smile would fade from his lips, Zeno was thinking to himself on his way down the steps.

He found Sander, the head of the new production line, surrounded by a group of construction workers. It turned out that the concrete slab on which the scalding tank was to be installed was not up to specifications; it needed to be stripped of its top layer and then covered with a thicker new layer. As Zeno approached the group he was greeted deferentially and then immediately brought up to date on what was going on. Sander added his own opinion to the report. He believed the thickness of the foundation did not have to be increased, claiming the existing slab was already oversized. 'If you want I can give it to you in writing,' he claimed, but none of the others was paying attention to him. Zeno too walked away with a smile on his face.

When he got back into the office he found Dora's answering machine blinking. He pushed the playback button. Cameron's familiar voice came on:

'– This morning Barbara's Cessna disappeared soon after takeoff on an excursion flight. Walter was also aboard. Please call me at the office. Cameron –'

Since he was not really paying attention at the beginning, he had to replay the message and listen more intently. He grabbed a pen and made a note of the phone number. In the meantime the machine went on to an older but not yet erased message:

'– Hello Dora, thanks, I received the copies of the letters. Heavy stuff. I'll get back to you later.'

It was Sylvia's voice. He was petrified, staring at the red button that stopped blinking and stared back at him steadily. He would have suspected anyone except Dora.

So it's come to this. Even my old flame has turned against me; the painful thought stabbed him to the heart. He could not decide which one of the two emergencies to deal with first.

He slumped down in his chair, too dumbstruck to make a move.

I'll wait till Monday to deal with Dora, he decided. I'll call Cameron now. What can I say? I begged Walter to stay away from Barbara, it was a sure bet that affair would lead to no good. But no, no; he would not listen to me. But who am I to talk?

Zeno's call reached only Cameron's answering machine. When Cameron called back, Zeno was no longer in his office, but huddled on a bar stool of a nearby diner. He was eating a sandwich when he learned the full story of Walter and Barbara from a television newscast.

The report stunned him. He had known Walter for years and years. They had attended many of the same official functions and receptions. In addition he had often consulted Walter, the economist, when he was faced with a tricky business decision. My God, he thought, how unpredictable life is! Thursday we're sitting together in a TV studio, and on Saturday he's gone. That's it. That's life. Past history. A piece of chicken from the sandwich got stuck in his throat and he had to cough it into his napkin. He put down the sandwich and asked for more water. It was time for him to go home and change.

Earlier Wanda had called. He had been about to lock up the office. He had hurried back to pick up the phone, expecting Cameron with fresh news. He had to shout hello twice before Wanda's voice came on.

'I wanted to surprise you.' She sounded very cheerful. 'I wanted to reach you in the office. I got lucky.'

'And so did I, because another thirty seconds and I would have missed your call. I was getting ready to go home. Where are you now? Has your timetable been extended?'

'That's why I'm calling. New development. There's only one team of students from Vancouver. The other team we expected for tomorrow is not coming. We'll have to host them next Sunday. That means we can spend the whole day together.'

'And how about tonight? What are you doing tonight?'

'I'm free. I'm all yours, if you want me.'

'Terrific, let's go out,' suggested Zeno, who didn't feel like spending the night at home.

'Try to get to my place by eight, I should be home by then. Mom asked me to pick up some kind of a special soap from a downtown boutique. I have to deliver that, and then I'll be on my way. Don't bother with the doorbell, just walk right in.' Wanda's voice was sparkling with happiness.

'I'll be there.' Zeno looked at his watch. It was only five-thirty; he had two and a half hours to kill.

*   *   *

Cameron Fowler could no longer prolong the agony; he had to convene the members of the election committee, now again in their nominating capacity. He decided to hold a meeting without delay, that very day, Saturday.

The news of the tragedy had thrown the high command of the Conservative party into total disarray. They had already regarded Walter Wallmeyer a sure winner. None of the party stalwarts had had any doubts that he would win the election.

Old in-fights between Walter's supporters and detractors were rekindled. Cameron escaped being made a scapegoat, but among the second echelon of party activists there were many who criticised him for failing to maintain party discipline. Knowing about Walter's escapades he should have kept an eye on him, should have kept him in line. In the end though, they all again agreed to burden Cameron with the job of nominating a replacement candidate. Somehow he was to find another candidate that was as effective as Walter.

Cameron knew he had no chance of finding such a candidate. None of the aspirants had the slightest chance in the general election.

By eight o'clock all five members of the committee were seated in the conference room of the election headquarters.

Among those present, Ralph was the only one who was quick to restate his earlier opinion: it had been a grave mistake to nominate Walter in the first place. He immediately nominated himself as a replacement. He was, he said, the most qualified to run, having planned and pursued his whole career in conformity with the goals and the interests of the party. His achievements in his life-long struggle with liberals were, in his estimation, unparalleled.

In the hours preceding the conference he had contacted every party activist who might support him, from the national party chairman to the local politicos. He lobbied Cameron, too, trying to enlist him on his side, but Cameron made it clear that the field was wide open, and all four candidates had to be given an equal chance at the nomination.

It was Miriam who spoke first.

'It's as if we're hexed,' she said bitterly. 'We field the perfect candidate, and he's taken from us. Let's face it, none of us is capable of trouncing the Liberal candidate.'

'Speak for yourself, Miriam,' Ralph said immediately. 'We know your own family situation is no better than Walt's was.'

'You'd better explain yourself,' said Miriam, looking at him with eyes that might have pierced armour.

'It's immaterial,' said Ralph, 'whether your husband left you, or you left your husband. The main thing is, you're on your own, unattached. With this kind of a background you cannot face the electorate. That's it in a nutshell.'

'I'm leaving,' Miriam said angrily, rising to her feet. 'I refuse to have anything to do with this person.'

Cameron ran after her when she left the room, but Miriam was adamant, refusing to return to the table. 'You men can go to hell!' she told him and left the building.

After this scene not even Ralph was in a mood for further debate.

'I propose we conduct the meeting in such a way that we have a concrete result,' Cameron said, resuming his role as the chairman. 'Ralph, you first, maybe you'd better tell us why you feel you have the best qualifications?'

'Don't expect me to sing my praises, because I am not in the habit of doing that.'

The others burst into laughter.

'Maybe as a speaker I am not as distinguished and eloquent as Walter was, but I've devoted my life to the party and stayed with it through thick and thin, even when its popularity was at its lowest ebb. All of you know that my entire life has been an open book, and I shall keep it that way.'

Ralph paused here looking at the remaining members.

'You, Mark, and you Alfred...' His finger wavered between them. 'Has either of you considered seeking the nomination?'

Neither of them answered.

'Does this mean you'll vote for me? What do you say?' and he kept shifting his gaze from one to the other.

'Yes, I think I'll vote for you, because I don't consider myself tough enough to take a beating,' said Mark with finality.

Since Alfred remained silent, Ralph now turned to him.

'I don't deny it,' Alfred spoke slowly and deliberately. 'It has occurred to me to ask for your votes. But recently I've been finding I get tired very easily. My health is not what it used to be. On the other hand, I'm very sorry that Miriam is not with us, and of course, Walter's death came as a terrible blow. Yes, Ralph, I am voting for you,' he concluded by casting a look around the table and snapping shut the notebook he had been holding in his hand.

'Ralph, you can have my vote too. So, long live the new king! Let's celebrate!' said Cameron with a smile and started to clap.

The others joined in the applause.

—*Chapter 55*—

Murder in Hotel Odéon
—XVIII—

It seemed to Hugo that everything was going against him. It had reached the point now where he was sitting at his desk, staring into space, paralysed. What was bothering him most was that the accidental concatenation of recent events might cause a drastic change in his life.

If Viktor had not got himself murdered, the spotlight would never have been directed at the members of the secret society. He was deeply disturbed by the real possibility that the press would get wind of the true nature of their parties at the Club; that would inevitably lead to a scandal of enormous proportions with consequences too frightening to contemplate.

For the past few days, he had even been toying with the idea of escape. Leaving behind the office of the Mayor, family, everything, and taking to the mountains.

Running away was not all that new to him; he had done it once before in his youth.

The memory of the adventure was still painfully vivid in his mind.

One summer morning he went through the ritual of getting ready to go to work. He was an intern at a multinational marketing company. Before going to the railroad station he mustered up all his fortitude as he laid the makings of a sandwich on the kitchen table. He spread butter on two slices of bread. Using the large butcher knife he produced thin, even slices from the salami, cut a piece of cheese and green peppers to go with it, and then placed the little meal into his lunch box.

He let his gaze wander around the kitchen once more, like someone taking his leave of the furniture. He let out a barely audible sigh, and then shut the door behind him.

Although his heart was beating furiously, he did not let it dictate his pace. In fact, he was walking a little slower than usual. At the tram stop he did not get on the first streetcar, which was jam-packed, but instead waited leisurely for the next one.

At the station he looked at the list of departures, picked out the next long-distance express, and bought a coach-class ticket for it. He ambled out to the track with a canvas shopping bag hanging from one shoulder, containing the lunch box.

The train pulled in five minutes late, but he hardly noticed; he was in no hurry to get anywhere. In his compartment he was the only passenger. He wasted no time in taking out his sandwich and slowly and methodically consuming it.

The train had been speeding along for more than half an hour when the conductor appeared. Hugo realized he sounded timid, almost suspiciously so, when he asked what the next stop was.

The conductor named Marosvar as the next city.

Hugo remembered an old classmate from high school who lived in that provincial town with his parents.

Soon the train squealed to a halt in front of a neat little station, decorated with planters full of begonias.

Hugo got off, and spotted a post office just steps away. Inside, there was a clerk who paid no attention to him and, in a corner, a table with a phone book. He looked up his classmate's phone number.

His call was answered by a warm feminine voice.

In less than a minute he was on his way to the house. He and his classmate had not seen each other for two years, but greeted each other as if they had parted only the day before.

He was led into the guest room.

The family members went back to their work on the industrial-scale vegetable garden stretching far behind the backyard, and sent the unexpected visitor to rest in the arbour closer to the house.

He went from fruit tree to fruit tree, admiring each of them, as well as the fresh shoots growing out of the recently pruned grapevines.

Then he went back to the house, asking what he could do to help.

'The guest is a guest, he doesn't come to work,' they said and put him at ease, handing him a bunch of glossy magazines. They encouraged him to sit at the picnic table under the walnut tree and relax there while supper was prepared.

After supper they all sat under the walnut tree late into the evening, talking about the past.

He woke with a heavy heart in the morning, hardly able to get out of bed. No doubt his parents had already reported him missing to the police. Maybe there was a search already on for him. His picture was probably shown on TV with the news, and that thought gripped his heart even tighter. He pulled on his clothing quickly. He was fully dressed, standing in the middle of the room when he realized his footgear was missing. His shoes were nowhere to be found. They were not where he had left them the night before. Finally he decided to look in the entrance hall in case he may have left them there. To his great astonishment he found his shoes in front of the door when he opened it. They were polished to the brightness of a mirror. Just like Grandma at home, he thought, overcome by emotion and even tears.

He bade a hasty and somewhat uneasy goodbye to his hosts, like someone with a bad conscience. But to be on the safe side, he thanked them at least three times for everything, and then, with his bag slung over one shoulder, he hurried back to the railroad station.

It was only on the train that he noticed that his lunch box was filled with all kinds of snacks for the road.

He didn't get back to his home town until late afternoon. He found himself facing his father's gaze, a look fired by rage. They stared at each other for a while without a word.

There was no smack across the face, not even harsh words.

They were already on their way out of the station when his father remarked in a very soft tone as if talking to himself: 'Boys are usually in their early teens when they run away.'

His mother on seeing him opened her arms, ready to embrace him; but in the last second she thought better of it and turned away with tears in her eyes.

There was never any discussion of this failed attempt at leaving home.

Now, reliving in his mind the details of his first escape and feeling the bitter aftertaste of the failed adventure, Hugo allowed a faint little smile to loosen his tightly closed lips. He dropped the ballpoint pen from his hand and, armed with a firm decision, he rushed out of the office.

He almost tripped over Elsa in the anteroom.

'I was just about to let you know that Artur Liptak, the attorney, is already here. Can I show him in?' she asked hurriedly, as they bumped into each other; but then, without waiting for the Mayor's answer, she opened the door to a small waiting room.

Artur quickly rose from a chair.

'I hope you don't mind my getting here ahead of my appointment,' said Artur apologizing profusely.

'Not at all. But you know I haven't eaten yet. I was invited by the Prefect for lunch, but he cancelled because

of some pressing business, and now I'm ravenous. So
would it suit you to have a bite with me?'

Artur nodded, and Hugo led the way out to the
corridor.

The lunch crowd was slowly thinning out and there
was no problem finding a table. The two of them sat
down far from inquisitive eyes and ordered cold salad
plates with mineral water from the young waiter who
followed them.

'I was anxious for this meeting with you, and that's
why I am here earlier than agreed,' said Artur but without
any trace of the nervousness that his words implied.

'Believe me, I was just as anxious to see you,' whispered
Hugo, patting the attorney's shoulder reassuringly.

The furrows in Artur's face, instead of relaxing,
tightened up, especially those around his eyes. 'I've
something to tell you. A detective named Fabian Mueller
ordered me to report to him at police headquarters,' he
said, watching for a reaction from the Mayor.

Hugo's face betrayed no surprise, and he responded
at his leisure.

'For what reason?'

'Actually nothing in particular. He claimed he just
wanted to have a chat with me.'

'And what did you say to that?'

'I just let him ramble on, hoping to see what he had
in store for us.'

'Did you know he called in Lidia, too?'

'Lidia?' Artur was surprised. 'What did he want from
her?'

'I'll tell you later; let's have your story first.'

'The detective wanted to know about my contacts
with Viktor. What was the nature of our relationship,
when was the last time I saw him, who were his friends,
and were you were among them. And he kept returning
to the question of the membership of our secret society:
what was it that we had in common, what brought us

together, what kind of meetings did we have. I have to confess my first thought was that Valerian was somehow involved in this line of questioning. I went to see him in the city jail and came to the conclusion that if he had blabbed anything to Detective Mueller, he'd never have the guts to admit to it. But let me go on with the details of my discussion with the detective: Mueller claims there were others who visited Viktor on the night of his death. I'm not sure what he meant by 'others' – two or three? – I wasn't in a position to ask questions. In any case, he was quite definite about one thing: one of Viktor's visitors was a woman.'

'Yes, he was right,' Hugo snapped back.

The attorney's jaw dropped.

'You know who she was?'

'Yes. It was Lidia who went up to Viktor's room.'

Artur turned a gloomy face toward the Mayor. But his voice was cold and expressionless.

'What was Lidia doing at Viktor's?'

'I asked her that. She says Viktor invited her over because he'd had an argument with Valerian, and he needed company, someone to chase away the blues.'

'Does Mueller know about Lidia?'

'No. Even though he questioned Lidia, she did not tell him that she spent any time with Viktor on the night of the murder.'

'What else?'

'I don't know, Artur. All Lidia told me was that she's letting Fabian find out if she was the female visitor he was talking about. That's his business.'

'Lidia's acting pretty cocky!'

'Cocky, yes, because she has an alibi.'

'Lidia?'

'Yes. She says the superintendent let her into the building at two in the morning, because she had left her key at home.'

'I suspected it wasn't Valerian who did it, because

now it's obvious that it was after his visit that Lidia went to see Viktor,' Artur said as he quietly drummed his fingers on the table.

'According to the pathologist, death occurred between five-thirty and six in the morning,' Hugo remarked meditatively.

'In that case another theory of mine may turn out to be the right one. It's quite possible that Valerian went back to Viktor, and perhaps not by himself. Or else what?' Artur snapped his fingers. 'I always had the feeling that if Valerian did not kill Viktor, then he is the only one who knows the identity of the killer.'

'What makes you think that?'

'I'm inferring it from Valerian's behaviour. Yesterday I confronted him with the question: Did you kill Viktor? He denied it in no uncertain terms.'

They both remained silent for a while. The young waiter brought the salads. With leisurely movements he arranged the forks and knives to line up with the napkins.

'The thing that bothers me most,' Hugo went on when they were finally alone again, 'is that the press might get wind of Viktor's association with us, however tenuous it was. And then everyone will forget about looking for the murderer; instead, they'll switch their attention to our little group and busy themselves tearing us apart.'

'Yes, exactly,' Artur said as he twirled his fork on the plate. 'We must do something to prevent that happening. The sooner the better. If possible, I'll go back to Fabian today and tell him Lidia was the female visitor.'

'And what if he asks you how you found out?'

'Why should he?'

'Most likely he will.'

'He hasn't put all his cards on the table either. In exchange for this information I'll ask him who the other visitors were, if he's succeeded in identifying them. Don't you see? It's all a game. Mueller is rummaging among us knowing perfectly well we had nothing to do with the crime. And yet he summons me, puts me on the spot, questions me, lording it over me. Why? Because he expects the key to the solution of the crime from us. He's trying to provoke us into helping him. All right, we'll help. But I'll suggest to him that he give us something in exchange, something to our advantage, such as assuring us that there will be no public exposure.' Artur stopped as if to weigh his words. Then suddenly he turned to Hugo. 'By the way, where were you on the night of Viktor's death?'

'I don't really know. I believe I was home. I was supposed to go to the theatre, but I can't recall now actually going.'

'What do you mean you can't recall?

'Just that. It's as if somehow someone had wiped the evening from my memory.'

'You're pulling my leg,' Artur retorted.

'No, I'm not. I'm serious. This morning I checked my appointment diary. For that night there is a play slated – *The Physicists* by Dürrenmatt. But I have never seen that play in my life.'

'So you have no alibi?'

'No!'

'And if Fabian asks you about it, what are you going to say?'

'I don't know. I'll check it out. I'll have to go over it in my mind, or make something up… I'll ask Nina.'

—*Chapter 56*—

SUMMER ASSERTED ITSELF with exceptional force that year. At times, it turned the city into a fiery furnace, baking the streets and buildings. These hot spells were interspersed by waves of cold air bringing heavy black clouds with them that closed down upon the city wedged between the Rockies and the prairie. The resulting showers could go on a week at a time, making the helpless inhabitants yearn for sunshine again.

'I'd like to have your child,' Wanda whispered passionately into Zeno's ear.

'A golden-haired little girl with pigtails,' he answered.

'Not a girl, but a boy.'

'I'd really like to have a little girl,' said Zeno. 'Sylvia wants a divorce,' he added.

'Because of me?'

'Yes. She claims my relationship with you does not belong in the category of minor, insignificant missteps.'

'So where does it belong?'

'With fatal love affairs.'

'With star-crossed lovers?'

'Maybe. Are you capable of being faithful, capable of true love?'

'I love no one else. I have no one else. I sent Paul away once and for all. I truly fell head over heels in love with you, Zeno – have no doubts about me. Please.' She pressed herself passionately against him.

Zeno was drunk on passion, on Wanda's searing touch. The world again seemed far away and wrapped in fog, unreal. Sylvia's image too flew away, along with the impending divorce, the loss of his life's work for the company, and the prospect of becoming a nobody.

'I'm following on Walter's tracks,' he announced suddenly.

'Walter? What do you mean?' she asked startled.

'Into non-existence.' Zeno gave a nervous laugh.

'Come now, stop scaring me!'

'I'll have nothing to fight for.'

'How about me?' the girl snapped back. 'Me! Look at me! Am I not worth fighting for?'

'Perhaps next week I can stop going into work because Sylvia's going to fire me.' Zeno was whispering the words as if to himself, as if no longer listening to the girl.

'Oh, stop turning this into a tragedy. With your experience, you'll have no problem finding another job. If nowhere else, with one of your competitors.'

'That would be the lowest thing I could do. To say nothing of the humiliation. How could you even think of such a thing?'

'It seems like an obvious solution.'

'Did you consider the consequences?'

'Not right now. I just want to make love now.' She put her arms around him again.

It was Sunday. They had the whole morning and the whole afternoon ahead of them. And a whole lifetime.

Chapter 57

'A SINGLE ROSE?' the florist raised a dark eyebrow to confirm the unusual order.

'Yes, red, if possible.' Tamas pointed at a plastic bucket on the floor filled with at least two dozen long-stem roses. His finger stopped at one that was only half open and then he went on with his request: 'Please, wrap this in green foil to keep it from drying out.'

The shopkeeper looked piqued by the small purchase.

Tamas handed over the five dollars as if he were pulling a tooth. He was so shocked by the price of the flower that he took it and walked out of the place without even saying goodbye.

It took him two bus rides and a streetcar to reach Christine's address. The Karady house was a modest, ranch-style, single-family home with an attached one-car garage directly facing the street. It was standing in a patch of grass, without a fence to protect it, just like the other houses around it. It looked strange to Tamas, coming from Europe where a house is not considered complete without a fence. And without a gate. There were three steps leading up to the front door, with a path leading to them directly from the sidewalk.

He gave a short, rather diffident push to the doorbell. Nothing. After about two minutes he wondered if he had pushed the bell hard enough, so he pressed his finger on the button two more times. This time there was an almost instantaneous response. The door swung open to reveal a middle-aged man. In his momentary confusion, Tamas shifted the rose to his left hand so he could hold out the right for a greeting, but he didn't know what to say.

'You must be Tamas.' The man smiled indulgently.

'Yes, Tamas. Good morning.'

'Henrik. Welcome, come inside,' he said opening the door wider.

Christine emerged from indoors wearing a flower-print apron.

Tamas awkwardly handed over the single rose.

'That's very nice of you,' the woman said with genuine feeling. Her eyes told the tale: it had been a long time since anyone had given her a flower. Perhaps Henrik didn't bother with such frills.

A young boy came running up to see who was at the door.

'Hi. I'm Patrick. Do you know my sister, Wanda? She goes to college. She has a summer job at Farm-Fresh meat-packing company. She has a nerd for a boyfriend called Paul. He's awful.' The words came tumbling out of him in one breath. He then quickly retreated to a room off the long inner hallway.

'Listen to him,' Christine said and turned around to follow the boy. 'Just listen to my son. Is that any way to behave? To entertain everyone with stories about the family?'

But Henrik waved a pacifying hand to stop her.

'Leave it alone, Christine, this is the way kids are nowadays. They've no idea how to carry on a polite conversation – they just blurt out whatever comes into their head.'

Tamas was charmed by this family scene; he was reminded of his own two little boys.

'Come in, make yourself comfortable.' Henrik led him into the living room and pointed at a deep easy chair.

It was the room of a warm family home. At the centre, a coffee table was surrounded by a sofa and two easy chairs. One wall was covered by a floor-to-ceiling bookcase, and the opposite wall was decorated with a set of abstract paintings, most likely prints.

'What would you like to drink?' asked Henrik, stepping over to the liquor cabinet.

'Nothing strong, thank you.' Tamas smiled apologetically.

'In that case I'll keep you company,' Henrik declared and went to the kitchen for juice and glasses.

'Christine has spoken about you,' Henrik said as he sat down by the coffee table and poured red juice into two glasses. He placed one of them in front of Tamas. 'Blood orange,' he announced and started sipping from his glass.

'Thank you for having me here today,' Tamas answered, looking the room over again.

'Why don't you two sit outside in the backyard,' Christine called out from the kitchen. 'At least you can keep an eye on Patrick. He's always up to no good.'

There was a patio with outdoor furniture, chairs around a table with a large sunshade in the middle. Henrik talked about his job, complaining that he was working a lot and earning not enough. At first Tamas listened only out of duty, but he perked up when the host started talking about his work with computers. It was intellectually satisfying work, he said, and even exciting. Then it was Tamas's turn. He spoke about his background and his plans for the future until Christine broke into the conversation.

'You must come to the dinner table,' she said. 'Henrik, will you go and see that Patrick washes his hands.'

An attractive table was waiting for them in the dining room. The centre place was taken by a tall and slender vase with Tamas's rose in it.

'I invited Wanda, too, but she can't come. She has something important to do at the university,' said Christine while serving the appetizers. 'It's a little cold meat salad, it's got a bit of everything in it.'

'Wanda always finds something important to do when we get together for a family dinner. We're used to it,' said Henrik, heaping three spoonfuls of salad on his plate. 'She's quite a beauty, and she knows it. Her picture is on the wall.' He called Tamas's attention to a large photo.

The portrait showed a girl with a high forehead and a smile that flashed a perfect set of teeth. For a few minutes everyone was quiet. Patrick smeared some of the mayonnaise on the tablecloth. By the time Christine noticed what was going on, it was too late, the damage had been done. She whipped the plate out of her son's hands and covered up the spot with an extra napkin.

'The employment situation is not very encouraging.' Henrik turned to Tamas to resume their earlier talk, while he wiped his plate with a piece of bread.

'That's what Eugene keeps saying all day,' Christine noted with a peevish glance at her husband. 'You two should be sent to a mood-rehabilitation programme.'

'Last week two real estate investors' – here Henrik raised his left hand with two fingers extended – 'two of them took a leap from the top floor because their apartment towers are standing empty. The owners could no longer make payments on the bank loans, and now of course their real estate will be foreclosed and sold to recover some of the investment for the bank. Not for the owners. And the tenants end up in the street, children and furniture and all. That's capitalism for you. You're insolvent? Then you're finished, move on. Let someone else take your place. It's as simple as that. The stores in the mall are closing down one after another. They don't have enough income to pay the monthly rent, business is slow. There's no work, no money!' declared Henrik nervously.

'You paint a very depressing picture of the world, Henrik. Tamas arrived here to the new world two weeks ago. It would be irresponsible of us to dampen his determination to succeed.'

'Am I responsible for the depression?' Henrik snapped back.

'Well, save it for later. You can continue after the soup.'

'Sorry.' He held his soup bowl closer to the tureen.

'I invited Tamas here for a nice home-cooked meal, the kind he grew up with, and not to have his spirit broken.

He's already got plenty to worry about. He was told they will not even consider his application to bring his family here until he can get a permanent job. He doesn't speak the language. He'll have to attend a language course. His family is thousands of kilometres from here, and he worries about them, too,' she explained while ladling soup into her husband's bowl.

'I wasn't aware of that.' Henrik turned toward Tamas.

'It happened Thursday.'

'Eugene is working very hard to find Tamas a job,' Christine said. 'We are hopeful.' She turned to her husband on that last word for emphasis. 'It should help that Tamas is a jack-of-all-trades, and while he's learning the language, he's willing to do anything. Even office-cleaning. Anything. He's sure to be hired somewhere.'

After dinner the men went into the living room. Patrick was sent to his room to take a nap. Christine retired to the kitchen to restore order.

'Have you heard the news?' Henrik asked.

'News?'

'Some time yesterday morning Walter Wallmeyer was killed in an airplane crash. He was a second-generation fellow countryman of ours, and the Conservative party candidate for the National Assembly.'

'What? Walter? I don't understand. What happened?' Tamas asked, as if he had not heard Henrik's words.

'Yes. We're all stunned. He was on a leisure flight with someone called Barbara Redwick, and their aircraft vanished from the radar scope some time after takeoff. Later in the afternoon the search helicopters found it burnt out and burrowed into a farm building.'

Tamas closed his eyes. He was striving to fight back his tears.

'I think the last time I saw him was Wednesday,' he answered finally with sadness. 'He stopped by my apartment. He was helping a new immigrant who had been arrested for shoplifting. No, I can't believe it, it seems impossible,' he kept repeating. He could see Walter's good-humoured face, the coke-bottle glasses, his measured gestures, each detail over and over again.

'I didn't know you knew Walter.' Henrik looked at his visitor in surprise.

'A welfare worker in the refugee camp gave me his name,' Tamas explained.

'I'm surprised you missed the news, they even had televised reports from the scene.'

'I didn't turn on the radio yesterday, and I don't have a TV. I spent the entire afternoon in the park behind my apartment building. The grass along the creek was tall enough to bathe in.'

By the time Christine finished with the kitchen and joined them, Tamas was getting ready to leave. He felt it was time for him to go home. It was Sunday afternoon – the Karadys should be allowed to enjoy it on their own, he was thinking, before he announced his intention to take his leave.

Christine urged him to relax and stay a while, but Henrik seemed to welcome the visitor's intention to take off. He even whispered to his wife: 'A well-brought-up young man. He learned good manners from his grandparents.'

On the doorstep Tamas thanked them for having had him for dinner. He could not praise Christine's cooking highly enough.

'See you tomorrow morning at nine at the language class,' he said to Christine and gave an old-fashioned bow.

Feeling disconsolate and lonelier than ever, Tamas ambled to the streetcar stop. He could not get Walter's jovial face out of his mind.

*   *   *

It was midnight on Sunday when Zeno left Wanda's apartment.

'What are you going to tell Sylvia about where you spent the weekend?' Wanda asked him at the apartment door.

'I doubt if she'll ask. But if she does, I'll tell her the truth.'

'That you were with me?' Wanda eyed him carefully.

'Yes. If she hired someone to tail me, she'll find out anyway. And besides, I've already admitted to her that I am in love with you.'

'Yes, I know.' The girl gave Zeno another parting kiss. 'Sleep well!' she whispered, pulling him close to her again.

*   *   *

At the usual Monday morning session of the *Monitor*, Joseph Singer and the editorial board paid tribute to Walter Wallmeyer's memory with a minute's silence.

Bradley was delayed that morning – his car would not start. He had to take the bus to work. He tried to slip into his office unnoticed but, to his surprise, Joseph was waiting for him, sitting on the desk.

Joseph rose and remained standing, silently and in a formal pose, while Bradley took off his linen jacket and hung it on the back of his chair.

'Sorry, Chief, for missing this morning's meeting. I don't know what happened to my car, but it refused to come alive. And I had it serviced just last Saturday, and it was working fine then.' Bradley sounded casually apologetic.

'You didn't miss anything. We held a brief memorial service for Walter. I expect you, too, liked him.'

'He was a very good colleague,' Bradley exclaimed, but he did not risk looking his boss in the eye.

'Yes, I know he acted as a midwife for many of your articles. He kept saying how talented and promising you were.'

'We understood each other,' Bradley mumbled.

'You understood?' The chief emphasized the last word.

'Yes, we had a good relationship.'

'Is that so? Even when you followed him around, took pictures of him, and wrote reports about his activities? Even when you blackmailed him?'

Bradley said nothing.

'Even then? I asked you a question.'

Bradley still didn't answer. He was tracing the pattern of the rug with the tip of his shoe.

Joseph felt like stepping on him and grinding him into the ground. But seeing how miserable and helpless the man looked, he felt his fury dissipate.

'Mr Northrup, as your final official duty I want you to write your letter of resignation and bring it to my office. I'll have a cheque for three weeks' salary for you. Starting tomorrow, you're free – you needn't come in. If you start looking for a job at another newspaper, don't expect a letter of recommendation from me. Frankly I think you're trash. You have no place among us.'

—Chapter 58—

T HERE WERE about thirty students of all ages, nationalities, and abilities in Tamas's language class. The instructor, Mary Dalton, was said by Christine to be one of the best. She spoke slowly and in carefully articulated sentences. She repeated every new word several times to make sure it would stick even with the poorest students. She was very patient. She would never scold anyone for making a mistake. In the first break Tamas sought out Christine.

'I wanted to thank you for the special dinner yesterday. You treated me to authentic home cooking of the old world.' He bowed with old-fashioned courtesy.

'Come now, stop embarrassing me.' She smiled at the young man. 'Everyone enjoys getting compliments, but don't spoil me. You may have an opportunity in the future to return the favour.'

At noon, before leaving the welfare centre, Tamas asked Christine, 'Do you know the plans for Walter's memorial service?'

'I think it'll be Wednesday. But I'll know for sure tomorrow. Henrik mentioned that Walter had taken you under his wing.'

'Please let me know by phone,' Tamas asked.

'Do you have a phone already?'

'They promised it for today.' He wrote down his number for her.

'Easy to remember. Good, I'll call you as soon as Henrik lets me know.'

With his notebook and new language manual tucked under his arm, Tamas walked out into the bright sunlight. Although he was eager to get home, he chose to walk all the way. It was not only to save the fare but to put off the pleasure waiting for him, the phone conversation with Iren.

The telephone was delivered by a man with curly hair and a walrus moustache. He handed over a box to Tamas, along with a folded sheet of paper and a pen, which he laid on the box. 'Please sign on the line. Assemble the set according to the instructions included in the box. You can plug it into any of the telephone jacks in the apartment and it will be immediately in operation,' he explained at a speed Tamas could not follow. Still this didn't bother him now; he would be able to figure out what it was all about. The main thing was he had the set; now he could talk to his family.

The man said, 'Good luck,' and hurried off.

Tamas opened the box. He slipped one end of the cable into the set and the other into the phone jack in the wall. He lifted the receiver. Never in his life had he been so delighted to hear a dial tone.

Right away he dialled his home number. There was ringing at the other end, but instead of Iren, it was the operator. She informed him that the number he was calling could only be reached through the overseas operator. She took the order and assured Tamas that in a few minutes she would have the connection, and would call back as long as the lines were open within the country he was calling.

Ten minutes went by, and then another ten.

And then he waited another half an hour. To save telephone time he rehearsed his conversation with Iren, concentrating on the latest news; he didn't have a job yet, the application for their immigration was not accepted yet, the economy unfortunately was in a depression, and jobs were scarce and hard to come by. He was also trying find the words to express how much he was missing them, and how many times a day he thought about them, and to convey somehow his loneliness and his desperate state of mind without unduly alarming her. Added to all that was the tragic loss of Walter, who had been such a good friend to him.

Another hour went by, but the telephone placed in the middle of the coffee table remained stubbornly silent.

He reminded himself to ask Iren if they had received the picture postcard he had sent them showing a bird's eye view of the city. What did they think? Could they get an idea of what it was like from the photo? Did it seem like a place they would like to live? And he had not spoken to his boys for a month.

There were two short rings from the phone. Tamas grabbed the receiver. He spoke into it: 'Hello, hello, Iren, is that you?' Only metallic noise answered from the phone. Then the connection broke off. He clicked several times on the disconnect button, hoping against hope, but he could get no response.

In a few seconds the phone rang again. 'Sorry Sir,' a friendly female voice came on, 'we tried connecting you to the number you wanted, but the line went dead again. If you wish we can try again later.' Tamas listened intently and recognized one word 'later' and he immediately answered, 'Yes.'

The world seemed to cave in around him. He suddenly lost interest in the whole business. He really didn't feel like talking to Iren. It would make more sense to call her when he had a job and when the application for the immigration of the family was in progress, but now what did he have to report? Nothing but bad news, the economic crisis, his loss of confidence, his wretched mood, Walter's death, his hopelessness?

He slumped into bed without undressing. He felt thoroughly exhausted. I'll take a nap, he thought, as his eyelids were getting heavy.

He was startled by the ringing of the phone. At first he didn't know how to respond or where he was. The phone kept ringing, but it was hard to find it in the dark.

'Hello, hello!' he shouted into the phone several times

until he finally heard a barely audible voice at the other end which seemed very far away. 'Iren? Is that you?'

'Yes, Tamas, I can hardly hear you.'

'All I wanted to say –' he repeated the phrase with his mouth going dry from the excitement, '– all I wanted to say is that I'm doing fine. And how about you and the boys?'

'We're all right too,' came the faint voice again.

'I'll write to you. A long letter, tomorrow,' he shouted.

'Good, I'm looking forward to it. The boys are sending their love, too.'

'I love them, and I love you Iren.' There was no answer. They got disconnected. Tamas dropped the receiver back in its cradle, and he staggered out to the bathroom. Coming back to the bedroom he glanced at the alarm clock. It was three A.M. He practically passed out falling into bed. I only hope I can get up on time in the morning, he thought as he slipped back into deep sleep.

Chapter 59

MURDER IN HOTEL ODÉON
—XIX—

DETECTIVE MUELLER closed the cover of the file devoted to the Viktor case with a careworn sigh. For some time at the beginning he had the feeling he had the case well in hand. The security cameras of Hotel Odéon kept surveillance over the first floor and the entrance to the building. There was, however, a half-hour gap in the recordings made on the night of the murder. The detective had managed to learn from the janitor and the doorman on duty that night that Viktor had only two visitors. One of them was definitely a woman. But they were unable to provide a reliable description of the other person, because that person was seen only by the janitor and only for a fleeting second. The description spoke of a full figure that could have belonged to a woman, and that was as far as the janitor could go, no matter how hard he was pressed to conjure up the image in his mind. Concerning the first visitor, Fabian Mueller was quite certain it was Lidia. That was why he had summoned her for questioning; he was curious to see if she would tell him about her visit to Viktor's room that night. He was puzzled by her saying nothing about the visit. That was why he had cut the questioning short. The woman's impertinent brazenness seemed to suggest that her self-confidence came from innocence.

'I must find that person,' the detective said to the wall, exhausted, 'but if I don't, the world will not come to an end. How many of us are guilty and get away with it?'

His eyes came to rest on a photo on his desk: it was

of his wife. It had been only a few months since he lost
her in a freakish automobile accident.

It was a Saturday morning. The time they usually
went to do their weekly shopping. His wife was in
an exceptionally good mood at breakfast. That little
detail struck him as odd, now that he thought about
the tragedy; she was usually tense before a shopping
expedition, but that fateful morning she was even telling
a joke.

They planned on going to a large suburban shopping
mall, to a supermarket for the groceries. Where their
residential street joined the main road to the suburbs at
a stop sign, both roads passed through a patch of forest.
Trees and undergrowth obstructed the view of those
trying to enter the faster road from behind the stop
sign, which made pulling out a risky business. Fabian,
as always, approached the intersection cautiously, poking
his nose out to look left and right; when he deemed
it safe to proceed, he stepped on the gas to clear out
of the intersection as fast as possible. On that fateful
morning though, all his usual precautions failed. He
didn't see the pickup truck approaching at a high speed
behind a lumbering van, which it was in the process of
overtaking, and he could not complete the turn before
he found himself across the path of the speeding vehicle,
smack in front of it. In the collision their car was hit
with an enormous bang on the passenger side. The
impact wrenched the steering wheel out of Fabian's hand
and knocked him unconscious. When he came to and
managed to free himself of the tangled mass, the first
thing he did was to look at his wife. She had passed
out and her head was lying back on the headrest. He
pushed his door open and ran around the front to the
other side to pull his wife out of the wreckage. Her door
was crumpled and stuck shut, impossible to open. In the
meantime the driver of the other vehicle hurried over to
help. The two of them together could not get it open.

By the time the ambulance arrived, it was too late. The paramedics could only pronounce her dead.

After the accident, Fabian started having nightmares. Every time it was the same: he sees the same endless field where he's walking with his wife, just the two of them. They soon get into an automobile, and when they start rolling a huge rock falls on top of them. He doesn't feel frightened or anything else for that matter; it's as if he were floating in outer space. He reaches out to touch his wife's crushed body, trying to revive her. But here the dream breaks off.

Fabian now reached out for the photo on his desk, picked it up, turned it toward the light, and then, with a swift, decisive move he slipped it into one of the desk drawers.

There's no way of recovering from a tragedy like this.

The vehicular homicide charge was dropped as soon as his police affiliation was revealed, but he could not forgive himself as easily. I'm no better than the poor bastards I put in jail, a voice inside him said relentlessly.

For weeks he felt the need to see a psychologist friend of his, sometimes even two or three days in a row. They had long talks about the marriage, the circumstances of the accident, and his guilt feelings about it. In these sessions his friend eventually convinced Fabian of his innocence in his wife's death, but that was not enough to bring him relief from the pain of his loss.

He was almost glad to hear the phone ring.

'Dr Artur Liptak, the attorney, is here,' trumpeted the voice of the gate guard in the receiver. 'He'd like to see you. Do you want me to send him up?'

'Yes, send him up.'

Artur entered the detective's office with an official air. Fabian greeted him also in a businesslike manner.

'Can I offer you some refreshment, Counsellor? Coffee, or perhaps tea, mineral water?' he asked.

'A glass of water would do nicely,' answered Artur as he sat down.

Fabian got up, placed two glasses on the desk. He extracted a bottle from a tiny refrigerator built into the bookshelf, filled the two glasses, and pushed one of them toward Artur.

'Last time we parted with the agreement that if I learn anything about the identity of the female visitor I would share it with you.'

'Is that what brought you here?' asked Fabian with a show of surprise.

'Yes. To me it's important that I keep my word.'

'And what is it you hope to get in return?'

'If I help you, Inspector, then I am sure you'll help me. Yes, that's the idea.'

'Help you? How could I possibly help you?'

'You can help me by telling the press no more than is essential for the detection and capture of the perpetrator, no more than concerns the case.'

'In my opinion reporters are concerned about everything that has to do with the murder.' Fabian assumed a grim expression.

'Look, I know that you know what I am thinking about.'

'The little matter of the gentlemen's secret society?'

'Yes. Yes. I have the feeling you know a lot more about us than I suspected the last time we talked.'

'Look, Sir,' said Fabian taking a sip from the glass, 'it is not my intention to give you and your friends any adverse publicity. That would be too hard on all of you. Knowing the way our reporters work at the slightest hint of a scandal, I can just see them placing all your Club members under a magnifying glass, and examining the professional and private lives of all of you. You understand what I am talking about. Talking of despair, I am speaking from experience.' Artur returned his gaze without comprehension.

'Yes, it concerned my wife.' Fabian bent his head down in a penitent mode. 'So I know from experience what it means when...'

The detective put his glass on the desk, got up from his chair, stepped over to the window, and peered out between the slats of the shutter as if looking for someone in the street.

'You have to realize my first duty is to do my job, which is to track down the criminal.' Fabian turned away from the window.

'But you don't have to look for the criminal among us, Inspector,' said Artur folding his arms on his chest.

Fabian looked thoughtfully at the attorney. 'Who do you think hated Viktor with so much passion?'

'I keep asking myself the same question.'

'And how do you answer it?'

'I can't. Anyone can commit a *crime passionelle* under extreme duress.'

'Well, then let me sketch out to you a scenario,' said Fabian, leaning back in his chair without taking his eyes off the attorney. 'Valerian was seen by the doorman leaving the building shortly after midnight. Soon after that a woman entered the victim's room. She's known as...'

'You know that already?' Artur's voice betrayed his astonishment. 'That's what I came here to tell you.'

'Yes, I know,' said the detective dryly. 'That lady is called Lidia Novak.'

'Did she come forward with this?'

'Let me go on. That night Viktor had a quarrel with Valerian. This latter gentleman bore resentment against our Mayor who did not want to give up Viktor, his lover, for the benefit of Valerian. Considering this unhappy triangle, we are justified in saying that both Valerian and Hugo had a motive for murder – one prompted by the quarrel, and the other by jealousy. Lidia had no motive. It's common knowledge she's everybody's friend, and ready to help all her friends. She's always at the service of anyone in any capacity. In addition, I checked her alibi. She got home by two in the morning. However, there is another fact, or let's say a factor, that tends to muddy the water. I have clear evidence from reliable sources that there was yet another person visiting Viktor that night, and that person could very well be the culprit. I considered the possibility of Valerian returning later but reached no definite conclusion. As it stands now, we have three suspects: Valerian Lang, Mr Hugo Wagner, and that unidentified third visitor.'

The attorney listened to Fabian Mueller in astonishment, his eyes downcast, trying hard to hide his forebodings.

Poor Hugo, he thought, it's going to cause quite a stir when it comes out he's among the suspects. Now, in retrospect, he wondered why he had never suspected Hugo, not even when the Mayor confessed he had no recollection as to his activities on the night of the murder.

'I can't bring myself to believe the Mayor would have been capable of such a horrible crime.' Artur cleared his throat. 'I've known him for a long time and I could not see him doing it even in my worst nightmares.'

'And how about Valerian? Could you see him doing it?'

'Him neither,' said Artur, after a moment's hesitation.

'If you're right, we're stuck with the third suspect, the unidentified person. It's that person we must find. Rest assured, I am not ready to go public with any of this, and I am asking you not to reveal my thinking to anyone. Not even to the Mayor. No one. If you comply, I can also promise you I am not going to harass the members of your secret society. Well, do we have a deal?'

'Certainly, but there's one thing I can't understand,' said Artur in a low voice. 'What do you get out of this agreement?'

'Nothing. Let's just say this is a friendly gesture on my part.'

Artur felt devastated when he stepped out into the street; he had the sensation the world was spinning out of control. It sat heavy on his mind that Hugo was among the suspects. Now both of his friends were in serious trouble.

—Chapter 60—

S ITTING ON A CHAIR by the bed, Wanda watched Paul lying on his right side, breathing evenly. She was trying to guess at what time of the night he had dropped in unexpectedly. She had not heard him come in, only noticed his warm body snuggling up to hers.

She remained sitting there for a while. She didn't yet feel up to taking a shower. Finally she made her way to the bathroom on tiptoe. She didn't find the face looking back at her from the mirror very attractive. With a fingertip she felt the pimple budding on her chin, and then wiped it several times with a piece of gauze soaked with rubbing alcohol. In the meantime she noticed on the shelf the pregnancy test kit she had bought the week before. Still yawning, she picked up the kit and opened it. She went through the prescribed process, and when she was done, she left the long test strip on the shelf. She turned on the shower tap, peeled off her diaphanous baby-doll, tested the temperature of the water with a hand, and stepped into the shower.

For a few minutes she let the stream of water massage her back; with eyes closed she delighted in feeling her body warming up. She thought of Zeno and how nice it would be to be soaking together.

Soon she was standing in front of the mirror again, working on her hair. She glanced casually at the test strip on the shelf. Then she snapped it up to take a better look. A blue streak was developing on the cream-coloured paper strip: a positive test for pregnancy! She ran into the bedroom, threw herself on Paul, and started pummelling him with both fists.

'Wake up!' she screamed. 'Wake up! I'm pregnant!'

Paul rose a little, propped up on an elbow, showing no

sign of comprehension or reaction of any kind to Wanda's hysterical outburst.

'No idea what you're talking about,' he mumbled and tried to turn away.

'I'm pregnant, you beast, can't you hear me?' she continued at the top of her voice.

The repeated word 'pregnant' acted like a bucket of cold water on Paul. He sat bolt upright, staring at Wanda with his eyes like saucers.

'Pregnant?' He tested the word with his reluctant tongue. 'That's just what we need!'

'I told you to be careful! Didn't I, you beast! Didn't I ask you not to rush into things without precautions? How many times did I warn you?'

'You didn't get pregnant from me. I was careful. I am sure it wasn't me.'

'It wasn't you, it wasn't you, is this all you can say? You're so self-centred and careless. You wouldn't think twice whether you were taking precautions or not.'

'It wasn't me!' Paul was getting grimly serious. 'It must have been your big-shot businessman friend. When was the last time you were with him?'

Wanda abruptly quieted down, looking pensively at Paul.

'You may be right,' she whispered as if to herself. 'But what now? What should I do?'

'Nothing. Do nothing. Have the baby. Every woman,' Paul said knowledgeably, 'needs to go through the experience of giving birth.'

'But not now, not just yet! I'm not prepared for it right now,' she said sadly. 'My God, I'll be late!' She hastily got her clothes ready for the day and started to dress.

Paul gazed at her nervous, jerky movements. His mind was elsewhere. He was thinking it was finally time for him to move out from Wanda's apartment, and start seriously looking for someone else. He was fantasizing about a safe, enduring, new relationship, with someone who would not shout at him, would not bawl him out a dozen times a day, who would not be seduced by another man, who would listen calmly to his troubles, his constant fears, and daily anxieties.

With a sour expression, he turned to the wall, in his mind already dissociating himself from the agitated girl.

On arriving at the plant, Wanda's first thought was to look up Zeno. She smuggled an envelope into the daily departmental mail with a quickly scribbled note.

> 'My Dear Love, I must see you at the earliest opportunity. Please! I have something very important to tell you.
> Burning kisses,
> W.'

Zeno received it only in the late afternoon; he had no idea what important news she couldn't wait to tell to him. He was so busy in the morning that he didn't even leave his office at lunchtime. He asked Dora to order in a ham sandwich. He didn't eat anything else all day.

He had gone in to work in the morning firmly resolved to fire his secretary. But there were so many other issues that had cropped up and needed his attention that he gradually relented; it seemed more expedient to do nothing at the moment and just let things go on as before.

No, I should not take revenge on Dora. She'll get her just deserts sooner or later. Fate or the higher powers will make sure that eventually she'll pay for her dirty deed. And besides, what difference would it make? The whole world is crumbling around me.

*   *   *

Earlier that afternoon, the lightning bolt he had been expecting struck. His attorney called to inform him that

Sylvia had filed for divorce. 'We should meet Wednesday,' he proposed briskly, adding, '– late afternoon would suit me best.'

'I can't make it then,' he said. 'Walter Wallmeyer's funeral. I don't know how late it may go on.'

'Well then, how about Thursday at five?'

Zeno flipped open the appointment calendar. 'Fine, my afternoon is free.'

It was getting on to six o'clock, but the summer sun was still strong. Dora had left half an hour earlier. Zeno reached for the telephone again and dialled the marketing department. He asked for Wanda. They said she had already left for the day.

During that day he had received two phone calls concerning Walter. One of them came from Cameron Fowler, asking Zeno to support the candidate who was Walter's replacement. He had been nominated on Saturday.

'Who is he?' Zeno asked.

'Ralph Grainger. You probably know him.'

'Oh yes, of course. Walter told me back at that time how hard Ralph had fought his nomination.'

'That's all in the past now,' Cameron observed in a mournful tone. 'Can we count on your support?'

Zeno hesitated for a moment. Soon he would no longer be with the company and in no position to support Ralph or anyone else. 'In principle, yes,' he blurted out finally.

The other call came from Joseph Singer, the editor-in-chief of the *Monitor*. 'I know you two were good friends. I'm inviting you on behalf of the editorial staff to Walter's funeral. We are taking care of all arrangements.'

'Yes, of course, I'll be there,' answered Zeno immediately. 'Has there been any new statement from the commission investigating the accident?'

'The aviation experts went over the wreck with a fine-tooth comb but couldn't come up with anything. One thing that puzzled them was that neither Mrs Redwick nor Mr Wallmeyer had their seat belts on at the time of the crash.'

'What's the significance of that?'

'The experts have no explanation.'

Zeno mulled over the conversation, but he found the question of the seat belts just a minor part of the bigger mystery of the whole flight.

He was already in the office parking area when he remembered Wanda. He had forgotten to call her at home. He turned around. She answered the phone after one ring. She sounded nervous and impatient. 'We've got to meet tonight,' she insisted. 'Come up to my place. But right now, if possible.'

Zeno tried to calm her by asking questions, but it was no use, the girl would not go into details.

She swung the door wide open for Zeno with a nervous smile.

'Come in, come in.'

He was mystified by her air of urgency.

'What's up?' he asked

'Let's sit down here.' She pointed to the table. 'How about a Campari? Would you like a drink?'

Zeno nodded. He loosened his tie and leaned back in the chair. In seconds she was back with the bottle and two sherry glasses.

'So tell me, what's so urgent?'

'Let me pour first, and then I'll tell you all about it,' she smiled.

Zeno took the bottle from the girl's shaking hands, unscrewed the cap and poured.

'Cheers! And to our health,' he added, taking a sip. 'I'm all ears.'

'I'm pregnant,' she announced without preamble.

It took a moment for the words to sink into Zeno's consciousness. When they did, he sprang to his feet exuberantly, hugged Wanda, then lifted her up and spun her around.

'Is this definite? Are you absolutely sure?' he demanded, like someone sobering up from revelry wanting to know if everything that's been happening is real and not just a dream.

'Yes indeed! Very much so!' she replied and ran into the bathroom for the proof, 'I did the test this morning,' and she handed the strip to Zeno.

'If blue is the sign, this sure looks proof positive.' He held up the cardboard strip.

'Our baby, Zeno,' she said looking at him through a haze of emotion. 'Are you happy?'

'Life is full of surprises, but this is something even beyond that, especially at my age.' He handed the test strip back to her and sank into his thoughts. Lately so many major events had been happening to him, enough for a lifetime for most people, not just for one day. The divorce proceedings, his career in shambles, Dora's betrayal, Walter's death – each event held a tragedy within it. And now a piece of good news: finally, a child of his was to be born. The child he used to dream about all his adult life, the child that he had given up on long ago.

He looked at the glass in Wanda's hand.

'Should you be drinking, now that you're pregnant?'

'This is a pretty light drink. And I barely stuck the tip of my tongue in it. I'm not sure I even swallowed it,' she laughed. 'So what do you say? Are you happy? Have I made you happy?'

C HRISTINE SHOWED UP at the language class looking unhappy and distracted. She barely acknowledged Tamas with a hello. She automatically got her notebook and pen out of her bag, apparently in deep thought.

'Anything wrong?' Tamas whispered to her. He too was feeling under the weather after the disappointing phone call in the middle of the night.

'Oh, nothing really. Just everyday problems. Henrik often starts the day in a foul mood, and he doesn't realize how much that upsets me. But now I'm getting over it.' She produced an anaemic smile. 'And how about you?'

'I tried to call Iren last night. I had to wait hours for a connection and then we kept getting disconnected. Finally at dawn we were able to exchange a few words.'

During class, Tamas's thoughts wandered. He could hear Iren's voice from far away.

After the break, while Mary was talking about irregular verbs, the classroom door opened unexpectedly and Eugene Mazur appeared. He hurried up to Mary and whispered something to her. The teacher beckoned to Tamas and Christine.

'Eugene has something important to say,' she said.

Tamas looked around hesitantly, but when Christine called out to him, he followed her out to the corridor without a word.

Eugene was waiting for them.

'Christine, translate.' He gestured toward Christine with excitement. 'The thing is, I've lined up a job interview for Tamas. There's an opening for a handyman in the maintenance department of a large suburban hotel. I talked to the manager. I agreed to send Tamas to the hotel this morning. Would you go along with him?' he asked, but without waiting for an answer he handed her a slip of paper torn from a notebook.

'Naturally,' she said, catching his excitement.

Tamas impatiently looked from one to the other.

'I'll translate in a second,' Christine reassured him, and then turned back to Eugene. 'Does the manager know Tamas doesn't speak English?'

'Yes, I told him. He said the job did not require great communication skills, and there's a compatriot of yours in the department,' explained the administrator. 'Get going now. I'll tell Mary you two will have to be excused for another hour or two. On this slip of paper you'll find the name and address of the hotel, and the name of the manager. Tell him I sent you.'

'Wait here,' she turned to Tamas again, 'while I collect my purse and my car keys.'

When she came back out to the hallway she was beaming. 'The gods have smiled on you,' she laughed.

'All I could make out was "job" and "hotel".'

'Yes, he found you a job prospect, that's where we're going.' She opened the car door and waited for Tamas to get in.

'A job? You mean I might start working?'

'It's not a hundred percent certain, not a job, only a job prospect. We're going to the hotel for an interview.'

'Is it far?' asked Tamas, worried about getting to the job if it was beyond the city transportation system.

'It's on the outskirts. Don't worry, there's a bus line nearby, and it should be an easy commute. The main thing is to get the job.'

When they pulled into the parking lot of the hotel, Tamas looked at the huge building with awe. He quickly counted the floors. Only fourteen; it had looked taller at first sight.

Above the entrance a green neon sign proclaimed the

name: CROSSWINDS. The same sign was also visible at just below roof level, but in much bigger letters.

Through the revolving door they entered a huge, two-storey lobby. The pool in the middle had a small island with flowers and a babbling fountain on it. This looks more like a fairy-tale land than a hotel, he thought, gaping at the luxurious décor. Am I really going to work here? Tamas kept asking himself, but not for very long, because Christine was dragging him along at a brisk pace to the concierge's desk. She unfolded Eugene's notebook page and showed it to the girl sitting there, who immediately dialled a number.

'Mr Vid, the manager, will be with you in a few minutes. In the meantime,' she said reaching into a half-open drawer in front of her, 'here's an employment application form. Have a seat in the waiting area and fill it out.'

Christine took the form and led the way to a corner furnished with comfortable easy chairs, sofas, and end tables like an elegant living room.

'You have your passport with you?' asked Christine.

'Yes, here it is.' He stuck his hand into his coat pocket.

'This is easy.' And as she scanned the questions she quickly started filling in the blanks. 'How young you are!' she exclaimed when she got to his date of birth. 'And now I need your help.' She lifted the pen from the form. 'The question is what kind of work can you do.'

'Every kind,' he said quickly, and then thought this sounded childish. 'I've done construction work, bricklaying, plastering walls, tile work, painting, and wallpapering.'

'Anything else?'

'I can do some carpentry. And yes, I have quite a bit of experience doing general janitorial work,' he added ruefully. He said nothing about his journalism work. He had no idea if it would help him or not, but it was a part of his past he did not want to be asked about just yet.

'Well, that should do. Sign here.' She handed him the pen pointing at the dotted line.

Guests were coming and going around them. More than fifteen minutes had passed, but there was no sign of Mr Vid, the manager. Christine went back to the young lady at the desk and asked for directions to the boss's office. Armed with the directions they made their way to the inner sanctum of the management and sat down on an office couch in the hallway. They had a good view of the office through a glass wall, and they could see no one inside.

Soon a lean, tall man came hurrying from the other direction.

'Christine Karady?' he asked. He paid no attention to Tamas.

'Yes, Eugene Mazur of the pastoral welfare centre sent us,' she said, rising from the couch.

'Let's stay right here,' the manager suggested and sat down with them.

Christine handed him the application form and Tamas's passport and permanent residence permit.

'He doesn't have a social insurance number yet. He'll get it in three weeks, by mail.'

The manager spent a minute or two studying the application form, and then he turned to Tamas.

'How's your command of the language?'

'So-so.' Tamas gestured with his hands.

'He's attending a language course right now,' Christine said hastening to his aid. 'He's making progress. I've been studying the language for years, and I'm still not perfect.'

'So he doesn't speak the language?'

'A little bit.' Tamas spoke up finally for himself. 'I can understand more than I can say.' He spoke the line close to perfection. He had rehearsed it over and over again, and it always seemed to impress whomever he was speaking to.

'Uh-uh.' Mr Vid, the manager nodded in approval.

'Okay. I'll give you a full-time job in the maintenance department. We need an all-around handyman, and I can see you have the experience the job requires. Your hourly rate will be three-forty,' he went on briskly. 'Do you accept the offer?'

'Yes,' Tamas replied without hesitation; he understood the words 'job' and 'offer' too.

Christine looked at him in shock.

'Did you understand what you accepted just now?'

'Yes, a job. I'll be working.'

'That's not all there's to it. Did you accept the wages he offered? Three dollars and forty cents an hour? That's what you accepted.'

'Yes, that's fine with me. Great!' Tamas was stuttering.

'Look at me and listen!' Christine admonished him. 'Do a little arithmetic. The work week has forty hours. Multiply that by three point four that makes one hundred and thirty-six. Subtract the income tax. Well, it may not be much, but at least thirty, which means you get one hundred and six. Multiply that by four weeks in a month, well, let's make that four and a half, and you get a monthly wage of four hundred and seventy-seven dollars. You know how much you get as the minimum aid if you're unemployed? Six hundred and thirty dollars. You will not even earn that much at the rate this man is offering, and you'll have to work hard.'

The manager listened to the foreign gibberish with a blank face.

'Any problems?' he asked finally, getting impatient. He even got back on his feet, indicating the meeting was over.

'He accepts the job,' answered Christine quickly.

'Fine. He can start Saturday morning at seven. He must bring a pair of steel-tipped work boots, but we provide a work uniform.' Mr Vid offered a hand in parting, first to Christine, then to Tamas.

She walked toward the exit, deep in thought.

'So you need the job that badly?' She looked sadly at the young man.

'Yes, I do,' he responded proudly. 'And you know why? Now I can apply for my family to join me.'

'Oh, yes, that's something I didn't consider.' She was getting into the car.

They were joining the main road when she spoke again. 'You're right. You don't have to stay here forever. This will be a good springboard to another job.' She was trying to convince herself more than Tamas. 'Good. With that thought, I can celebrate with you. You have an apartment, a telephone, and a job; now the only thing missing is the family.' She kept nodding, all the while trying to hide her feelings of pity for her protégé.

By the time they returned to the pastoral welfare centre Eugene was already well informed. He was impressed by Tamas's conduct and the way he was taking charge of his life.

'Every time someone in our care gets a job and goes out on his own, we celebrate the event. Tomorrow it'll be your turn. Coffee and cake.' Then he said goodbye and set off for his office. That cheap bastard Vid, he mumbled to himself. Three-forty an hour. I'd like to see him live on that.

During the last break the whole class was buzzing about Tamas's good fortune. Some of the classmates even congratulated him and shook his hand. Even people he had never had any contact with before. He received the good wishes with his head bowed, allowing himself a modest smile.

After classes Tamas sought out Christine again.

'I'm not going home yet, I have to stop in at the Immigration Office,' he told her as she was hurrying to her car.

'The one downtown?' she asked.

'Yes, my weekly visit to Bertold for the cash allowance.'

'Get in, I'll take you.'

When Tamas was getting out at the office, Christine had another thought: 'I was wondering if it's a good idea to tell Bertold about the job.'

'What else should I do? I'll tell him and see what happens.'

'They might stop giving you the weekly aid.' She was worried. 'And suppose the job doesn't work out for you, you get fired, then what?'

'You may be right. It crossed my mind. I'll think about it,' said Tamas and took his leave.

While waiting to see Bertold, Tamas got anxious. How was he going to communicate with the administrator without Walter's help? As it turned out his anxiety was unfounded. Entering Bertold's office, he noticed an older lady with him, most likely an interpreter.

'I was stunned by the news of Walter's death,' she said softly after the introductions. 'I've met very few of his kind – people who would so selflessly help others.'

'Unfortunately, our friendship was cut short.' Tamas sat down in front of the administrator's desk. 'But I'm not quite alone. Since then I've made the acquaintance of a lady. Christine Karady is her name. She even had me over for a family dinner, and today she took me to my first...' He got stuck here, sensing that he had inadvertently let slip what he was supposed to keep from Bertold.

'Where did she take you?' asked the alert administrator.

'Well...Eugene...well, I was at a job interview,' he finally blurted out.

'And how did it go? Did you get the job?' Bertold was very curious.

'Yes.' The young man forced himself to smile.

'That's terrific. Congratulations. Among my clients you're the only one who's managed to get a job in a matter of days. What kind of work is it?'

'I'll be working as a general handyman in the maintenance department of Crosswinds Hotel.'

'That's wonderful. And how much are they paying you?'

'Three-forty an hour.'

'What?' The administrator's mouth stayed open.

'That's it, three-forty an hour,' Tamas repeated.

'But that's hardly anything. It's barely more than the welfare payment you've been getting. How can that be?' he sighed, saying the last words softly, as if to himself, and then looked at the old lady shaking his head.

'I'll manage somehow.' Tamas held up his head proudly.

'Great, then let's get down to business,' the administrator went on. 'For the time being, you'll get your rent paid. This month and the next. We don't want to rush things yet. That'll give us enough time to see how your job works out. I'll let you have the food aid for the next two weeks, one hundred for clothing and the telephone. You will not have to come in next week unless you run into any problems. Good luck to you, Tamas.' Bertold shook hands with the young man and followed him with his eyes as he left the room.

The recognition flashed through Tamas's mind that now he was really on his own.

—Chapter 62—

Murder in Hotel Odéon
—XX—

AFTER HIS MEETING with Detective Mueller, Artur came to the conclusion that he had to work out what had happened at the Hotel Odéon. First he would fortify himself with a strong drink and then he would find Hugo.

In the meantime the tower clock of City Hall was striking five as Elsa hurried into Hugo's office to report that the Prefect was on his way and might arrive any moment.

Hugo found this unannounced visit surprising; earlier that day Geza Kolomar, the Prefect, had cancelled a lunch date in the Hotel Odéon's restaurant on account of some last minute emergency.

'Sorry about this interruption,' Geza said when he appeared a few minutes later. The expression on his face was unusually stony.

The Mayor jumped up from his chair and hurried to greet him and offer him a seat. They settled down in the two easy chairs in the corner of the spacious office. Elsa soon brought coffee, tea, and mineral water on a tray, and then looked at her boss questioningly. Hugo waved to her, indicating she was free to quit for the day; if there was anything they needed he would take care of it.

'What happened? I was wondering why you had to cancel lunch?' Hugo said as he placed the tray on a small coffee table between them.

'It was not something I could say on the phone. I thought I'd better come here myself and give you a full report.' Geza fingered his tie. It was a habit of his, but

350

only when he was nervous. He cleared his throat, looked toward the window as if expecting a pigeon to fly in with a message, and then he remained silent.

Hugo was getting impatient. He didn't know how to interpret this strange behaviour. 'Well?'

'I hope you don't mind I held back so long telling you about this, but…'

'Tell me, for Heaven's sake, what's happened?' Hugo said urgently, suspecting the Prefect had bad news.

'I'm afraid it's about your wife…'

'Nina? What about her?' Hugo felt the strength suddenly drain from his body. 'Tell me!'

'Jonas asked me to tell you,' Geza said, finally facing the Mayor with a veiled glow of sorrow in his eyes. 'The police found Nina bleeding profusely from several stab wounds beside her car on Route 31.'

'And…how she is?' Hugo asked in panic. 'Is she okay?'

'I'm afraid she passed away before reaching the hospital.'

'Passed away?' For a moment the room was spinning around Hugo. His heart was pounding so hard it seemed about to break through his ribcage. He reached for his glass with a trembling hand and took sips from it.

'Just take your time, when you're ready I'll tell you all about it.' Geza too took some water, to give Hugo time to collect himself and digest the news. Minutes went by in silence before he launched into his report.

'A highway patrol came upon Nina's car on Route 31 after they got a report of a car stranded near the 34-kilometre mark, and maybe in trouble or involved in an accident.'

'That's the highway we take to our holiday home,' Hugo said.

'Yes, we think she must have been on her way there. The highway patrol was on the spot almost immediately, and they found her soaked in blood lying in the open door on the driver's side. But she was still alive in spite of the significant loss of blood. The ambulance too was there in record time, believe me. They were at the scene in less than twenty minutes. Jonas sent the best team of paramedics he had.'

Hugo looked at Geza with vacant eyes.

'Unfortunately, it was just too late. The doctor who came with the ambulance said she had no chance of surviving those wounds. One of them even pierced the lower end of her heart. The likely scenario is that the killer or killers flagged down Nina, pretending to ask for help, and when Nina stopped they attacked and robbed her. From the multiple wounds the experts conclude your wife resisted and that's why they kept stabbing her. She obviously didn't know the kind of ruthless people she was up against.'

'And where is Nina now?' Hugo asked in a faint voice.

'In the autopsy room of the emergency hospital. Actually, I am here to escort you there whenever you're ready.'

The ringing of the phone interrupted the exchange.

'I'll have to pick it up, I've let Elsa go home already,' said Hugo, apologetically, and made his way to the desk. It was Artur on the line, but on hearing Hugo's listless voice he said he was going to join them very shortly.

In five minutes Artur was knocking on the door. He could see by Hugo's expression that something terrible had happened.

'How is it possible that no one saw the perpetrators? Route 31 is a very busy road. How is it possible for anyone to stop a car, stab the driver, and then move on as if nothing had happened? I can't understand it!' The questions came tumbling out of Artur.

'Nothing like this in recent memory ever happened in our district,' Geza explained. 'This case is an anomaly, it's beyond comprehension.'

'Are you coming with us to the hospital?' Hugo had to force himself to speak as he turned to Artur.

'Of course,' he replied quietly.

In the emergency hospital the executive director was waiting for them. The Prefect excused himself from going all the way to the autopsy room. He wanted to avoid viewing Nina's dead body. With some embarrassment, he said goodbye to those present.

The place reeked of formaldehyde, and when they entered Hugo almost passed out. Artur grabbed him by the arm.

Their faces were ashen when they left.

The mayoral limo was waiting in front of the hospital. Miklos, the driver, opened the doors to the back seat with a sombre look. He was sure something momentous had happened. But he said nothing.

Artur got out in front of Eddy's Bar. Hugo said he was going back to his office; he had a few things to take care of, and then he'd join his friend.

Left alone in the limo, however, he was suddenly overwhelmed by an inexplicable feeling of mortal fear. He could not understand why he had said to Artur that he had to take care of some urgent business. What could he accomplish after seven in the evening?

For one thing, he told himself, he had to call Jonas Balog, the Police Chief, for a firsthand report on the case. He was hoping to catch him still in his office.

When he telephoned, Jonas himself answered the phone.

'I hope you're not too angry with me, Hugo,' he said apologetically, 'I just couldn't do it, I just didn't have the guts to be the first to bring you the news about Nina. I asked Geza Kolomar to be the bearer of the bad news. You two work together on an almost daily basis, and he knows you better... Yes, I know you've been to the hospital... For the time being we have not informed the media, although two pushy reporters have been sniffing around already and giving me a hard time... Tomorrow, yes, tomorrow will be soon enough, we'll meet in the morning. If you want, we can come to your office... What time do you usually get in?... We'll be there by ten, latest... Yes... And I'll bring Detective Mueller with me, and the head of the crime scene investigation unit... Once more, my apologies, and I hope you don't hold my lack of nerve against me... And my sincere condolences...on behalf of my family, too.'

Hugo hung up. He buried his face in his hands. Nina had no family to be notified; her parents were gone, there were no brothers or sisters. She had a distant aunt living in Bucharest, the capital, but she was elderly, and he didn't want to alarm her with a call at this late hour. He had a lot of friends, but none that he felt like seeing and sharing this pain with. Everybody will know about it in due course.

There's nothing else left for me to do but follow Artur to Eddy's Bar, he thought and started walking down the grand staircase.

Chapter 63

'F OR WALTER NOW, the struggles and pains of life have crumbled to dust. The sorrow of parting only belongs to us. It is with a heavy heart that we, your colleagues, say goodbye to you, Walter.' Joseph Singer folded up the sheet of paper containing his farewell and stepped away from the grave, back into the ranks of the mourners. Melanie broke into sobs again. Caroline put an arm around her.

At least four hundred mourners came to pay their last respects. Joseph was preceded by Cameron, who delivered such an emotion-laden oration that there were tears in many eyes when he finished.

Then, slowly, in the outer ranks of the crowd the sounds of soft whispering conversations arose. 'Why was he sitting with Elmer's wife in a private plane on a Saturday morning if he was such a moral human being?' whispered an older lady to a tall, gaunt man standing next to her, who had to bend down to hear.

'Who cares?' He waved a hand. 'You have no idea, my dear lady, what it means to fly. It gives the sensation of freedom, an uplifting experience, the pleasure of having wings...'

'They were probably making out in the privacy of the plane up there,' remarked another young woman cheerfully.

'You have a dirty mind!' the gaunt man rebuked her angrily, earning the reprimanding shush of the crowd around them.

Zeno was standing right behind the grieving family. His mind though was far away, on Wanda's pregnancy. He was trying to consider the alternatives open to them; one obvious way to deal with the situation was to move away, to another part of the country and start a new life;

on the other hand, why shouldn't they stay and build a future here? He no longer had any doubts in his mind. He was going to marry Wanda right after the divorce was finalized, and if possible, raise a family. He was thinking about taking her on a trip the coming weekend, when they could talk about their future.

After the farewell speeches, Father Garnini resumed the funeral rites. He added a few remarks of his own, praising Walter's magnanimous soul and unwavering faith in God: 'Yes, he stumbled sometimes, but he never lost his faith in God's infinite grace and mercy. Yes, he was praised for his humanist spirit, but he was not a secular humanist, he always stood up for the Church, and he always preached the gospel as if he had been ordained to do so. His graceful spirit, his deep concern for his fellow man, and his abiding humanism will remain an example to us all,' Father Garnini concluded.

Tamas joined a row not too far from the grave. He was listening to the eulogies with respectful reverence. But he could not stop his thoughts wondering off, back home, to Iren and the children. He was looking forward to Saturday when he was going to start working. With the money he had received from Bertold he had bought a second-hand television set the day before. He set it up immediately and then he never turned it off again, so obsessed was he with the idea of total immersion in the language, even in his sleep.

He looked around when the slab covering the grave was being removed to make way for the urn, and he spotted Christine and Henrik. He thought about joining them, but then he changed his mind. It would be better to wait until it was over and they could talk more freely.

Ralph, Mark, Alfred, and Miriam lined up behind Cameron Fowler. They paid their respects to Walter with heads bowed in a sombre pose but without a word.

Finally, everybody's attention returned to the bier wrapped in a black sheet where now Walter's urn was lifted up and placed in a hole in the ground already lined with black-dyed rush. Melanie broke into sobs again and staggered to one side. She looked to be on the verge of collapse. A nearby mourner took her elbow.

Tamas took this opportunity to get closer to the Karadys. He quietly greeted them both.

'Terrible,' Christine whispered, 'and how young he was still.'

'Did you know him?' asked Tamas.

'Not personally, only by sight. But he was a very good-looking man.'

'To you every man is good-looking,' Henrik said with a sour smile.

But the ceremony was over and the crowd of mourners was breaking up.

Tamas tagged along when Henrik and Christine set off toward the cemetery gate. She offered to drop him off at home.

Zeno lingered with the slowly dispersing group of mourners. He wanted to express his condolences to Melanie and to squeeze her hand, but she was surrounded by the party politicos, so he turned around and headed for the exit. But not before he noticed a man in a dark jacket lurking near the spot where Walter's remains had been placed in eternal rest. He thought he recognized Elmer, but then that figure veered off in the opposite direction on a narrow path. When is Barbara's funeral? Zeno wondered.

Walter's accident was no longer front-page news in the papers, and the TV channels were already churning out newer stories. Even the news summaries had dropped the subject. Has the cause of the accident ever been uncovered? he wondered. He regretted now rushing away without talking to Melanie. And he could have asked Cameron about any new developments in the crash investigation.

He also thought about the simple urn containing Walter's ashes, and was reminded of something Heraclitus of Ephesus had said: that fire is the beginning and end of all things, that all objects burn, including the body and soul.

Cameron had an unfocused look as he led Melanie by the arm away from the grave. He felt worn out, drained. Ralph was in no better shape. His first public speech as a candidate on the Monday morning television news programmes had not gone well. His calm demeanour, his intelligent and well-composed sentences, earned Ralph some praise, but polls showed that he had dropped far behind the opposition. For the first time he was beginning to doubt himself.

—Chapter 64—

L ouis Terentini Esq. had his law offices on a side
street of the downtown area.
A silent elevator took Zeno up to the second
floor of a crypt-like office building. In the anteroom a
serious-looking secretary waited. She begged his patience
while she announced him to the attorney.

An inner door opened and a spry old man of small
stature and with bald head hurried to greet Zeno.

'Come in,' he said.

He had a manila folder in his hand, and now he
opened it.

'Your wife's attorney has filed for divorce as you know.
The grounds for divorce: the abandonment of house
and hearth, the habitual conduct of extramarital affairs
during the marriage. She must have material evidence for
the accusations; my counterpart showed me a fat folder
containing written reports and photos. I did not care to
examine it in detail; there will be no need for that unless
you wish to contest the case and attack the validity of the
evidence.'

Zeno was watching every move the tiny fingers of the
lawyer were making, and he thought: What a laughable
little man, and yet how much power and determination
he possesses.

'Yes,' he answered without taking his eyes off the hands
holding the evidence. 'I know all about it. Sylvia informed
me of the contents of the written material, and what can
be seen in the photos.'

'You mean to say the evidence is not in dispute?' asked
Terentini, adjusting the glasses on his short nose.

'No, the evidence is not in dispute.'

'Am I to understand you and your wife see the facts in the same light?'

'Yes.'

'And you, too, want a divorce?'

Zeno hesitated for a few seconds, even though he knew his marriage was not salvageable.

'Yes, I do want a divorce.' He finally managed to utter the words.

'In that case,' the attorney went on, 'the only business that concerns us is how the property is to be distributed.'

'Yes, I know,' Zeno hurried to agree.

'Your wife's lawyer has provided me with a list of assets subject to distribution. As I mentioned before, the company remains her property alone as it is privately held in her name.'

Zeno found it strange that during their conversation Terentini never once referred to Sylvia by her name. It sounded like maybe he too disapproved of her.

The attorney was leafing through the documents in the folder, apparently looking for something missing.

'It's supposed to be here somewhere, the copy of the notarized declaration in which you acknowledge your father-in-law's wish concerning the property rights to the company.'

'Yes, I know the document and I confirm the acknowledgment.'

'Well, then we can get on to the list of assets.' He pointed at a sheet of paper on top of the stack. 'According to this, the joint bank account shows 183,656 dollars plus 250,000 in equities.'

'I checked up on the current value, and it shows about a ten percent appreciation, which makes the total roughly 270,000 dollars,' Zeno intervened.

'Also on the list is your single-family dwelling on Herman Road. Last week three real estate agents appraised it. The approximate fair market price is about one million. Did you know about that?' The lawyer looked at Zeno.

'Yes, Sylvia mentioned something about having the house appraised but never got back to me with the results. The figure seems reasonable, about one million.'

'Furthermore your wife wants each of you to keep the automobile now in your use. We can forget about them. Well, that's all.' The old man snapped the cover shut on the folder. 'And one more minor detail, but I think it is to your benefit. Her lawyer made an offer on behalf of your wife: she's willing to buy your interest in your house with one half of the appraised value in cash.'

'Which means she wants to keep the house?'

'Yes, it would seem so. All in all, adding up everything, you'll end up with a significant amount of funds in your bank account.'

'Roughly three-quarters of a million, if half of the real estate value is included.'

'That's right.'

There was a momentary pause, or maybe a carefully calculated delay, before the interview could be politely brought to an end.

'So that's it, after all these years of marriage, after all these years of work, worry, after all those sleepless nights...' Zeno gave tentative expression to the sore feelings built up inside him, leaving his eyes on the lawyer and the sentence unfinished.

Terentini took off his glasses, picked up a wad of paper tissues and wiped his forehead. It was more out of habit than necessity, because there was not one bead of perspiration on his balding head, as Zeno observed. He was watching every move the lawyer made. He formed the impression the lawyer was a tough old bird who might see things his way.

'...Yes, I acknowledge that I gave up all rights to the company, but I've spent more than two decades managing it and developing it to its present state. Don't you think –' he intensified his stare at the attorney, 'don't you think I am entitled to some kind of compensation for that?

A golden parachute or something like that? Something
executives get on separation from the company?'

'Did you have a contract with the owner of the
company...?'

'You mean with my wife?' Zeno interrupted again.

'Yes, with her. Did you draw up a managerial
employment contract that was to be renewed every two,
three or five years, whatever the terms might be?'

'No. Never occurred to me. We were a family, our
financial interests coincided. Yes, I received a salary and,
in addition, yearly bonuses, but I turned them over to our
household account, and we both lived on that. Sylvia had
no other income except what she received as a distribution
from the company's profit. True, we ploughed two-thirds
of it back into the business. I too was entitled to a
percentage of the company profit every year. To be more
precise...' Zeno zeroed in with his gaze at the attorney,
'what I am leading up to here is that it was not only my
energy, my expertise, and talent that contributed to the
progressive development of the company but the funds
that we reinvested in it over the years. And half of those
funds were mine. Looking at it from that perspective,
what do you think? Am I not entitled to a piece of the
business?' asked Zeno, and then without waiting for an
answer continued: 'What I am saying is that beyond
the personal financial settlement involving the house
and household account, there's the business side of this
divorce. I have a right to some sort of severance pay like
any high-level executive. I've invested a lot of money in
the firm and I have a right to an equal share in it. Don't
you agree?'

'I most certainly do.' The attorney placed the glasses
back on his nose and flipped to a fresh page in his yellow
legal-size pad.

'Not quite three months ago I paid over three million
for a new poultry processing plant from our joint account.
Suppose this divorce had been filed six months earlier.

In that case I would not be handed three-quarters of a million but one and a half a million in addition. Don't you think?'

'I have it down here. First thing tomorrow morning I'll call your wife's lawyer and inform him of our demands. What total figure did you have in mind?'

'Since I took charge of the company we've reinvested about eight million. But I have detailed records of that in my office.'

'For the moment I don't need exact figures and documents but a sum you feel you're entitled to.' Terentini put down his gold fountain pen. 'After all, we can ask for more and if your wife doesn't have the cash in hand, she'll have to take out a mortgage on the plant.'

'What do you say we ask for four million?'

'We can ask for any amount you say, but how much we get will depend on what final settlement we can agree on.'

'Let's ask for four million,' said Zeno; he was getting tired of the conference.

'I'll get back to you right after I have a talk with your wife's lawyer.' Terentini rose from his desk and reached out for a handshake. 'Don't worry, I'll put up a good fight on your behalf.' And he patted Zeno's arm as he saw him off to the elevator.

Zeno had a lot to think about in the car. He started juggling the figures; if he could get three million at least as severance from the firm that would make nearly four million together with the personal divorce settlement. A tidy sum, enough for him and Wanda to live on pretty comfortably. He felt suddenly liberated and unburdened by the worries of recent days.

He was driving home, but home for him was not the old place where he used to return weary and tired at night, but some other place that meant a new beginning. A place, he thought wistfully, where joy and happiness also would have a home.

Chapter 65

TAMAS WAS DEADLY AFRAID he would be late on his first day at work. He had an alarm, but he didn't trust it. Even after testing it again and again in the middle of the night, he was still worried it wasn't working. Finally he gave up and got out of bed, opened the window, and went to take a shower.

From the hundred dollars Bertold had given him, he had purchased a pair of work boots in addition to the used TV set the day before. He had also got bread and some cold cuts, enough for lunch and dinner. On the city transportation map he had looked up the bus routes he had to take to work, which buses at what stops. To his surprise he only had to change buses once. The bus just around the corner could take him downtown, and from the downtown depot another bus would drop him off right in front of the hotel.

He stepped out of the apartment at five-thirty. He had to wait ten minutes for the first bus. Travel time was fourteen minutes. The next bus was already waiting there and whisked him to the hotel in twenty-three minutes. He was on the sidewalk a few minutes before half past six, his face bathed in lukewarm morning air. This being Saturday, he knew Monday's trip would take longer.

He held a plastic shopping bag with the boots and a sandwich in it. He slowly set off in the direction of the hotel building. He cut across the huge parking lot, across the endless lines of cars. The flashy green sign over the entrance gave him a friendly welcome. The concierge desk was unattended, but there was a young man hanging out at reception. While Tamas was trying to get his bearings, he was passed by two others. One of them was a woman in a maroon-coloured dress with a white collar, much like a chambermaid's uniform. Most likely an employee, he thought and followed her. She headed for the elevators in a hallway off the lobby. The sign above the door said: Staff Elevator, for the use of Employees Only. The door opened. Tamas followed the woman into the elevator. She pushed 'LEVEL A' inside. The trip down to the basement took only seconds. They stepped out into a recess where three hallways faced him, running left and right. The woman turned to the left. Tamas followed her again. Most of the doors on either side of the hallway were open. He peeked into one of them. Ironing boards were lined up all across the room. Behind one of them, a thin little woman was ironing a bed sheet. He walked on. The next door opened into a laundry room, filled with churning and buzzing washing machines. Two women were sorting through clothes on a workbench. One of them gave a questioning look to Tamas. 'Good morning. Maintenance,' he recited the well-rehearsed words, and added: 'New here.' The woman nodded and said something about finding Lester. 'Wait here,' she gestured pointing to the door. In a little while she returned with a man in blue overalls. He had short-cropped grey hair.

'You're lucky I got in early today.' He held out a hand. 'Mr Vid said you were going to start today, and assigned me to the job of supervising you. The big boss is not here yet, but I have the key to the locker room, I can let you in.' He was trumpeting his words, which seemed to be his usual way of speaking, while he led the way to a door further down the corridor. The room behind it had a penetrating smell of paint.

'Why did you dress up like a clown?' he asked with a big laugh, pointing at the necktie Tamas was wearing. 'This is a flunky job, son. I don't want to see you in this executive get-up.' He spoke with authority. 'Here's your padlock with two keys, and I'll keep the third in case you lose yours.'

'This is the only suit I have,' Tamas protested feebly.

'Okay, okay, but forget the tie.' Lester muttered. He was already busy with something else, rummaging through a box containing coverall uniforms. He picked one out, held it up to see how it would fit Tamas, but then he looked for another. Soon he came upon one that seemed to be Tamas's size and handed it to him.

'Try this on. Do you have a pair of boots?'

'Yes, I do.' Tamas was glad to show off the plastic bag hanging from his hand. 'I bought them yesterday.'

'Well, how does it fit?' Lester surveyed Tamas in the overalls.

'It pinches under the arms, but otherwise it feels fine,' Tamas answered.

'Okay, so that's taken care of. Did you bring something for lunch and snack?' asked Lester while he busied himself with the piece of pipe he had retrieved from a shelf.

'Yes, I did,' said Tamas.

'In there.' Lester pointed at a refrigerator in the corner. He unrolled an enormous black garbage bag from another box and pressed it into Tamas's hand. 'Go out to the parking lot and pick up all the trash you find. When the bag gets full, into the dumpster! And come in for another one. There are plenty more in the box.'

Tamas worked hard for two hours. He did not even notice Lester approaching among the cars.

'You're making progress,' he observed dryly. 'You'll have to finish this job later. At ten this morning they're having a meeting in the downstairs conference room. You'll have to clean up the restrooms. Mr Vid is not yet in, and we can't get going on the dance floor repair job in the nightclub.'

Tamas tagged along with Lester without a word. He tossed the half-full trash bag into a dumpster behind the hotel.

They entered the building through a service entrance. In the basement Lester showed Tamas where the cleaning tools were stored and how they were to be used, and then left him alone.

Time passed quickly. Tamas didn't know how long he had been working in the lavatories. He was getting his tools together in preparation to return to the maintenance workshop when Lester reappeared.

'I figured you were just about done here, that's why I'm back.' He blared it out while inspecting the washbasins and the wall-to-wall mirrors. He could see everything was shining clean.

'How do you like it?' the young man asked as they were leaving.

'Not bad, not bad.' The old man nodded and then issued a new command, 'Take these tools back, I'll wait for you here.'

Only a few minutes later they were already looking at the peeling tapestry in the bathroom of a suite up on the ninth floor.

'We'll have to work on the walls in room 917 and 926, both,' said Lester while marking the door frame with a black felt-tip pen. 'They're like wild animals, the way they carry on,' he added angrily and waved to his assistant to follow him out into the corridor.

The restoration of the wall surface and the tapestry took longer than Tamas had expected. He didn't get back to the workshop until a quarter to one. Lester had finished his lunch already and he was turning the pages of a newspaper.

'That's what happens to slowpokes.' Lester looked up from the newspaper with glee. 'Don't worry, you still have fifteen minutes left of your lunch break, plenty of time to stuff your face.' And he had a good laugh at his own joke.

Tamas washed his hands and retrieved his lunch bag from the refrigerator. He devoured the first sandwich in less than a minute. Then his eyes latched on the other one. If I eat it now I'll have nothing for the afternoon break, he thought. But then he stopped thinking about it and unwrapped the second sandwich. He took a big bite of it, still keeping his eyes on Lester while he continued eating.

Mr Vid arrived at three in the afternoon. He immediately summoned both of them. Lester, who had been following Tamas around all day, was now leading the way. The big boss was waiting for them in his office. For the project of repairing the dance floor he had requisitioned two extra workers from the technical support group, which made five people in the room.

'How is the new help working out?' he asked the old man.

'He's learning slowly, boss. I'll beat it into him,' Lester announced boisterously and then produced another loud laugh.

At seven in the evening Mr Vid inspected the new grout in the dance floor with visible satisfaction. He even tested it by skipping and hopping around on the half-inch-thick milk-white vinyl tiles. He wanted to make doubly sure that none of them would curl up at the corners. He nodded several times, indicating all was well and everybody was free to go home.

On saying goodnight to Lester and Tamas, he ordered them to come in at eight Sunday morning.

'In compensation, you two can take Monday off,' he assured them briskly.

On the bus heading downtown Tamas was half asleep. This time he took no notice of the balmy summer evening passing by the windows.

As soon as he got home he fell right into bed without bothering to undress. He was aching all over. Fatigue poured like lead all over his body.

—Chapter 66—

MURDER IN HOTEL ODÉON
—XXI—

BY THE TIME Hugo got to Eddy's Bar, Artur's eyes were beginning to be out of focus from shots of brandy already consumed. He was sitting at the bar with only a tumbler for company. Silently, almost without being noticed, Hugo sat down beside him. He too ordered a shot of brandy and looked at his friend with an expression of misery, feeling tired and burned out.

'We should know a lot more by tomorrow,' Hugo said quietly.

'For me this whole business seems unreal; I feel as if we had just stepped out of a cinema where we watched a mystery. As I said before, I went to see Fabian this afternoon. He promised to keep the membership roll and the activities of our Club confidential and out of the tabloids.'

'And how about Valerian?'

'If Mueller succeeds in identifying that mysterious third visitor, then he feels he'll have the case wrapped up,' reported Artur.

He didn't go into details. He didn't mention that Hugo's name was also on the detective's list of suspects.

*   *   *

They lingered in Eddy's Bar, but Hugo's depression made the conversation difficult. Artur kept changing the subject and bringing up things that had nothing to do with the tragedy. He refused to talk about Nina, or anything related to her, and he even avoided any speculation about

Hugo's future. He talked only in generalities, musing about the trivial things of the everyday world and how meaningless they were now.

They had stopped drinking and were just sitting there next to each other, looking into the distance.

Hugo was the first to stand up. By that time his eyes, too, were out of focus. He said he needed to go outside and get some fresh air.

Miklos was still waiting with the limo parked by the curb, but Hugo sent him home, telling him he wanted to walk, he needed to air out his head. He told the driver to pick him up at eight in the morning as usual.

Slowly he set off for home on the main down-town thoroughfare. The oncoming traffic's headlights bombarded his eyes, unsettling him. The fearful shadows of loneliness and despair flitted around him; they came trudging with him. He let them.

He got home from his wanderings around midnight. He searched his pockets for the keys to the house, and was almost surprised when he found them. He had put them there mechanically, without noticing.

He stepped over the threshold, turned on the lights, and then in the mirror of the entrance foyer he caught sight of a stranger. When he looked over the rooms of the house he got the feeling he was in an unknown place; the walls and the furniture between them looked as unfamiliar as if he were an intruder in a strange house.

Somewhere far away, dogs were barking desperately.

He stopped in his tracks, frozen, waiting for Nina to come through the kitchen door with a cheerful face and a melancholy, crooked smile:

Look at the time, why are you so late again? I had dinner waiting for you. It must be stone cold by now! Let me go and warm it up. Put your slippers on in the meantime. Did you have a hard day?

The door to the kitchen slowly swung open. He

looked dreamily in the direction of the squeak. But then nothing. Nothing moved.

He stepped back to the front door and shut it, turning the key twice in the lock.

The wind, he thought, putting his slippers on. The lights were on in the kitchen. On the stove, it seemed the dinner stew was simmering.

'Nina,' he called out her name softly. 'Nina,' he repeated it more loudly. The third time he bellowed.

*   *   *

Hugo woke at seven thirty. He could hardly open his eyes, they seemed glued shut.

Suddenly the realization struck him. Nina was dead, and last night he had slept alone in the house. Yesterday's events started to surface into his memory. The most vividly reproduced among them was the long walk home at night. Mechanically he took a shower and dressed. A few minutes after eight he was already closing the front door behind him.

Miklos sprang out of the driver's seat and opened the door to the back seat, greeting the mayor awkwardly and with some distress.

'To the office as usual?'

'Yes,' Hugo answered curtly.

The secretary welcomed him with tear-soaked eyes. 'I'll get your tea in a minute.' She said turning around to attend to the chore. She seemed at pains to avoid Hugo's eyes.

It was obvious she knew about the tragedy, but felt awkward talking about it, the Mayor thought. He thanked her for her attentiveness. When the door closed behind Elsa, Hugo looked around in panic.

'The Prefect is on line one,' came the voice of the secretary.

'Good morning!' Geza's voice rang out, followed by a little pause while he cleared his throat several times.

'I'm not going to ask how you slept last night.' He paused again to clear his throat. 'I got a call early this morning from Bucharest. The police there issued an arrest warrant for two young men who had been implicated in another murder-robbery case. They are accused of stabbing two women and a man last week in the same way as Nina was attacked, and then they robbed their victims. We expect these fellows will be in custody soon. Jonas says he'll be seeing you in an hour and you'll be able to learn more from him.

'Can I do anything for you in the meantime?' the Prefect asked then.

Hugo remained silent.

'Jonas and I decided to hold off on the press conference, perhaps until the afternoon. I'll keep in touch and keep you informed,' the Prefect said finally and hung up.

Hugo kept the receiver at his ear for almost another minute before he slowly realized he was listening to the dial tone.

The previous evening he had wondered what Nina had been doing on Route 31. Then he remembered Nina telling him about her plans to go out to the country house yesterday morning. Only twenty-four hours ago.

For minutes more he sat at his desk, hoping for more illumination on the subject, but then he gave up and called Elsa into his office. The secretary discreetly knocked on the door before pushing it open.

'Please take a seat,' the mayor said in a tone more like usual. 'I need your help. This may turn into a very long day.' He glanced at Elsa from the corner of his eye and then went on, 'I ask you, however, to keep everything I tell you confidential until such time as it is made public. I'm sure you heard that my wife was killed in her car yesterday. The police think they know who did it. They think it was two young men who did the same thing before. A few minutes ago, the Prefect told me the Bucharest police issued an arrest warrant for them.'

Now that he managed to put it into words, the realization came to him that at last he was able to accept as fact what he had known all this time.

'Should I cancel all meetings and appointments for today?' she asked on her way out the door.

'Yes, please, and thank you for reminding me.'

After she left, he just sat there.

*   *   *

Police Chief Jonas Balog, Detective Fabian Mueller, and Sergeant Leo Radich, the head of the crime scene investigation unit within the criminal department, were soon seated in Hugo's office.

Sergeant Radich reported finding fingerprints and scraps of fabric in Nina's car that were not hers. With this evidence, they expected to be able to tie the two suspects to Nina's murder and soon arrest them.

'Even before the attack on your wife,' Chief Balog added, 'the descriptions and the police artist's sketches of the suspects were widely circulated all over the country, in news reports, and even in handouts. I've no doubt we'll soon have them in custody.'

'I'd like to go over the press release with you,' the Police Chief said awkwardly, as he produced a document from his briefcase and placed it on the desk in front of the Mayor. 'I promised Geza that we'd be ready to face the media by two o'clock this afternoon.'

Hugo quickly read through the text, which was terse, giving only a matter-of-fact description of the events as reconstructed from the evidence. There was a paragraph at the end addressed to the members of the press, asking that the case should be handled respectfully and with understanding, being mindful of the grieving Mayor.

Hugo nodded his approval of the document.

The Police Chief lingered after his two subordinates had left the office. 'I know it's none of my business,' he said awkwardly, 'but as far as the funeral arrangements are concerned…the memorial service…well…so far the subject hasn't come up, but I just wanted to offer my help, the whole Department's help…' here he looked at the Mayor again, and then quickly finished what he had to say with a big sigh, 'since I owe you so much, a great debt of gratitude.'

'You do me a great honour,' Hugo answered in a voice that he could not keep from cracking. 'Very nice of you to offer.'

He accompanied Jonas all the way to the staircase. They walked side by side in silence.

—*Chapter 67*—

FRIDAY EVENING Wanda got home upset by another run-in with her parents. Christine had wanted her to babysit Patrick on Sunday; but Wanda had arranged with the vice-chairman of the student association that she would act as a tour guide to a visiting delegation of students from the University of British Columbia and would provide transportation. It happened that the visitors had chosen this particular Sunday for their visit, which meant she would have to spend the whole day with them.

'I've told you a hundred times –' she ended the fight with Christine, 'I am not a babysitter. I go to school. I work. I have my own life to live.'

Henrik had listened to their quarrel with studied indifference. He did not intervene in the dispute between mother and daughter. Finally he mediated. 'We hoped you'd help us out, but maybe you'll be free the following Sunday. As you know, it's just a visit to friends we were planning, and we could put it off till next Sunday if that suited your schedule. Or do you have plans for that day, too?'

'The Sunday after this, I'll be free to take care of Patrick,' Wanda agreed, but took her leave still sulking. She drove home with her nerves tattered. She checked the mailbox at the entrance. Among other things there was a letter from Paul. She ripped open the envelope on the spot.

Hi Wanda,
   I meant to say goodbye with this letter, but I changed my mind. Why should I say goodbye to someone I still love?

375

I am sorry if I ever hurt you in any way in the past. And I am sorry if I failed to please you, no matter how hard I tried. I don't think I'll ever be able to change or ever learn to enjoy doing the dishes.

I'm writing to let you know I'm leaving town soon. I wanted you to get the news directly from me and not at second hand.

I'll remember you forever.

That's all.

Bye, Paul

The lines got blurred in front of her eyes. She took her time refolding the letter and putting it back in the torn envelope.

I'll remember you too, forever, she whispered to herself.

*   *   *

Zeno had made some progress in the divorce settlement. At first his attorney had only bad news. His wife's lawyer had told him that Sylvia didn't even want to hear of the four million in compensation. In Sylvia's view, the money ploughed back into the poultry business was shared expenditure by agreement of both spouses.

'But in case of divorce, assets acquired by shared expenditure are subject to equal sharing,' Zeno had argued. Terentini accepted the objection and asked for more time for further negotiations.

That afternoon, Terentini reported back on new developments. Sylvia's lawyer had called and conceded her willingness to bargain about the compensation, but of course the sum of four million was out of the question.

Terentini sounded unusually elated this time around, saying he had managed to achieve something. Zeno was not quite as sanguine about the results. 'Let's keep the champagne on ice until the money is deposited in my bank account.'

The sad political rally Zeno had just attended had not helped his mood. The replacement candidate's presentation was lethargic and uninspired. Cameron had been pleased to see Zeno there.

'Walter's absence is sorely felt, isn't it?' said Zeno, squeezing Cameron's hand. 'Two months ago, we presented a whole different team to the voters. What they see now is pretty hopeless, isn't it?'

'I wish I could contradict you. We're fighting a losing battle now. And not even for an election victory, but just for the survival of the party.'

Driving to Wanda's on Friday night, Zeno spotted a florist's and quickly pulled up to the curb. He enjoyed teasing the teenage salesgirl who was eager to show off her freshest flowers. She was trying to convince him to buy orchids because they were more expressive than any other. Zeno finally decided on yellow roses, and asked for a bouquet of them.

'But why yellow? If it's roses you want, why not red? Like these.' And she went over to a solitary, but huge, full glass vase at the edge of the display table.

'Because I like yellow roses,' Zeno insisted with a smile, pointing out the stems he wanted to be included in his bouquet. 'It's the colour of acquiescence, merriment, and unbounded love.'

The girl examined the finished bouquet from every angle before handing it over with a satisfied smile.

'I wouldn't mind receiving a bouquet like this from a boyfriend,' she said wistfully.

Zeno entered the apartment holding the bouquet behind his back.

He found Wanda waiting for him, looking as happy as he had ever seen her. Laughing, she grabbed the roses from his hand.

During dinner Zeno several times sank back into his thoughts, staring blankly in front of him. 'Don't you like my cooking?' Wanda asked, trying to recapture her lover's attention.

'I most certainly do,' he responded with a relaxed smile, 'I've never had anything better.'

'Did you have a bad day?'

'Well, it ended well,' he said and proceeded to give a full account of his telephone conversations with Terentini.

'That's terrific, now you are getting somewhere,' she said. 'We must celebrate the occasion.'

She dug out a bottle of rosé champagne from the refrigerator, took glasses from the shelf and handed him the bottle, asking him to open it. The pink liquid frothed up in the glasses; Zeno had to wait to fill them to the rim. 'To our health, my one and only,' he said as they clinked glasses.

Afterwards she grabbed Zeno's hand. 'Come with me,' she told him, 'I'll change your mood.' She dragged him into the bedroom.

'Let me help you,' she whispered while pulling the shirt off her lover. 'Today you'll be under my command and do as I tell you,' she said as she planted a passionate kiss on his mouth.

*   *   *

Zeno and Wanda were driving to a vacation resort about seventy kilometres from the city when they heard on the radio the official findings about the accident in which Walter died:

'...Yesterday the inquiry into the air traffic accident that claimed two lives, including that of Walter Wallmeyer, the candidate of the Conservative Party for the National Assembly, came to an end. After a thorough investigation the safety commission found nothing amiss in the wreckage of the Cessna type aircraft, nothing that might have caused the tragedy. In their final report, made public last night, they described the accident as inexplicable and mysterious. The weather forecast for today: a cloudy sky with the wind picking up from the southwest...'

Zeno turned down the volume on the radio.

'Inexplicable and mysterious...' He repeated the words from the news report while giving Wanda's hand a squeeze. 'What they mean is that we will never know what happened to Walter and Barbara.'

It had been Wanda who had suggested they drive up there and spend Saturday in the lap of nature, since she was going to be busy the next day with the visitors to her university. The popular and now luxurious resort was an extension of a small town at the foot of a mountain range. Its natural hot springs and outdoor pools attracted a lot of visitors, especially on weekends.

For some time they were both quiet, watching the road before them. Each had retreated into his or her own thoughts.

There's no turning back now. I must finish what I've started. I wonder how Sylvia will manage on her own? he asked himself, but then banished the thought from his mind. Terentini says she's planning to take over the management of the company. It'll be quite a challenge for her! She was never very good at technical problems; she always needed my help even with new household appliances. But she'll have Dora to guide her, he reassured himself with a thin smile. I hadn't thought of that. But how will the others adjust to Sylvia as the big boss? Will they accept her?

Wanda too was lost in thought, although in a different direction. When my mother finds out what I've done, she'll surely beat the living daylights out of me. I'm carrying the child of man who is much older, and I'm not even sure I'm in love with him. Okay, let's say I am, but not madly in love with him. I'm leading the poor fool down the garden path. I broke up his marriage.

What kind of a person am I? I don't like myself for that. What's my graduation going to look like, with a baby in my arms? What are my girlfriends going to say? So what, who cares? It's not their life that is at stake but mine. Let them mind their own business. I wonder what it's going to be? A boy or a girl? I'd like to have a boy. He'd not have to suffer as I have.

And what's my new life going to be like? Zeno is pleasant and attentive, but he's going to age much faster than me. And then what's going to happen to me? What indeed? I'll have to get myself a younger man. Maybe two. I certainly deserve it. My god, what will I think up next?

She suddenly turned to Zeno and let her beaming look scan his face.

'I am madly in love with you. Did you know that?' she said with emotion.

The man squeezed her hand.

By the time they reached the spa, the parking lot was already full. But eventually they managed to find a room for the night. They decided to stay until Sunday morning and then drive back to the city very early.

—*Chapter 68*—

A T DAWN Tamas woke from his sleep, again with the frightening thought that he was late for work. One glance at the TV digital clock, however, assured him it was only four thirty-two; he had roughly two more hours before leaving the house. That was when he realized he had dropped on the bed and fallen asleep in his street clothes the evening before. He undressed and slipped under the covers with the idea of getting a little more sleep, come what may.

He reached the hotel ten minutes before eight. There was a group of pilots and flight attendants waiting in front of the reception desk. The young man behind the desk beckoned to Tamas as soon as he saw him enter.

'Do you have a driver's licence?' the receptionist asked.

'Yes, I do.'

'Then I'll ask you to do me a big favour. There's no one here to take them out to the airport.' He pointed at the group. 'Could you help me out?'

'Yes,' Tamas blurted out without thinking about it, and just to make sure he understood what was going on, he pointed at the group asking, 'To airport?'

'Great, you got the idea. Here is the key to the minibus, it's parked in the reserved lot. Go and pull up at the entrance.'

'I do not know where airport,' said Tamas, surprising himself with how well he put the words together.

'You take this road to the freeway going south.'

'South?'

'Yes.'

Tamas had never driven anything like a minibus in his life, but he had handled trucks before, and the size did not daunt him, but the alien road signs did. He took his place behind the wheel with considerable trepidation and drove the vehicle slowly and carefully to the hotel entrance. The airline personnel hopped aboard without any questions. They continued their lively discussion that had been disrupted a minute earlier. One of them told Tamas he could get rolling.

He had to go around the block twice before he found the southbound ramp to the freeway; but from then on, all he had to do was follow the airplane signs to the airport, and he arrived there without any further problems. His passengers disembarked still engaged in their loud banter. One of them, a blonde stewardess, put a twenty-dollar bill in Tamas's hand. He was so astonished that at first he wanted to give it back, but the young lady gently pushed his hand away. 'Keep it, it's yours. Thank you for the favour.' She smiled and hurried after the others.

In fifteen minutes Tamas was back at the hotel. He handed the keys to the receptionist, and he was already on his way towards the staff elevator to the basement when the young man called him back. 'How about the tip?' He gave Tamas a stern look. Seeing that he was not understood he reworded the question: 'Money? Did you get any money?'

'Yes,' Tamas stuttered. He reached into his pocket and fished out the twenty-dollar bill. 'Here.' He was disgruntled about handing over the little extra earnings, coming as it did almost as if from heaven; on his way back to the hotel he was already making plans for it.

'The custom here is that we share tips,' said the young man handing over a ten-dollar bill to Tamas. 'I lined up the job for you, so we go half and half – we split the money. Now we're all set.'

When Tamas entered the maintenance workshop Lester looked at his watch with undisguised peevishness. It was eight thirty-seven.

'Where have you been?' he growled.

'I drove a group of pilots and stewardesses to the airport.'

'Who authorized that?' The old man's voice was unrelenting.

'You don't really think I did it on my own, do you? The receptionist sent me.'

'What the hell? Is he trying to be another Mr Vid?' The old man went on grumbling but more to himself as he unrolled another big black trash bag and sent Tamas outside to pick up the trash in the parking lot and the walkways.

Through the morning, Tamas worked as hard as he had the day before. To his astonishment, at lunchtime Lester called him in. They sat down to the workbench for their meal. While they were eating their sandwiches the old man questioned Tamas about his life in every detail. Where he came from. What his job was back home. What his childhood was like. When he learned that the application for the immigration of the young man's family had been rejected, his face turned sombre and he said with meaningful emphasis: 'Come in tomorrow morning at ten and go to the accounting office. I'll call the chief accountant and ask him to fill out a hotel ID card for your name plus a deposition proving that you have a job here with a steady income. Let's see what those high and mighty bureaucrats in the Immigration Office will have to say.' He patted the young man's shoulder. Tamas was lost for words, he was so surprised.

By three in the afternoon they struck up a friendship. They went together from one chore to the next. Even Mr Vid remarked on it. He ran into them at the main entrance where Tamas was changing light bulbs while Lester was holding the ladder.

'What happened?' he asked Lester. 'You two become inseparable?'

The old man mumbled something into his moustache to the effect that, 'It's none of your business.' It was unusual for the manager to drop in on a Sunday, but he wanted to inspect the dance floor again, and make sure the repair work had successfully held up under the Saturday night crowd. He didn't linger; in a few minutes he took off again without saying goodbye but visibly satisfied.

That day the old man did not let Tamas wait for the bus but gave him a ride downtown in his car.

'And come Tuesday morning, I want you to report to work with good news!' he yelled after Tamas, who got off at the downtown central bus stop.

Walking home on his street, Tamas was full of dreams and hopes. He felt like skipping all the way. He stopped several times to take in the view of the modest little single-family homes nestled in a continuous green lawn under protective trees, and he gave a neighbourly nod to a flower bed here and there. For the first time since his arrival he felt – yes, he could start a new life in his new country.

—*Chapter 69*—

Z ENO AND WANDA got into the car a few minutes
before seven Sunday morning. It had been worth
it to stay for the whole of Saturday. The growing
familiarity with each other's body guided them in new
explorations, new ways of connecting skin to skin, flesh
to flesh, and soul to soul. Zeno could feel the last icicles
of reservation melt inside him. He was feverishly looking
forward to what the future held for them.

By eight-thirty they pulled into Wanda's parking lot
and stopped beside the girl's ancient car. Zeno stood out
to help her with her overnight bag.

'I don't feel like spending the day without you,' Wanda
told him, raising her face and puckering her lips. 'I hope I
can get away early and maybe we can go out to dinner,' she
said wistfully. She began to ransack her voluminous purse
for her car keys without much success. 'This bottomless
purse, it holds everything, but I can't find anything in it.'

Zeno was looking on with amusement.

'Found it!' she yelled, lifting high a bunch of keys like
a trophy of a hunt.

'See you tonight,' Zeno said to her departing car as it
rolled out of the parking lot.

He didn't feel up to seeing anyone and just kept
driving through the city for almost an hour. Everything
looked different to him that morning – enchanted almost.
He surrendered himself to the pleasant sensation of flying
high, to a mood that quickened the blood in his limbs.

Suddenly a limo pulled out in front of him from a
side street, and if Zeno had not jerked the steering wheel
in the right direction, they would have collided. By the
time he recovered from the shock and looked behind
him the unruly limo had cut across the main road and

385

disappeared down an alley. This close shave brought Zeno back to his senses, and he changed his direction toward the plant. He decided to spend the day in his office until Wanda got home, going through all his papers and getting ready to hand over the management of the company to his successor, whoever that might be.

*   *   *

The visitors were supposed to arrive by nine-thirty at the latest, but Wanda was still waiting for them in front of the university at ten o'clock. They finally showed up at ten-fifteen, three girls, arriving in a beat-up small sedan. They seemed likable to Wanda. After just a few words they were all tuned in to the same frequency. Kitty was slender, with a high forehead, short-cropped hair and a challenging personality. Edina was short and pudgy, with piano legs; her face was freckled and she had a lisp. Claudia on the other hand could be described as beautiful, with blue eyes, a pixie nose and thin, sensitive lips. The three of them kept up a constant patter. Kitty was too politically correct, Edina a bit of a spoiled child, and Claudia acted a bit superior, but Wanda listened tolerantly to all of them. In the morning she showed them the most important university buildings, leading them through the central library and let them have a look at the chemistry and physics laboratories.

At noon they went to lunch in the most popular cafeteria on campus, which was also the only one that stayed open over the summer when the university was functioning at a much lower capacity. During the meal the girls hotly debated the merits of the latest style; the almost ankle-long skirt was unanimously rejected. Kitty asked Wanda's opinion on the subject, but Wanda, brushing the question aside, asked them if they had read any exciting books in the summer vacation. Of the three, it was only Edina who piped up with a report – she said Nabokov's *Lolita* was a great read, she could hardly put it down, and she recommended it wholeheartedly to everyone present. Claudia immediately dismissed the book: 'I can't see what's so great about the love affair of a paedophile professor and a teenage girl. To hell with all those child-molesting, perverted men!'

'Did you read it, too?' Edina asked, surprised.

'Yes, I did some years ago, but it almost made me puke.'

After lunch Wanda drove the girls to an ethnographic display in the museum downtown, an authentic recreation of the life of the early settlers. During their visit Claudia was bored, yawning at the old-style homes, stores and workshops. Edina, in spite of her pudginess, hurried with unexpected nimbleness from one place to another, providing a lively commentary on the sights. Wanda and Kitty hit upon men as a subject they were both interested in, and they kept up a non-stop conversation comparing experiences.

They didn't realize how late it was getting. It was close to seven in the evening, almost closing time, when they became aware of how famished they were. Luckily the Ye Olde Style cafeteria in the museum stayed open late. The speciality of the day was breaded pork chop with French fries. After dinner, they piled into Wanda's car. She was to drop them back to the student dormitory at the university. The long day seemed to have put Claudia in a melancholy mood, and she kept asking her friends to simmer down.

Wanda, keeping her eyes on the road, was the only one silent in the car. Her thoughts were somewhere else; they were centred on Zeno and their child on the way – on the new life ahead of her. They were stopped by the traffic light at an intersection with a major artery of the city that had streetcars running on it. The traffic light was changing to yellow, but she didn't want to risk slipping through and stepped on the brake.

It seemed to take forever for a streetcar to make its way across with a clatter that was given an accompaniment by a low-flying airplane heading in to land at the airport.

Wanda's eyes were fixed on the traffic light, waiting impatiently for it to turn green. She was thinking of Zeno and the night ahead. Well behind the tram train, maybe four hundred meters away, was a thirty-ton truck loaded with quarry stones, moving at a pace far above the legal speed limit.

The driver was a man well past thirty and covered with a three-or-four-days' growth of bristle. He was nervously shifting his eyes from one side of the avenue to the other. The rapidly approaching behemoth vehicle caught the attention of pedestrians on the sidewalk, out for a stroll in the pleasant evening air, and they later described the event as it unfolded before their eyes.

The truck must have been about eighty metres from the intersection that had stalled Wanda's progress when the traffic light turned yellow in front of the unshaven truck driver. His first instinct was to step on the brake, but at that speed he figured there was no way of stopping that vehicle with the heavy load of quarry stones it was carrying. At the moment when the light changed from yellow to red, the truck was about forty meters from the crossing.

Wanda, who by then had joined in the girls' chat, already had her foot over the gas pedal, ready to step on it as soon as the way was open to her; she was letting out a pure-hearted laugh when they shot across the avenue under the fresh green traffic light. Claudia happened to glance to the right as they were reaching the middle of the intersection, and she saw the huge truck zooming toward them, but she had no time to cry out.

*   *   *

Zeno spent all day Sunday sorting out two decades of personal correspondence: long-expired subscription notices, parking tickets, various projections and evaluations, and other musty memorabilia.

From one of the drawers a stack of long-forgotten photos came to light. They had been taken at a seaside resort. Sylvia was still young. Her smile was so enticing in the picture that it made Zeno's heart jump. Only for a second though, because then he returned to the present, and that moment immortalized by the photo seemed so distant that it lacked all reality. He slipped the photo back into an envelope with the rest of them.

By nine o'clock in the evening he was surprised he had not yet heard from Wanda. He telephoned her, and listened to the ring a dozen times. Uneasy, he decided to go to Wanda's flat and wait for her there.

He got there by nine-thirty, pushed the intercom three times at short intervals, and waited. There was no answer. He pushed the intercom again, longer and harder. And then again and again. No response.

He started to get worried. Finally he ambled back to the car to while away the time listening to the radio. A Haydn sonata calmed him for a time, and then he decided to switch stations, finding one with the news on:

> '...The economy is taking centre stage in the election platform of the incumbent liberal party. A tragic traffic accident in the downtown area this evening claimed the lives of four young women, all college students. The national council of labour unions...'

He turned off the radio and jumped out of the car. He had a dreadful premonition. Four girls, the words echoed in his mind. That boy, Paul, is not such a hapless creature after all, he wasn't in the car... But those four girls...

He glanced up and down the street in panic.

There was a bar on the corner where he and Wanda once had a cup of coffee. He practically ran there. He stepped inside the almost empty place and looked up at the TV screen suspended above the far end of the bar...

*   *   *

Christine was busy in the kitchen, taking the clean plates, pots, and pans out of the dishwasher one by one. She stopped for a second with a bowl in her hand when she noticed an abrupt change in the sound coming from the TV set in the living room, indicating that they had broken off the usual programming. This happens all the time, she thought. Somewhere in the world some madmen have taken hostages again or robbed a bank. She shrugged, and she continued with her chore.

'Mommy, Mommy, hurry, come in here!' Patrick ran into the kitchen, grabbed hold of his mother's hand and started dragging her into the living room.

'What's the matter, my dear?' Christine followed her son to humour him.

'Look!' Patrick pointed at the TV screen.

'…the driver and the three passengers in the sedan were college students. Witnesses at the scene say the speed of the truck was well over eighty kilometres an hour when it roared into the intersection against the red light, ploughing directly into the side of the passenger car that had the green light. Paramedics pronounced the four girls in the car dead at the scene. Of the victims of the accident that happened about ninety minutes ago…'

– and then shown on the screen were the ID photos of Kitty, Edina, Claudia, and Wanda –

'…three of them were visiting from a nearby university…'

Christine saw the room turn black as she collapsed in a faint. Patrick, seeing his mother lying in a helpless heap on the floor, broke into hysterical sobs and ran to find his father in the study.

—Chapter 70—

MURDER IN HOTEL ODÉON
—XXII—

HUGO FELT INCREASINGLY UNCOMFORTABLE in his house, almost like a guest who's overstayed his welcome, finding it more and more impossible to settle down and rest up from the tragedy. Finally, with time on his hands, he decided to do a thorough clean-up job and get rid of every item that had belonged to Nina. They suddenly lost their meaning without their owner present.

He started the clean-up with the pantry. Obviously, the first order of business was to discard goods that would spoil and any container or can he could not identify. If in doubt, out it went.

The dressing room, however, turned out to be a harder nut to crack. He ran into an insurmountable pile of scarves, shoes, belts, caps, hats, and other articles of clothing, all things he had seen before without taking notice.

Who would have thought a family of two needed so many possessions? He started furiously stuffing everything he considered useless into a huge black plastic trash bag.

The bag was more than half full when he changed his mind and dumped its contents in the middle of the living room.

He decided it would be better if he called a charity and let them take whatever they could sell in their thrift store for the needy, and then he would dump the rest in the garbage. Having made his decision, he closed the door of the small dressing room. He looked over the bedroom as his next target when his eyes alighted on a book on Nina's night table. He bent down for the small brown hardcover book, without a title or anything else printed on the outside.

He opened it absent-absentmindedly. It was a diary, and he could immediately recognize Nina's handwriting in it. At the same time everything became a blur again.

No, I can't go on like this! I'll be no good for anything if this keeps happening to me – if every time I touch something related to Nina, my guilty conscience plunges me into despair. He sat down into an easy chair, the elegant, gilt-edged diary still in his hand. He took a deep breath, and opened it once more.

He began to read, sampling the diary at randomly selected entries —

> This is not a 'diary'. I never liked the idea of a diary as a refuge. I write only little notes, simple sketches of whatever goes through my mind, to fill my solitude or simply to relieve my impatience with day-to-day life.

> ### THIRD ENTRY
> 'In my well-considered opinion, the best way to gain the will to live...is through the pleasure that accompanies sexual union... That pleasure is the essence and core of all things in nature, the purpose and meaning of all existence.'
> I don't recall now where I found the above quote, but it impressed me so much that I copied it into my notebook. I came upon it today while I was looking through my notes. The idea of the 'will to live' resonated with me. This 'will to live' was the secret source of my energy, this is what

has helped me through my difficulties, given me the strength to manage crises and conflicts, and maybe it also provided a balm for the pain of my infertility.

I have never broached the subject of this will to live with Hugo, because it has never occurred to him to give up the struggle. He was made of different clay. He's combative, he's always ready to respond to the challenges of life, and he can muster his physical and intellectual resources at a moment's notice. In many ways, he is the man of my dreams, the one I had always wanted. As soon as I met him I too felt stronger, I felt I could achieve fulfilment; with him beside me my self-confidence increased more than I would have dreamed possible.

In female company, I am often asked about my self-confidence. Is Hugo really the man he seems to be, the well-balanced, thoughtful, gentle, and pleasant partner? In response to a question like this I sing his praises.

True enough, our love was self-explanatory, taken for granted, always at hand, inexhaustible; it only goes up and down in intensity, just like one's mood. I always enjoy Hugo's company; our sex life, even at its most mundane, always satisfies me. I find gratification with him, I can surrender myself to him without ever worrying about anything and without the slightest hint of the nausea I hear about from some other women. On the contrary, I am the selfish one who tends to forget about the world while I have him on top of me; I can't see, can't hear, I simply surrender myself to the moment, to the pleasure of the moment, reeling in the arms of the sensation that overpowers me so much that I couldn't escape its sweet embrace if I wanted to. While writing these lines I cannot help but feel it's a good thing Hugo is not around to see what I am scribbling; he would probably be surprised by my praise, because I have never confessed such passion to him with such sincerity, not even in my most sentimental moments.

We talk about our life in a very matter-of-fact manner. Although I consider him a sensitive soul, I have never seen him go overly sentimental, or let himself get carried away on the wings of the moment, as I often do. He's completely pragmatic; he approaches every problem from its everyday, material side. 'Problems and difficulties exist for us to solve, because that's our business,' he always says. Hugo doesn't think the way I do. Perhaps that's the reason we get along so well. Whenever I wear myself out worrying about some problem, he concentrates on the logical and pragmatic solution. Often it turns out he was right. What I really enjoy though, and what makes me secretly value him so highly, is that he never exploits his triumph over a problem but presents it in such a way that at the end I turn out to be the mastermind, with him simply approving what I proposed.

NINTH ENTRY

Today I had lunch with Artur. We ran
into each other in one of the downtown
department stores. He's a pleasant man,
somewhat of a ham, and thinks highly
of himself; nevertheless, he can be a lot
of fun. He made me laugh a lot – his
nonsense and silly jokes were almost too
much for me to take.

And needless to say, he's extremely
attentive. I don't think his pleasant attitude
toward me is thanks only to his friendship
with Hugo.

He invited me to have lunch with
him. I had no special plans for lunch that
day, except for a quick bite in one of my
usual restaurants. I was glad to accept his
invitation. I don't like to be alone when
eating out.

My escort surpassed himself; I don't
know how, but he managed to conjure up
a red rose for me, and he handed it over
with a gallant gesture. We had an excellent
red wine. Artur was all smiles. While we
were sipping coffee, he reached over the
table, took my hand, looked deep into
my eyes, and said: 'Nina, I was always in
love with you, but I could not help it that
Hugo was faster and more convincing.'
This confession came as a surprise to me.
I've known Artur for decades now, but his
behaviour, the way he looked at me, never
hinted that he might be carrying a torch
for me. It was all so unexpected that I
didn't know how to deal with it. At the
end, probably with a blush, I replied that
the wild days of my life were over. But I

was grateful for the compliment, for that was how I chose to regard his revelation.

Twenty-first Entry

I had another chance meeting with Artur. He seemed a little uneasy, almost sheepish talking to me. I think he must feel ashamed of himself for his declarations a few weeks ago. In any case I consider the whole business over and done with. From somewhere, with a magician's skill, he again produced a single red rose and presented it to me. Before I could thank him for his kindness, he disappeared and I could see no trace of him. Only men are capable of such things.

I did not mention this latest meeting with Artur to Hugo, but to tell the truth I had not told the whole story about the first meeting either. For obvious reasons I hadn't mentioned the declaration of love.

Twenty-fourth Entry

This morning I took a walk around the pond in the park. The sun was shining, and lifted my spirit, but at the end I was sad. I felt something was missing from my life. Something that would have stood for movement, jubilation, the feeling of achievement. So far I have come through many crises, but I always needed some external stimulus, some adventure to electrify me, to jump-start me. I promised myself to seek out something that would cause me pain, torture me, and put me to the test.

Thirty-sixth Entry

I feel Artur is serious about being in love with me. But I feel no attraction of any kind to him. I have no idea how to say this to him, how to deal with his ever-increasing compliments, his persistent advances, his unnerving propositions. It has occurred to me that I had better tell Hugo and ask him to have a word with Artur. Of course, I would not want a showdown, only a tactful and sensitive heart-to-heart talk so as to avoid offending him.

Forty-fourth Entry

I had some chores to take care of in the city. Hugo is careful not to abuse his office and have city employees involved in any of our private business dealings with government departments, and he usually asks me to attend to them. I was in the tax office where, as always, they called me ahead of other clients as soon as I signed in, not letting me stand at the end of the line. As I left the building I suddenly saw Artur. He was again very courteous, oozing charm. He introduced the man he was with as an old friend, a college classmate, by the name of Valerian. From the first moment he seemed familiar to me. After the exchange of names I even mentioned I must have seen him somewhere before. Valerian is a handsome man who exudes an animal magnetism. They invited me to have coffee with them. We went into the bistro across the street from the tax office. As I was leaving, Valerian gently

kissed my hand, an old-fashioned gesture
that nevertheless made me appreciate his
gallantry. Artur on the other hand, to
my surprise, acted rather cold in parting.
Which was all right with me; I didn't
relish the idea of a sentimental farewell
witnessed by the other man.

FIFTY-FIRST ENTRY

We were awakened in the middle of the
night with the news of a four-storey
apartment house collapsing near the lake.
Poor Hugo, pulled from a deep sleep,
could hardly understand what was going
on. He was running around like a headless
chicken, couldn't find his clothes. He
seemed really frightened by the news.

FIFTY-EIGHTH ENTRY

I find Hugo impossible to talk to. He walks
around like a man in a dream, or someone
spellbound. He talks only to himself. At
this stage, I'm beginning to worry about
his mental health.

SIXTY-FIRST ENTRY

The whole city is still talking about
the collapsed building. So many killed.
Nothing like it has happened in this city
since the war. Hugo has thrown himself
into the rescue operations. He never gets
home before midnight. I don't know
what I should do for him, how I can
make him relax. This morning we briefly
talked about the drama of the collapsed
apartment house, but it ended with Hugo
withdrawing into gloomy silence again.

Seventy-second Entry

Ran into Artur again. He was his old pleasant, gentlemanly self. This time it was I who invited him for coffee. He kept me entertained with his usual banter. At the end I asked him to say something about the Club that both he and Hugo are members of. He looked surprised and asked me what Club I was talking about. I told him what I knew, what Hugo had told me about it, how much he enjoyed the place, and how it was a favourite of the élite. I don't understand why, but he changed the subject and would not get back to it no matter how hard I pressed him to say more. His sudden air of mystery came as a surprise. So if Artur doesn't want to talk about the Club, he must have good reasons – but what are they? I keep asking myself. Tomorrow I'll ask Hugo to take me there.

Eighty-first Entry

Something unusual happened last night. Hugo came home early, before ten o'clock. I was overjoyed; this has not happened for weeks. I quickly prepared dinner. Hugo uncorked a bottle of red from Péter, our neighbour in the country. He was still in that strange mood, just as in the last few weeks. Obviously, the apartment house disaster has been bothering him, but I can't help feeling there is also something else. I wonder if I should talk to Artur; it's possible that his feelings for me might loosen his tongue. My mind is made up; I'm going to use all my feminine guile if necessary to get to the bottom of Hugo's depression.

Ninety-fifth Entry

So far I have never paid much attention to the fact that somebody might live by a different pattern of thinking and behaviour; I regarded such an alternative life style as the expression of basic human freedom. Whoever engaged in it, it was their business. I can see homosexuality quite clearly in people I have nothing to do with, but now the more I see of it, the less I am able to accept it. I could never have imagined Hugo might be attracted to men. When I first met Viktor I had no idea of his true nature (but then I didn't think about it much either). But Hugo!

Hugo's manliness, his attraction to the female sex left no room for doubt in me. Hugo is astonishingly good in bed. Although I have not had all that many men in my life, none of them has ever brought me to the heights of pleasure that I achieved with him. I really believe I have received from Hugo all the sexual pleasure a woman can expect.

One Hundred and Second Entry

Hugo is seriously involved with Viktor. They're practically living together. For me this discovery means disaster. I have no idea how to deal with it. I have no close girlfriends, or friends of any kind, I could share my problems with. But this is a subject one cannot discuss with friends, with any degree of certainty that tomorrow they may not blab about it to another circle of friends – if not in public. And then the confidant would claim it was unintentional, a slip of the tongue. The best thing would be to discuss it with Hugo. I wonder how he would react to the news. Am I going to turn him against me? Am I going to force him into embarrassment, with no way out for either of us? What if I ask Viktor to give up Hugo? Yes, no doubt about it – that will be the solution to all my problems. I'll use my own money. I'll ask him to name his price if he's reluctant to agree.

ONE HUNDRED AND SEVENTH ENTRY

I hate Artur from the bottom of my heart. I always thought he was a sincere and truthful man. But he isn't; he's a coward, a nobody. He's nothing but talk, empty talk. He's a liar who puts on airs; he's an arrogant and conceited bastard. And a congenital liar. My God, how could I have been such a poor judge of character? If Lidia had not been so helpful and so forthcoming, I would never have learned of the relationship between Hugo and Viktor. When I asked Artur to help me and to corroborate Lidia's statements, he talked to me like a teacher to an elementary school student, he practically threatened to punish me for talking out of turn and – in his words – for daring to come out with such tactless questions. He pretended to know nothing about the affair. And he even upbraided me for imagining such filthy – yes, filthy, that's how he expressed himself

– things about his good friend, the Mayor of our town. He almost threw me out of his office.

ONE HUNDRED AND EIGHTEENTH ENTRY
I finally got to meet Viktor. While waiting for him I suddenly got a bad case of the nerves; my pulse started racing and there seemed no way of stopping it. Maybe it was all the coffee I had had that morning, plus the fact that the night before I had drunk a little too much. Hugo came home in a good mood. It had been a long time since I last saw him so calm, so well-balanced. I learned from Viktor that they had been together in the course of the morning. I was pained to hear that. I tried to imagine my husband making love to this man sitting in front of me; but in a strange way, it was not loathing and disgust that gripped my soul, but jealousy. That made me realize how much I still love Hugo.

Yes, I love my husband. I have considered the possibility that over the years I might have to fight off a woman for him, but it has never occurred to me that I might have to compete with a man.

Viktor too realizes that his relationship with Hugo is dangerous for both of them. He promised to break it off with Hugo. He gave me his word of honour. When I offered money in exchange, he turned it down most emphatically. Also he was angry with me for making what he called a disgraceful proposition. He said he was not for sale. He wanted me to be fully aware of that. Before we parted I think

I managed to make peace. He agreed to call me when he was able to make a clean break with Hugo.

I went home happy and relieved. Finally a battle won.

—Chapter 71—

Murder in Hotel Odéon
—XXIII—

H<small>UGO</small> <small>KEPT TURNING</small> the pages of Nina's small brown book –

O<small>NE</small> H<small>UNDRED AND</small> T<small>WENTY-FIFTH</small> E<small>NTRY</small>
Last night Hugo came home worn out and in a bad mood. I questioned him – cautiously – about what was wrong, about why he was feeling so blue. He answered my questions unwillingly and tersely. So I gave up trying to get anything out of him. Instead, I prepared supper because he complained he was hungry; he had been served only drinks at the Club, as the chef was out sick, and there was no one else working in the kitchen.

This morning Viktor called with the news that last night he broke up with Hugo.

O<small>NE</small> H<small>UNDRED AND</small> T<small>WENTY-EIGHTH</small> E<small>NTRY</small>
Today I fired my cleaning woman. Hugo of course left that to me, since it was I who had hired her in the first place. I simply can't put up with hired help who neglect to do the work. I asked this woman to do a certain thing but she kept putting me off with promises. On the bookshelves the layer of dust is now so thick that I hate to touch my own books.

Hugo is in better spirits now. Lidia

promised to keep an eye on him. In the Club he was served something to eat instead of just brandy as usual, one shot after another.

ONE HUNDRED AND TWENTY-NINTH ENTRY
I had a date with Lidia today. We had lunch together in a bistro downtown. During our conversation she volunteered the information that she likes men and women equally. And then, as an aside, she went on to say that she found me exciting, and asked if I'd be interested in trying something new. I was completely floored. It came out of the blue, just like that. Only back home, while taking a bath, I allowed myself to imagine what it might be like with Lidia. I gave free reign to my imagination. I decided to sleep on my decision about this venture.

ONE HUNDRED AND THIRTY-SECOND ENTRY
Fantastical, unforgettable, wondrous, these are the words to describe the exaltation I experienced today. I don't know how I worked up the courage to make up my mind to see Lidia. The one thing that's a turn-off for me is her chain-smoking, not to speak of the way she can put away one bottle of champagne after another. Her body, however, is a surprising source of pleasure. I cannot get over it; it'll take me some time.

ONE HUNDRED AND THIRTY-THIRD ENTRY
I am soaring again. Have I been born again? I can hardly recognize myself. I

am suddenly interested in everything, even things that I hardly ever noticed before. I like Lidia. I pine for her. I'd like to have her with me all the time – with me and with no one else. This feeling is so powerful that it has taken over my whole being. Hugo noticed I seemed to be more absent-minded lately, and he even remarked he had not seen me like this in a long time, staring into space in a reverie.

Yes, lately I've been daydreaming like I used to as a teenager. Some years ago I buried passion so deep inside me I never expected it to re-emerge from the depths and overpower me. What I am experiencing now, the constant longing, the weird and inexplicable turmoil in my soul, the lust for pleasure, they all unite in driving me crazy. I can't recognize myself. I am not the same Nina I was a few weeks ago, after learning about Hugo and Victor, when my spirits sank to previously unknown depths. Since then I've sprouted wings. I am no longer trudging on earth but flying high in heaven.

Yesterday I was struck by a new thought: how would Hugo react if he found out I had a lover, and not just any kind of lover? What would he do? Would he behave as I did? Would he ignore it? Would he be capable of the manoeuvre I performed with Viktor when I convinced him to betray Hugo? How is my love affair different from Hugo's? Am I any different from him? Any better? What a double-dealing, immoral, spiritual swamp I have become! I pray to God to forgive my sins.

This morning I started out with a prayer. I did it out of some inner need. Some kind of inexplicable, invisible force pushed me into the ritual of atonement that could purify the soul and body. I prayed to someone I do not know, someone whose sacrifice has expiated our sins of the past, present and future. It was while praying that I suddenly realized I do not know this God; I've only seen pictures of him, heard other people talk about him, and read mythical stories about him. I've been going to church; and every time I enter, I feel I am stepping out of reality, and into a world of a higher level of consciousness where I can sit among those soaring walls garlanded with the myrrh of suffering and forgiveness, but where now I look for myself in vain. I believe the reason I cannot find myself in church is that I am evil personified. A devilish force has me in its power, and no matter how I hard I try, I cannot achieve the remission of my sins – forgiveness is denied to me.

I often ask myself why should I need the help of supernatural forces, why can't I solve my own problems? What kind of morality is it to commit a sinful act, time and time again, thinking that it's no matter, it will be forgiven?

I cannot wash myself clean of sins unless I get to know them better. I'll have to familiarize myself with them, become one with evil – sense it in my body, taste it in my mouth as I've been doing recently – revelling in the fever of pleasure, hearing the gradually diminishing clamour of the material world as I leave it behind me.

Have I got my just desserts? My sins call for an executioner, but that job is reserved for me!

ONE HUNDRED AND THIRTY-EIGHTH ENTRY
Here is something again that could have happened only to me. Lidia called me in the morning hours, asking for a date. I told her to jump into a cab and come up to the house. Hugo took off early morning on a day-long business trip to some place not too far, but out of town, and I did not expect him back till late evening. I sacked the cleaning woman two weeks ago and have not found a replacement yet, so there was no one to disturb us.

It didn't take long for Lidia to arrive. She looked terrific and in high spirits. She asked for champagne at once. I told her sorry, but I was out of champagne. I could offer a glass of red wine. When I said I didn't like anyone to smoke inside the house, she became very agitated, calling me all sorts of names. At first I rather enjoyed the hysterical show. It contained the elements of something sublime, unbridled, fascinating, ravishing. But when I saw she had no intention of ending it, I asked her to leave immediately. She responded by leaping out of the chair and charging at me, only to start a hot bout of kissing. When I began to warm to her approach she unglued her lips from mine, took my face into her hands, looked deep into my eyes and hissed at me with great dramatic force: 'I've cheated on you, I have a new lover. Don't you want to know his name?' she asked, breaking into seemingly unstoppable laughter. She was about to let herself out by the front door when she turned back to toss the words in my face: 'Viktor's my new lover!'

I wanted to run after her, but I felt paralysed, my limbs would not obey me. From the balcony I could barely catch a glimpse of her figure, light as air, as it disappeared around the corner.

I must do something.

ONE HUNDRED AND FORTY-FOURTH ENTRY
I've been trailing them for several days now. I've had neither time nor appetite to eat. I've become the victim of a sick love affair. I can see and feel I'll never get over it.

And I was so happy to see Hugo's problems slowly resolving themselves. The monstrous clouds that used to cast their shadows over his face have moved on to me. And now it's me, I am the one in a crisis. I must look for a way out.

I wanted too much, too fast. I was selfish, dissipated, my soul is demolished. Am I to be a murderer, or am I one already?

ONE HUNDRED AND FORTY-SEVENTH ENTRY
On the surface things are hum-drumming along as usual; in the depths, I've been laid waste, put to shame,

Yet what a good show I can put on! As soon as Hugo gets home, I become cheerful, serve him dinner, ask him about his day; I pretend inner calm, good cheer, a carefree spirit. We even discussed that fatal night, at least in part. As if nothing had happened.

True, nothing really did. Or did something? Good God, how far have I strayed, what will become of me?

Every day I hear a new theory about the murder. How well fog can blindfold reason!

Hugo was devastated by the news of Viktor's murder. He cannot get over it. I am living in the midst of a crisis. We both are. I wonder if he really loved Viktor as much as I loved Lidia. Was he as mad about him as I am about Lidia?

Viktor was cruel! And yet how easily, how readily, and unselfishly he immediately gave up Hugo when I asked him to. He showed no sign of lovesickness over it, not even the slightest cloud of doubt passed across his face.

No? Viktor never loved Hugo with all his heart, with every particle of his soul. He was playing with Hugo! Hugo's high position enthralled him, befuddled his mind. And he, too, was scared when he was confronted with the possibility of someone making their relationship public.

Viktor was a selfish predator. He was always lying in ambush, waiting for his prey.

Poor Valerian! Please God save him who is expiating for my sins!

That Eddy's Bar Club and Artur are to be blamed for the whole mess! He orchestrated it, he was the one to lead us to the border of madness, and now he's observing how his empire, built on wretchedness, is crumbling and falling apart.

Can love be craven? Can it be degrading? Can anyone mired in the tendrils of carnal and spiritual forces ever be rescued? Can she ever find escape? Can anyone partaking of the opiate of fever and euphoria ever rescue love back into palpable reality?

I'd like to rebel, but what for? My life is sinking.

ONE HUNDRED AND FORTY-NINTH ENTRY
Artur must suspect something. He had a talk with Lidia.

ONE HUNDRED AND FIFTY-FIRST ENTRY
Lidia was asked to come into police headquarters for an interview. I've never met a person like her, more perverse, more deceitful, more of an evildoer.

I had no good reason for it, but I simply had to laugh when she described her meeting with Detective Fabian Mueller. Lidia enjoys taking chances; she is not aware of her vulnerability, and that she is at the mercy of others. She is relying on her verifiable alibi. She doesn't even consider that I...

She says it is enough for me to know that she knows something that no one else needs to know, and that's the way things should stay forever.

I am afraid of Lidia. I am afraid of her unbridled, reckless personality, and I am afraid of the future, what it might have in store for me.

I considered asking Hugo to let me go abroad for a while. I'd like to go to a mountain retreat, an inn somewhere out in the country with plenty of fresh air. I'd like to spend at least three months in relaxing and nourishing mountain air, and in the meantime all the problems would be resolved without me.

Nothing will be solved. I am the one who knows that only too well.

ONE HUNDRED AND FIFTY-FIFTH ENTRY
It's becoming harder and harder for me to bear up under this pressure. I am conscience-stricken. I have nauseating dreams every night. I am in bed with Lidia and Viktor, making love. Viktor suddenly gets up and starts for the door. Blood is gushing from his crotch. Lidia says something loudly enough for me to hear but I can't make it out; the hotel room catches fire, and we all try to escape. We run out to a clearing in a forest.

I wake to someone screaming. I look around, frightened. Hugo is fast asleep by my side. The patch of light from the lamp post out in the street seems to lurch slightly now and then.

ONE HUNDRED AND FIFTY-EIGHTH ENTRY
Hugo gave me a suspicious look this morning while he was reading the police report to me. From that look, from the

way he glanced at me, I have the feeling he knows. For a second or two, I was waiting for him to read me the awful indictment. But I was thoroughly mistaken. Hugo is only torturing himself, suspecting only himself. But why in heaven's name would he suspect himself?

ONE HUNDRED AND FIFTY-NINTH ENTRY
Lidia refuses to see me. I called her this morning. She was curt and unapproachable. She said she didn't care for me any longer.

So she doesn't? I don't love her any more either. But I did not bring that up now. It's best we don't see each other ever again.

ONE HUNDRED AND SEVENTY-FIRST ENTRY
It's all over. I shall suffer no more. Hugo will manage without me. Too bad I can't tell him how much I love him. With pure, sincere, and true love. There's just one person I must phone. Then I'll go out to our country house. And then I shall see what I'll see...

It was with a transfixed, sombre face that Hugo got up from the easy chair where he had settled down an hour and a half earlier, holding the diary with the brown cover in his hand. He went over to the bathroom and turned on the cold water tap. He cupped his hands under it until they filled up, bent down, and dunked his face in the ice-cold water. He repeated this several more times.

With the towel in his hand he went into the kitchen and used the wall phone there to call Artur. He asked him to meet him in an hour at Eddy's Bar.

Chapter 72

MURDER IN HOTEL ODÉON
—XXIV—

'WHAT IS THIS supposed to mean?' Markus Frankel, the Cultural Affairs Editor, asked, poking a finger at Vilmos's manuscript. 'What you wrote about is erotica and passion.'

'It means,' Vilmos replied, raising his voice slightly, 'it means that erotica has nothing to do with sexuality.' Markus had managed to get his goat again, and right then and there he swore it was the last time, the very last time that he would show his writing to this man. He was about to stand up to snatch back the manuscript when Artur stepped into the office.

'Ah, my favourite editor! How are you doing?' He produced a thin smile. Then he turned to Vilmos, shook hands with him too, and patted his back. 'Don't let him get you down, my boy, every editor is conceited and fancies himself the guardian of the language. Of course I am joking, but I expect you two to take it seriously,' he added, flopping down into an armchair.

He seemed to be well-rested and in a good mood. The wrinkles on his face seemed a little smoother, and the purple spots under his eyes were gone.

'You have any news?' Markus straightened up in his chair with a sour expression, obviously annoyed by Artur's remark.

'You already know that the Mayor resigned this morning?'

'Yes, we heard about that. At the press conference. He was vague, but I presume it's because of his wife's murder.'

Markus looked back at Artur with a question mark, as if expecting him to be the repository of insider information.

'I went to see Valerian in prison today,' Arthur said. 'It looks like he'll be set free soon.'

'What's happened?' Markus asked, surprised. 'Have they found who murdered the barber?'

'Actually, the case has been solved.' Artur sent a noncommittal look into the far distance.

'So who did it?' Markus was getting impatient.

'You mean "whodunnit"? That will have to be answered by Detective Fabian Mueller.'

'That's all very mysterious. You know who the murderer is, but you're not going to tell us?' the editor protested.

'Markus, my dear friend.' Artur softened his tone as he quoted: 'All in due time. There's a time for everything.'

'But you already know who it is?'

'Now, what makes you think that?' He waved airily.

It was the first time in his life that he actually enjoyed withholding sensational information.

*   *   *

Vilmos was the last to leave Markus's office. Still miffed by the reaction of the Cultural Affairs Editor to his manuscript, it took him a minute to go over to the editor's desk to retrieve it. He was on his way out the door when he noticed the attaché case on a shelf beside the chair where Artur had been sitting.

He suspected the lawyer had left it behind. He didn't like Artur that much, but he thought he should try to restore the case to him if he could. He wondered if he could catch up with him.

Unless, of course, the case belonged to Markus. He decided he'd better check before running after the lawyer. All that was inside the case was a bundle of photocopied sheets, but it was not readily apparent to whom the papers belonged. There was no name or office stamp. It looked to him like they were pages photocopied from a diary. He flipped through them idly for a moment. Then the names of some people and places caught his eye, and he began to wonder what it was he had stumbled on. He flipped to the end of the document.

At first, he felt just disbelief, but that was quickly followed by fear.

The safest course of action would be to put the document back in the case, and put the case back where he found it, but curiosity, and his instinct as an aspiring journalist that he was holding the scoop of a lifetime in his hands, made him hesitate. He took a chance. He closed the office door, put his back to it, and read the sensational contents right through to the end.

He was astonished by the diary. At first he wanted to believe it was not genuine. He considered himself a man of the world, but what was in that diary was almost beyond his imagination. Looking down at the pages, he began to feel more and more frightened. There already were rumours of a hush-up circulating around the city. Now he knew that those rumours were true. It was certain that the information in these pages was never going to be made public. The more he thought about it, the more frightened he became. His shock quickly began to turn to fear. If it became known that he had read what was in those pages... There was no reason, of course, that anyone should ever know. He would put them back quickly. He tried to remember how exactly they had lain inside the attaché case. He put them down on the editor's desk in order to straighten them, and noticed with horror that his hands had been sweating so much while reading them that impressions had been left on the pages. He wondered if that meant he had left fingerprints on them. If that frightening lawyer, Artur, suspected the document had been read, he would be the type to check for fingerprints. Vilmos thought immediately about his wife and children. What on earth was he going to do?

Unable to think of anything else, he decided to take the documents with him and destroy them. Quickly he put them into the envelope in which he had brought his own manuscript. He tried to remember where he might have touched the attaché case, rubbed down those areas with his handkerchief, and put it back where he had found it. All the time, he had his ears tuned to footsteps in the corridor, picking up his own manuscript once or twice when someone was close.

As he made his way through the corridors of the newspaper building to the street, he was more frightened than he had ever been in his life. Once outside on the bustling pavement, he became acutely aware that he could not risk bringing that document back to his house – to his wife's home. What on earth had possessed him to look inside that lawyer's case and touch that document? He would have to get rid of it immediately, but where? He could drop it into a garbage bin, but beggars often went through those, looking for something they could sell. If he dropped it into the river, the pages would probably float away and be seen by everyone. He wasn't likely to chance upon a bonfire, which would be the fantasy solution. No, it would have to be a garbage bin. He decided on one by a bus stop, but not on a route that served his house. He would have liked to tear up the papers, but he felt he would just call attention to himself if he did.

Beside one particularly busy stop, there was a street vendor selling fried potatoes. The smell of rancid fat was so strong that he had never before considered stopping to buy any, but tonight he bought a portion. They tasted the same as they smelled, but he ate all of them. No one would be surprised to see someone who had finished a portion of fried potatoes dropping the greasy paper wrappers into the bin. He crumpled it with the photocopied pages, pushed the wad far down into the bin, and went on his way.

Well, the deed was done. It was most likely, he told himself, that the photocopied pages would disappear later that night or early in the morning, along with the fried potato wrappers, empty water bottles, and whatever else was in that bin. If he was being followed or watched, the papers would probably be found, but there was no reason for anyone to be watching him.

That night, he said nothing to his wife, but quietly he started to sort his possessions. He didn't want to frighten her, and he also knew she was not a good liar. She would be safe only if she knew nothing. When she asked him once what he was doing, he said he was looking for a sock that had gone missing.

When the doorbell rang, he was not surprised, but he was terrified. Remembering what he had said to his wife, he went to the door holding a sock in his hands. Before he opened it, he practised a surprised but relaxed welcoming smile. As he had expected, the caller was Artur.

'Well, this is a surprise…' he began, trying to look pleased.

Artur wasted no time. 'Where is it?' he asked, in the tone of a seasoned interrogator. 'Don't try to play dumb with me! If you don't get it back to me by tomorrow, you'll have to deal with the consequences.'

'Vilmos…?' His wife had come to the hall to see what was happening.

Vilmos introduced her to Artur with a degree of calm that impressed himself.

'By tomorrow,' Artur repeated.

'Vilmos, what's this about?' his wife asked.

'I don't know,' Vilmos said, feeling surprisingly calm. 'There must be some mix-up.' Obviously Artur suspected him, but more importantly, it seemed he had not been seen dumping the photocopied pages. Which meant, he had to believe, there was no proof. 'I met Artur today in Markus's office when I was showing Markus my manuscript. Artur says he wants something by tomorrow, but I'm not sure what it is that he wants.'

Artur said nothing more, but turned and walked away.

'Vilmos, you'd better tell me what's happening. That man looks dangerous. What were you talking about in Markus's office?'

'Nothing to do with me. We were talking about the Hotel Odéon murder. He said the police know now who did it, but he wouldn't tell us who it was.'

'I just heard about that on the television. Some police detective was saying that two robbers had committed the murder. He said they had committed other murders as well, and there's a big manhunt going on for them now.'

Vilmos didn't sleep at all that night. He had assembled everything he would take with him if he had to leave the country quickly, but he wouldn't let himself think that it might really come to that. But then the process started. The next day, two plain-clothes officers from State Security came to the house and asked him to come with them to police headquarters. They had been told he had been reading poems in a café, and they had been overheard by other patrons. Some of them, it seemed, were subversive. He had been questioned all night in the basement of police headquarters.

Two days later, his neighbours had visits from the State Security men. Three days later, Vilmos had disappeared. Only his wife knew that he was fleeing the country.

As for the murders of Nina and Victor, Detective Mueller officially closed both cases by pinning the blame on the two already-wanted highway robbers who conveniently died in a gunfight with the police when they tried to cross the border, according to the official reports.

Chapter 73

AFTER GETTING CONFIRMATION on TV of the disaster that had befallen Wanda, Zeno decided, in spite of the lateness of the hour, to leave the bar and drive directly up to the resort hotel where they had spent the previous night.

Before taking off, he stopped by his office to pick up a small box from a locked drawer. Wanting to make sure it still contained what he was looking for, he snapped open the lid, glanced inside, re-closed it, and buried the box in his pocket. In his mind's eye he could see Walter's grim face reminding him to put that box back in its place when they were touring Countess Pellegrini's mansion. In an entirely uncharacteristic act, and for reasons he still could not understand, he had decided to pocket it when Walter wasn't looking.

Most of the guests had already departed from the hotel before Sunday evening. There were plenty of vacant rooms. He would have liked to return to the same room where they had enjoyed the night before, but it was occupied. The room right next to it though was available.

He unlocked the door, and switched on the light. He looked around with eyes clouded by a rush of memories. 'Everything's in order,' he whispered to the empty room.

He took the little box out of his pocket, opened the lid and held the slender glass ampoule up to the light.

He rolled it between his fingertips just a half a turn and then put it in his mouth.

He could feel the cool touch of the glass and its brittle hardness between his teeth. All that was needed was a tiny move, the clenching of his jaws. Simply bite down once, and he'd be covered by the wind-blown sands of oblivion.

Forgetting and forgotten.

'Forgetting…' Zeno found he was repeating the word to himself as he stepped closer to the window.

Finally he said the word out loud: 'Forgetting.'

Curiously, it was the sound of his own voice that seemed to break the spell cast by the decision he had made more than an hour earlier. His mind began to clear, but it only told him he was governed now by nerves. The time having come for him to act on his decision, he seemed to have lost his resolution.

He felt desperately alone.

The choices were plain: a moment of panic on one side, and on the other a life without a future, in a world that had forsaken him.

He felt worn-out, unfit for further struggles, indifferent to new challenges. So what was there to hold him back?

As if hoping for a sign, he looked out the window. It was an idyllic night. A stray breeze blew gently through a maple tree. The hotel courtyard below was bathed in the misty light of garden lanterns. The road was lit occasionally by car headlights, but on the other side, there was total darkness. It was a vision of tranquillity.

He wondered if there was anything left of his life – anything he could claim as his own. Yet the serenity of the night was washing over him.

I can see this park below, he thought. I can see every piece of furniture in this room, I can hear myself breathe. If I were to open the window, I could reach out, and with my fingertips touch that velvety darkness out there, the soft flesh of the night. He suddenly jerked open the window.

He caught a raindrop on his hand. It was cold, almost icy. It was followed by more, but they felt hot like sparks flaring up from dying ashes.

There was something smouldering out there. It was as if his own cremation had already begun to spew hot cinders into the night.

Chapter 74

W HEN TAMAS FINALLY arrived home late Sunday afternoon, he made a resolution: come what may, whatever might happen to the world, he was going to get a good night's rest for once – he was so tired and worn out. Before falling asleep though he managed to conjure up the images of his wife and boys.

Next morning, walking into the hotel through the main entrance, he suddenly realized he had put on a tie again. But he decided it was too late to take it off now, in the lobby, where he would have called unwanted attention to himself. What the heck, I'm not here to report for work, he calmed himself while trying to sneak unnoticed past Mr Vid's office. Luckily Mr Vid was not at his desk. After a sigh of relief Tamas made his way toward the accounting office. The young lady inside gave him a questioning look when he entered and quietly closed the door behind him. If Lester did indeed call ahead about this, then they should be expecting me, he reasoned and gave his name.

'Oh, yes, I know all about it.' The secretary leaped to her feet and hurried into the neighbouring office cubicle. In a little while she returned with an envelope in her hand. 'Here you go.' She handed it over, and even managed to accompany it with an anaemic smile, more like a professional pout, deftly placed on her lips. 'Your ID card will be ready tomorrow, but in the meantime you can use this.'

When he was alone again in the hallway, the door to the office safely closed behind him, he quickly opened the unsealed business-size envelope and pried a sheet of paper out of it. It was the hotel's stationery with its logo and address embossed in the letterhead. Typed in the middle of the sheet were a few lines with the name and phone number of the personnel manager under it, completed by a decisive signature. He scanned the letter of deposition with eager eyes. And then he did it again. At the bus stop he felt the inside pocket of his jacket to make sure the envelope was still there. He took a step or two, pulled the document out again, and reread it three more times. He was overwhelmed by joy, but it was mixed with intolerable impatience. He felt his family already so close to him that at first he did not sense the shadows of a doubt creeping into his jubilation. And what if they still find my application premature? He felt himself getting unsure. Come now, isn't this what they demanded, a steady job with regular income? The internal debate went on and on inside him.

He stepped over the threshold of the Immigration Office with his heart pounding against the letter in his inside pocket. The large waiting room was conspicuously empty. Most people are at work in the morning hours; he assured himself that the place was indeed open for business. He took a number from the dispenser and sat down. The electronic display high above the counter showed NO. 147 being served. The ticket in his hand showed NO. 158.

It shouldn't take long before they call my number, he thought, but every passing moment felt like a lead brick being handed to him to hold.

The counter was served by only three officials that day. None of them looked familiar. That boded well for the upcoming encounter with officialdom.

His attention was caught by a client, a short, stocky, bald man who was getting into a loud and demonstrative argument with one of the agents. Tamas was too far from them to make out the substance of the altercation, but the scene reawakened his anxiety and his resolve to remain calm no matter what. There were only two more clients ahead of him.

He did not even hear when his number was called. If he had not happened to glance at the display, he would have remained fidgeting in his seat. He jumped to his feet and hurried to the counter before he might lose his turn. On his way, he fished out the passport and the hotel letter from his pocket.

'I would like to apply for my family to immigrate...' He said it almost syllable by syllable to the official serving him, but then he got stuck.

The official, a middle-aged man in a grey suit, took the passport and the white hotel envelope and disappeared behind a door in the back. In a little while he returned accompanied by a short middle-aged woman.

'The interpreter,' he said, while spreading out Tamas's papers on the counter.

'Your address?' he went on, producing a fresh form.

'I have my address and phone number written down on a slip of paper inside my passport.' With hands shaking, Tamas opened the passport to the information written in print.

'Your place of employment?'

'A hotel called Crosswinds,' Tamas answered pointing to the return address on the envelope from its personnel department.

'What is your job there?'

'I work in maintenance.'

'And what kind of work do you do there?' the official asked somewhat hurriedly.

'Whatever needs to be done. I do wallpapering, cleaning, repair work... I am an all-around handyman,' said Tamas with the help of the patiently smiling interpreter.

'Uh-huh.' The grey suit went on filling out the form.

'How many persons are you sponsoring?'

'My wife and my two sons.'

'Their names?' he asked, but before Tamas could answer he waved him off. 'Never mind, I've got it all here,' he said cryptically.

Tamas was steeling himself for the next question, whatever it was, but it did not come.

'This will do it. Please check the information.' The official pushed the form in front of his client.

Tamas could see the first few lines quite clearly, but as he went on to the body of the document the words all turned into a misty blur. 'Yes, it's all correct,' he grunted finally, through the fog of anxiety engulfing his head.

'The processing will take from a year to eighteen months. If you're lucky, maybe less,' explained the official in a grey tone and, seeing the client's hesitancy, he added, 'We're finished, you can go now. Who's next?'

'Good-bye and good luck!' The lady interpreted, nodding encouragingly.

Tamas was close to fainting when he finally walked away from the counter. It was only a few minutes later that he realized he had forgotten to thank the interpreter for her help. In the cavernous, all-steel-and-glass lobby he was already about to step on the down escalator when he was suddenly overcome by a laughing fit. He could not control himself. After all that worrying, all that headache, how simple it had turned out to be! No angel from heaven, no devil to pay – just a simple step in the bureaucratic process. But what a huge leap for him and his loved ones!

Descending slowly to the ground floor he already started composing the phone call he was going to make as soon as he got home:

'Success! Iren, we've made it!'

Zoltán Böszörményi

THE AUTHOR

Zoltán Böszörményi was born in Cold War Transylvania in 1951, in the Hungarian community of Arad. He studied for seven years at the Ballet School in Cluj and finished school in Arad, where he published two books of Hungarian-language poetry, the second of which resulted in his arrest and interrogation.

He fled to the West, through Yugoslavia, spent seven months at Traiskirchen Refugee Camp in Austria, then was admitted to Canada, where he learned English and studied at York University in Toronto.

After returning to Eastern Europe in the 1990s, he became a successful industrialist, setting up Romania's most modern lighting company.

Subsequently, he retired from industry to return to writing, and in 2009 received the Gundel Arts Award for the Hungarian version of *The Club at Eddy's Bar*, and in 2012 the József Attila Award for Hungarian literature.

He has had works published in Hungarian, Romanian, Russian, and English, and is editor-in-chief of a Hungarian-language daily and monthly journal based in Arad and Budapest. He is married and has two daughters.

THE ARTIST FERENC MARTYN

THE ILLUSTRATIONS on the cover of *The Club at Eddy's Bar* are by Ferenc MARTYN (1899–1986), an influential Hungarian artist with an Irish great-grandfather. Among his Irish kinsmen are Edward Martyn, co-founder of the Abbey Theatre in Dublin, and Richard Martin (often called 'Humanity Dick'), a founder of the Society for the Prevention of Cruelty to Animals.

FERENC MARTYN
SELF-PORTRAIT

Ferenc Martyn was born in Kaposvár, Hungary, in 1899. His mother died when he was five, and he grew up in the house of (and was the apprentice of) his relative, the portrait-painter József Rippl-Rónai. In World War I Martyn served in the Austro-Hungarian army on the Italian front. After the war, he studied at the Hungarian Academy of Fine Arts in Budapest (under the Transylvanian artist, István Réti, among others).

In 1926, he moved to Paris. His interesting early style can be seen in images used in this book: *Kávéházban* [*At the Bistro*] – on the front cover and frontispiece – was drawn in Paris

1927 PASTEL 'PARISIAN SCENE'

in 1927; and the back cover shows an excerpt from his *Párizsi látkép* [*Parisian Scene*] *(above)*, of the same year.

428

In 1934 he joined the international exhibiting group, *Abstraction-Création*, founded by artists Vantongerloo, Hélion, and Herbin, for the promotion of abstract art. Other members of that group were Irish artists Mainie Jellett and Evie Hone. This body was succeeded in 1946 by another group with the same aim, the *Salon des Réalités Nouvelles*, and Martyn's work was featured in its 1947 exhibition in Paris. By then he had settled in Pécs, Hungary, where he spent the rest of his life.

During most of the 1950s, official discouragement of the abstract style caused him to work in some obscurity; in 1958, however, after images of ten of his works were published in Pécs in the Janus Pannonius Museum Yearbook, he came to be regarded as the foremost exponent of Hungarian abstract art; and he was a major influence in the creation of the

ULYSSES ILLUSTRATION
[IMMA, DUBLIN]

Hungarian museum of modern art. Although primarily known as a painter, he was also a sculptor, graphic artist, and book illustrator (of James Joyce's *Ulysses (above)*, *Madame Bovary*, and *Don Quixote*, among others). He died in Pécs in 1986, where his work is on permanent display within the Janus Pannonius Múzeum in the Martyn Ferenc Múzeum.

Ferenc Martyn was generous to Ireland, donating works to it in the 1940s. Abstract paintings by him can be' seen in the < Highlanes Gallery in Drogheda, in the Crawford Gallery in Cork, and Greyfriars Gallery in Waterford *(overleaf)*, and in NUI Galway library. Martyn drawings (including *Ulysses* illustrations) are in the IMMA in Dublin, and a

WATERCOLOUR [HIGHLANES]

Martyn abstract donated by
painter Sylvia Cooke-Collis
(a student of Mainie Jellett)
is in the Niland Collection
in Sligo.

WATERCOLOUR [CRAWFORD GALLERY]

OIL ON BOARD [GREYFRIARS GALLERY]

The artist's Irish ancestors,
the Martyns/Martins, were
one of the fourteen merchant
families called 'The Tribes of
Galway,' who gained wealth
and power from trade with Europe between the 13th and
16th centuries, and who dominated the politics and social
life of Galway during that time. The Cromwellian conquest
of Ireland in the mid-17th century cost them their power,
which they never fully regained.
It was Cromwellian forces who
applied to them the term 'Tribes
of Galway,' intending it to be
derogatory; but the families later
claimed it, using it with pride.

Peter Martyn (the great-
grandfather of the artist, born
1772 in Castlebar) emigrated from
Ireland in 1790, joined the Austria-
Hungary Imperial Army as a
Second Lieutenant Cuirassier, and
advanced by 1812 to the rank of

ENSIGNS OF THE 14 'TRIBES'
OF GALWAY (1820)

Major in Kleanu's Light Cavalry Regiment; in 1822 he
retired and settled in Hungary, where he died in 1827 at
Arad – the birthplace of the author of this book.

Ferenc Martyn married twice but outlived both wives.
In his final years he was cared for by Marianne Polgár, a
friend of poet and translator Paul Sohar who assisted the
author with the adaptation into English of this novel.

FRENCH CINEMA IN CLOSE-UP
— La Vie d'un acteur pour moi
edited by Michaël ABECASSIS with Marcelline BLOCK

350 pages (royal octavo size), 170 illustrations
ISBN (PAPERBACK): 9781908420114

Not just biographies, but personal sketches of
170 French cinema actors and actresses (by a
worldwide panel of contributors), looking at their
personalities as well as their acting careers, to give a
deeper understanding of them and their work.

    The book profiles actors from Adjani to
Zylberstein, and its contributors include academics –
from universities in Australia, Austria, Canada, Cyprus,
France, Ireland, Malaysia, New Zealand, the United Kingdom, and throughout
the United States – as well as journalists, film curators, and lovers of French
Cinema, both francophones and francophiles.

    Each actor's profile is illustrated with a portrait drawing/caricature by artists
Jenny BATLAY (PhD. Columbia University) and Igor BRATUSEK (Sorbonne).

AN ILLUSTRATED MINI-DICTIONARY OF FRENCH ACTORS   edited by
Dr Michaël ABECASSIS (University of Oxford)
with Marcelline BLOCK (Princeton University)

PHAETON PUBLISHING LTD.   DUBLIN   WWW·PHAETON·IE

EXTREMELY ENTERTAINING SHORT STORIES
—Classic Works of a Master
by Stacy AUMONIER

576 pages : biography, 29 stories, 1 essay
ISBNS (PBK): 9780955375637 (HBK): 9780955375651

Stories of World War I & the 1920s
in England & France

'Stacy Aumonier is one of the best short story writers
of all time. His humour is sly and dry and frequent…
And can't he write!' —JOHN GALSWORTHY (winner
of the Nobel Prize for Literature).

'…a very elegant volume…short stories that invite comparison with
those of Saki, O.Henry and even Guy de Maupassant.'—BOOKS IRELAND

BROADCAST ON BBC RADIO 4 *Afternoon Readings* in 2011.

'… in England, my first trip there in 25 years … I bought the new Phaeton
collection of *Extremely Entertaining Short Stories* by Stacy Aumonier …
greatly appreciated in his time for his wit and neatly contrived plots. Back now
in New York, it's a heavy volume to cart back and forth as subway reading,
but it's well worth the weight!' —*LIBRARY JOURNAL*, NEW YORK, 2009

'…a great holiday read.' —BRENTANO'S, PARIS

BRIGHTER FRENCH

—Colloquial & Idiomatic, for Bright Young People (who already know some) *by* Harry Thompson RUSSELL
illustrated by Eric FRASER

340 pages, (incl. author's & illustrator's biographies)
20 drawings & 28 photos ISBN (PBK): 9780955375675

Volume I of the *Brighter French* Series

'When did readers last read a really good dialogue in
a language textbook with a real sense of conversation
and a good punchline? ... these books provide a breath
of fresh air, quite a few laughs and some really useful
idiomatic French...'—ELSEVIER *SYSTEM* JOURNAL, 2010
R. VANDERPLANK, DIRECTOR, LANGUAGE CENTRE, UNIVERSITY OF OXFORD

1. 'What did he die of?'	1. « *De quoi* est-il mort ?
—'Nobody knows.	—On ne sait pas.
But then nobody knew	D'ailleurs on ne savait
what he lived on, either.'	non plus de quoi il vivait. »

'...that brilliant volume *Brighter French*...'
—PREFACE TO *TEACH YOURSELF FRENCH* (36th impression, 1980)

'Great Fun.' —*BOOKS IRELAND*, 2010

'Regarded as one of the best French language learning guides ever
written.' —*WILTSHIRE TIMES*, 2010

PHAETON PUBLISHING LTD.   DUBLIN   WWW·PHAETON·IE

The BRIGHTER FRENCH WORD-BOOK
—A Guide to 'the Right Word' for Bright Young People
by Harry Thompson RUSSELL

352 pages, 32 illustrations ISBN (PBK.): 9780955375699

Volume II in the classic *Brighter French* Series,
written in the 1920s for 'Bright Young People
who already know some'

Vocabulary on a wide range of subjects—both
of universal interest—*the House, the Town, Illness,
the Weather, etc.*—and more specialised—*Horses,
Firearms and Target Shooting, Finance and Business,
Nautical Matters, etc.*—with distinctions that are hard to find in a dictionary.

'...remarkable for the amazing detail that is presented. The Motoring
section would have come in handy many years ago when I broke down
in France. ...Television and computers make no appearance, of course,
but just about everything else is present in this handy paperback.'
—ELSEVIER *SYSTEM* JOURNAL, 2010, ROBERT VANDERPLANK, DIRECTOR,
LANGUAGE CENTRE, UNIVERSITY OF OXFORD

'It is a book unique of its kind, and if anybody who has occasion ever
to speak French is content to do without it, then he is either a perfect
French scholar—or else very conceited!' —*TRUTH MAGAZINE*, 1929

STILL BRIGHTER FRENCH
—for Bright Young People (who now know more)
by Harry Thompson RUSSELL with illustrations by Emil VAN HAUTH

330 pages, 20 illustrations (in colour and b+w)
ISBN (PBK): 9780956105516

Volume III in the *Brighter French* Series

'...H–T–R– doesn't just want you to parrot French phrases, the essential of fluent speech is to think as the French do. ...'—ELSEVIER SYSTEM JOURNAL [2010], R. VANDERPLANK, DIRECTOR, LANGUAGE CENTRE, UNIVERSITY OF OXFORD

53. 'I don't mean to say that you never see married people there, only they're not married to one another.'

53. « Je ne veux pas dire qu'on n'y voit pas de gens mariés, mais ils ne sont pas *mariés ensemble*. »

377. 'He must have quite a lot to say! The less people do, the more they have to talk about.'

377. « Il doit *en avoir à dire* ! *Moins* les gens *en font, et plus* ils en ont à rencontrer. »

'*Brighter French*— when you start to read you giggle. This naughty guide to flappers' French is full of useful phrases. ...'—*EVENING HERALD*, DUBLIN, [2011]

PHAETON PUBLISHING LTD.   DUBLIN   WWW·PHAETON·IE

NO MATTER WHERE I AM, I SEE THE DANUBE
Autobiography of Thomas KABDEBO

SHORTLISTED FOR THE PRIX DU LIVRE EUROPÉEN 2012

ISBN (HBK): 9781908420046 (EBOOK): 9781908420053
216 pages, 57 photo illustrations

With Foreword by Árpád Göncz, President of Hungary 1990-2000

'...he witnessed many traumatic historical episodes during his life and his account of his part in the Rising is gripping. His is one of those lives that serve as a European history lesson.' —*BOOKS IRELAND*, 2012

'...evokes the old settled life of the Hungary of his ancestors and parents, but for himself Hungary under the Communists after WWII took on a different aspect. Like so many of his contemporaries, he fled west after the collapse of the 1956 rising, leading for some years the life of a wandering intellectual before settling in Ireland, ...this book provides vivid insights into the convulsions of recent Eastern European history, changes which many suspect may not yet be at an end.' —*THE IRISH CATHOLIC*.

'...Kabdebó's first-hand experience of the often cruel reality of life in Central and Eastern Europe after World War II, and of the hardships (as well as the infinite possibilities) of life as a refugee, has been captured unforgettably in this compelling, deeply honest book.' —*HUNGARIAN NEWS AGENCY* (MTI)